TAPESTRY OF LIGHT

A Circle Sleuth Mystery

Titles by Betty Lucke

FICTION

Circle Sleuth Mystery Series
Circle of Power
Family of the Heart
Secrets of the Past
Angels of Justice
Tapestry of Light

NONFICTION

Festival Planning Guide:
Creating Community Events with Big Hearts and Small Budgets

TAPESTRY OF LIGHT

A Circle Sleuth Mystery

Betty Lucke

Spearmint Books

Tapestry of Light
A Circle Sleuth Mystery, Book 5

Published by Spearmint Books.

This novel is a work of fiction. Any references to real people, living or dead, business establishments, places, organizations, or events are intended only to give the fiction a sense of reality. These references are used as background in which the fictional characters live, move, and have their being. The fictional law enforcement entities portrayed in this book may or may not reflect how their real-life counterparts function. All other names, places, characters, and incidents portrayed in this book are the product of the author's imagination.

To contact the publisher, please email: spearmintbooks@gmail.com.
Editor: Wendy VanHatten
Cover Design: Tara Baumann
Loom photo on cover is from Harrisville Designs

Library of Congress Cataloging-in-Publication Data

Lucke, Betty, Author
Tapestry of Light: a circle sleuth novel / Betty Lucke
First Edition   Spearmint Books, 2023
Library of Congress Control Number: 2016910487
    ISBN 978-0-9884631-0-3

1. Bjornson, Karen (Fictitious Character)—Fiction
2. Mystery—Detective—New Mexico—Santa Fe—Fiction
3. New Mexico—Santa Fe—Fiction
4. Immigration—Fiction
5. Weaving—Fiction
    FIC LUC   813.6 DD   PS – LCC   1. Title

Printed in The United States of America

This book is dedicated to the memory of Jean, my big sister, best friend, and advice nurse. Always supportive, always ready to listen.

In these past years, she lived more than a thousand miles away, but we talked every day. She always wanted to know how my book was coming. I would read chapters to her—she called them her bedtime stories.

She left this earth before Karen's book was complete. I miss her, but I'm sure she's still listening.

Acknowledgements

Karen's journey in using her art to make the world a better place and to let her light shine has been challenging. I've grown and explored with my characters. The brainstorming with other writers has been, in turn, fraught with clashes, tears, frustration, awe, and pure joy. I've deep gratitude for those who supported me in telling Karen's story with courage and conviction.

I wish to thank the following for their expertise and encouragement. My "What If" group and the Fiction Writers' Coffee Klatsch folks. Thanks to all who welcomed Karen, Dom, and all the rest into their lives and helped the story come alive.

Draft and Beta Readers Abbie Vick, Cheryl Filarsky, Cheryl Potts, Dwight Blackstock, Emily Brown, Judy Leonetti, Kelly Hess, Lacy Smith, Lauren Filarsky, Laurie Rawlinson Evans, PJ Loomer, Page Frechette, Peggy Lucke, Rachel Lewis, Rebecca Mezoff, Sadye Reddick, Sierra Janisse, Su Schlagel, Syl Bestwick, Terry Murray, Tom Markle, and the Fiction Writers' Coffee Klatsch of the Town Square Writers.

Consultants: Allegra Love, Cheryl Potts, David Barthelmess, Don Bestwick, Dotty Schenk, Jean Norrbom, Kelly Hess, Lauren Filarsky, Laurie Rawlinson Evans, Marty Markovitz, Nick Costales, Peggy Lucke, Rebecca Mezoff, Su Schlagel, Syl Bestwick, and Tom Markle.

Editing: Wendy VanHatten
Loom photo - Harrisville Designs
Cover Design – Tara Baumann

Cast of Characters for *Tapestry of Light* as the book begins

Not all the **Circle Sleuths** came out to play in *Tapestry of Light*. Rest assured they have been busy living, loving, and learning. When the Circle needs them again to celebrate or sleuth, they will be ready.

Adelle Gupta. 54. Exhibit coordinator for Swift & Adams Galleries.

Akiko Schultz. 51. Married to Pete. Mother of Lou and four others.

Algie (Albert Grayson) Adams. 15. Son of William.

Anton Bjornson. 34. Married to Skyla. Son of Karen. Father of Krista.

Bruno Keller. 25. Security guard at Swift & Adams Gallery, Santa Fe.

Cecil Dupre. 45. Owner of Dupre Security Systems.

Cheveyo Loloma. 45. Detective, Santa Fe PD.

Costain. 44. Digital artist.

Diego Quispe. 50. Manager of the Bjornson Ranch.

Dolores Martinez. 51. Married to Frank. Daughter of Dom. Mother of Sam and five others.

Dom (Domingo) Baca. 70. Widower. Father of Dolores. Grandfather of Sam and five others.

Dulcie Rodriguez. 30. Widow. Mother of Santos. Employee of Lemon Élan.

Elena Ruiz. 49. Detective, Santa Fe PD.

Farah Martinez. 29. Married to Sam. Mother of Leyla.

Frank Martinez. 53. Married to Dolores. Father of Sam and five others.

Guy Roquet. 47. Financial Officer for Swift & Adams Galleries.

Herb Nelson. 35. Married to Yolanda. History professor, El Paso. Former colleague of Dom's.

Joaquin Jimenez. 32. Sculptor.

Karen Bjornson. 56. Widow. Mother of Anton. Grandmother of Krista.

Krista Bjornson. 11. Daughter of Anton.

Leyla Martinez. 11. Daughter of Farah, adopted by Sam.

Lou McCreath. 29. Married to Cliff. Daughter of Pete and Akiko. Mother of Dougie. Illustrator.

Lucas Edvar Bjornson. Born May 16, 2017, to Skyla and Anton.

Maria Segura. 38. Housekeeper at Bjornson Ranch.

Otto Griffin. 62. Manager of Swift & Adams Gallery, Santa Fe.

Pete Schultz. 53. Married to Akiko. Father of Lou and four others. Lead detective, Santa Fe PD.

Purity Gold. 39. Artist.

Ruben Turner. 36. Art world mover and shaker.

Sam Martinez. 29. Married to Farah. Oldest child of Dolores and Frank. Father of Leyla.

Santos Rodriguez. 11. Son of Dulcie.

Skyla Bjornson. 30. Married to Anton. Stepmother of Krista.

Tuttle. 45. FBI Agent.

Vidar Bjornson. Nephew of Karen. Worked as sheriff's deputy. Killed in the Line of Duty.

William Adams. 44. Widower. Father of Algie. Owner of Swift & Adams Galleries.

Yolanda Nelson. 35. Married to Herb. Music professor, El Paso.

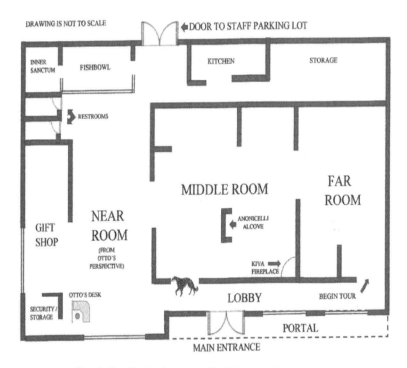

Smith & Adams Gallery, Santa Fe

The Niemöller Quote

First they came for the Socialists,
    And I did not speak out—
    Because I was not a Socialist.

Then they came for the Trade Unionists,
    And I did not speak out—
    Because I was not a Trade Unionist.

Then they came for the Jews,
    And I did not speak out—
    Because I was not a Jew.

Then they came for me—
    And there was no one left to speak for me.

Attributed to: Martin Niemöller, (1892-1984)

Niemöller was a Lutheran pastor in Germany.
These words attributed to him are displayed in the
United States Holocaust Memorial Museum.
Many people in our time have heard the quote,
but few know about the man who gave voice to it.

Prologue

In Santa Fe, New Mexico, the eve of the year 2017 promised exciting changes for Karen Bjornson, a tapestry weaver. She and Domingo Baca celebrated quietly, cuddled on the couch in her sitting room, sipping champagne and watching the flames snap in the kiva fireplace.

She and Dom were newly engaged. Who'd have thought that they—both widowed, both grandparents—would find the joy of loving and being loved again?

No date was set. No ring yet graced her finger. Only promises, leaving a wistful vagueness in their wake. And, if Karen were truthful, the slightest sense of uneasiness.

The year ahead promised more adventures—like starting a new tapestry. Her last commission was done and delivered. Now free, the next design was bound by nothing but her imagination.

With freedom came challenge. Confident in her ability to create beauty, she wondered if it were possible to also make a difference in people's lives, to bring them into harmony. But how?

Weavers must have patience. They work slowly. Doggedly. Hour by hour. Day by day. Week by week.

Passing weft threads over and under the warp threads held in tension.

Back and forth. Tenacity under tension.

◆ ❖ ◆

As December waned, a fired art gallery manager drove erratically through a dark, icy Minneapolis suburb. The effort to drown her despair in a sea of margaritas had not succeeded. Her job was gone. Unfair, since she had no clue about how her gallery had been robbed. They'd summoned her for another interview tomorrow at the police station. Why? What more could she tell them?

A car pulled alongside hers. She blinked to bring it into focus, vaguely wondering why its window was down in this freezing cold. Lights flashed. Shots sounded. Windows shattered into tiny glass cubes. Her car slammed against a barrier of dirty plowed snow. She slumped over the wheel, bloody, permanently relieved of her troubles.

◆ ❖ ◆

In the dim bowels of a Miami parking garage, a young courier entered a limousine, sat across from his boss, and handed a large, flat parcel to him. The elderly gentleman, whose features appeared sickly in the dome light, creeped him out.

"Have you seen it?"

The courier nodded. "I verified it was what you wanted."

"Open it."

In the scant light, the courier opened the package, uncovering an old painting in dark hues. A mother nursing an infant, another child pressing against her side.

The old man wiped the moisture from his rheumy eyes. "At last, another Anonicelli comes to me. Look! The way the light bathes their faces. *Bellissima*."

The courier shrugged. "Sir, here are your receipts for the final payment and the down payment for your last painting."

"Leave. Now."

The courier got out with a sigh of relief. It had gone well. This time.

◆ ❖ ◆

In Santa Fe, a middle-aged professor and his wife left on sabbatical. Their arrangements were concluded—all their personal papers and valuables safely secured, the details about bills and upkeep arranged through a property management firm. The man handed over the keys to their modest home for the house sitter.

Just after dark that night, the house sitter let himself in to explore his new home. Upstairs, he scoped out the neighborhood through all the windows. He opened the garage door and found two vehicles. Identifying their keys on the ring that management had given him, he smiled. People were so gullible.

Up until Minneapolis, everything had gone smoothly with no violence. But that escalation had been surprisingly satisfying. He liked—even favored—the finality.

Loose ends could unravel.

In Washington, D.C., FBI Agent Tuttle scowled as he left his boss's office. Only nine Anonicellis in existence, four of them in commercial art galleries. Three of those four stolen in three years. Same modus operandi. All with help from the inside. Nothing the FBI had found tied the galleries or personnel to each other. Until the last, there had been no physical violence. Even now, they weren't sure the drive-by shooting was connected. Random? Mistaken identity? Or the thief silencing that witness forever.

Only one Anonicelli remained in an art gallery—*Lady in White*—in the Swift & Adams Gallery in Santa Fe. The others were secured in museums or in the hands of unknown collectors.

His boss said Santa Fe would be next. He was seldom wrong.

As Tuttle boarded his flight, he formed his plans. He'd lean on his former partner, perfectly placed, owning the security company, serving the Swift & Adams Gallery. Cecil Dupre would resist, but, hey, he could twist his arm.

Bad things had happened. One must power on through.

Justice must prevail.

The owner of the Swift & Adams Gallery leaned against the abruptly closed door of his office, hearing the footsteps of his teenaged son receding. They'd argued again. Such a stubborn kid. Why couldn't he take no for an answer instead of always coming back with the same plea—to take lessons in digital art. Fake art. Where was the future in that?

Why couldn't his son follow his mother's path? She'd been an outstanding portrait artist, in oils.

He missed her with every fiber of his being.

He sat at his desk and picked up a promotional card, caressing its glossy surface. He'd continued the "Art for Social Change" competitions, begun by his late wife, as a way of keeping her memory close. In a thick folder of his wife's painting ideas, he'd found the scribbled quote by Niemöller and pounced upon it as the next theme in the series.

What would she have done with these words? What vision would they have brought to her mind? He knew it would have been profound, moving. Full of emotion.

He'd made sure to leave digital art out of the list of accepted media for this competition. Neither he nor his child was going down that road.

That was final.

Shadows crept toward Karen from the obscurity of the future, some threads coming from afar. Invisible, elusive. Not yet touching Karen or her world … but stretching …

Living strands reaching to tug, tangle, and intertwine with the fabric of her life to leave knots, puckers, and the threat of unraveling hanging overall.

Events seemingly unrelated.

So far.

CHAPTER ONE

Santa Fe, New Mexico
Thursday, February 9, 2017

Outside Books and Bearclaws, shoppers hunched in their jackets and hastened about their business in downtown Santa Fe. The wind whistled through the eaves, whipped flags, and sent a plastic bag hopscotching along the street and into the plaza. As Karen Bjornson watched, a tree reached out to snag it. There it stayed, flapping impotently.

Karen turned from the window to the cozy cheerfulness inside the crowded bookstore coffeeshop and to Domingo Baca. He set down a plate with a chocolate-chunk scone. His warm smile, the noisy chatter, and the aromas of freshly brewed coffee and pastries hot from the oven pulled her away from the scene outside and her unsettling thoughts.

"Be right back," said Dom. "Need two hands for the coffees."

She smiled after him, this silver-haired man who brought such joy to her life.

"Nobody's going to bully my kid."

That snippet of conversation from two men at the next table caught her attention.

One, wearing a tan flat cap, stirred his coffee. He leaned across the table toward the other, clad in a sports jacket. "He's your child. Of course you don't want him bullied. I can help you with people like that."

"I'd be grateful to you," said Mr. Sports Jacket.

Bullying. It seemed to Karen that just as the public was becoming sensitive to the problem, and schools were finally combatting it, there was a backlash against change. Why did some think it was okay to pick on the weak?

How nice to hear these men talk about helping.

Her gaze drifted to a dark-haired mother with a little girl, who appeared to be about four, looking at Valentine plush toys near the coffee area. The girl's eyes shone as she pointed at a snow-white bear with a red bow. The mother checked the price and handed her the bear. The girl hugged it as they set off toward the cash register in the bookstore area.

Dom came back with their drinks. Karen warmed her hands around the mug, appreciating the bear created by the barista in foam. Karen sipped her brew, distorting the bear into oblivion. Dom bit into his scone.

She grinned. Dom really was a chocoholic. "May I have a bite?"

With seeming reluctance, he broke off a piece for her and took another bite. "Mmm. Nothing's better than chocolate."

"Uff da! I thought you loved me. Am I second to chocolate?"

He pressed his finger into a chocolate morsel on the plate and licked it off. "Maybe I misspoke. How can I forget my grandchildren, my border collie, a good book, and talking history with old friends? Hard to rank them against chocolate."

She raised an eyebrow. Could he extricate himself from this?

"But then …" He leaned closer, covering her hand with his, dropping his voice to a near whisper. "Chocolate doesn't hold a candle to waking by your side, warm together in a cocoon of blankets on a dark winter's morn and knowing that you love me."

She squeezed his hand. The side door opened, allowing a wintery blast to reach their table and send their napkins aloft. He snatched them before they blew away.

"Good save, Dom, in more ways than one."

Near them, the mother seated the girl with her new bear before going off to order drinks.

Karen smiled at the tyke. Shyly ducking her head, the girl made the bear's paw wave at Karen. How delightful! The mother returned with two mugs of cocoa and spoke with her daughter in Spanish.

Soon, another child came in, followed by a man Karen took to be her father. The child, who seemed to be ten-going-on-thirty, flounced across the room toward the plush animals. She was dressed in a jacket open to show a shirt with sequined writing, leggings, and pale pink suede boots.

Pink Boots stopped at the display. "No! It's gone. How could Mom do this to me?" She turned away from the toys with a petulant look.

The father scowled. "She should have gotten it. Moron. Maybe they moved it." He started toward the counter, stopping when his daughter screeched.

"There it is! That's the one I want."

Her voice grated on Karen. She felt sorry for the father. Almost.

"I saw it first. Get it for me, Daddy."

The man reached out and snatched the bear, his sleeve riding up to uncover a tattoo, saying PROUD BOY. What did that mean?

The little girl jumped up, open-mouthed, a look of shock on her face.

Her mother stood and said in a shaky, accented voice, *"¡Un momento, señor!* I pay for bear."

"Liar. Go back where you came from. You're not welcome here."

The woman gasped. The child edged behind her, fear in her wide brown eyes.

Karen flicked a glance toward Mr. Sports Jacket. Would he stand up against this bullying? He only sent a disgusted look at the child before resuming his conversation with Tan Flat Cap.

7

The man holding the bear raised his voice. "Dirty, filthy Mexicans. Stealing from children."

Karen rose. How dare he? When did it become okay to pick on immigrants or those who were different? What chance did Pink Boots have with a father like that? She heard the scrape of a chair, and Dom stood right beside her.

A clerk came over from the book area. "Is there a problem?"

"That illegal alien brat stole my daughter's bear."

"That's not true," said Karen.

The man glared at her. "Mind your own business, bitch."

Karen sucked in a breath.

Dom's voice was quiet, firm. "Your language is offensive."

Oh, my God. Karen's eyes flew from the Proud Boy in his thirties to Dom, a scholar of seventy years. He stood relaxed, confident, his eyes holding those of the young, muscular father.

No one moved.

The father's eyes shifted to the onlookers, the store clerk, then to Pink Boots. "That alien touched it. It's filthy. Let's get the hell out of here." He flung the bear to the floor.

"But I want that—"

"Don't you talk back to me." He turned and strode to the exit.

Karen threw a glance at Dom, impressed by his act of courage. Then she sat. With a final look at the departing father, Dom joined her.

The dark-haired girl rescued her bear and cuddled him. Her eyes were huge as she whispered in the bear's ear. Her mother looked apologetically at the few watching and picked up her cocoa. Her hand shook, and she set the mug down.

Pink Boots hung back. She glared at the child comforting her bear.

The man yelled from the door. "Get a move on, you little shit."

Suddenly, his daughter darted to where the little girl sat. She yelled a slur and swiped her arm across the table, sending their mugs flying. Steamy hot chocolate drenched the girl, her mother, and the new bear. The little girl screamed. Pink Boots ran outside.

Karen stood again, seething with anger.

The barista hurried over with damp towels for the woman to wipe her child's face.

"Please, no want trouble," the mother pleaded.

"Dom," said Karen, "help me with my Spanish." It seemed right to speak in the child's language. She picked up the bear from where it lay and turned to the mother. "May I say something to your daughter?"

Carefully dabbing at the redness on her daughter's face, the mother nodded.

Karen knelt in front of the girl and began in Spanish, "What's your name, sweetheart?"

The girl pressed closer to her mother. "Adoncia."

"Adoncia, some people do mean things. But most people aren't like that." Every so often Karen asked Dom for the right word. "Your bear is very sad now. He hurts where the cocoa splashed him. He needs someone to take care of him and to kiss him better."

Adoncia sniffed, her eyes meeting Karen's.

Karen continued in her halting Spanish. Sometimes the girl looked puzzled, until Dom repeated the words. "Maybe your mommy can run him through the washing machine. But even if the spots never go away, he'll always need you."

Karen handed the bear to the child. Adoncia held him tenderly, straightening his red bow.

"Your bear is special. He was waiting, hoping today would be the day you came for him."

The little girl kissed one of the red-heart pawprints embroidered on the bear's feet.

"He wants you to be kind to people because that's what's important. What's his name?"

Adoncia shrugged and brushed her hand over his wet fur.

"If you hold him real close to your ear, will he tell you?"

The girl tucked her head next to the bear's sewn-on smile. Her expression changed, and she squeezed him tighter. A ghost of a smile began to play on her lips.

"He told you, didn't he?" Karen rocked back on her heels.

Adoncia nodded.

"What did he say?"

Dom translated Adoncia's soft Spanish. "Cocoa-spot. He's glad I found him."

"He's so lucky to have you." Karen swallowed against the lump in her throat. "You take good care of each other."

"*Gracias*," said the woman. "*Ven*, Adoncia."

Dom helped Karen to her feet as mother, daughter, and Cocoa-spot left.

Trembling, Karen turned into Dom's arms. "I couldn't let her leave without giving her good memories for that bear. I couldn't let her be reminded of ugliness whenever she looked at him." She drew in a shuddering sigh. "What an awful man. How dare he teach his daughter to be like that."

She pulled back and looked up. "You stood up to him. He could have flattened you."

"It was the right thing to do." Then Dom grinned. "Bullies are often cowards."

"When they're faced with courage, yes."

"I love you, Karen." Dom touched her cheek with his thumb. "Just now you touched their hearts. You made it better for Adoncia and her mother."

Karen became aware of the room, now back to normal. Adoncia and her mother were gone. Almost as if they had never been there at all—out of sight, out of mind. And life was unchanged.

She frowned. "But don't you see, Dom? It's not enough. The darkness spreads so far. People don't care." She searched his eyes and saw only compassion.

Maybe he didn't have an answer for her.

Maybe there was no answer. She felt woefully inadequate.

"It needs so much more." She put on her jacket. "What can I do? I'm only a weaver. Let's go."

Dom caught her arm and stopped her. She turned in surprise.

"A weaver, yes," he said, "and an excellent artist. Artists have changed hearts in the past."

He zipped up his jacket. "It's something to think about."

They made their way to the door and out into the chilly morning, buffeted by winds over which she felt no control.

CHAPTER TWO

The Bjornson ranch, where Karen lived with her son, his wife, and his daughter, nestled in hills covered with piñon and juniper near the northern edge of Santa Fe. Karen followed their long drive along a ridge top, past the horse corral, several alpaca pens and outbuildings, to the parking area between her two-story home and the duplex. The duplex was home to Maria Segura, their housekeeper, and Diego Quispe, the ranch manager.

The wind pushed a pair of bouncing tumbleweeds in front of her to settle against the outside door of her weaving studio. As she parked, Diego came from an alpaca shed, pulling on his gloves.

She waved to the tumbleweeds. "Sorry, I didn't invite them."

"It's the wind direction." Diego gathered the prickly weeds.

He chuckled as she turned to check the other outside door, which led to a long hallway between her suite and the studio. No tumbleweeds there.

"Your studio doorway is their choice today," said Diego. "Third time I've cleared it. I put the mail in the kitchen. We got letters from the shearers. They'll be here mid-May."

A little later, Karen finished her solitary lunch and turned off the TV news in disgust. Polarization. Folks couldn't even agree on what was good and what was bad. She pictured God sitting in heaven, shaking her head, and saying, "Oy vey."

Irreverent? Perhaps, but heartfelt.

Karen inhaled the steamy fragrance of her ginger-apricot tea. She left the kitchen, walked down the long hall, and into her studio.

She loved this large, bright room. The high clerestory windows brought shifting patterns of light as the sun battled storm clouds scudding across the sky. Intermittent sunbeams caught drifting dust motes and swept over several floor looms, an array of spinning wheels, and worktables. Light danced over spools of alpaca yarn in brilliant colors in cedar cubbyholes before being blocked by heavy gray clouds.

Art that changed minds. Is that what Dom had said as they left the bookstore? What had he meant? While confident in her weaving skill, she had no clue how to express her societal concern in a compelling way. If she came up with an image that touched minds and hearts—and that was a big if—it would have to be seen by people who were inspired to make a difference. A public space, certainly.

The grandfather clock near the door bonged one. An uninterrupted stretch of peace and quiet until two-thirty for brainstorming. Then her beginning-weaving students would arrive for their lesson. She collected her sketchbook and pencils, leaned back against the cushions in the window seat, and rested her book against raised knees.

She'd thought of doing another tapestry with a Viking motif like the one hanging in her family room. Cool tones of sea, sky, mountains, and fjords. Viking ships plowing through the waves, gulls circling overhead, and crashing waves. Strange. She'd grown up in New Mexico—a land-locked high desert. There must be genetic memory calling to her from those rugged vistas, frigid waters, and salt-scented air. Though such a tapestry would be enjoyable to work on, sell well, and bring her a certain acclaim, it wouldn't change a thing about the world she lived in.

Wouldn't her work have to focus on a theme to inspire change? But what?

The incident this morning? It was larger than bullying. Pink Boots needed a better role model. Dom showed courage.

Kindness, empathy, immigration might also be themes. She jotted all the ideas down.

The clock chimed one-thirty. *Uff da.* Her page held only words. Not even concrete words, but intellectual concepts, which didn't easily lend themselves to compelling visual images.

She picked up her mug and finished the remaining tepid swallow. Maybe in the give and take of conversation with Dom, she'd find inspiration.

Her attention drifted to the scene beyond the window, a section of her alpaca pens, where movement caught her eyes. Curious alpacas of white, cream, and gray crowded their fence. Somebody must be arriving.

A small yellow car came up the driveway and parked. Dulcie Rodriguez, one of her students, a cheerful, outgoing soul.

Seeing the young woman's struggle with the gusty wind against her plastic-wrapped loom and her supply tote, Karen opened the studio door.

"*Gracias.* I thought the wind would steal my loom." Dulcie set her load down on a table. "I hope it's okay I'm early. I wanted to show you this." She pulled a tapestry from her bag and unrolled it carefully on the table. "My father wove it. I wish I'd paid more attention when he worked. None of us knew he'd die so young."

Karen smoothed the woolen threads, tracing the colorful birds and animals in a stylized jungle scene. "This is beautifully done, Dulcie. That's why you learn so fast. I wondered after you said you were a beginner."

"Once I learned how to get started, some of what my father did came back to me." She rolled up the weaving and tucked it away before taking the cover off her loom. She began straightening the small skeins dangling from unfinished rows.

"Thanks for being so generous and giving me lessons. Weaving connects me with my father again."

Karen smiled. Dulcie's accent was melodious and her English quite good. "Exchanging cleaning for lessons means I benefit, too, and Maria certainly appreciates your help. There was a lot to do. It was only on Sunday that all of our company left, and we have another gathering this weekend."

"Maria's wonderful. She said she's worked here a long time."

"Ever since my son, Anton, was in high school. He's thirty-four now."

Karen collected yarn spools, two of blues and one of green, sat near Dulcie, and began winding the colored strands around her fingers, blending them into small, manageable skeins which she tied off in a butterfly shape. These butterfly skeins would become the weft yarn. Using a succession of different blended skeins gave her the colors, which allowed her to show contour and shading in her design.

Dulcie began practicing the weave introduced the previous week. "I saw a sculpture in one of the galleries where I clean. It made me weep, that one. How could something metal like that bring out such feeling?"

"Which gallery?"

"Swift and Adams." Dulcie looked up. "It opened before Christmas on Canyon Road. It got added to my cleaning list."

"Who's the artist?"

"Joaquin Jimenez. They have a bunch of his work."

"I know him—he's local. He's had his bronzes at events I've been in. I'll have to see his show. Tell me more."

"The statue was a young woman, kneeling at a grave. She was touching the name of a soldier on the headstone. She looked so sad. I felt like he'd captured me." She blinked rapidly. "I miss my husband. I wish he was here. Not only for me, but for Santos. He needs a father. He needs someone to look up to, to show him how to be a man."

"The Iraq war took a lot from you, Dulcie. I'm sorry," said Karen. "When Anton was thrust into the role of a single parent, it was tough, moving forward. I know what you mean—having someone to look up to. Children need good role models these days. Character matters."

Karen finished the butterfly skein, tied it off, and began another. "Speaking of role models, Sam says your son is doing well on the police activities basketball team."

Dulcie's brown eyes opened wide. "Sam? Oh, you mean Officer—Coach Martinez. Santos adores him. I bless the day he came into our lives. Funny that Santos getting in trouble could turn out so good. Do you know the coach well?"

"Sam's a good friend. Why don't you bring Santos with you some day? He would love the alpacas and horses."

"He'd be no trouble?"

"Diego, my manager, could show him around. He's patient with kids. I'll talk with him."

Karen heard excited barks in the hall. Two young Airedales raced in, skidding on the polished hardwood floor. They greeted her with torpedo-like kisses, ran to Dulcie, barking, sniffing her, and circling their table, before facing off with each other, fronts down, butts in the air, tails wagging, and then tearing around the large room. Dulcie sat back in laughter.

Pleasure filled Karen as Dom entered, his silver hair tousled by the wind. Quixote, his border collie, followed at his heel.

"Sorry," said Dom. "When I got here, they got all excited." He touched Karen's shoulder, running his hand over her sweater. "Are you feeling better after that scene downtown?"

Dulcie's brown eyes filled with concern. "What happened?"

"I don't think you've met." Karen introduced them and told Dulcie about Adoncia.

"I feel for that mother. It's awful when that happens to you."

"You've experienced that kind of bullying?"

"Many times," said Dulcie. "Lately more often. It's scary."

Karen saw again the pain in Adoncia's eyes. Maybe she had made a difference with Adoncia, but that was only a drop in an ocean when it came to bullying.

Karen spotted Twitch taking a spool of yarn from a cubbyhole. "Twitch, leave it!" The dog dropped the spool and came to put his head in her lap. She rubbed his wiry fur.

"I'd better get these guys out of here," said Dom as he picked up the spool. "Sorry for interrupting. Dulcie, good to meet you. Twitch, Shadow, come."

"Your husband reminds me of someone," said Dulcie.

"Oh," said Karen. "Dom and I aren't married." Good Lord, how she'd like to be.

"Sorry," said Dulcie. "I didn't mean to … put my toe in it."

"Toe?"

"Was that wrong? How do you say, 'step in it'?"

"Foot, not toe."

Dulcie still frowned.

Karen tried to smooth it over. "I know who Dom reminds you of. He's Sam's—Officer Martinez's—grandfather. There's a strong family resemblance."

Dulcie's face cleared. "Oh, I see."

As Dulcie started weaving again, Karen's thoughts of Dom wandered on. When they became engaged, she expected things to move more quickly to setting their date and tying the knot. Because he was becoming part of the household, many of his things were here already—mostly clothes, his laptop, and books. A huge, towering stack of books leaned precariously in her suite. Once, while straightening books a dog knocked over, she'd found some Dom himself had written. Impressive. She hadn't thought much about the pressure on the university faculty to "publish or perish."

But when it came to what Dom called sticky wickets, he moved at the speed of a glacier. At one time she thought he was a peacemaker, never showing anger but being calm. But unfolding before her eyes? Real skill in avoiding conflict rather than confronting it head on and working through it.

Karen heard more commotion outside. "The other students must be here. I'll get the door."

Chapter Three

In a community west of downtown Santa Fe, a car door slammed outside Cecil Dupre's home. Cecil shut his eyes, sat back in his office chair, and dug his fingertips through his hair. Tuttle was back. Why couldn't he take no for an answer? The situation sucked any way he looked at it. Shit.

Striding to the front door, he flung it open. His former FBI partner walked toward him past the ornamental grasses in his miniscule yard.

Tuttle. If he had a first name, Cecil didn't remember what it was. Probably Agent. The guy was like a robot, programed for efficiency. Perfectly suited for his vocation as a member of the FBI Art Crime Team, he seemed to have ingested the book on art history and kept it catalogued in a highly organized brain from which detail spewed on demand.

Still, Cecil liked Tuttle. He didn't even mind the dry, humorless personality. They were the same age—mid-forties— and physically fit. Tuttle was a good man to have your back.

"Why did you have to move way out here to Aldea?" demanded Tuttle as soon as he got in the door.

"It's only about fifteen minutes from downtown, and I like it. Out here I can walk without tripping over tourists. Clear the cobwebs from my brain in fresh air."

"Obviously, you don't remember working in Denver. Santa Fe air is fresh."

Cecil led the way to his office. "I don't want to remember it. That was more than ten years ago. Why haven't you got somebody else to harass? I quit, remember?"

"Believe me," said Tuttle, "if I could get the information I need without putting up with your surly self, I would."

"When you came the first time, telling me the Anonicelli is a target, I gave you my decision. William Adams is my friend. I'm not going to investigate him and his employees behind his back."

"Cecil, this thief weasels himself into the confidence of the employees and uses them to gain entry. As William's friend and as the owner of his security company, there's no one better than you to help block this theft."

"Don't push it, Tuttle."

"Consider this. Helping us out may be the only thing that keeps William and his employees safe."

Cecil sent him a sharp glance. "Meaning?"

"I can't prove it yet, but I'm sure the Anonicelli thief killed the Minneapolis manager because she knew too much. She was a loose end, expendable. End of story."

Cecil slammed his fist on the armrest of his chair. "Far as I'm concerned, the FBI has a dismal record of keeping innocents safe."

Tuttle cleared his throat. "There are only nine Anonicellis. Three are in European museums. Not our problem. Two are owned by private collectors. Four paintings were in private galleries. Then those in D.C., New York, and Minneapolis were stolen. Santa Fe is the only one left. It doesn't take a rocket scientist to figure out what'll come down."

"Back off, Tuttle."

"You could protect your friends by helping us."

Cecil's loss haunted him. As much as he tried to lock away the memories, they had a way of emerging to knock him for a loop. "Damn you," he whispered. "You know just how to slide in that knife and just where to twist it."

Tuttle had won.

Cecil knew it.

If he could keep William and his son safe, he'd play it Tuttle's way. Cecil exhaled, the sound loud against the silence. "You have more resources to dig into lives than I do."

"Your advantage is knowing them as people, not collections of facts and dates. You can get into their heads, talk with them, feed us inside information. You're good at discovering what makes people tick."

"Can I assume you're mostly concerned with those who have access to security codes?"

Tuttle nodded.

"There's only two in Santa Fe—William Adams, the owner and Otto Griffin, the manager—who are privy to the whole system—building and art."

"None of the gift-shop folks? How about the janitors?"

"Cleaning service. They have keys but know nothing beyond what will let them in and out of the building. Same with the rest. The manager cleans the secure area around the Anonicelli."

"What's your take on him?"

"Otto Griffin is a devoted nanny for the Anonicelli. He speaks of *Lady in White* like she's a real person. But then, he speaks of all the old masters in worshipful tones."

"Adams just hired security guards."

"You've been busy. Bruno Keller is full-time. There's another part-time. I showed them what they need to know. Good records," said Cecil.

"Our investigation shows two more who have security access to all seven Adams galleries."

Cecil nodded. "Adelle Gupta, the woman in charge of all the special exhibits and Guy Roquet, the chief financial officer."

"Why the hell does the financial officer need access to the galleries outside hours?" asked Tuttle.

"He wanted it. Says he can concentrate better on his work with no one around."

"That's a lame reason."

Cecil shrugged. "William trusts him."

"He's been in all the cities where there've been thefts."

"No surprise. William has galleries in those cities. Roquet has been with William as long as I have, but I don't know him well. He bothers me. Too pale, too perfect. Shook his hand once. I'm used to palm against palm—good honest sweaty firmness. This guy latches onto your fingers, presses them, and pulls back." Cecil shuddered. "Has your digging raised any red flags?"

Tuttle picked up a fat little droid figure from Cecil's desk. He hefted the five-inch bronze in his hand, examining the booted feet barely visible under the warrior's cloak. "Guy Roquet did manage to get himself onto our radar—lives very well for the salary he's making."

"Maybe he's independently wealthy."

Tuttle ran his finger over the droid's sides. "This wealth didn't start showing up until about five years ago."

"Inheritance?"

"Not that we've found. Owns a condo in L.A., but he's hardly ever there."

"William told me he rotates his time among all seven galleries. Spends two to three weeks, sometimes more, then goes on to the next. Otto says he's scheduled in Santa Fe the last half of February. William keeps telling me how fortunate he is to have him. He hates the finance side of business."

"Why the hell does Roquet need an expensive condo in L.A.? Keep your eye on him."

Cecil nodded. "William set up a staff meeting tomorrow morning for me to go over the new security features. I'm glad he's finally taking the threat of someone targeting the Anonicelli seriously."

"Will Roquet be there?"

"Shouldn't think. Otto expects him Monday, the thirteenth."

Tuttle began pressing things on the bullet-shaped warrior.

Cecil watched in amusement. He knew it wouldn't open for Tuttle. "I studied the systems of those galleries where the

Anonicellis were stolen and patched holes in the system here. I also added a few gizmos of my own."

"Like?"

"A tiny tracking device on the Anonicelli frame. It should send signals to my cell phone if it's moved."

"I see you're still making mechanical toys."

Cecil shrugged. "It's an amusing hobby. The original of the one in your hand was a toy I made for Algie about five years ago. He named it Didion—he liked the sound of the name."

"Algie?"

"William's son."

Tuttle ran his thumb over the nosepiece of the squat figure's medieval-looking helmet. "This guy has a hell of an attitude."

"I patterned him after you."

"Funny, Dupre. What's it programed to do?"

Cecil picked up a remote. "Put him back. I'll show you."

With a slight rocking motion, the figure shuffled toward Tuttle, each deliberate step sounding, "*Whirr-clunk. Whirr-clunk.*" It stopped in front of him with a click, tipped forward, and its eyes lit up green. The droid remained motionless for a few seconds before the eyes dimmed.

"Iris scan complete," said a computerized voice from the straightening droid.

Tuttle sat back, "You've got—"

The cloaked figure threw its arms wide, opening his cloak like a flasher, revealing a camera lens. Tuttle recoiled as a flash lit his face, and the lens opened and shut with a whiney whir. Then with a chugging sound, an instant picture emerged from the back of the warrior's cloak and curled away to lie facedown against the desk. The figure closed his cloak.

Tuttle reached for the figure. It shot into Cecil's waiting hand. Laughter sounded, growing fainter as if it were disappearing in the distance.

"Are you serious, Dupre? That thing can't do iris scans. Let me see that picture."

"Of course, it can't do scans. I'm good, but not that good."
He showed him the picture.

"Damn thing's blank." Tuttle handed it back.

"It's a prototype. It has potential." Cecil reset the picture back
into the droid.

"Your brain is strange, Dupre. All the same, it's clever."
Tuttle drained his cup and stood. "Keep in touch."

Cecil frowned as he closed the door behind the agent. The
intrigue of the puzzle, the quest to outthink and out maneuver the
crook had set hooks into him, and it scared him. His addiction
was too strong. He didn't want to be sucked back into the same
job that had shattered his life.

Yet how could he say no? How could he not act to keep his
friends safe? Algie was a great kid. Moments over the past years
stood out, like when Algie first started calling him Uncle Cecil.
Moments when his eyes gleamed with mischief and delight.
Moments after his mother died when he'd held him close as he
cried. Moments now when he glimpsed the promise of the future
adult, the bright inquisitive mind. The talent for creating art.

He wandered back to his desk and picked up the little
mechanical figure.

William was so lucky.

If only ...

CHAPTER FOUR

Friday, February 10

William Adams stepped into the shelter of the Swift & Adams Gallery portal. He set the box of pastries he was carrying on a bench and tugged his cashmere scarf up to protect his ears from the chill breeze coming down Canyon Road. With fingers encased in fur-lined leather, he slid his sleeve up to check his watch. Just past seven. Guy should have been here by now.

The light of dawn struck the Hog Bristle Bistro across the street, accentuating its logo of artist brushes and color palette and transforming the stucco walls to gold.

Next to him, his son, Albert Grayson Adams—known as Algie—pushed off from his slouch against the wall. He tightened the drawstring on his charcoal hoodie and stuffed his hands back into his pockets.

William did an about-take as the fifteen-year-old's lanky length straightened. When had his son gotten that tall? "You warm enough? Otto's here. You could wait inside."

"I'm cool."

There was irony for you. Obviously, he was cool—probably bordering on frostbite. Why was it so hard to get a teenager into a decent winter jacket? Had he ever been that ornery?

William's breath fogged the air. "When I suggested Guy meet us on the portal, all I got was a blank look. But he hasn't been in New Mexico much. I explained that in other places it'd be called a porch. Then he asked why they didn't call it that."

"Guy has zilch imagination."

"You're right. Must be the bean-counter brain, but that's why I hired him." He laughed. "Guy thought I was talking about some portal or gateway to something weird, like in one of those fantasy paintings."

Algie scowled. "Why do you use the word weird when you talk about fantasy?"

"I believe in calling a spade a spade."

Algie rolled his eyes and withdrew into silence.

Just looking at his son still sucked the air from William's lungs—a cruel reminder that his wife was gone. Algie's eyes and wavy dark hair were Gloria's. Hopefully he would hang on to that thick hair and not be like his old man. William's hair had grayed and receded into a fringe that curved from ear to ear across the back of his head.

William jerked out of his thoughts as a neat, dapper man in a suit hurried across the street toward them. "Ah, here comes Guy."

"Brrr," called Guy as he neared. "This far south, why isn't it warmer?"

William picked up the pastries. "We're at more than seven thousand feet. I have to get Algie to school by quarter to nine."

"Sorry I'm late. Still learning my way around."

William preceded his son and Guy into his newest gallery, which had opened last October. Santa Fe, third largest art market in the United States, now joined six other cities in which he owned art galleries. He'd been patient, waiting to acquire just the right property on the prestigious Canyon Road. In a pedestrian-friendly one-half mile, set in the old-world charm of historic Santa Fe, more than a hundred art galleries, boutiques, and restaurants lined the street and spilled into courtyards—a mecca for art lovers.

Inside, opposite the front doors, graceful lettering on the wall welcomed visitors to Swift & Adams, Galleries of Distinction. In all his locations, a life-size bronze statue of a borzoi stood proudly under the gallery name.

Just as the borzoi, impressively elegant, towered over its cousins in the world of dogs, William believed his gallery stood out among its Canyon Road competitors not only in the quality of its authentic, tourist-pleasing Southwestern architecture, but the well-chosen art for sale inside.

William caressed the bronze dog lightly. How he missed Swift. Couch potato, comical, affectionate with his family, yet aloof to others. People often asked him who Swift was in the gallery name. All he would say is that Swift was deceased, and he would rather not talk about it. That quieted them, and he'd smile inside, pleased to honor his wolfhound in cryptic fashion.

After the warm air from inside hit them, Guy removed his glasses to wipe them clean. "You've done yourself proud, William."

William felt his heart swell with pride, glad for an opportunity to show off what he'd accomplished.

He set the pastries on the front desk to his left. "Otto must be in the back. Since you weren't here for the grand opening, I want you to see the changes we've made, Guy. We'll start in the Far Room."

William was pleased—surprised, actually—when his son turned and went with them. He'd expected that Algie would disappear into the back and get lost playing with his phone.

"I like the sign," said Guy. "But Far, Middle, and Near? Such boring names. Why not name them after artists like so many galleries do? The Vermeer, Picasso, or the Warhol Room?"

"Part of the answer is in your question. 'Like so many galleries do.' I didn't want to follow the herd. Also, I feel an artist's name implies a promise of the contents to the customer. No sense in setting up disappointment."

"Isn't it confusing?" asked Guy. "Which end is Near?"

In accordance with the signage, William led them down the lobby to the right to the Far Room. "It's from Otto's perspective. The Near Room is where his desk is. I admit I was tired of calling them Far, Middle, and Near. I thought of names that would convey an image connected to New Mexico. Names that would roll off the tongue and be easy to use."

He and Algie had worked on the names—one of the most enjoyable evenings William had ever spent with his son. They'd brainstormed Latin, Spanish, and German terms. They'd considered names of artists they'd admired. They'd even tried fantasy and literary terms, and made-up words. They laughed, thinking of how Otto would struggle with those. Finally, they came full circle to Far, Middle, and Near.

That exercise had become a favorite memory. He felt good inside when he looked at the tastefully done diagram in the lobby announcing what was shown in each room.

The Far Room was narrow and typical of adobe interiors with high ceilings showing peeled wooden beams, or vigas. Brightly colored Southwestern-themed art hung on white walls. Dark wooden tables held small sculptures. The hardwood floor gleamed in a walnut hue.

William tucked his gloves into his pocket and opened his coat. "*The Painters of the American West* exhibit will be opening March first in this room."

They passed through a wide archway into a larger room with a tiled floor—the Middle Room. In the corner, a fire burned merrily in the kiva fireplace. The built-in bench held a display of pottery and other *objets d'art*.

Guy frowned. "You have a fire? In the same room as the art? What are you thinking?"

William laughed. "Calm down. It looks real, but it's only digital. No smoke, no heat."

"On a day like today," said Algie, "it makes me want to stay for a while."

William smiled at his son. That was exactly the reaction he wanted visitors to feel. "This space is where our Niemöller-themed exhibit will begin its tour."

"Another one of your art-for-social-change exhibits?" asked Guy.

"Yes. I have great expectations for this theme."

"As long as it makes a profit."

William threw a glance at him. Why couldn't Guy, just once, get excited about the art? Why was it always about crunching numbers?

"Will you move the Anonicelli?" asked Guy, motioning toward *Lady in White*, a seventeenth-century portrait hanging in a recessed, Aegean-blue alcove.

"I don't believe so. That spot has security features that would be difficult to achieve elsewhere."

When William had purchased the Anonicelli from an estate sale, it'd been in a frame that had been clumsily cut down to fit. He'd reframed it in a reproduction frame that enhanced the colors in the painting. Delicate three-dimensional acanthus leaves twined in a repeated pattern between gilded edges.

William looked closer. Odd. He'd never noticed how the center leaf on the bottom stood out. Must be the lighting here.

"Any interest shown in the painting? I've mentioned it to several of our more discerning collectors."

Ah, William felt a bit of excitement from the businessman whose mousey, spectacled persona kept him in the background. Guy did enjoy alerting William to estate sales featuring art—not that Guy cared about art per se, but he excelled at cultivating art lovers with dollars to spend. When they attended sales, William would be engrossed in the art and provenances. Guy schmoozed with collectors, adding them to their network. William's talent lay in putting art and collector together and in growing clientele for emerging artists. His galleries had prospered under this cooperation.

"Not yet," said William, "by anyone with pockets that deep. I appreciate your dropping those hints. She's become a bit of a liability. I'm glad you were able to catch a flight that got you here in time for our meeting."

The little entourage stepped through another wide arch into the Near Room, which included a gift shop and the manager's desk, completing their circle.

"The Niemöller exhibit will need part of this room as well. Presently we have an exhibit of Joaquin Jimenez's figurative sculptures here. You know his work from my other galleries, but he lives in Santa Fe." William motioned to the rear of the room. "Otto should have coffee back there. I'll get the pastries. We'll meet in the fishbowl."

"Fishbowl?" Guy sounded confused.

"What Algie calls the workroom. It's glassed-in with windows."

Sotto voce muttering came from his son behind him, "Oh, crap. Gnome alert. All he needs is a red pointy hat. Why did you keep him, of all people, from the old gallery, Dad?"

A pudgy man with a shock of white hair and a neatly trimmed white beard rose from the desk to greet them.

William spoke softly. "Don't be rude, Algie. He's knowledgeable and a good salesperson." Raising his voice to a normal level, he walked toward the desk to shake the manager's hand.

A man entered the front door. He sported a short, dark beard and wore a deerstalker hat with untied flaps hanging over his ears.

"Uncle Cecil's here, Dad."

William heard the change of tone in his son's voice. Somehow Cecil Dupre had found the key to unlocking the blasé teenager's attitude and finding the excitement inside. Even more amazing was Algie's crawling out of bed before dawn to come to the meeting because Cecil would be there. What did those two have up their sleeves now?

"Welcome." William returned Cecil's firm handshake. They'd been friends long before William had moved to Santa Fe, but he always had the feeling that he didn't really know Cecil. What did that confident manner hide? It was almost as though Cecil were an actor in a play, and when he removed his makeup and went home, no one would recognize him.

Where had that thought come from?

He jerked himself back to the present. This security update hadn't come a moment too soon for his peace of mind. Ever since the Santa Fe detective had stopped by to warn him that Anonicellis were being targeted by thieves, he'd been itching to get those upgrades done.

Jokingly, William challenged Cecil. "Dupre, you should add Algie to your payroll. Lately, when he hasn't been in school, he's been following you around."

Cecil fist-bumped Algie before doffing his deerstalker. "He was a big help. My crew enjoyed him too. He catches on fast."

Algie shrugged. "It was fun."

William compared his two friends, Guy and Cecil, from way back. So different. Both were a few years older than he was, but Cecil always seemed to be in motion even when sitting at a computer manipulating designs and components in his CAD program, brown eyes snapping with life. Guy faded into the background, a monochromatic, quiet calculator. His intelligent eyes behind those lenses were reserved.

William glanced at Otto. Very different again. Pudgy, old-worldly, and decidedly gnome like.

He waved toward the fishbowl. "Let's get started. I want to see what magic Cecil's wrought in our security system."

◆ ❖ ◆

Otto Griffin liked Algie's name of fishbowl for the area doubling as the breakroom and workroom. From the fishbowl, Otto could keep an eye on activity anywhere in the gallery—up front through the glass, and the rest of the gallery from security monitors, not visible to the public, arranged under the workroom's windows.

One had to go through the fishbowl to get to William's private office, dubbed the inner sanctum. The division between fishbowl and inner sanctum was also glass.

They gathered around the worktable as William distributed a short agenda. Otto watched the others interact as William covered the more mundane items. Then William surprised him by deviating from the written agenda.

"I would like to acknowledge Otto's brilliant performance since the gallery opened. Guy told me that the sales for this gallery are excellent compared with my other galleries. His sales have consistently rated in first or second place. Oh, I've heard the grumbling. Why haven't I made more business-like decisions and hired a younger, more technologically astute manager who can handle digital needs with more ease?"

William turned to Otto. "So, thank you. I am very pleased with you as my manager here."

Otto felt his face grow warm and stuttered a thank you. Oh, my. To be called brilliant, excellent in front of these men. Right then his resolve grew to try and master the technology too. Maybe he could.

As William moved on, Otto basked in the glow of praise, only half listening. Then a name from the ongoing conversation caught his ear.

"Purity Gold," said Cecil. "I laughed when she introduced herself."

"Purity Gold! Oh, my." Otto bristled. "Did you hear about the stink she made at the Gellerud Gallery? In front of patrons! All because the manager didn't choose her work for their show."

"I heard about it," said William. "I didn't know who it was."

Otto shuddered just thinking about her acrylics. "She doesn't even have a passing acquaintance with talent. Chimps throwing paint at a canvas do better."

"Are you saying Gold does abstracts?" Algie shifted in his chair. "Not everyone shares your antiquated opinions of what true art is."

"She's an abomination, not an artist."

"I get the feeling you don't like her," said Algie.

Otto looked down his nose at the young man before turning to William. "You know where I stand. She gets shown in this gallery over my dead body."

Oh, my, had he really told his boss whose work he was allowed to show? Why had he let Algie rile him enough to lose his good sense?

"Sign her up, Dad." The teenager laughed.

Otto jerked up straight and pulled in his chin.

"Algie, Otto manages this gallery. You, my son, are just visiting." William straightened his papers with a decisive click on the table. "Let's move on. Guy, did you get the paperwork for our new security guards?"

"Yes. Bruno Keller full-time?"

"I know Keller." Cecil smiled broadly. "If you ever want to thank him, forget the bonus or the employee of the month. Give him chocolate. He'll bend over backwards to make sure your gallery is secure as Fort Knox."

"But Keller knows diddly about art," said Otto.

"As long as he can keep it safe, that's okay." William's voice took on an exasperated tone. "Algie, would you mind putting away that phone and acting like an adult for a change? You might learn something about running a business."

Algie flushed and put his phone away.

Otto recoiled. That seemed harsh. For several months now, he'd watched the back-and-forth tension between father and son. He couldn't figure either of them out.

Next, William covered the coming Niemöller-themed exhibit. "The call for entries ran in this month's art magazines and in major newspapers, including the *Santa Fe New Mexican*. Otto, have plenty of the information packets on hand."

"Certainly." Otto glanced at his planner. Over five months away. He thought ahead to all the work involved in the frequent changes of displays. One of William's new purchases really pleased him—the art hanging system. A discreet mini rail went around the ceilings and supported paintings on almost invisible cables. Much easier to hang than the old-fashioned way.

◆ ❖ ◆

As the meeting wore on, Cecil Dupre fought against a headache by massaging the bridge of his nose. What the hell was Guy doing here? He was sure Otto said he was coming Monday. William hadn't said anything.

Cecil had reviewed Tuttle's findings about Guy's too-lavish lifestyle. Now he looked at him with new eyes, noting the impeccable, tailored clothing, making the most of his average stature. First class all the way.

He wished William would take the threat against the Anonicelli more seriously. When the alert first came of Anonicellis being targeted, Tuttle had given a heads up to a Santa Fe police detective, Lieutenant Pete Schultz, who had, in turn, contacted William. Cecil hadn't been invited to that meeting. He only knew about it because of Tuttle.

William was too trusting—with both people and his reliance on a security system. He'd brushed it off, telling Cecil, "Police say thieves are after the Anonicelli. You can fix it, so it'll be safe. Do your magic."

Magic. Right.

At least William had the good sense to hire guards. That was how William operated. He delegated. Found good people. Made sure they had the training and resources to do the job, then let them get on with it. He didn't micromanage—just trusted them to do it right.

"Cecil?"

He heard his name and realized everyone was looking at him.

Shit. William had come to the meeting's main purpose.

"Cecil's going to show us our new security features. I told Guy about this meeting and am glad he arranged his schedule to be here."

Cecil hesitated. Not now. Not with Guy. How many times had he told William the dangers of sharing security secrets with too many people?

His displeasure must have shown on his face because William jumped on him. "What's the matter?"

"Nothing," he lied. "Could we do this later? It's good policy to only have those who need the information be in the know."

"Come on, man," said William. "This is why we're here. I trust everyone here."

Reluctantly Cecil reviewed the security changes. Otto soon wore that deer-in-the-headlights look. He was furiously scribbling notes. Hell, this was only the beginning. What would the poor sod do with the more complicated features surrounding the Anonicelli?

Cecil paused. "Are you still with me, Otto?"

"Not totally." Worry creased Otto's forehead. "I'm afraid I'm going to key in wrong numbers and set off alarms or break something."

"We'll have you run through it several times before I leave. I'll fix a cheat sheet with step-by-step instructions."

Algie smiled at Otto. "I'll be glad to help when you have questions. People my age aren't intimidated by electronics the way old folks are."

"Thank you." Otto looked surprised by Algie's helpful attitude.

"I can fix mnemonic devices to remember your codes too," said Algie. "I like doing stuff like that."

God love him, thought Cecil. Ever since he'd installed a system in William's first gallery, Algie had followed him around, peppering him with questions. Eight years, six galleries and systems later, Cecil knew Algie really did understand.

Cecil patiently went through all the steps and noticed Otto felt better when much of the instructions had to be repeated for William. Guy just seemed bored.

"William, if you forget," Otto said, "I'll put all these notes in a file in the back of the top drawer."

Cecil closed his eyes briefly. "It's okay to have it written down, but don't label it SECURITY SYSTEM."

Otto's look was grave. "No. That'd be silly. All my codes and passwords go in a file named AUNT MARY."

Shit. Otto was a security nightmare. Maybe when Guy left, Cecil would change the codes again. Just tell William it was part of the magic.

He took a deep breath. "We've a new feature Otto will appreciate. He complains about running back and forth from the main keypad by the backdoor to work the Anonicelli systems."

Cecil led everyone to the Anonicelli display. He showed them how the informative placard could now be swung aside for Otto to access a second keypad. He went on to describe other features protecting various artworks, like magnets that would set off alarms if art was moved. Only Otto, and William, if he wanted, would know which works were alarmed at any one time. He showed them how a code with a certain prefix would automatically alert the Police Department. He talked about codes that would override features, allowing Otto to dust and clean in sensitive areas.

"Did you take out that old grille that came down over the alcove at night?" asked William. "I don't see any sign of it."

"Glad you mentioned that," said Cecil. "It's still there, but now even a sharp observer will probably miss it when the gallery is open."

"One of the first things I noticed," said William, "was how clean and uncluttered it looks. Much better."

Cecil entered a code that lowered the grille over the recessed alcove where the Anonicelli hung, an area about three by five feet. "Imagine that a thief gets in at night, and somehow makes it past security and the guard and tries to take the Anonicelli. He has no way of knowing ahead of time about this grille. Do not tell anyone about these features you see today. I don't care if you are the owner, the manager, the CFO, or the owner's son."

His eyes met each in turn.

"The other Anonicellis were stolen because the thief used employees to gain information and access. He manipulated people to learn their secrets. Is that understood?"

Cecil waited for the gravity of his statement to penetrate his small audience. Then he went on. "If you're a thief, what would you try first to get the painting? Remember, you can assume that a silent alarm will have gone to the police station when you came in. You have only minutes to take your prize and disappear."

"Shake the bars to feel how secure they are," said William.

"Good. That will activate the next surprise." Cecil winked at Algie, standing behind the three men. The teen's eyes were alight with anticipation, but he hadn't seen this either. "Try it, William."

Cecil watched the audience. William's shaking activated part of the floor of the recessed area behind the grille to fold up, uncovering a metal plate. Simultaneously a small door to the left of the plate slid up to reveal a bullet-shaped droid standing at the edge of the opening.

"Didion!" Algie's face split in a grin.

Out of reach behind the grille, the figure moved out along the metal plate. With each *whirr-clunk*, he moved closer to the center of the grille.

"What on earth?" growled William.

"This is Re-Didion." Cecil saluted Algie.

"Algie, did you know about this?" asked William.

"No. Honestly. Cecil just said I'd get a kick out of seeing one of the security features."

The droid reached the center, faced them, and went through the same routine with the iris scans and camera that Tuttle had seen.

Otto's mouth hung open in a round O of surprise. Guy still looked bored. William just showed puzzlement.

Algie frowned. "Iris scans? Really? I guess. Even with a ski mask, eyes show."

"There's an instant camera in there too?" William reached a couple of fingers through the grill to snag the photo. The metal under the droid swung down like a trap door, and Re-Didion dropped out of sight. The trap door snapped shut above him.

"Oh, my," said Otto, clapping his hands. "The thief thinks he can be identified now, his picture has been taken, and he can't get it."

"But the thief's already on the security camera," said William. "Why this elaborate charade?"

"This must cost a fortune. How much are we paying you for this toy, Dupre?" Guy's voice challenged him.

"Now the robber is worried," said Algie. "Cool. How long did the routine take?"

"Seventy-three seconds." Cecil grinned at Algie.

"How much?" repeated Guy.

"Seventy-three dollars, my friend. One dollar for every second that the thief stands watching while the cops come closer."

Guy snorted. "Isn't real. Not at that price."

"Doesn't matter," said Cecil. "Somebody up to no good doesn't know what's possible or what you paid. William's right about the security camera. Except now, thieves worry about being identified. And the police might have gained an extra minute and thirteen seconds to catch them."

"Wouldn't they skedaddle when they first heard the noise and saw it?" asked William.

"Maybe. Or they might be so bemused they'll watch the whole routine. Either way, your Anonicelli is safe."

"Re-Didion didn't go down the trap door until I tried to get the picture," said William. "What'll he do if the thief runs?"

"He has a motion sensor. He'd stay put if no one is there."

"I like it," declared Otto, "but will I have to fiddle with him?"

Cecil shook his head. "He can wait under the trap door until the excitement is over, the police have gone, and I can get here to set him up again."

"Are we done with your school-boy tricks?" asked Guy.

Cecil shrugged one shoulder. "You may see it as a toy. Algie said something that put this idea in my head. Was there anything that would give the cops more time to catch a thief? Something totally unexpected and startling? I thought it wouldn't hurt to worry the hell out of the thief either. Hence the iris scan threat. Even if the thief doesn't think it's possible, he'll still worry."

"I can't see anyone believing this," said Guy.

Cecil laughed. "Of course, it's not going to be standard in a security system, but given the configuration with the grille, the wide ledge behind it, and the size of the alcove setback where the painting hangs, I thought I could make it work. I enjoy tinkering."

"Can we see it again?" asked Algie.

"No," said William. "You have to get to school."

"Two minutes is all it takes. I'm going to be early if we leave now."

"Who knows what traffic will be like?" William started for the back door. "Get your things. We're leaving. Now."

Algie scowled. Cecil touched his sleeve and mouthed "Later." The kid brightened and followed his dad. Cecil reset the droid and patiently answered Otto's questions.

After Cecil collected his jacket and deerstalker from the fishbowl, he took the long way out through the showrooms, glancing at the Anonicelli when he passed by.

Guy stood before it, looking thoughtful, stroking his chin absently.

CHAPTER FIVE

"Mmm. Smells wonderful," said Karen as she entered the kitchen. "What are we having, Maria?"

"Dijon-tarragon chicken, mashed potatoes with Brie, and green beans."

"Goodness! Who's cooking tonight?"

"Dom volunteered."

"Dom? Really?" Karen knew from his grandson Sam, he was a good cook, but this menu suggested gourmet status.

"He'll be right back." Maria Segura twitched her long black braid over her shoulder. "Hang on to that man, Karen."

"I plan to. How many tonight?"

"Full house with no extras. No one's told me different."

Karen counted out plates, placemats, napkins, and silverware for seven and set them on the serving cart.

Diego came in, hung his well-worn Stetson and sheepskin jacket on the coat tree, standing where the long hall ended near the stairs, and immediately went to Maria in the kitchen. "Let me help you with that heavy pan."

Karen grinned. Diego was always so solicitous of Maria. Pulling out her chair, getting things from high shelves, even though he wasn't that much taller than Maria. Old-fashioned—even courtly. She paused. Courtly? Hmm. She knew their ranch manager and their housekeeper enjoyed each other's company, but was that all?

She added a water pitcher and glasses to the cart. Her son, Anton, and his wife, Skyla, came in, with Twitch, their Airedale.

Skyla rolled the cart into the breakfast room where most of the family meals were eaten. Her baby bump was obvious now. A new grandchild due in May.

"Sure smells good!" At six-foot-two, Anton hovered over Maria as she turned the chicken in the sauce. He grabbed a fork, stabbed a small piece, and blew on it. Maria swatted him away. He laughed, stepped back, and slid the stolen morsel into his mouth.

Dom entered, chuckling at their play. He checked the chicken and began mashing potatoes. His movements were confident.

To think Karen had once worried if Dom would feel he belonged. No problem—he fit in very comfortably.

Anton ran his tongue over his lips. "A chardonnay should go well with this."

"Perfect," said Dom.

Shadow and Quixote came in with Krista right behind. She was wearing jeans and a baggy blue sweatshirt, her blonde hair pulled back in a messy ponytail. She collected the trivets and serving spoons and disappeared into the breakfast room. What a delight her granddaughter was. No artifice, unlike Pink Boots. Krista, eleven, was rapidly getting taller. Karen figured she would be close to her own five-foot-nine when she stopped growing.

Karen took her place at the head of the table. After grace was said, she tasted the chicken. Tender. Flavorful. And the potatoes? A new and tasty version. Karen glanced at Dom, sitting on her right, basking in his culinary success.

A keeper. Dom was here many nights, and sometimes she stayed with him in town.

"How are your weaving classes going, Mom?" Anton's question interrupted her thoughts.

Karen took a sip of her wine. "Quite well. Dulcie especially catches on quickly."

"I like Dulcie," said Maria. "She's a hard worker."

"She told me about an exhibit of Joaquin Jimenez sculptures at the new Swift and Adams Gallery. I'd like to see it. Dom, would you like to go with me, maybe Sunday?"

"After Mass," said Dom.

"You going to Mass, Mom?" asked Anton.

Karen shrugged a shoulder.

"I like that sculptor's work," said Skyla.

Karen smiled at her daughter-in-law. She was a ranger at Pecos National Historical Park. She and Anton were thinking about a joint business venture, using his drone expertise and her love of archaeology. Karen couldn't imagine a better mate for her son than Skyla.

"Is that the gallery you took me to once, Daddy? Where I thought the guy working there looked like the Tomten in my book? All he needed was a long, red knit cap."

"Good memory, Krista," said Anton, "but he's probably gone."

"What's a Tomten?" asked Skyla.

"One of the wee folk, sort of like a gnome," said Karen. "He comes out at night, keeping children and farm animals safe."

"One lives in our stables," said Diego. "Sometimes when I go in, there's a flash of movement like something leaving in a hurry. The animals look annoyed with me for scaring him away."

"Really?" asked Krista. "Aww, you're joking. Don't believe you."

"I'm hurt." The expression Diego put on his swarthy face didn't match the twinkle in his dark eyes.

"You're not either." Krista sipped her milk. "Saying he was like a Tomten. That's a simile, isn't it? We were studying figures of speech today in English. For my homework I'm supposed to write a paragraph comparing somebody in my family to a bird."

"Uff da. Who are you going to choose?" asked Anton.

Krista looked innocent. "I think I'll write about you."

"You'd do better with your gramma," he responded. "A swan, long necked and graceful."

Karen watched as Krista considered that.

"I see Gramma more as a dove. She's always seeking peace or kindness." Krista took a bite and turned back to her dad.

Uh-oh. What did that mischievous glint in Krista's eyes portend? Karen shot a glance at her son, his dark blond hair, rugged, clean-shaven features so much like his father's. She'd always seen him as handsome.

"But I still think I'll do you."

"Okay," said Anton, "what kind of bird do I strike you as?"

"Big Bird!" Krista smiled triumphantly.

"Why am I like a yellow puppet?" asked Anton.

"No, silly. I was trying to find a tall bird. Or a smart bird that knows all about flying—like a swallow. That would fit the good flying super-neat, but the size isn't right."

"A flamingo?" suggested Maria.

"How about a crane?" asked Dom. "They're tall, and they're always sticking their necks out."

"Pulleeze. I refuse to be compared to a bright pink lawn decoration, and I'd fall over if I had to stand on one leg very long."

Krista tilted her head. "If there's a bird that's into technology, that'd work."

Karen chuckled. "Do you mean a mechanical bird, a cuckoo on a clock maybe?"

"Thanks, Mom."

Skyla rubbed her back. "What do you want to capture in your comparison? Looks or character? It's hard to do both."

"I know," said Krista. "I thought about you, Skyla, with your goldy-hazel eyes, your brown hair with its red highlights, and your favorite color to wear being teal. Your coloring is like a kingfisher, but I can't see you diving into a pond and spearing a fish with your beak."

Laughter rippled around the table.

"Then there's Dom," said Krista furrowing her brows.

Interesting. Karen looked at him. What bird would Krista pounce on? Songbird? Domestic? Waterfowl? Raptor?

"I'm thinking owl. Lots of my story books showed owls as wise old birds. But what kind of owl? Snowy owl? Maybe a great gray or great horned. Not a dinky one like a saw-whet."

"And how about Maria?" asked Karen.

Krista sent a teasing glance to Maria and Diego. "Maria? A mourning dove. Looks soft, rounded, she hugs good. Quiet."

"Quiet?" asked Anton. "I hear mourning doves all the time around here."

"That's partly why it's a good bird for her," said Krista. "Their call isn't all cackle and noise but comforting. Dependable. Always there, but in the background."

Maria lifted an eyebrow and smiled. Karen caught the wink Diego sent to her.

Krista focused on Diego. "Maybe the easiest person to get both in one bird is Diego."

"Me?"

"Yeah. Like a California quail. From a distance, brown and ordinary. I've tried painting quail. When you look close, they're not plain at all, but real interesting and colorful. Diego's protective of his flock like them too."

Diego smoothed his black mustache. "Don't want to be a California quail. Can you imagine life with a tennis ball bobbing between your eyes?"

Karen chuckled at the image, a sound that echoed around the table.

Krista lowered her fork. "You can only take figures of speech so far. Then they get stupid."

Karen swallowed the last of her wine. What a delicious meal.

"Gramma, can I ask you something?"

"Sure, sweetheart."

"When are you and Dom getting married? Can Leyla and I be bridesmaids?"

Silence like a heavy blanket dropped over the room.

Anton cleared his throat. "Krista, that's a pretty personal question, especially out of the blue in front of everyone."

Karen felt her face getting pink. She kept reminding herself she was content to let things slide, but damn, it was getting harder.

She looked at Dom, trying to gauge his thoughts. There was an intensity as his eyes met hers.

Now Krista was visibly upset. "I'm sorry. I didn't know I shouldn't ask. I thought that's how it worked. Skyla moved in with Daddy when they got engaged, then they got married. So, when Dom and Gramma got engaged and he started sleeping in her room, I thought … I know he's already Leyla's grandpa, but I wanted him to belong to me too."

Karen couldn't come up with a coherent sentence. She didn't want them forced into this public moment.

Into the hush, Skyla spoke. "Krista, honey, when the time is right, they'll let you know. For every couple, it's different."

"No matter what, I'm proud to be Grandpa to both you and Leyla." Dom reached out an arm toward Krista. She shot out of her chair and ran to his hug.

Then she turned into Karen's arms. "I'm sorry, Gramma. I didn't mean—"

"You surprised us. If we have bridesmaids, you and Leyla will certainly be among them."

Karen picked up the empty serving dishes to carry them to the kitchen. Good Lord. You'd think two adults could have come to a solution long ago. She knew every fold, wrinkle, and texture on Dom's body, and he hers.

But did you ever really get to know someone? Weren't there always secret places where no one was allowed? What thoughts did Dom hold deep inside?

Every time this date question came up, shutters closed. Was he too comfortable? Fitting in so easily he'd no motivation to make their marriage real?

❖

That evening, Dom leaned back against the pillows in Karen's four-poster bed. A notebook lay open against his bent knees. His mind struggled with the novel he wanted to write. Random ideas of characters caught in conflict, snippets of dialogue, and settings filled several pages. Nothing had grabbed him yet, but ideas came as fast as he could jot them down.

Rrrrip.

Startled, he looked at Karen, posed much the same as he, but with a sketchbook. An exasperated *aaacch* left her lips. She crumpled the page she'd torn out of the book and threw it with force to land by the wastebasket next to another sheet discarded earlier.

On other occasions, he'd seen ideas flow from her pencil, filling pages with mini sketches. Not tonight. At the moment she was frowning, biting her lip as she began drawing on a fresh page.

He folded down the corner of his notepaper. "What's wrong? This doesn't seem like the normal muse that won't cooperate."

She snorted. "What muse? This morning you said something about artists changing hearts. What did you mean?"

Dom shrugged. "Every so often, an artist creates a work of art that touches people. It takes hold of them and won't let go. They're compelled to respond."

"What kind of art?"

"I suppose photos come first to mind. One like that little Vietnamese girl running naked away from the napalm. It had a profound impact on the way the war was seen. But not just photos. Paintings like Norman Rockwell's Rosie the Riveter. Can you imagine how inspiring that was for ordinary women? How it motivated them to join the war effort? Rockwell was a genius for painting average Americans one identified with."

"I'm having trouble coming up with my next image to weave." She sighed. "If only I could do something that made people think." She picked up her pencil again. "Sorry. Didn't mean to interrupt your muse."

Dom went back to his notes, jotting down fictional characters that might spring from historical periods that would be fun to research. Mini flow charts littered the borders and ran through his notes.

Karen's pencil tip snapped. She slammed her sketchbook shut and sat, moodily looking across the room. He filled another page before responding to her stillness and the thoughtful, almost sad look on her face.

Dom closed his notebook. "Now what?"

"Krista's question. It seems since we decided to marry, all we do is drag our feet." She set her sketchbook and pencil on the nightstand with her reading glasses and angled her body toward him. "Why can't we pick a date?"

"Don't get me wrong. I love you, and I want to marry you, but—" Dom set his own glasses aside, turned out his light, and lay down. "If we can resolve those sticky wickets …"

Karen turned out her light. "And another thing bothers me. I wanted it to go away, but it won't."

"What, love?"

"Role models," she said in a small voice. "I've always gone on about them. Yet here we are. Living together. I know we're engaged, but …" Her voice trailed off. "Krista and Leyla are watching what we do. I'm not living up to my own standards. I'm a hypocrite."

"I guess I am too."

"Then can't we deal with the rest of the sticky wickets? We've worked out so much. What can be left?"

Dom heaved a small sigh and lay in silence.

"Dom?"

"Two things. My daughter for one." He smiled wryly as Karen stiffened. "That's no surprise, is it? Unlike Anton, she's dead set against us."

"I don't have a problem with Dolores. It's silly to act as a stepmother to someone just five years younger, but surely, we can get along."

"It's not going to be easy. I haven't seen much of her since we got serious. She's feeling left out. I told her I'd make some special time for her. She suggested we go to Mass and dinner together on Thursdays."

"That's a good idea. Rather sweet, really." She slid down in bed and took his hand.

"The other? A real sticky wicket." He frowned. "Religion. Tough barrier to work through."

"This might sound stupid, but do you want us to give up sleeping together?"

"And tear my heart out? No." He squeezed her hand. "I can't give you up."

"I'm not asking you to."

Dom thumb rubbed her hand lightly. "Until we deal with those, I don't feel right about setting our date."

"Can we move ahead with the pre-nuptial paperwork? The trusts, the estates, and all that?"

"I suppose. We don't have to sign them until—"

He heard a quiet sniff. Was she crying? "Hey, it's okay. We'll work it out. I promise."

He'd talk to Dolores. Surely he could fix that problem. Well, maybe.

But what of the other?

Dom lay still, staring into the darkness, long after Karen's lax fingers and rhythmic breathing told him she slept.

It had never been a problem in his first marriage. Isabel had shared his Catholic faith. He wanted to be able to worship together with his wife, for her to believe what he did. What was he supposed to do? Examine a lifetime of conviction?

He felt caught in the middle. God, he hated conflict.

His church said he was not in a state of grace.

A love unsought, but surely Karen was all that was right and good.

It was unfair to ask this choice of any man.

Should he be here with her?

But he belonged here.

His throat ached in anguish. A state of grace. Or love that gave joy to his soul.

They had time. Or did they? He wanted more years but was afraid he wouldn't see them.

The moon tracked its way across the heavens, and still his eyes would not close. He lay quietly, a tear sliding down past his ear to dampen the pillow.

CHAPTER SIX

Sunday, February 12

Karen and Dom parked in the small public lot next to the Hog Bristle Bistro on Canyon Road after they'd left Mass. She looked across at the Swift & Adams Gallery. "They've spruced it up."

"About time." Dom took her hand as they crossed the street. "It's nice without the ratty junipers."

Karen glanced at the strip of land between the low wall bordering the sidewalk and the building. "Those red berries are great against the adobe— Look!" She paused near the entrance, fascinated by a small flock of bluebirds flitting from branch to branch, happily devouring the winterberry fruit.

"We timed our visit well. When we come out, that bush will be bare." He held the door open for Karen and followed her in.

She hadn't visited an art gallery with Dom before, but it was obvious he knew his way around Canyon Road. Not surprising— his ancestral home he shared with his grandson, Sam, was nearby.

Karen admired the bronze borzoi. "He calls out to be petted, but I suppose that's a no-no."

"Hasn't stopped some." Dom gestured toward the gleaming gold on its head.

They followed the diagram and signage guiding them to the right and the first of three showrooms, the Far Room.

Dom paused in front of a portrait in oils. "I like this. It has a sense of peace and timelessness." It depicted an old Navajo looking into the distance of Monument Valley. Wisps of white hair escaped his rolled-cloth headband to caress the blue material covering the rounded shoulders.

Karen read the placard. "Stella Von Fluss, 1896 to 1979. Not familiar with her."

"Me either. I wonder what else she did."

They went into the Middle Room, stopping before a stand-alone wall, painted in an Aegean blue. Within its recessed alcove, a single small painting held pride of place.

"That's not Southwestern," said Dom. "European, I believe, and very old."

"It has a curious appeal," said Karen. "The woman looks as though she could be sharing a secret with you."

"*Lady in White* by Anonicelli the Younger, painted in the late 1600s," read Dom. "One of only nine of his paintings still existing."

"I'm sure it's worth a pretty penny."

"Wonder how they came by it."

"I'd expect to see it in a museum."

They went past the blue wall, wandering the Middle Room's offerings of paintings, sculptures, and pottery.

"The Jimenez exhibit is in the next room," said Dom.

They walked into the showroom dubbed Near. Windows gave this space a different quality of light. A portly, white-haired man was seated at a desk in front near the gift shop.

Uff da. Karen felt a mischievous smile curve her lips. The man still worked here and did look like the Tomten from Krista's book. He was dressed in a suit and tie that would have been fashionable decades ago.

She faced Joaquin's work. A dozen figurative bronzes were arranged on podiums and tables. Karen found the sculpture of the young woman at the gravestone that Dulcie had admired.

"Dulcie's right. The sorrow on the woman's face tugs at your heart."

"It's not just her face," said Dom. "Look at her posture."

Karen stepped back to look at the whole group. "That's what I like about Joaquin's work. He has a real gift for capturing emotion."

Dom touched her elbow. "I'll check out the gift shop. Take your time."

Karen couldn't help but smile. Dom had spotted books. He always did.

As she meandered around the sculptures, a man with a muscular, wiry build, dark hair, mustache, and a light brown complexion came in. She recognized Joaquin. Good. Dom would enjoy meeting him.

Joaquin stopped to talk to the man seated at the desk. His energy stood out against the Tomten's sleepiness.

Karen waited until they finished talking. When Joaquin turned and saw her, his eyes lit up in recognition. His eyes were one of his most memorable features—dark, almost black, conveying warmth and interest. Karen wondered if he had felt the intensity of emotions he'd imbued into his sculptures.

"Karen, isn't it? I remember your work from the Cathedral Park Festival."

"It is. I'm impressed with your exhibit. You've added several new pieces since then."

"Have you met the gallery manager?"

The Tomten smiled. "I'm Otto Griffin."

"Karen Bjornson—"

Joaquin interrupted. "Karen, have you heard about the Niemöller competition this gallery is sponsoring? When I exhibited my work at their Phoenix gallery, they had a show about art as a catalyst for change. Now there's a new one. That's a hallmark of your galleries, isn't it, Otto?"

"Yes, it's a tradition the owner, William Adams, feels strongly about. There's more than one exhibit making the rounds at any one time. Do you plan to enter, Joaquin?"

"Yes, William gave me the entry packet last week."

Karen's interest was piqued. "Art as a catalyst for change? Tell me more."

"Are you an artist?" asked Otto.

"Yes, I am."

He handed her a promotional card. Could this be her answer? Dom left the gift shop and came to stand nearby. She introduced Dom and gave him the card. His eyebrows raised in interest.

Joaquin encouraged her. "Why don't you enter?"

"When is the call?"

"Entries are submitted in June," said Joaquin. "Winners are announced on July 14. Give her a packet, Otto. She does fine work."

Otto took a manila envelope from a desk drawer. "What is your medium?"

"I do art tapestries."

He hesitated. "This is not a craft fair for ladies and their handicrafts."

"I wouldn't expect so," said Karen.

Joaquin reacted. "Otto, have you seen her work?"

"Well, no, but—"

"Then you can be forgiven for your ignorance. Give her the damn packet."

Otto relinquished it.

"Thank you." Karen held her head high.

Dom gave her a quick wink over the manager's head. "The other day your son was talking about looking for something special for Skyla. I'm wondering if he'd consider one of these bronzes."

Karen noticed Otto didn't make any more disparaging remarks to her. He was smart enough not to antagonize a potential customer. A Tomten? Maybe not. He looked the part, but his sour expression was at odds with friendly care of children and animals.

Karen heard the raised voice of a young person from a glassed-in work area in the rear. She glanced back to see a teenager and an older man.

"You don't make sense. Just because it's digital, doesn't mean it isn't good art."

A more subdued voice, words unintelligible, replied.

The first speaker countered. "Why won't you even take a look?"

Otto winced. "I'd like to show you a special painting." He led the way into the Middle Room.

Karen knew they were being drawn away from the strident voice but played along. As they neared the archway, she heard a door slam hard enough to make the work-area windows rattle and saw the teenager running past, a scowl on his face. What was all that about?

They dutifully looked at the painting Otto pointed out.

As they left, Karen paused to sign the guest book, then glanced toward the borzoi statue. A large glob of viscous liquid was dripping down the bronze head.

"E-yew! Is that spit?"

"Gross. Who would have done such a thing?" Dom opened the door for Karen.

Karen had a good idea of who, but the why was beyond her.

As they left, she glanced toward the winterberry bush. The bluebirds were gone, the bush stripped bare.

"Well, that was a worthwhile adventure," said Dom. "How about I take you to lunch, and we can see what this Niemöller exhibit involves?"

Dom drove to the upscale Museum Hill Café, one of his favorite restaurants, part of a museum complex set in the more rugged terrain where Santa Fe edged onto the foothills of Mount

Atalaya. He could count on excellent service and delicious food presented artistically. The restaurant's wall of windows afforded a vista across the Botanical Garden. Native piñon and juniper obscured the homes and buildings of Santa Fe, self-dubbed the City Different, where the tallest building was the Cathedral Basilica, two miles away downtown.

After the waiter took their order and brought their wine, Karen opened the seal on the packet. The top item was a card with the quote by Martin Niemöller, "First They Came."

"These words are familiar," said Karen. "I didn't know who said them."

"Does it say who Niemöller was?" asked Dom.

"It says, 'How can your art express Niemöller's message to our present-day world?' Do you know of him?"

Dom sipped his Chardonnay. "Niemöller was a German pastor from the Second World War. At first, he was a staunch supporter of the Nazi regime."

The waiter placed their entrees in front of them—mixed greens with grilled salmon and roasted asparagus.

"Glad you recommended this. It looks great." Karen set aside her papers and began to eat. "At first you said. What happened to Niemöller?"

"The quote is autobiographical. As each of the groups, Jews, or others, succumbed to the Third Reich, people let it happen. Then Hitler tried controlling the church. Some resisted, Niemöller among them. They found themselves alone. Niemöller and many others spent years in concentration camps until the Allies liberated them in 1945. He survived. Many clergy didn't."

"What did he do after he was freed?"

"He'd learned a lesson in those concentration camps. He believed his countrymen had a moral obligation to acknowledge their guilt, to repent and change their ways. He led by example, speaking out against racism and bigotry till he died, an old man in his nineties."

"I'm beginning to see what the organizers of this competition are looking for. I should learn more about Niemöller."

"When we get back, I'll crank up my laptop. This old history professor will tell you more than you want to know."

Karen smiled. "I pressed the right button, didn't I?"

"Indeed." When Dom finished, he leaned back and sipped his wine, watching Karen enjoy her last bites. He smiled as she sent another yearning glance at the packet. He signaled their waiter and ordered coffees.

Finally, Karen placed her utensils on her plate and picked up a sheet of vellum from the packet. "Here are the rules. Each entry should include a statement about the art and its vision for change. Oooh, I like this. Winners will get national recognition from the exhibit tour."

Her look was sparkly. He loved seeing her like this.

"This is wonderful, Dom. To use my art to make a difference. Do you suppose I could?"

"Why not?" Dom grinned. "How many winners will there be?"

"Uff da. The competition will be fierce. Around sixty works will be chosen."

"Does it list fiber arts?"

"Yes." Karen put that page down. "I get so tired of attitudes like that manager's. Ladies' handicrafts!"

"Joaquin gave him a proper put-down."

Karen chuckled. "I saw you struggling not to laugh."

She picked up the next page. "June thirtieth is the deadline. Less than five months. Uff da. I don't know, Dom. Weaving is time-consuming—designing, planning the colors, warping the loom—let alone the actual weaving and finishing."

"You're in control of a lot of that. The size, the complexity."

"But it still has to win." She sipped her coffee. "I could start right away. But in the middle of it, the shearers will be coming. Anton and Skyla's baby will be born. Nothing, not even weaving, will keep me from my new grandbaby."

55

"Could your students help?"

"Dulcie, maybe. She learns quickly. She could do butterfly skeins and help me warp the loom. She'd jump at the chance to get extra income for what she loves to do."

"Could I help? I'm good at rubbing kinks out of tired shoulders."

"You are. And having you with me—reading, working on your novel, listening to music, and solving the problems of the world as I work—that's such a gift." Karen sat back with a sigh, letting her glasses fall on their leash. "I'd love to have a go at this."

"Do you have a vision for what it might look like?"

"I've been playing with sketches ever since last fall when the light-on-the-hill idea became important to me. I wonder if any could grow into this concept. Would you mind looking at my sketches with me? Bounce ideas around?"

"Happy to." Dom laid his napkin down and took her hands. "You're positively glowing. I have high hopes for your creation. Show the world what this weaver can do."

"It means a lot that you believe in me. But it will take all my time. You don't know how obsessed I get. What about time for us? Hashing out all the financial and legal stuff? It's not fair to you to devote all my time and energy to this."

"Listen. I want you to do this. Create your art. When your tapestry of light is done, then we'll tackle those sticky wickets."

"You're sure?"

"Absolutely positive."

A reprieve? Meant to be?

He was of two minds.

On one hand, it would only put off eventual pain, no matter which alternative he chose.

On the other, a sense of relief flooded him. *Carpe diem.* Enjoy it while it lasts.

CHAPTER SEVEN

That night in Dom's bedroom of his Eastside home, Karen added another idea to her list of possible themes for her tapestry.

"I've found one biography on Niemöller," said Dom. "Shall I start reading it to you?"

"It'll keep till tomorrow. I'm bushed." Karen held out a hand to him. "Will we ever be living together without two places?"

"God, I hope so. Living out of a suitcase gets old." Dom tugged on her hand, and she went willingly into his arms. "It'll be odd when I leave here. This adobe has been home all my life. I'm glad it will still be in the family."

"Sam and Farah could fill it with more children."

"I like that thought," said Dom.

"I was thinking about the old pictures on your walls. Some Sam will keep. But you will want some—to make your new home your space."

"Mm-hmm."

"You know the long hallway by my studio? We could turn that into a family gallery of sorts. Ancestors, your family, my family, Skyla's too."

"I'd love that. A nice visual of belonging."

"You do belong."

"You know the picture of the young blond man on your bookshelf? I've seen you trail your fingers over it like his absence was painful. Is that your nephew, Vidar?"

Karen was surprised. "Yes, how did you know about him?"

"Sam told me. That whole incident affected so many lives. Sam very nearly left the police force after that."

"Of course, I didn't think. Vidar was a troubled soul. Tough childhood. His death had a profound impact on me. It made me wonder." Her eyes searched his. "Was there a way I could have stepped in? Edvar and I tried to intervene. But we didn't have the right, and his father hated us. I feel I owe Vidar. I know I can't bring him back." She paused. "I'm still here. My life has to make a difference."

His arms tightened around her as they stood quietly.

Her voice broke the silence. "Do you have second thoughts about moving in with me, rather than the other way around?"

"We chose the practical way. The ranch and the studio are your business. Me, I'm retired. If you're there, and I have space for my books and my computer, I'm content."

"With all your books, I'm glad our house is so big." Karen reached a hand to the polished bulbous carving on the Jacobean-style poster nearest her. A top frame connected the four posters and the solid carved headboard. She wondered if there had once been a canopy and curtains. "This is a massive bed. It looks really old."

Dom grinned. "This four-poster has been in the Baca family for over two hundred years. Many generations of our family were conceived in this bed, including me and my daughter. Dolores told me she wanted the bed to stay in her family."

"It should go to your blood-kin. Put that in our pre-nup."

"When I do move my furniture, I'd like it to be our bed."

"Okay by me. Mine could go into a guest room."

He pulled her down with him, so they lay across the bed. "Remember that night at your place when we finally knew something was happening between us?"

"I had just put away my wedding ring."

"You were so beautiful. I didn't know if you could love this old man."

"I wanted you to stay."

"Then you came up with those chocolate-chunk cookies you'd set on the hearth. All melty. You minx, you knew what would happen."

"I hoped for what did."

"You said I had chocolate on my lips and wiped it off with your finger. You made such a production of licking your finger clean of that gooey chocolate. I couldn't look away. My God, Karen, what a siren you can be."

She smiled, enjoying the memories.

Dom propped himself up on an elbow to look down at her. "Remember the time when Anton came home from Skyla's in the wee hours and caught us?"

"I don't know who was more surprised."

"I wish Dolores could accept you like Anton does me." Dom flopped back down.

"Do you suppose it's harder for daughters to accept new relationships for their widowed fathers?"

"Seems true for her. She's my only child. I want her to be happy we are together."

CHAPTER EIGHT

Monday, February 13

The next morning, they returned to the ranch. Thoughts of her tapestry consumed Karen, no matter where she was or what task she did. Her folder with ideas burgeoned with colored sketches and ideas she struggled to capture before they fled her brain.

Karen printed out the Niemöller quote in a large font and hung it in her studio. It had to guide her work.

She set goals. It was now February 13. By the month's end, the size and the design must be nailed down, her loom warped, and the major blocks of color and how the eye would move through the vision mapped out.

Karen perused images woven by Maximo Laura, a weaver with whom she'd studied. He never failed to inspire her—not to copy—but just to drink in the color, the vibrancy, the light, the shadow, what made his figures stand out. To imagine how her vision might be created.

She hired Dulcie and started her on inventorying yarn colors. Over the years, Karen had developed binders with samples of all her yarn colors and the blends made from them. Every hue, tone, and shade had its own number. Dulcie's task would be making butterfly skeins with all the subtle hues Karen would need.

Most of the weft yarn that formed the design would be woven from small butterfly skeins, which Karen could manipulate over and under the warp threads. Each figure on her design might contain colors from several skeins, allowing form, shadows, and gradations to emerge.

What would be the focal point of her tapestry?

Dom read to her from Niemöller's writing, and a picture of the man, his flaws, and his mission formed in her mind.

Gradually, themes emerged that seemed right. Movement from dark to light. Bridges, not walls. She felt a growing certainty that Niemöller, if he were alive today, would have expressed deep concerns over the plight of immigrants and how they were treated.

This work had to be her best; it had to win over the judges if it were to be awarded a spot in the exhibit. She felt overwhelmed. Unable to see the clear task ahead because of the clutter of details.

Could she bring some of the Circle Sleuths together and pose the problem? The Sleuths were a group of friends who had bonded in the process of solving the mystery behind the danger that threatened the Bjornsons almost two years ago. Would the Sleuths help clarify her vision? Their dialogue would be lively and provocative. These kindred spirits never stopped challenging her, inspiring her, and giving her hope.

She set a date for a gathering on Saturday, February 18, a buffet supper in the Bjornson family room.

She hadn't thought about it before, but there was the complete spectrum of immigration patterns within the Sleuths. Maria's ancestors had lived here before it was part of the United States. Dom's forebears had come with the conquistadors four hundred years ago. Her own people and her husband's had come to America from Norway with the waves of immigrants in the late nineteenth century. The parents of Pete Schultz, their detective friend, came from Germany, and Diego's from Peru, making them first-generation Americans, as was Dulcie's son. Pete's wife, Akiko, had been born in Japan, Dulcie in Mexico, and Farah and Leyla, Sam's wife and adopted daughter, in Syria.

Each had a story to tell. It was time to listen.

CHAPTER NINE

Wednesday, February 15

Otto arrived early for work at the gallery—a habit he'd formed decades ago. Fewer mistakes were made when one had plenty of time to be methodical.

He parked behind the gallery, fished his security system notes from his pocket, and gingerly punched in a sequence of numbers. Then he unlocked the door and hurried to input the rest of the codes. The unit remained quiet, and the digital security panel behaved.

He breathed a sigh of relief. Practice and Algie's coaching had paid off.

Humming a Barry Manilow tune, he turned on the lights and walked through all the rooms to see that everything was in order. Then he stopped in front of *Lady in White*. It was not a large painting, fourteen by sixteen inches with its ornate frame.

"Good morning, my lady. Don't worry about thieves. Not while I'm here."

He marveled at the way her eyes seemed to look directly at him. Her luxurious dark hair was drawn up with a ribbon, but one tendril had escaped to caress the delicate line of her neck. She was dressed in filmy, white softness. The low neckline showed the sweet curve of her upper breast. Demure, yet he felt an incredible pull. The young woman's hand hovered above her neckline and its slightly loosened ties. Her cheeks held a light blush, and her lips were parted as though she were about to speak. He often fantasized that she would whisper his name.

Someday—a day that would tear his heart out—a buyer would take his lady away forever. Shortly after the gallery had reopened under William's ownership and this exquisite piece had gone on display, a burly businessman had been taken with the Anonicelli. He'd asked Otto the price. Otto looked at his gaudy, custom cowboy boots, his florid face with piggy eyes, and smelled his stink of fine whisky and stale smoke.

Otto lied, all the time shaking in his shoes. He'd rattled off a price close to three million, triple what William wanted. The man leered at the Lady for several minutes. Otto cringed inside.

Then the man said he wouldn't pay more than two million. God forbid William ever found out what Otto had done.

But his lady would have despised belonging to that man. He knew she looked to him for protection. He'd promised to keep her safe.

Otto went to his front desk to tackle the day's tasks. One part of the desk was raised, forming a shelf for brochures. Underneath that section, discreet screens allowed him to see activity in any of the rooms. He'd learned to take the interruptions of visitors in stride, watching them on the monitors.

A young man, neatly dressed in a brown leather jacket and tan flat cap, entered the gallery lobby. He unzipped his jacket and tucked his gloves into his pockets. Then he turned toward the right and disappeared into the Far Room.

Otto's internal timer, set from long years' experience, began ticking down. He knew how long visitors would take to travel through the two rooms into the area where he sat. Some he pegged for a quick trip. If they took longer, he would check the monitors and see what captured their attention. He would seek them out and begin a conversation to determine their interest in making a purchase.

The young man didn't show, and Otto found him on the monitor, standing in the Middle Room studying *Lady in White*. His heartbeat quickened. Oh, my. A buyer? Or possibly a thief?

But as Otto approached, his trepidation diminished. This man had a respectful demeanor. He was maybe thirty years old, with brown wavy hair, just a tad bit longer than stylish. Clean shaven.

"Welcome to the Swift and Adams Gallery. I'm the manager. Let me know if I can answer any questions."

The young man smiled. "Ruben Turner."

"Pleased to meet you, Mr. Turner."

"Ruben, please. I'm in awe of this painting. It's almost as if she will come alive and speak. Is there a story behind this exquisite work?"

Otto recited the dry details. Was it at all possible this man could purchase his lady? Not many visitors were interested in the history of a piece, but this man seemed rapt, hanging on Otto's every word.

"I'm impressed by your knowledge. Do you have time to tell me about other paintings?"

After Otto expounded on several other works, they paused again in front of *Lady in White*.

"I hesitate to ask, but what is the price of this painting?"

Otto told him the true price. If he had to let the lady leave him, she could go to this charming man who saw that she was real. He was impressed with his easy smile and the sincerity in his brown eyes.

Ruben shook his head and turned to Otto. "Too rich for me. But I am looking for a painting that I can relate to."

The flood of relief Otto felt was interrupted by the sound of people entering. "Excuse me, I'll be right back."

"I'll be here."

Otto hurried away to greet the newcomers. He rang up several greeting cards before scurrying back. The young man was still there, gazing at the Anonicelli.

"I'm drawn to her. Isn't it unusual to have an old masterpiece hanging in a gallery rather than a museum? Security must cost a fortune."

"The lady is well-protected."

"Maybe you can give me some advice. My friends tell me I should think like an investor when I buy art, but I want something that makes me feel pleasure, not just a work that may increase in value."

Otto launched into his salesman mode. "You are absolutely correct. Are you interested in a portrait?" He was certain he could find the right work. "What price range are you considering?"

He heard more visitors and stepped away to greet them.

Would Ruben stay through these interruptions? Or would he use them as an excuse to leave? It was never this busy on a weekday morning! He started back, only to find Ruben approaching his desk.

"Look," said Ruben. "I shouldn't keep you from your work, but I enjoy listening to you."

Otto saw Ruben glance at the crystal candy dish on his desk—today it was filled with individually wrapped chocolates. "Please, take one."

"I do like good chocolate. I see you have the best."

Otto chuckled. "We just hired a guard. I can leave the money in the cash register, but I have to put the chocolates in the safe. Isn't that absurd?"

"He should be trustworthy with the money. Not absurd at all."

Otto blinked. Maybe he didn't get the joke.

Ruben smiled. "I wondered if we could meet for a drink after you finish work some day? You could tell me more."

"I'd like that."

"Do you know the Blue Goose over by the train station?"

"I've heard of it, but I've not been there," said Otto.

They arranged to meet there the following week. Such a nice young man. Otto scurried off, humming snatches of "I Can't Smile Without You," to greet another group of visitors.

CHAPTER TEN

Saturday, February 18

In his home office, Cecil rolled back from his desk with a sound of disgust to look out the window. The view of his enclosed patio with its dormant young tree was just about as exciting as what he'd found digging into the backgrounds of Otto and Guy. Nothing. Why couldn't the FBI catch the thief and get out of his hair?

It was Saturday, and he planned to work at home. In peace and quiet, he'd get a head start on the security schematic for a new client. But then Tuttle had called. Said he was dropping by to show him something.

Resigned, Cecil fixed a pot of coffee, not that he felt that hospitable toward Tuttle. Rather than disturb the plans spread out in his office, he and Tuttle could meet in the kitchen.

Tuttle got right to the point when he arrived. "Haven't found anything in common between the owners and staff of the galleries with stolen Anonicellis, so I started looking for patterns in the thief's MO. We know security was breached through an employee connection, but all swore their innocence."

Cecil leaned back in his chair. "What kind of employees did he target?"

"In New York, apparently a lower level keyholder, an employee responsible for closing. In L.A., it was through the security guards. In Minneapolis, it seems to be the manager. She was fired before she was killed."

"Could whoever fired her have set her up to take the blame? Then conveniently shut her up?"

"Yes, we're looking at the owners." Tuttle shifted in his seat. "Why the sudden frown?"

"I can see Guy schmoozing with managers. But I'm having a hard time putting Guy together in my mind with the little people. Seems out of character for him."

"Would he hold his nose and do it if it helped him get what he wanted?"

Cecil shrugged.

"You have a good mind, Dupre. I wish you'd come back to our team."

Cecil doodled on a scratch pad, thinking about the staff at Swift & Adams. "You said no ties between any staff in the three galleries. How about all the individuals visiting them? Certainly you have security camera footage. Did you run any of it through your fancy face-recognition software?"

"A few repeats. That's what I wanted you to see." Tuttle scrolled on his phone to several photos.

Cecil pointed at one of them. "I know this one. A sculptor. Joaquin Jimenez. He's got a show currently in Swift and Adams."

"What else can you tell me?"

"Does quality figurative art. Sells well. He shows in all of William's galleries. Fairly aggressive about marketing his work. Travels a lot. He has a combo residence / studio on Canyon Road, not far from Swift and Adams."

Tuttle raised an eyebrow. "An average property there is in the millions. How can he afford that?"

Cecil shrugged. "Oddly enough, he's never volunteered that information to me."

Tuttle looked at his watch. "Check him out. Keep in touch."

Cecil closed the door behind the agent. That was all he wanted? Tuttle could have emailed the photos and saved himself a trip. Translation—he knew it would be harder for Cecil to resist the pressure when he was in his face.

He didn't know Joaquin Jimenez well, but he'd always wondered about him. Behind the smokescreen of success, was there someone worth keeping an eye on?

Needing a change of scenery, he decided to go downtown to Books & Bearclaws and see if they had anything new by John Grisham. Much of crime fiction he found laughable, written by people who didn't know what they were talking about, but Grisham's legal thrillers sometimes captivated him.

Cecil walked into Books & Bearclaws a short time later. He saw a tall blond man picking up his coffee, recognizing him from the few Chamber meetings he'd attended. Nice guy, maybe even more into gadgets than he was.

Cecil extended his hand. "Bjornson. Anything new with the Chamber? I've been out of town a lot."

Anton's grip was firm. "Good to see you, Dupre. You're asking the wrong person. My attendance hasn't been great."

"Drone business keep you busy over the holidays?"

"That, and I've married again." Anton waved at the empty chair. "Join me? I'm upgrading my security system. I'd like to pick your brain."

"Sure. Let me get some coffee."

When Cecil sat, Anton explained what he was looking for. "Our ranch is huge. I have a good monitoring system, but it's impossible to set up cameras on all the access points."

"Can you show me a rough idea?"

Anton grabbed a pen and started drawing roads, his gate, and his driveway on a napkin.

A visibly pregnant woman pulled a chair to their table as Anton's face lit up. "This is Skyla, my wife. She's a park ranger at Pecos."

"Hi, I'm Cecil Dupre." Cecil smiled, not only in welcome, but at the pride in Anton's voice. Lucky man. Park ranger. That would account for her athletic look.

"I do believe you're the first real Cecil I've met," said Skyla.

Cecil laughed. "Here it comes. All my life those words have been followed by, 'Of course I've heard of Cecil B. DeMille.' "

Anton smirked. "Don't forget Beany and Cecil."

A blonde, blue-eyed girl put a couple of books on their table and sat down. "Who are Beany and Cecil?"

"Thank you, young lady," said Cecil. "You made my day."

"My daughter, Krista," said Anton. "Beany and Cecil were cartoon characters from way back."

"Cecil was the likeable, but not-very-bright sea monster. I took a lot of ribbing about my name growing up." Married again, Anton had said. Krista could be a teenager. He wondered what happened to her mother.

Krista began showing her books to Skyla, and he and Anton went back to the makeshift map.

"There must be natural trails. How about motion-triggered cameras?"

"They'd be going off all the time. Wildlife."

Cecil leaned back to sip his coffee. "I've read about artificial intelligence ways of filtering out wildlife. I'll look that up again. It'd be easier to actually see your place, to see what you're up against."

Anton waved the napkin. "You mean my map isn't doing it? Could you come out some afternoon? I'll knock off work early."

Skyla looked over at him. "Bring your family, stay for dinner."

"No family, but I'd love dinner."

"Great." Anton picked up his phone. "Is Wednesday okay? February 22? I'm not asking for a freebie here. I'll pay you for your time."

Cecil shook his head. "Make you a deal. I'll come early enough for you to show me your latest in drones. I've a shitload of questions for you. Drones have always intrigued me. Fair trade?"

Anton shook his hand. "Deal. Fun too. The only thing I like better than showing off my gadgets, is exploring other gadgets."

"Isn't that the truth?" Skyla grinned. "He loves new toys."

Chapter Eleven

After lunch, Diego Quispe climbed the outside stairs to the covered deck of the barn overlooking the alpaca pens, horse corral, and the driveway of the Bjornson ranch. With his coffee, he settled into the sturdy wooden swing seat, setting it in motion with a push of his foot. This was a favorite spot to think, plan, and renew his energy while looking out over the critters under his care.

The air was fine for mid-February. The morning chill had given way to the sun's warmth. To his left, the Sangre de Cristos rose across the valley. Puffy white clouds sent ever-shifting shadows over the distant terrain of tans, blues, and snowcaps.

Nearby sprawled the two-story Bjornson faux-dobe home. The side nearest him held Karen's wing with her weaving studio. The driveway split, one branch coming into the small lot outside the studio, and the other branch circling past the front of the house to the garages connected to Anton's wing.

Movement in the alpaca pens caught his eye and he grinned at the playful yearlings. They pronked, moving for the sheer joy of it, like exuberant children skipping.

Beyond in the horse corral, his Peruvian Paso dozed with the other horses in the sun. The animals raised their heads as a car came up the long drive. Dulcie was coming to help Maria get ready for the gathering that evening. The alpacas crowded toward the fence, watching as she parked her yellow car outside the studio.

Diego sipped his coffee, using his foot to keep the swing in motion on well-oiled chains. Dulcie got out of the car, as did a boy about Krista's age. He looked around, his eyes settling on the animals. This must be Santos, Dulcie Rodriguez's son, the one Karen had told him to keep an eye out for.

Dulcie, the breeze catching her long brown hair, motioned to Santos, and they went inside.

After a while the boy came out and walked to the alpaca pens. Diego watched. Some kids didn't know how to behave around animals. The creatures of white, brown, gray, black, and cream crowded closer. The boy backed up.

Diego sipped slowly, approving of his quiet manner. He knew Santos was in Krista's class at school and had been a bully, but Sam had stepped in and gotten him involved in PAL sports. Since then, Krista only had good things to say about him. He knew the boy's father had been killed in service. It had to be tough to be without a dad.

He set his cup aside and went quietly down the steps. His feet crunched on the gravel as he walked toward the pens. The boy spun around, alarm on his face, brown eyes wide.

"I wasn't doing anything wrong."

"Never said you were."

"Is it okay if I watch them?"

"You're Dulcie's son, Santos. I've heard her talk about you. I'm Diego. You like animals?"

"Yeah, I have a cat named Tuffy. Can I pet them?"

"If you're quiet and don't make any sudden moves, they might let you."

Santos reached for the head of a nearby alpaca. It swerved and moved away.

"When the next one comes close, keep your palm up and lower, to scratch their neck. Blanca thought you were trying to grab her."

"Oh, sorry. Do they all have names?" Santos extended his hand slowly to a small gray alpaca.

Diego smiled. The kid listened well. "They do. The gray one sniffing your fingers is Thunderbump. He's not a year old yet. Baby alpacas are called crias."

Santos gently touched the cria's neck. "Gosh, he's soft."

Diego chuckled. "There's nothing finer than baby alpaca."

"Will he bite me?"

"Alpacas can't bite, not really. They only have lower teeth. Just a hard pad on top."

As he talked with Santos, Diego felt more comfortable. He listened as Santos told him all about Tuffy. He found himself inviting the boy to help feed the animals. He grinned as Santos peppered him with questions. How come? What's this? How do you know that? Why?

Dulcie came out after a while to check on her son, and Santos pulled her toward the pens, telling her what he'd learned.

Diego was surprised at how fast the time had flown. He'd enjoyed the kid's company. His own daughter lived so far away, and because of his divorce, she hadn't been around him much as she was growing up. It was a shame he had no one to pass his knowledge to. If only he had a son that he could teach, but that wasn't how life had played out.

CHAPTER TWELVE

Everyone Karen had invited for brainstorming night had come.

Pete and Akiko were the first to arrive. Then came Sam, his wife, Farah, and their daughter, Leyla, who was Krista's best friend. Karen had included Dulcie and her son, not only because Dulcie was helping with her tapestry, but because their stories were important.

When they'd gotten to the cherry-pie-and-coffee stage, Karen began. "You know my motive for this gathering." She described the competition rules, gave a few facts about Niemöller, and read the "First They Came" quote. "I'm leaning toward the theme of immigrants and voices speaking up on their behalf. I want to hear what would touch people's hearts and fit with the quote. I'm looking for ideas that would express that theme." She set aside her pie and picked up her pencil. "Fair warning. I'm taking notes. What you say is valuable."

Dom cut a forkful of cherry pie. "I've heard many off-the-wall paraphrases of Niemöller's words. They could come for any group—the blue-eyed, the Baptists, the Canadians, or those on the other side of the tracks—any name you want to plug in there. Because you weren't any of those folks, you did nothing. Then when they finally came for you, there was no one left to stand up for you." The bite disappeared into his mouth.

Karen turned to Farah, sitting next to Sam on the sofa. "What did you think when you heard Niemöller's words?"

Farah tucked an errant light-brown curl behind her ear. "I thought of overflowing Syrian refugee boats. The little boy who drowned and washed up on the beach. That horrific photo forced people to confront how desperate the situation was."

Farah looked over at her daughter, listening from the counter with her friends, then turned back to Karen. "When you called, strong feelings flooded my memory. Sadness at leaving home. Grief and anger when my husband, Halim, was killed. Fear of the unknown. America held promise and hope, but when we came, I did not feel welcome. I felt hate. Some did not see me at all, just a terrible Syrian. I ached with loneliness. Above all I wanted a place to belong."

Sam, dark-haired and gentle, took Farah's hand.

Karen's pencil hovered over her page. "How can I put those feelings into images?"

Anton stretched out his long legs on a hassock. "How about opposites? Movement, like from despair to hope?"

"That's good," said Karen, "But what images do you see?"

A chorus started, slowly at first, and growing, until Karen struggled to keep up on paper.

"A solitary figure, looking at a group."

"Statue of Liberty."

"Generic figures in action, fighting, running, hitting, reaching out."

"Fists."

"Or the opposite. Open hands."

"Barbed wire."

"Deep, intense colors."

"What color is loneliness?" asked Skyla.

"I think it is light blue," said Farah.

Dulcie said, "We come from different places, Farah, but my story is like yours. In our Mexican village, life was scary. Violence took part of my family. We came to America to find a better future. My husband joined the U.S. Army and died fighting for this country. I worked hard for citizenship."

Pete's voice came from across the room. "I'm glad Santa Fe is a sanctuary city. We need to take a good look at the whole immigration ball of wax. There's not a one-size-fits-all."

"Ball of wax?" asked Dulcie.

"Sorry," said Pete. "A comprehensive look at the whole topic."

Skyla chuckled. "The other day we had a group of visitors come through the gift shop at Pecos. One of them had a sweatshirt with a Native American on it. The slogan said, FIGHTING TERRORISM SINCE 1492."

"I've seen that one," said Sam. "Thought about getting it."

Diego spoke up. "People ask why immigrants leave their homes. Why don't they stay where they belong and just fix things? That annoys me."

Anton huffed. "Have you ever noticed who's asking? Some hypocrite with a short memory whose ancestors came not long ago."

Pete looked serious. "They're showing ignorance and lack of empathy. They've no clue about the agonizing situations that force people to leave home. Both sets of my grandparents left Germany after the Second World War. My parents were only small children—just old enough to remember the bombings and chaos. They witnessed friends and neighbors being taken suddenly, never to be seen again."

He paused, seemingly struggling to verbalize something very personal. "My paternal grandmother never talked about the war. She'd seen things, maybe even done things, that troubled her deeply. She wrote a poem when she left Germany. I found it after she died. Translated roughly, it said you don't leave home unless home chases you away. It has become a beast with teeth of hatred and intolerance, mouth wide open to devour you. Home is no more."

"More images for you, Karen," said Sam.

"Beasts, scary monsters," said Krista.

"Beasts or predators?" asked Skyla. "Is this going to be a classic good-versus-evil image?"

"Is that good?" asked Karen. "I don't want to create a cliché."

"You have duality built into your work already," said Dom. "Darkness versus light. Universal ideas often work well. They don't have to be cliché."

Karen smiled at him. "Dulcie and Farah spoke of hope. When I turn on the news these days, I don't hear about the promised land, the America I love and believe in. Now I hear about walls. It makes me sad."

"That guy's quote," said Diego, "makes me think of protecting what can't protect itself, like the animals. My people herded alpacas in Peru. Alpacas and the land were their whole life."

Her ranch manager was generally quiet. Karen didn't often think about his ancestry, but his dark eyes, high cheekbones, and strong straight nose were those of the long-ago Incas.

"Hundreds of years ago, my people were taken over by the Spanish." Diego set down his pie plate. "They didn't care about us, just wealth. Alpacas ate the grass they wanted for their sheep. They slaughtered alpacas for meat and almost wiped them out. My people fled high into the mountains, saving alpacas from extinction."

Dom set his cup carefully into its saucer. "I've had to come to terms with the legacy my Spanish forebears brought to American shores. Many of them were ignorant and cruel."

"Dom, I didn't mean you," Diego's voice was alarmed.

"I know, Diego. We may be shaped by our ancestors, but we are not them. We choose our own roads, and hopefully, make better choices than they made."

"Empathy," said Sam. "We should ask ourselves what we would feel if the roles were switched."

Santos looked over at Sam, his coach on the PAL basketball team. "We put ourselves in their shoes."

"Exactly." He and Santos exchanged a long-distance high five.

"Friends are important," said Leyla. "It was hard moving to a new country. To speak English without silly mistakes. Friends made the difference."

"A big difference." Farah smiled at her daughter.

Pete frowned into his empty coffee cup. Anton brought the pot over and filled it.

"Oaths are important," said Pete. "If I want justice for myself, then I must protect my neighbor's justice. Why didn't *Niemöller* know that? He read the same Bible I do."

Anton snorted as he continued around the room with the coffee pot. "And we know how all Christians today believe the same things and always agree on everything."

"Okay, okay, point taken," Pete grumbled.

Dom held out his cup for Anton. "Fascism is insidious. It creeps along, gaining strength, masquerading innocently as a good thing, until, like what happened to Niemöller, you find yourself with freedom and friends gone. Today's world is no exception. We can be blind as to what is happening around us."

Dom added cream to his coffee and looked around. "Sorry, sometimes the history professor in me won't quit. We're getting off topic. Karen hasn't written any notes now for several minutes."

"Sorry, Karen," said Pete. "We got carried away."

"It's all pertinent," she said. "I want to ask. What colors do you see in what you've been saying?"

"Huh? That's a non-sequitur," said Anton.

"What's a non-seck-wit?" asked Santos.

Farah chuckled. "Something that does not logically follow what went before."

"It does follow," said Skyla, adding another cushion behind her back. "Feelings and ideas are often connected with colors in your mind. If you said the word violence or hate, you'd probably think of red or black. If you said growth, green would likely come to mind. Farah said earlier that loneliness was light blue. That was brilliant."

Karen gave her daughter-in-law a thumbs-up.

"Red. Blood red."

"Oranges, colors of flame."

"Tell you what I didn't see," said Sam. "Blues, greens, peaceful colors."

"Not a pale shade to be found," said Akiko.

"Are you going to save all the yellow hues for the light?" asked Krista.

"Here's an idea," said Dulcie. "Include all the colors humans come in."

"Maybe you should mix all the race colors into one," said Skyla.

"You mean like a melting pot?" asked Maria.

"Yeah. What color would you end up with?" asked Diego.

"Probably puce," said Pete.

"What's puce?" asked Leyla. "It sounds icky."

"Pukey green," said Anton.

"E-yew," said Krista.

Dom chuckled. "Many people think it's greenish, but it's actually a reddish-brown color. It comes from the French word for flea."

"Double e-yew," said Krista.

"W," said Leyla with a giggle.

A passionate voice cut into the joking. "I hate the idea of a melting pot."

Karen twisted around in surprise to Akiko at the opposite end of their roomy sofa.

Akiko sat on the edge of the cushion, dark eyes flashing. "A melting pot is what people talk about when they want you to lose your cultural identity. They want you to be like them, so you don't make them uncomfortable. It's just wrong!"

"But isn't that the goal? So differences don't get in the way of getting along?" asked Maria.

Akiko's voice shook in her vehemence. "Not if we have to hide who we truly are. Not if I have to lose my identity in order to fit in. My people came from Japan. I have a heritage and family traditions I am not willing to give up. I am not a melting pot."

Pete set his cup down and crossed the room to squat in front of his wife, taking her hands. "You are you, my angel. A unique blend of Japanese, a little bit of rubbed-off German, and as American as any of us. Not melted into anything. We've taken good from our cultures and built something new."

Akiko looked into his upturned face for long seconds, then closed her eyes and leaned into his surrounding arms, laying her head on his shoulder.

Karen's eyes traveled around the room, stopping at the three kids at the counter. They were quiet, watching, listening. What a beautiful moment for them to experience. How often did they see the tender side of a marriage outside their own families? She jotted down role models once again.

"What color is this moment, Karen?" asked Sam, obviously impressed by his boss's action.

"I don't know," she said. "But it glows. It's part of the light."

Sam nodded.

"My mind keeps coming back to Adoncia." Karen told the story of what happened in Books and Bearclaws several mornings ago. "Who will be the role models who shape her world?"

Dom leaned back on the sofa and crossed an ankle over his knee. "You know, Niemöller was far from perfect. Truly, he did nothing to stop others from being attacked. But he learned hard lessons in those concentration camps. He never forgot, and he handed on the task with his teaching and his writing."

Pete rose and sat next to Akiko, the others shuffling to make room. "Tell me, Karen, what do you see in this tapestry of yours? Have we helped at all?"

"What will it look like? You've given me a lot to play with. Someone giving light to the darkness. A bridge. A wall. Figures reaching for and giving help. Fingers stretching, fists clenching, hands clutching weapons, hands extended in welcome. And hope."

She looked around the circle of friends and family, each of them so dear. "Has it helped? Yes. Your sharing means a lot to me. But the vision in my head still isn't focused."

"Can you combine elements?" asked Skyla. "Like a bridge made of hands?"

"That's a thought." She frowned. "I don't want it tied to our time, to 2017. I'd rather it be timeless."

"From what vantage point are you seeing this vision of hope?" asked Dom. "Is it through that damn wall we hear about so often?"

"The wall isn't from Niemöller's day," Karen responded. "It's now. I don't know that I want that."

Dom's voice was sure in its conviction. "Walls aren't just stone and steel. They are built with prejudice, hate, and greed. Those were just as much in play in Niemöller's day as ours."

"I just realized something," said Akiko. "What's really sad is that the physical wall isn't the worst part of this struggle. You get to the physical wall in your journey, and you get past it— over, under, around, through. It's the walls of hatred, racism, lies, and injustice that truly divide—for generations. They fester. They poison from within. They are much, much harder to overcome."

The group was quiet, reflecting on Akiko's words.

The small voice of Santos broke the stillness. "You need somebody to show you the way."

Karen smiled at Santos. "Role models. It keeps coming up. I believe Niemöller was saying we are all in this together. Any blessing we want for ourselves we must grant to others as well."

"There you have it, Mom. Show that," said Anton.

"But how?"

CHAPTER THIRTEEN

Tuesday, February 21

Dulcie hurried down the sidewalk of the Lemon Élan office toward her friend Vicky. "Wait," she called in Spanish.

Vicky set a tub of cleaning supplies down by her bright yellow car and straightened. The company cars, like their uniforms, were advertisements for Lemon Élan, the cleaning service they worked for. Vicky's black jacket, identical to Dulcie's own with its logo of lemons, was open in the pleasant morning air.

"My weaving teacher, Karen, just hired me to help with a big tapestry she's doing for a contest."

Vicky opened her arms and met Dulcie's warm hug. "Lucky you. You quit your cleaning job?"

Dulcie shook her head. Lemon Élan was where she and Vicky had met and become friends. "I'll do both. She's willing to work around my cleaning schedule. It's only till the end of June."

"Why don't you and Santos come over for dinner anymore? I miss you doing that."

"Your boyfriend and I don't get along," said Dulcie. "I don't want Santos around Rafa."

Vicky opened her hatchback and bent to pick up her tub. Dulcie's sharp eyes noticed her friend's sudden wince and intake of breath. Vicky rested the tub on the opening and paused, slightly hunched, eyes shut. Then she shoved the tub into its spot. She turned with a wan smile, holding her ribcage below her heart.

"You're hurting. What happened?"

"Nothing." Vicky's response was instant, her tone defensive. "Strained muscle. Damn tub weighs a ton." She shut the hatchback.

"Vicky, did Rafa hit you again?"

"Of course not."

Dulcie raised her eyebrows.

Vicky scowled. "I made him mad. My fault."

"Bull. There's no excuse to hit you."

Vicky twitched her long dark ponytail over her shoulder. "He said he got a job driving a forklift for a big company. I asked him how without a green card. He didn't like it."

"Rafa's no good. He's not going to change." Dulcie took in the lines of pain and worry on her friend's face. She was glad Vicky was starting to push back from the abuse she took way too often.

Vicky opened her car door. "Sometimes Rafa's really sweet. You should find a man, Dulcie. Your husband died ages ago."

"I'm fine. I'd like Santos to have a father, but he deserves the best. Amiga, so do you."

"I wish …" Vicky looked up, her face strained. "I never said this before. Sometimes I wish ICE would pick him up and deport him."

"Vicky!"

"Then it would be out of my hands. Gotta go. Can't be late."

CHAPTER FOURTEEN

Guy Roquet looked up from his laptop in the fishbowl as he heard Otto approach. The door was open, so he not only had a clear view of the exhibit space up front, but the back area with the hallway, kitchen, and storage area as well. William's inner sanctum was dark.

He'd grown used to knowing Otto's whereabouts by the man's obnoxious humming and could even predict Otto's mood by his choice of songs. The fixation on Barry Manilow tunes and his not staying in the same key from the tune's beginning to end unnerved Guy.

"Mail came." Otto handed him two envelopes. "Want coffee?"

"No, thanks."

Guy had a condo in L.A. but was seldom there. His nomadic lifestyle, traveling between seven cities, was aided by the L.A. gallery forwarding mail to him per his schedule—for the business he couldn't handle online. These envelopes were from his personal stockbroker's firm. This should be the good news he'd been waiting for. His previous investments had paid off handsomely. This one risked much more, but he'd been assured the prospects were sound.

Guy opened the statement. He glanced down the right-hand side of the page and stared at the amount. "What?" He looked up at the top of the sheet. Had they put someone else's statement in his envelope?

His name stared at him from the top. Surely the amount was wrong. It couldn't be zero. He'd invested five hundred thousand dollars! He blinked and checked again, raising shaky, clammy fingers to his forehead.

Wait, the other envelope. This first one had to be a mistake; the second would be the corrected statement. He slit open the envelope and unfolded the single page.

This was no statement. Just a form letter saying that his broker was no longer with the company and that Guy had been assigned, pending his approval, to another.

He sucked in a breath.

What the hell would he do now? That money hadn't been his—it was William's big certificate of deposit—borrowed from William's business. He'd pay it back. He always had before.

Except this amount was huge compared to the others. And except for the small matter that William had no idea that Guy was borrowing and using his money.

Guy felt sweat beading on his brow.

Humming again. Otto, carrying his coffee. Guy quickly tucked the letters inside the breast pocket of his suit.

Otto paused and gave him a strange look. "You okay, Guy? You look like somebody died."

"Uh, I'm fine. Felt dizzy for a moment. Didn't eat breakfast."

"Might be the altitude. Take a break, hop over to the bistro, and get something."

Guy nodded. He'd go to the bistro, but it was a scotch he needed. Then he'd find out what the hell was going on.

After Guy returned, he thought long and hard. He followed up online research with a call to his brokerage. The money was gone. How could he even complain? What could he do except lie low and not draw attention to himself?

As Guy sat in the fishbowl in early afternoon, William came in. "Otto said you weren't feeling well. Altitude sickness. Better now?"

Guy managed a smile. "Yes, thanks."

"When I travel and get back here, I often feel shitty for a day or so. I take it easy, and it goes away."

With great mental effort, Guy stretched and grasped the lifebuoy of an idea. "William, it's been too long since we reviewed the art in storage to see if what's there is reflected accurately on our balance sheets. Some may need to be shuffled to where the market is better for them or need repair or restoration. I'd be happy to take that on."

"Wonderful idea. Do you want Adelle's help?"

"She wouldn't welcome the extra chore. This will add to my workload, but I don't mind."

William clapped Guy's shoulder. "Go for it. What would I do without you?" He went into his inner sanctum.

Guy tried to smile. Maybe he could fix this without William knowing.

◆ ❖ ◆

Algie liked working in the fishbowl. He was alone there since Guy had left shortly after Algie had come from school. The monitors proved handy for letting him know who was where.

Algie looked up from the English assignment on his laptop as his dad walked out of the inner sanctum to meet someone up front. He recognized that fellow, knew he was a talkative artist. They walked off into the Middle Room. With luck, they'd be gone a while.

Good. Algie switched from his homework and brought up the Adobe Illustrator screen. He was aching to try what Costain, a digital artist whom he admired from another Canyon Road gallery, had demonstrated in a workshop. He retrieved his notes from his computer case and picked up from where he'd left off last night.

Ten minutes later he stopped with a growl of frustration. What he'd written made no sense. The program didn't do what his notes indicated.

He jumped as the door opened, his finger hovering over the minimize button.

Uncle Cecil. Not to worry.

"Your dad around?"

"Somewhere, talking with the guy who does the cactus and flower paintings."

"Long-winded Lonny. I like his art, but he's bo-o-ring. I'll give them another ten, then rescue your dad." He looked at Algie's screen. "Wow. Is that your work?"

"Yeah. But I'm stuck. I was trying to remember what Costain said in his workshop, but I can't read my scribbles."

"I like where you're going with this piece. Impressive."

"Maybe you could help. Is there a way I could record his workshops and maybe school classes on my phone? I miss stuff he's doing on screen when I'm trying to write down what he says. I'd rather concentrate on watching him."

"Sure. I can show you different apps, and you can download the one you like. Check with your teachers first to see if they mind being recorded."

Algie switched his screen back to his homework and pulled out his phone. "Cool. Thanks."

After several minutes, his dad walked in. Algie put away his phone, satisfied with what he'd learned. Cecil was great—they spoke the same language when it came to digital stuff.

But his dad was annoying. He admired technical knowledge when it came to his own needs. He was willing to rely on Guy when it came to online finances and Cecil for security systems, but when it came to Algie, he labeled computers a waste of time.

♦ ❖ ♦

Just before six, Algie put his laptop into his case. He watched his dad clear his desk, then lock the inner sanctum door.

Algie waited till his dad turned. "I've been thinking about what college I want to go to. I'm looking at the University of New Mexico. They have a B.A. in Fine Arts that's interesting."

William sat at the worktable with a big smile. "Really? I'm glad to hear it, son. What do you want to concentrate in? Your mother was in Art Studio."

His dad's face grew sad. "She was so talented. I'd like to see you follow her footsteps."

Sure, retreat into your old memories. Make your kid feel guilty because she's gone. Crap.

Otto came in. "All finished up front. Lights are out." He put some files in the drawer.

William nodded, though Algie doubted his father even heard Otto.

"I'm glad you're thinking of going back to real art, rather than playing with that computer all the time. You're never going to get anywhere with digital art."

Algie gritted his teeth. "You always do that. Put down what I love to do. Just because I paint with pixels rather than oils, you say I'm not doing real art. UNM has good programs in digital art. I want to take those too."

"Oh, no. I won't finance fake art."

"It's not fake. When I use a computer, it doesn't mean I'm not using all the composition, perspective, and all the other skills that I would if I painted with oil on canvas. It's only the medium that's different, not the creative work of art. The computer is a tool, Dad."

Algie felt like he was losing control. His own fault. He just couldn't help it when his dad pressed his buttons. "You won't even look at what I've done."

Why couldn't his dad see how unfair he was being? "The art world can be stupid sometimes. When impressionists started displaying their work, they were shamed because it wasn't realistic enough. When a painter like Norman Rockwell came along, he was put down because he was only an illustrator. When somebody like Robert Bateman paints nature and wildlife, they put him down." Algie's voice took on a snide tone. "It's only representational. It's not real art."

"At least they use paint and brushes. I happen to like Bateman."

"I do too. But you have to admit the art snobs are slow to accept anything new. Oil painters turned up their noses at watercolor. It's what women dabbled in."

Algie realized Otto was listening, his head turning back and forth like he was watching a ping-pong game.

Algie stood and slung his computer case over his shoulder. "Then along comes a guy who drips paint on canvas, and the art world goes bonkers. They pay millions for it. I suppose you'd like me to pull that off so I could make millions too. Quite a role model."

"I didn't say anything about role models, and money doesn't make a person happy."

"Don't get me going on conceptual art. Duct tape a piece of fruit to a wall and call it art." Algie snorted. "The only art involved in that is convincing some idiot that it's art." He went into the hall.

"I'll agree with you on that." William looked at the man standing by the filing cabinet. "Otto, what is it? Did you want to say something?"

Otto put his finger on the file-drawer lock. "Didn't want to interrupt. Just checking to see if there's anything more to put away before I lock this."

"No, as you can see, I'm done." William turned out the light.

They left, leaving Otto to set the alarm.

"So can I go to UNM?"

"I'll think about it."

CHAPTER FIFTEEN

Otto had to admit the Blue Goose Restaurant had an old-fashioned charm—like a movie set from *The Orient Express*. The Blue Goose was two train cars long, attached to the front of a larger building housing the kitchen. He wondered if the train cars had once been a part of the Atchison, Topeka, and Santa Fe Line or if they were just clever facsimiles.

Ruben had told him he might be late as he'd promised to help an elderly woman he'd met at an art show. "Just wait for me in the bar."

Otto entered in the middle with the restaurant car on his left. He peeked into it to see tables with snowy-white linens lining the long narrow space with large windows.

"Table for one?"

Otto turned to find a fellow wearing a black jacket with gold stripes on the cuffs. He'd call him the maître d', except his brass name tag said CONDUCTOR.

"I'm supposed to meet someone in the bar," Otto said.

The conductor waved him to the right. This car was decorated much like the other, but in place of tables, shelves ran under the windows, wide enough to hold menus and drinks. Upholstered swivel chairs faced the windows. Midway down the car was the bar, staffed by white-coated waiters.

Otto claimed two chairs near the bar and ordered a draft beer. The window looked out upon the real Santa Fe trains. He watched as passengers from the Rail Runner commuter entered the bar. Otto nursed his drink, occasionally glancing at his watch.

He looked up when a waiter hailed someone with a greeting. "Yo, Ruben. How's it going?"

"Fine, Joe. How's that new dog? Glad I found him a forever home."

Ruben made his way to the empty seat by Otto. "Sorry I made you wait, old chap, but my friend was lonely, and she tends to talk a lot."

"Moscow mule, as usual, Ruben?" Otto's waiter was back, a friendly smile on his face.

Otto felt out of his element. What was a Moscow mule? The waiter left.

"You're well-known here, Ruben."

"Great place. Great people." Ruben swiveled his chair to face Otto. "I'm told your gallery has new ownership. How do you like the new owner?"

"So far I've been pleased."

"How is it, working with a chain? Do you ever even see the owner?"

"Oh, yes. Mr. Adams lives where he opens up a new gallery, getting a feel for the community. He's a hands-on owner."

"What does his wife think about being uprooted every couple of years?"

"He has a teenage son, but he's never talked about his wife. Of course, I haven't asked."

"Where does his son live?"

"Here with his father."

"Is he interested in the art world too?"

"He's mostly into computers. Young people are, you know. I struggle with technology."

The waiter arrived with Ruben's drink in a copper cup with a glass rod. Lime slices peeked out from the ice.

Ruben thanked the waiter. "I have a cousin, Neville Hayes, who's opening a new gallery soon in Dallas. Have you heard of him, Otto?"

"Sorry. Don't know Dallas."

"He's known in the art world." Ruben stirred his drink. "Anyway, he's about fifteen years older than me, and intimidated by all the electronics, paperless banking, and accounting systems. Right now, he's looking into different security companies."

"It's important that he finds one that knows about the art business."

"I'm glad you said that. He was going with a large commercial outfit that does mostly homes, but I said it's better to find one that deals with museums and galleries. Do you mind if I ask what system your gallery uses? He'd appreciate a recommendation."

"Dupre Security Systems. Based here in Santa Fe. They specialize in galleries."

"Thanks. I'll let him know." Ruben sipped his drink. "Maybe your boss's son could get a job with them if he's into technology. That'd be a great future for him."

"I might mention that to Algie. His father complains about the time the boy spends on his computer. But Algie was very helpful when I was learning our new system. Very patient."

"Algie. Hell of a name. Short for Algernon?"

"It's from his full name—Albert Grayson. Al G." Otto sipped his beer. "Algie does digital art."

"I know several galleries in Santa Fe who show digital art. Maybe I could help him. Is his work any good?"

Otto frowned. "I haven't seen any. His father's dead set against it. Some of their arguments have been quite loud."

"How old is he?"

"About sixteen."

"If you think I could help, I could meet with him somewhere outside the gallery." Ruben stirred his drink. "You never know when some kid will turn out to be famous. It makes me feel good when I can help a young person."

"I'll have to think about that. Don't want to cross his father, but—"

"Just giving him pointers wouldn't hurt. Oh, look at the time. I have to run. I'll get the tip." Ruben pulled out his wallet, then looked inside, a dismayed expression on his face. "Darn, I just have a couple of dollars."

"Let me." Otto placed a ten on the shelf, anchoring it with his glass.

"Come on, man, don't be stingy. These guys work hard for a living."

Otto drew another ten and placed it with the first. Ruben had a generous heart.

CHAPTER SIXTEEN

Wednesday, February 22

In the deep of night, images tugged at Karen's consciousness. Hands fought for her attention in a frenzied land, over a seething sea that morphed into a vast pit filled with dark and evil. A little girl struggled over a tenuous bridge made of hands of red, brown, yellow, white, and black. She reached for the hand extended toward her. A huge hand, stalwart, calm, solid.

Karen's eyes opened to the darkness. Dom slept soundly beside her. She pulled the softness of the blanket around her shoulders, tucking her hand under the pillow and closing her eyes, snuggling toward Dom's warmth.

Light, color, and shapes warred in her mind, pushing sleep away. Images sharpened. Now she could see the expression on the girl's face. The fear, the yearning. The girl, who was holding a teddy bear, reached out toward the hand. Toward the pale, greenish hue, lit by the flickering light of a torch held high by the giant's other hand.

Now Karen's eyes opened again, and she embraced the vision.

A strong inner voice urged, "Get up, get up."

Another voice argued, "No, wait 'til morning. You need sleep."

"You won't remember. It'll be gone. It'll be too late."

"I'll remember. I'm all cozy. It's too cold to get up."

"Get up. Get it on paper. Now! Then the muse will let you sleep."

Reluctantly Karen slipped from under the covers, reaching back to tuck them over Dom. She grabbed her warm, hooded robe and slippers. As she went through her sitting room, she picked up a soft, plush throw from the window seat and her sketch pad and pencils. Going to the family room, she turned on a light and cuddled under the throw in the corner of an overstuffed couch. She drew up her knees to brace the pad and began sketching.

Now she was wide awake, filled with urgency, for the magic of the waking vision was elusive. She didn't stop to make a hot drink, just pulled her hood up to keep the draft from tormenting her neck. Her fingers flew over the paper. She caught more details, erasing, adding, filling more pages.

Her eyes blurred, and she impatiently wiped her hand over them only to realize she was crying. Still, she worked until the vision was complete.

Then she stopped and fixed a mug of cocoa. She got her pastels and added colors, contrasting them, blending them.

The vision was captured now. It would go through changes yet, but she was moved by what she saw, and felt deeply satisfied.

Her eye was drawn first to a massive, greenish metal lady with a torch held high, who knelt in compassion. Behind the giant and across the top, other figures clustered, each with their own light.

Then her eye followed the lady's strong, verdigris hand stretched out over an abyss of terrors to a small girl, clutching a teddy bear. The child struggled to cross a fragile, shifting bridge made of supportive hands, hands of all colors. A bridge toward hope.

More figures followed the child, distinct in the forefront, but soon lost in a shadowed multitude. Waves of figures. So many—

of all colors, fearful, needy, desperately moving through the chaos of a desert wilderness on the lower right.

At the bottom left of the image stood a wall traveling diagonally up to the right, broken by light in places where hope reached across despair. Waves dashed against the wall, spray turning into hand-like claws to pull struggling figures under. Foam rode the surface of the waves like a distorted Munchian scream.

All across the bottom were cloying dragging hands—tense, clawing, or knotted into fists—warring with the figures struggling to reach the lady of hope and the beckoning figures with lights. The hands of the figures of light were extended too, but open in hope.

Karen's eyes came back to the girl with the bear, reaching to grasp the lady's strong, welcoming hand. The crown worn by the kneeling Statue of Liberty cast pointy shadows overall.

It was done.

Karen stood, arched her back to relieve her stiffness and felt an overwhelming tiredness. The light of dawn guided her back to bed, where she crept under the covers after leaning the open sketchbook against a chair where she could see. Dom stirred and spooned behind her, warming her body. He slept on.

In the dim light, she gazed, heavy-lidded, at the sketch. At last, suffused with warmth and her lashes resting against her cheeks, she drifted off in peaceful slumber.

CHAPTER SEVENTEEN

When Karen awoke, Dom was already gone. Propped next to her sketchbook was a note with his familiar half-printing, half-cursive writing. "I love it. The statue and Adoncia grabbed my attention. I'm off to pick up my mail before my alumni meeting. Love, Dom."

She smiled and tucked the note in her sketchbook. She was anxious to get started now that she had the images in her mind.

Now that the design was roughed out, some big decisions fell into place. Her colored sketch definitely called for landscape orientation. It must be big enough to allow for the image details she wanted to capture.

How big? Time dictated the size. It must be woven by mid-June, since the last part of June would be needed to take it off the loom, manage the ends, vacuuming, steaming, and all the other finishing steps.

She could have the loom warped and ready by March first; that gave her fourteen weeks. Experience said she could weave the equivalent of a square foot a week. If she pushed herself with longer days and weekends, she might do more.

She could handle that. Simplifying her design would buy more time.

Deciding the size told her what loom she'd use—her largest, a four-shaft, countermarche floor loom. She calculated the amount of warp thread she'd need and checked her stock. She had plenty of white cotton warp on hand in the right weight for a sett of eight warps per inch.

She'd tell her weaving students classes would end after this month. There just wasn't time.

Dulcie would come today after her work. Dressing the loom, getting it warped and ready, went much faster with two.

With all those details decided, she began what she was itching to do—look again at her colored sketch and improve on her initial vision. She made lots of sketches, thinking about the composition, how to draw the eye in and lead the viewer through the art.

As she worked, she made notes: ideas for colors, for light. She followed her sketch closely, but one section refused to cooperate. In her dream that area on the lower right had morphed from sea to abyss. Evil roiled and tumbled there, but of what stuff was it made? Maybe—

"Karen? Maria told me I'd find you here. May I come in?"

The thought flew out of her head. Drat.

Pete was standing near the door. What time was it? Twelve-thirty? She wanted to get this nailed down before she grabbed a bite of lunch.

"Of course," she said. "I'm working on my design."

"I stopped by to see Dom. Had to use some comp time."

"He's at an alumni meeting."

Pete stood by her chair looking at her colored sketch. "I like what you've done with the kneeling Statue of Liberty and the little girl. It's powerful, personal. Good symbolism. But …"

She waited for him to finish his thought. He wore a frown.

"But what, Pete?"

"Don't take this wrong."

Already miffed, she figured she wouldn't like what he was about to say.

He pointed to the lower right quadrant of the sketch. "What's this?"

"That's the chaos, the canyon, the abyss, the desert the immigrants must cross."

"I thought it was supposed to be a sea." He pointed to the left. "What you've shown here looks like a sea. I'm sure you meant those to be waves. Why do you have the sea changing into a desert? It doesn't make sense."

He wasn't the artist. Annoyance puffed up inside and Karen leaped to defend her work. Then, as if pricked by a pin, she realized he'd nailed what bothered her. Part sea, part wildland obstacle course. Uff da.

"Well, I haven't finished that area yet. It's full of danger and bad things." She was fuzzy about how the sea, the wall, the abyss of terrors, and the bridge fit together. "It represents struggle, conflict, chaos and is a barrier to what the seeker seeks." Even to her it sounded lame.

"But you will have a sea?"

Now she was feeling contrary. "I might leave it out. After all, there's no sea in New Mexico."

"There's no Statue of Liberty either."

"The Statue of Liberty is a concept—the promised land. I want it there."

"Your instinct is good. Many immigrants come over the sea."

Karen took a calming breath. "You have a point. Pete, what do your instincts tell you that area should be?"

"The sea. Goes with the statue."

Karen admitted his suggestion had merit. The colors the sea introduced attracted her. The blues and greens would make a more dramatic image. Turbulence in a cooler palette, providing a contrast with the hands of color and the light.

She looked up at Pete, patiently watching her. "How about the wall idea? I rather like that symbolism."

"A sea wall? Extending into the sea like a jetty? I wouldn't want you to leave it out. I can hardly wait to see this emerge as a tapestry. You have a gift for using color and light."

Pete raised issues she knew had to be fixed. She gave it grudging thought.

Pete chuckled. "I've seen that look on my detectives when they deduced what happened, narrowed down the suspects, and reached a conclusion. They weren't happy with me when I burst their bubble by pointing out something they missed or chose to ignore."

"You can be annoying, Pete, but I'm glad you brought it up. I was fuzzy about that area, and you're helping me clarify my vision."

Pete's expression grew more serious. "I didn't say the other night, but I wanted you to know how honored Akiko and I were to be included and how important this tapestry is."

His jaw worked. She waited.

Suddenly she knew these comments were the real reason for his visit—not to see Dom at all. He'd come clear out here to see her design, to say this in person, giving his words tremendous weight.

"It wasn't always easy to be the child of immigrants. It's been even more difficult for Akiko, leaving Japan and coming here to make a life with me. I have high hopes for your tapestry of light and the other entries in the Niemöller competition. I had to tell you."

Then he smiled. "Tell Dom I was here."

Karen stood, feeling both uplifted and yet very small in relation to the gargantuan task ahead. "Thank you, Pete. I'll do my best."

"I know you will. But no pressure. Your art is always wonderful." He turned and left.

No pressure.

Right.

Now this creation not only had to show her light and be her voice, but speak for Pete, Akiko, and countless others as well. Dear God, if ever she needed inspiration.

CHAPTER EIGHTEEN

Purity Gold made a kissing motion at her face in the bathroom mirror. Congratulations on keeping her beauty even as that dreaded fortieth year came closer. No one would ever guess. They'd say twenty-five—not a day older.

Her makeup routine provided plenty of time for organizing her day's work. By the time lashes were spiked with mascara, she had decided to go ahead with the goal of getting her paintings into the Avant-Garde Gallery.

That gallery had become her target after she'd happened upon it while meeting a friend for lunch at the Blue Goose. Avant-garde was a new word to her, and at first she mispronounced it. Then someone told her it meant innovative and just a bit out in front of what was accepted. Sounded Frenchy. A perfect name for her own work.

She overdrew her lips with a dark liner, using a steady hand and taking care to exaggerate the too-flat Cupid's bow. She'd take three paintings to show the manager at Avant-Garde and gauge his ability to be friendly. Yesterday's visit showed what paintings they had to offer. Her work was just as good. They'd had painting after painting with cubes, stripes, and diagonal shapes of color shaded dark to light. Hers were more exciting, with curvy lines and splotches of color.

With her favorite dark lipstick, she carefully filled in the space between her new lip line and the natural one, blending it with skill. She selected a lipstick just a shade lighter than the first and covered her mouth.

Her paintings had better texture than those she'd seen yesterday. Lately she'd tried applying paint with a palette knife. It was a good way to avoid waste. Any acrylic paint left over on the palette dried up and had to be thrown away. Now with the knife, it was all applied to her row of paintings in progress. Another clever reason for painting more than one at a time.

She inspected her lips, using a critical eye, trying a smile, a pucker, and then relaxed. Picking up a thin brush, she dabbed concealer along her bottom lip line to cover a color bleed.

Perfect.

This evening she had a date with Bruno Keller. They'd been out several times now. Such a sweetie, more innocent than most men she'd slept with. A big bear of a man from a small town in eastern New Mexico, Bruno had landed a job as a security guard at the Swift & Adams Gallery. A perfect target for her plan to advance in the art world.

At least, that had been the idea. Her first try at seducing a guard at another gallery had failed. She'd been making headway until his wife found out.

Bruno Keller surprised her. He was such a contrast to the slam-bam-thank-you-ma'am men she was used to. Bruno really cared about her. It was a new feeling, warm and appealing. It was tempting to let herself care about Bruno.

She arranged spikey blond hair into a calculated disheveled look, then fastened the slim black choker ribbon around her neck, centering the tiny gold heart above the hollow of her throat. Ready to go.

She went into her studio, the second bedroom of her apartment. She chose three framed, fourteen-by-sixteen paintings from the stacks leaning against the wall, put them into her roomy tote bag, and left on her quest for Avant-Garde.

CHAPTER NINETEEN

Cecil drove to Anton's place, anticipating the afternoon with pleasure. Conversation talking gadgets and technology and what he hoped would be a home-cooked meal.

Though he knew Anton well from business and the odd social gathering, he'd never been to his ranch. He only remembered it being described as huge. Property between the Tano Road and Monte Sereno Road areas could be anything from a multimillion-dollar, showcase home with spectacular views to a rundown, generations-old horse property.

Drone Tech's Research and Development facility was at another location, so why did Anton need more than a residential security system for his ranch?

The substantive gate at the Bjornson Ranch gave him his first clue about the property and the cluster of mailboxes his second. More than one family lived here. He appraised this important threshold before punching in the gate code and driving through.

The driveway dipped through a shallow arroyo before climbing to the top of the ridge. It followed the ridgeline, at one point doubling back on itself and opening to a view of the ranch buildings and home. As a bird flew, gate to home, it wouldn't be far, but the road had to be a half-mile long.

At the overlook, Cecil surprised a few deer, which bounded away, demonstrating the futility of ordinary motion sensors in a wildlife area. But what a great spot this would be for a surveillance camera.

Anton met him in the parking area between the home and outbuildings. "We can do two things at once. Demonstrate drones and show you the lay of our land in the process. This drone is the workhorse from my fleet." He motioned with the gadget in his hand to a sleek, white quadcopter resting on a smooth landing area several feet away.

"And you're holding the transmitter?" asked Cecil. "With a video monitor? Is that usual?"

"Incorporating the monitor is handy," said Anton. "No extra tablet to haul around to see what you're capturing." He sent up the drone and spoke over the whine, sending Cecil a sideways look. "This drone would never let you spy on someone unnoticed. We do have quieter ones."

Anton gave a virtual tour—first of the buildings, then the property, pointing out the trail around the perimeter and all of the spots where an intruder might be able to spy on family activities. When the drone returned, Cecil tried the same maneuvers. He made a point of checking out the overlook area.

"Cool. This is helpful." Cecil grinned. "Much more informative than your napkin scribblings."

"Pretty bad, weren't they? After dark, I'll show you the drone carrying the thermal imaging camera. Let's go look at my monitor setup."

Anton led Cecil through a door that opened onto a long hall. Two Airedales came running. After their enthusiastic greeting, Cecil noticed double doors to the right, opening into a large, sunny room where classical choral music played.

"That's Mom's weaving studio," said Anton. "She's in the throes of designing at the moment. You'll meet her at dinner."

Anton continued down the hall to an open great room with a cathedral ceiling. A staircase curved up to a balcony, off which Cecil saw several doors before the upstairs hall went on out of sight.

Under the balcony, a family room, with seating for about twenty people, adjoined the kitchen. A woman about Anton's age stood at the counter forming bread dough into balls and placing them into a pan.

"Maria," said Anton, "this is Cecil, our guest tonight. Maria is our housekeeper."

"Something smells wonderful," said Cecil. His anticipation for dinner ramped up another notch.

"Nothing fancy. Just pot roast." Maria's smile was warm.

Anton was already on the move, going farther down another hall into an office. "This is the hub for our system."

Cecil's eyes feasted. An impressive layout and a peer who spoke his language. Questions and answers flew in a comfortable exchange.

"I looked into that artificial intelligence surveillance system we talked about," said Cecil. "It can distinguish between bipeds and four-footed animals, alerting you to one while ignoring the other."

"How about someone on a bicycle?" Anton leaned back in his chair. "Or horseback? Would the AI see them as four-footed animals?"

"No problem." Cecil switched to the AI system's website that showed how the system recognized human skeletal structure.

"Several times, Mom has given sanctuary here to people fleeing some kind of danger. Part of why we're secure is our remoteness and the fact the bad guys don't know anything about our place. But the distance means a delay in getting law enforcement here if there is an intruder."

"So early detection is important."

"Exactly," said Anton. "So is getting good images so the cops have a prayer of getting positive identification."

"That overlook just after the hairpin turn on your drive intrigues me. I'd put a camera there."

Anton pulled up an aerial shot that included the overlook. His brows drew together.

"What are you thinking?"

Anton rubbed his chin. "If somebody did spy there, I'd want to know what they were looking at. Could the cameras be synchronized? Get the spy and what interested them?"

"Interesting word, spy."

Anton shrugged.

"Any cameras can be synchronized," said Cecil. "I've got options to show you on my phone." They proceeded to discuss what would work best and to put together a package for Anton.

Skyla came to the door. "Almost six. We'll eat shortly."

Anton shut off the monitors. "We're pretty casual around here. For only eight people, we decided to eat in the breakfast room like we normally do."

"Fine." Only eight? When Cecil was used to television for dinner companionship?

Cecil excused himself. When he came back from the bathroom, he saw Skyla and Anton in the shadowed hallway. Anton stood behind her, massaging her lower back. Her head leaned against his shoulder, her eyes shut, a look of bliss on her face. Then Anton's hands slid forward to cradle her swollen belly. Whatever he whispered in her ear elicited a low husky laugh. Then they saw him and stepped apart.

He wondered again what had happened to Krista's mother. How and when had Skyla appeared in Anton's life? He felt an apprehension about Anton's system. Excellent, up to date, but still a puny defense for so many acres. So far from help. A feeling of unease crept over him as he followed them into the kitchen.

Anton introduced his mother. Cecil greeted the tall blonde in her mid-fifties. Then Anton introduced a silver-haired man, who was filling a pitcher with water. "Dom Baca, part of our family."

Who was he? How did he fit into the household?

"You've met Maria. This is Diego, our ranch manager." Diego, swarthy and outdoorsy looking, smiled in greeting. He held a huge crock from which Maria dished meat and vegetables into deep platters. Everybody seemed to be coordinated, like they'd done this hundreds of times, all with something to do.

Even Krista helped, arranging freshly baked rolls into a basket. He followed them into the breakfast room.

Cecil was surprised when Maria and Diego sat with them but shrugged it off. Everyone seemed to be family here. Anton opened a bottle of merlot and poured the wine before he sat. Dom filled the water glasses. Krista added sprigs of mint and lemon slices to each and set them beside the plates before taking the chair next to Cecil's. A border collie and the two Airedales settled on a long cushion under the windows. They, too, were used to the routine.

Cecil reached for his wine glass when Krista's hand stole into his, startling him. He realized everyone had lightly joined hands around the table. On his other side, Anton's hand was waiting. Good God, he'd missed the clue of sudden silence and quickly bowed his head.

Karen said a short grace. After the chorus of amens, chatter resumed, and dishes of food were passed.

Cecil tasted the fork-tender pot roast, drizzled with savory brown gravy. What a treat. Finding it too much bother to cook for one, he often resorted to meals of the frozen variety.

"Do you have a dog, Cecil?" asked Krista.

"I travel on business too much."

Anton buttered a roll. "After Krista met Gandalf, all we heard was how much she wanted a dog."

"Gandalf?" asked Cecil.

"He's the dog that helped me when I was kidnapped," said Krista.

Cecil lowered his fork. "Kidnapped?"

"About a year and a half ago—she was snatched at our gate," said Anton. "Back then we didn't have much of a security system and no cameras. She got away up near Tierra Amarilla. Gandalf's owner helped her get back home. It was tough for all of us getting back to normal after that."

Krista gave Cecil a somber look. "They shot Daddy."

Anton's hand brushed a scar on the side of his head. Cecil didn't even think Anton was aware of the action. Shit. It was beginning to dawn on him that he had even more in common with Anton than he'd thought.

He learned more about the kidnapping and the resolution of the case. Conversation flowed with newsy bits. Everyone participated. People cared here. They listened. Cecil found himself sharing humorous anecdotes from his business, even as he retreated to a more distant observation.

Then his plate was empty.

"There's more pot roast, folks." Skyla started the platters around the table again.

When they passed by Cecil, he helped himself and looked around. How could Anton possibly protect his family, short of keeping them locked up?

His uneasy feeling grew.

He directed a question at Dom. "How are you part of the Bjornson clan?"

Dom raised his wine glass toward Karen. "I'm marrying into it."

Cecil shot a glance at Anton, wondering what he thought of his mother marrying again.

Anton's face was relaxed. "I'm glad Mom and Dom found each other. Dad died a long time ago."

Cecil looked again toward Karen. Dom must have fifteen years on her. Likely, she'd watch Dom decline into old age and face the pain of being a widow all over again. Why put herself through that?

Something shifted in his mind that he didn't understand. The niceness of this household took on a different dimension. Suddenly he wanted to get away, to be outside. Illogically, Cecil wanted to retreat into his own safe solitary existence. To wall himself away from this syrupy happiness that wouldn't, couldn't ever be his.

The evening became a trial to endure. Apple pie was next, for God's sake. The American dream.

Cecil's cell phone vibrated in his hip pocket. He looked at the number. A scammer. but he excused himself anyway, stepping into the hallway, leaning against the wall, taking calming breaths before going back.

"Sorry," he said. "I have to leave. Customer with an emergency."

After protests of dismay, he was on his way down the drive, a container of apple pie on the seat next to him. He'd asked Anton for a rain check on his thermal drone demonstration.

He opened the car windows, relishing the sharpness of the cold air before reason made him close them again.

Didn't understand? Shit. It was crystal clear. The goodness of this family had come shockingly close to breaching that spot in his mind where the memories of his wife and son were hidden.

He was running scared.

CHAPTER TWENTY

A milestone for Karen had been reached.

The tedious process of warping the loom was finished. The designing part was done—on schedule even. From the initial small sketches, she'd considered where the viewer's eye would land, how it would travel through the design, and where the shadows would fall. She'd worked on colors, deciding which made key elements stand out and enhanced the vibrance of its neighbor. Which colors worked so that the whole appeared luminous and evoked feeling from the viewer.

Her final, full-color design was life-size. It broke down all the colors and listed them by number. Pleasure filled her at the result.

From her full-size rendition, she had made a cartoon, a line drawing on acetate. The first part of the design was already marked on the warp threads. The cartoon was kept on a roll under the weaving. When she was ready to advance to a new section of warp, when the so-far-finished portion rolled around the cloth bar, she would line up the cartoon with the last section and trace the next lines onto the warp threads with a marker.

Karen was jubilant—this day was for celebration. It had begun this morning in Dom's arms, awash in that lamborous feeling. Moments to cherish, never to take for granted.

Her celebration continued, going out for breakfast with Dom at the Hog Bristle Bistro. The warmth of the restaurant felt good after the chill, overcast skies marking the end of February.

After this break, she'd go home and begin the actual weaving.

As they walked into the restaurant, she saw Cecil Dupre seated at a table near the door. She didn't recognize the man with him, but he had a presence hard to ignore. Her first impression was of confidence and prosperity—not in an ostentatious way—just a quiet aura.

Cecil waved them over. "Please, join us. Have you met William Adams? He owns the gallery across the street."

Her interest sparked but left her confused about how to respond to the invitation. "Maybe not this time. I'm entering the contest Mr. Adams is sponsoring, and I want to play fair."

"Call me William," he said, waving a hand dismissively. "Don't worry about the contest. It's independent. One of my employees handles all the contest details, the judges, and the exhibits. I don't influence her. I need to be free to talk to artists who may want to show in my gallery."

Karen glanced at Dom. He gave a brief nod.

The server poured their coffees.

Dom stirred cream into his. "William, I admire what you're doing. Art as a catalyst for change is a brilliant exhibit idea."

"Gloria, my wife, started it. I do it to keep her memory, her work alive."

Cecil gave William a mock salute. "She'd have been proud."

"Is there a story behind your wife's tradition you can share?" asked Karen.

William sat back and took more sips of his coffee. "I'm used to fielding questions about the exhibits. I'm proud to, actually. It helps validate her legacy. She was a superb portrait artist. She entered a contest once to win a chance to paint a celebrity. She won, but in painting his portrait, she learned he was truly an odious man. She painted him as she saw him. The portrait never saw the light of day."

"I love this story," said Cecil.

William smiled. "She got the idea for a contest where people painted a role model. The prize was the chance to be in a touring exhibit, which would be seen by people in many cities. The overall effect of so many artists creating art to honor someone who had been a positive influence in their lives was powerful."

"I'd have loved to see it," said Karen.

"As the show toured," said William, "we saw something just as amazing—commercial success. The galleries, which exhibited it, took on a certain cachet. The idea for our own chain of galleries was born. First came New York, then L.A."

William pulled a photo from his wallet. "This is my favorite painting of Gloria's. A self-portrait with our son and our dog, finished shortly before she died. The original hangs in my home." His voice softened. "I find myself talking to that portrait. She was so vibrant." His fingers brushed over the photo lovingly before handing it to Karen.

As he handed it to her, she noticed his wedding ring, three diamonds tastefully set diagonally in what looked like platinum. Empathy flooded her at his loss. He hadn't reached the point where he was ready to set that symbol aside.

The photo showed a dark-haired woman and a boy, who must have been about eight, standing next to her. The boy's hand rested on the back of an elegant black and white borzoi. "She was beautiful." Karen passed the photo to Dom.

"Your son favors his mother," he said.

William nodded. "Albert Grayson. Algie. Sometimes it's painful to look at him. Like she's living in him, but that's fleeting, and who's standing there is an ornery teenager. It's hard to believe she's been gone almost eight years."

How sad the boy lost his mother when he was so young. Karen kept her voice soft. "May I ask what happened?"

"Gloria and I had scheduled a flight to D.C. one morning to visit our third gallery. Algie's school called. There was an accident on the playground, and they'd taken him to the hospital.

I flew out. Gloria saw to Algie and rescheduled her flight for the next day."

He paused and blinked several times. "Her plane went down. No one survived."

"Oh, I'm so sorry. How hard for you and your son."

"Is your son also an artist?" asked Dom.

William snorted. "If he'd turn off his computer long enough, he could be a fine artist. He showed talent as a youngster. I don't understand a teenager who wastes his time on computers all day."

"Has he completely given up on art?"

"I insist that he take oil painting lessons. He plays with digital art, but that won't get him anywhere or give him any recognition. It certainly won't prepare him to take over the reins of the empire I've built."

Cecil cleared his throat.

William sent a look across the table. "I know, but it's not what I want for him."

"My son was a computer geek in high school," said Karen. "Always playing with gadgets, trying to figure out how stuff worked. Designing his own gadgets became his passion."

"How old is he now?"

"He just turned thirty-five."

William's eyes flared, as though he were surprised. "And what does he do?"

"He owns his own company, Drone Tech, designing and manufacturing drones. He's done consulting for military projects, law enforcement. Right now, he's working with archaeologists on exploring ancient sites with thermal technology."

"He's found a way to make a living playing with his gadgets?"

"An excellent living," said Cecil. "His company is well-respected, and not just locally."

✦ ❖ ✦

When William got back to his office after meeting Karen and Dom, Adelle Gupta called.

Forthright, as always, she didn't waste time. "Why is Guy messing with the art in storage? What does his financial job have to do with that art? I'm the one who uses it."

"He's doing an art asset inventory for the financials."

"That's not what he told me. He made it sound like those records are in disarray. They're not. They're in perfect order."

William sighed. "I think he's right about updating the list for the reports. He's willing to do the work. Can you give him what he needs to get the job done?"

"I have a handle on where all of the stored art is. I don't want him sending stuff to other galleries."

"I didn't tell him to move any."

"Well, he has been." Adelle's exasperation came through loudly on the phone.

William hated being caught in disputes between employees. Both Guy and Adelle were excellent at their jobs. If either quit, they would be difficult to replace. They were crucial cogs in the well-oiled machinery of his empire.

William drummed his fingers on his desk. "He did say he might take care of any needing repair or restoration."

"Guy might know his numbers and have a superb mind for remembering collectors and their bank balances, but he is not trained as a curator. I'm the one with that expertise."

Dammit. Why can't they get along? "Look. We do need to update the assets for the balance sheets. He's doing me a favor. Can you work with him?"

"How?"

"Let him access your records."

Several seconds went by before Adelle answered. "I have good relationships with all your managers. I've worked hard on that. Now they're complaining to me about him."

"Adelle, please."

"Copies he can have. He's not getting my master list of the stored art."

"Thank you. I'm sure he'll be happy with that."

She hung up, mollified for the moment, he hoped.

Paintings in storage. The Hoogstra collection. Hadn't thought about them for a while.

He got up and walked down the hall to the storage area and flipped on the light. A few moments' search located them. Louis Hoogstra was a nineteenth-century painter who specialized in Southwestern landscapes. He flipped through the five, all painted at Canyon de Chelly. Marvelous, vivid colors. He was partial to these and had thought about hanging them in his own home. They'd enhance the dining room. He'd give it more thought.

CHAPTER TWENTY-ONE

Thursday, March 2

"March came in like a lion," said Cecil, holding the gallery door open for William against the blustery wind. He nodded at Otto, sitting at his desk, and followed William toward the back.

"I'll show you that—" William broke off his sentence as he opened the door to the fishbowl.

Algie, school done for the day, sat at the table, a book and papers in front of him, and his phone in hand.

"Algie, how many times do I have to tell you to put that phone away when you're supposed to be doing homework?"

The boy made no movement to acknowledge his dad. Then Cecil noticed Algie's earbuds.

"Algie!" William's voice sharpened. "Dammit." He reached out to snatch one of the offending earbuds from his child's ear.

"Ow!" Algie put a hand to his ear as he whipped around to face his father. "That hurt."

"Why aren't you doing your homework?"

"I am." Algie's voice cracked. "History."

"Don't lie to me. You were playing with your phone."

"I'm not playing." Algie punched the speaker button on his phone. The voice of his history teacher filled the space, talking about things to look for as they read about the civil rights movement in the sixties.

William's face reddened. "When did you start recording classes?"

"Since a friend of mine showed me how." Algie's glance flicked to Cecil.

Good for you, kid, thought Cecil.

"Why didn't you tell me?"

"I didn't know you cared."

"Don't get smart. Of course I care." William's face grew redder. "Go to the bistro. Grab a bite to eat. You must be hungry. You always are." He pulled a twenty from his wallet and handed it to Algie.

Algie pocketed the money, his phone, and stuffed his homework into his backpack. He sent a look to his father but didn't say a word. He picked up the soda he'd been drinking and left.

Cecil stood quietly, reminding himself it wasn't his place.

"Sorry about that," said William.

The words came out of Cecil over his better judgment. "William, what's wrong with the boy being on his phone? Were you afraid he was doing digital art? Even if he was, so what?"

William looked up, glaring. "It's not what I want for my son. Don't interfere."

William's words stung.

"If you'd ever had a child, you'd understand, but you don't."

Cecil jerked back. His jaw clenched. But he did have a son. Once. He'd give anything …

William was still talking. "Sorry, it's hard to be a single father. Here's that article about the new security idea."

Cecil looked without seeing at the magazine William handed him. He even carried on what he thought was a reasonably coherent conversation for shoring up their already-adequate security.

"Thanks," said Cecil. "I'll look into it." As soon as he could make a graceful exit, he left.

Some friend he was. He'd never shared his background with William. Now here he was, investigating William and his employees. Guilt ate at him for keeping secrets of that size from a friend he'd known almost ten years.

Cecil had loved being an FBI agent. Loved solving the puzzles, investigations, the chase, and the rush of adrenaline when he faced the bad guys. But because it had led to his wife and son being killed, he punished himself by resigning from the career he loved.

He'd thrown himself into the security company venture, doing what he was competent at, and he'd found success. When he found himself missing the excitement of his former life, he forced himself to look at his painful losses again.

William had been one of his first big clients. But by then Cecil's former life had become a secret compartment. He didn't want anyone entering, bringing up the pain. Tuttle knew, of course, but Tuttle would never say anything.

Even when William's wife was killed, Cecil had kept mum. He had expressed his support for the grieving William by drinking with him. Males were supposed to be stoic, to offer support in silence. Bullshit. He'd wanted to cuss out the gods, to scream in defiance. To cry.

He'd become Uncle Cecil during those dark weeks. He'd ached with sorrow when young Algie had thrown his arms around his neck, sobbing his heart out. If tears had run down Cecil's face then, Algie hadn't noticed. His dad had been too shell-shocked to see anything or even cope. Cecil had held Algie, his sorrow doubled because he couldn't ever hold his own son again; would never see him grow up.

As Cecil passed through the lobby, an out-of-place, red-colored object caught his eye. A Coke can, lying by the borzoi statue. Brown acidic drops dripped from the smooth bronze head to the floor. Algie's way of hitting back. He picked up the empty can and tossed it into the nearby wastebasket.

He crossed the street to his car, got in, but didn't start the engine.

Cecil's memory of that awful time was vividly etched. He wondered, not for the first time, if Algie felt responsible for his mother's death. If he hadn't been hurt on the playground, she would not have been on the plane that went down.

There were too many parallels. If Cecil hadn't been working as an FBI agent, his wife and son wouldn't have been the targets of a vengeful, crazed shooter. It was his fault.

Intellectually he knew that wasn't true. But it was how he felt.

Algie must be torn in the same way he'd been. This kid was going it alone, carrying that burden on those young shoulders. And the kid had no life experiences to draw on, no peers who could give him support and counsel. Being a teenager—figuring out what it meant to be a man? Dealing with jumping hormones and testosterone? He shouldn't have to carry that baggage from his childhood.

Cecil wavered. Should he say something to Algie? Interfere and listen to what the kid had to say?

Or should he leave well enough alone? He had enough secrets from William. He started to turn the car key but sat back, thinking again of William's stinging comment of his having no son.

Shit.

He got out of his car and walked into the bistro. May as well be hung for a sheep as for a lamb.

Cecil spotted a waitress carrying a burger and fries to the booth where Algie sat.

"Mind if I join you?"

Algie glanced up and shrugged. Cecil slid into the booth. "I'm sorry the app I recommended got you in trouble, but I'm not sorry you're putting it to good use."

He signaled to the waitress and ordered coffee.

"Not your fault I can't please the old man." Algie poured a puddle of ketchup onto his plate and swirled a fry in it.

"And it's not your fault your mom died."

Algie's eyes widened. "How did you …" He lowered the fry in his fingers to the plate. His voice was small. "It is, Uncle Cecil. If I hadn't been showing off on the jungle gym and fallen, Mom wouldn't have been on that plane."

"It's not a question of fault."

"But—"

"It was an accident. Something went wrong with the plane."

"My dad blames me." Algie blinked rapidly. "He hates me."

Cecil was aghast. "Algie, no."

"I can't be who he wants me to be."

"What do you mean?"

"He wants me to paint what Mom did—portraits in oils. I like oils, but … what I really want to do is digital art. He thinks it's crap."

"Has he ever said that about your work?"

"I have a painting in the school art exhibit that's running now."

Cecil's eyes flared. "I've heard acceptance in that show is tough. What did he say?"

"He won't go. My entry is digital."

Cecil was at a loss. Who was he to suggest ways of healing this rift between the two of them? He could barely keep his own shit together. On the other hand, he didn't think Algie would be truly happy until he did feel valued by his dad.

"Tell me about your art." Cecil sipped his coffee. He resolved to see the show and Algie's painting. The kid came alive as he talked about his art. He went from picking at his food to polishing it off.

They both looked up as Otto came in.

"Cecil, I didn't know you were here. Algie, your dad said to tell you he was going to leave after I had my break."

"I'd better go," said Algie, sliding out of the booth.

"Otto, have a seat," invited Cecil.

They watched as Algie left.

"His dad is really hard on him," said Otto. "I feel sorry for him. I don't always like him, but he's a good kid." Otto gave the waitress his order.

Most of the Bistro's tables were full now, and the noise level had risen.

"Do you suppose it's easier for someone from the outside to see what goes on in families? You and I observe, Cecil. We aren't all caught up in the emotions."

Cecil shrugged. Otto didn't know him at all if he thought he didn't feel the pain and the emotions of family relationships.

"I have a friend who really understands the art world," said Otto. "I've thought about introducing him to Algie."

The waitress brought Otto's pie and coffee.

"I told my friend about Algie and how he wants to please his father. He said he could help. He's such a generous person. He has a good network of artists and galleries where he's known. Not just in Santa Fe, but all over."

"Any kind deed is good, Otto, especially if your friend can relate to teenagers. Being a teenager is tough. I'm not so old that I can't remember that."

"I don't. Too long ago. Say, something happened this afternoon. Somebody came in, don't know when, dribbled something sticky on the dog statue, and left."

"Did you look at the surveillance footage?"

Otto looked sheepish. "I'm afraid that I didn't have the recordings going. I mean, I watch the monitors, we were all there most of the time. It seems a waste of tape."

"Otto, the system doesn't use tape. It's digital. What good is the system if you don't have it on? Did you tell William?"

"Didn't want to bother him. Should it be on, even if we're there and watching?"

"Yes, all the time." Cecil resisted the impulse to roll his eyes. Otto had no clue how things worked. He relied on a list of actions—punch this to make that happen, put in this sequence of numbers to avoid bells, alarms and cops showing up. If he hadn't dumbed it down, the poor sod might be saying to a criminal, "Wait right here. I have to look up the code for the panic button."

He tuned out Otto's chatter about this very kind man who was so helpful. He finished his coffee, lost in a world of pain, guilt, and what might have been.

Chapter Twenty-Two

Saturday, March 4

Karen exchanged grins with Dom at the sight of Krista, tugging Skyla and Anton ahead of them. Her granddaughter was almost dancing in her impatience as they approached the Convention Center for the Annual Art Show by Santa Fe School District students.

"There they are!"

Leyla's familiar voice made Karen turn to see her with Sam and Farah. Both Krista and Leyla had work hanging in the show, an honor to be chosen from so many.

"Come on!" said Krista.

Sam grinned at them. "It's a shame these kids can't work up any excitement."

Inside the high-ceiling interior, elementary school art stretched in a kaleidoscope of color around all four walls. In the center, display panels for middle and high school art snaked their way around the floor. Panels were interspersed with skirted tables showing off sculptures, papier-mâché, and pottery.

Dom's voice teased. "Shouldn't we start with kindergarten and work our way up?"

"No," said Krista. "After you've seen ours, you can do that."

They jostled with other students, proud parents, and members of Santa Fe's art community until they reached the sixth-grade art. As the work had been done in class, none of them had yet seen it.

Krista's expression was alight, her lower lip caught by her teeth, her face full of anticipation, pride, and delight. Her art wasn't hard to spot—the only Airedale on the display panels.

"She looks real enough to reach out and lick you," said Skyla.

Krista basked in the compliments from her family.

"Now see mine," cried Leyla.

They knew immediately that Sam had been her model, captured as he played his guitar. The lighting came from a fireplace, giving a minimalist feeling to Sam in shadow.

Karen was impressed. "Leyla, what a lovely moment you captured."

"Has Lou seen the show yet?" asked Anton. Lou, one of the Circle Sleuths, gave drawing and watercolor lessons to the girls.

"She and Cliff are coming tomorrow," said Leyla.

Krista nodded happily. "Now we can look around."

Karen and Dom wandered off at their own pace, beginning with the childish efforts of the kindergartners, following the talent as it blossomed year by year. They worked their way through middle school and finally came to the high school art.

Young artists in Santa Fe had opportunities galore with teachers, mentors, classes, and workshops, but the competition was fierce among so many talented youth. Karen and Dom stopped in front of a display panel that showed mostly fantasy art. The work of one student in particular caught her eye. It showed a young knight in chain mail, standing alone.

"This one seems different," said Karen. "This student understands anatomy, light, shadow. Look at the setting they've created."

"And the mood," said Dom. "You can imagine there has just been a battle. His world has changed."

"I see bewilderment, grief, and yet resolve to forge ahead. I want to know the rest of the story."

Dom pointed at the lower corner. "One complaint I've heard about digital art is that it's too perfect. But look at this wall. It's crumbling; there are lichens on the stone."

"It's uneven like it had been hand-hewn. Those subtle details are extraordinary."

Karen read aloud from the label posted next to the art: A.G. ADAMS, GRADE TEN. DIGITAL ART.

She became aware of someone a few feet away, listening.

"I suppose that means it isn't real art." The challenge was hurled from a dark-haired youth with a scowl on his face.

Karen turned in astonishment. "Why would I think that?"

"The artist didn't use paint. He used pixels."

"So?" Karen responded. "When an artist looks at a blank canvas and begins to create, they still have to know what they're doing. They have to consider composition, shadow, and form. They can use a paintbrush, pastels, a colored pencil—or pixels."

Karen took a step toward him. "They still have to get it from their head to create it, no matter what medium they're using. It still has to communicate with the viewer. The artist who did this knows that."

His scowl changed to grudging acceptance. "Are you an artist?"

"I am."

"What is your medium?"

"I'm a weaver."

Surprise flashed over his face. His eyebrows went up and his lip started to curl.

"I hope," she said, "you're not thinking weavers don't do real art."

He laughed. "I get your point. I thought you'd be like other old farts. They don't get digital art."

Disrespectful, even with strangers? Karen remembered where she had seen this young man before—last month in the Swift & Adams Gallery. Adams. Raised voices, a belligerent teenager striding past. She saw in him the young boy standing by the borzoi in Gloria's painting. Now it made sense.

"Maybe the experience of the others you referred to has been limited to those with mediocre talent. This artist shows promise.

I'd venture to say he could wield traditional pigments as well if he preferred. I believe he's paid his dues, so to speak. Would I be right?"

"Only shows promise?" Sarcasm was evident as he flung his hand dismissively at the painting. "You cut to the heart."

Karen shook her head. "I don't think so. He knows the emotion on the face he's done is good, but he also knows it could be better if only he knew how. He's a long way from being satisfied, but he's eager to learn. Isn't that right?" She looked directly at the youth. "Mr. Adams?"

The laugh this time was a genuine burst of delighted amusement. "Exactly right."

Then emotion shifted again in his face, sadness, but with a new vulnerability. He turned and walked away.

Karen's mouth dropped. She stood for a moment, processing his abrupt departure. "Dom, do you remember the other day when William was talking about his son?"

"I do. That must be Algie."

"Poor kid. I'm beginning to see what his father can't."

◆ ❖ ◆

Sunday, March 5

Not long before the Student Art Show closed on Sunday, Cecil walked into the Convention Center. He was determined to see Algie's work and to let him know he had. Algie's comments at the bistro still shocked him. For William not even to see the show and his son's work, just because he didn't like the medium? He'd seen how crushed Algie was.

He found the high school section and looked along the panels. He saw the knight in mail, glimpsed a style from the few times Algie had shown him work on his computer.

A man stood a few feet in front of it, hands clasped loosely behind his back, studying the work. Cecil waited, curious about the man's reaction. The man had what Cecil thought of as a rugged New England look, somewhere in his forties with graying, wind-tossed hair just long enough to brush his collar.

As though he'd become aware someone was waiting, the man stepped aside. Cecil looked at the name by the painting. A.G. ADAMS.

"Do you know this young artist?" asked the man.

"Friend of his family." Cecil recognized the keen, deep-set, perceptive gaze. "Costain. You do digital art demonstrations."

A smile moved under Costain's shaggy walrus mustache. "And you're the security company guy."

Cecil introduced himself. "Algie has watched several of your demonstrations. He always comes away excited with what he's learned."

"His father owns the Swift and Adams Gallery, if I'm not mistaken. I've seen Algie at my demos. He kind of hangs in the background, though he did ask if I minded if he recorded my sessions." Costain's eyes drifted back to Algie's painting. "I like to encourage young talent, and he has a shitload of it. I'm very impressed."

"I'm blown away," said Cecil. "He's only fifteen."

"I do teach digital art, but he's never shown interest beyond the demos." Costain paused. "Does he have a teacher? I wouldn't think the cost would hold him back."

Cecil cleared his throat. "He has lessons in oils. How can I say this? His father has not yet developed an appreciation of this medium."

"Pity." Costain moved on.

Cecil took another look at the knight, marveling how Algie seemed to have captured the moment the youth teetered on the brink of manhood. Remarkable.

Pity indeed.

Chapter Twenty-Three

Wednesday, March 15

In her studio, Karen checked the colored design hanging near her loom. She picked up a new skein, confirmed the number, and started weaving it into her tapestry. Gregorian chant played softly in the background.

Dom sat at a table near her loom, pecking away at his laptop.

"I hesitate to bring it up." Dom leaned back in his chair. "And I know we weren't going to let our sticky wickets interfere with your weaving, but I was curious. You've been to Mass with me a few times. What did you think?" He frowned. "This is probably the most rotten time to ask."

"Why is it a rotten time?"

"Ides of March. Certainly wasn't good for Caesar."

"You're not a superstitious person. You want my honest answer?" Karen glanced at him to see his nod. "I felt excluded. I don't mean the priest wouldn't give me communion if I went forward, I'm sure he would've. But Catholic church doctrine excludes me. It makes far more sense to me to be inclusive in communion when you look at Christ's words in the Bible."

"Have you thought about becoming a Catholic?"

"Have you thought about becoming a Lutheran? Or finding a community of faith that both of us would be comfortable in?"

"I don't want to talk about leaving my church."

That was a conversation stopper. She doubled back with her color on the row above.

When Dom spoke again, his voice was inquisitive, not testy. "Why is communion important to you? I want to know."

Karen let the skein rest and rubbed her wrist absently. She wasn't used to explaining her beliefs, and certainly not when so much tension swirled around them. "It's a shared meal that connects us in a special way with God and with each other. It gives us strength to go into the world to do his work of feeding the hungry, giving drink to the thirsty. Being a good Samaritan to our neighbors."

Dom seemed to be processing what she said. She worked on as the chanting flowed around her. Uff da. Her timing in choosing Gregorian chant sucked. Since they shared a love of classical choral music, this should have been pleasant audible wallpaper. Instead, had it provoked this discussion?

"It's more to you than your relationship with God?" he asked.

"Definitely. Shared meals are important. Think how families celebrate. Same thing with Eucharist. We are a family, God's family, doing his work together."

"Technically, I shouldn't be taking communion." Dom's voice was pensive. "I'm not in a state of grace. I'm sleeping with you, a non-Catholic, and we're not married."

"If we were married, would the problem go away?"

"Good question." His brows drew together. "Maybe not. I think it's more. It's worshipping together and sharing beliefs. It's not just … It's what's going on inside me."

"Inside you?"

Dom's mouth twisted wryly. "I—I'm not—I don't have the words to explain yet."

Karen wove in the dark, purple-hued skein in her hand, tapping it down with the tapestry fork. This was no casual conversation, but a tense glimpse into a stumbling block to their marriage.

"I'm caught in the middle." His exhale sounded his frustration. "I don't want to stop what has been an important part of my life for as long as I can remember and yet—I'm sorry. Let's talk about something else."

She raised her eyebrows and kept on weaving in silence. The roiling sea was well underway. The struggle to the bridge and the obstacle of the wall were beginning to emerge. She had already simplified the design. She didn't want her concept blurred by a too-busy-*Where's-Waldo* effect.

"I knew it was a bad time to bring it up," he muttered.

She changed the subject. "Are you going to read from Niemöller to me today? I'd like to finally move past the Dachau part to where he begins to change."

Nothing. She glanced at Dom. He'd made no move to pick up the book, stacked with others on the table. He just sat, seemingly lost in thought, rubbing his hands lightly.

"Dom, is your arthritis bothering you?"

"Huh? Arthritis? No, not particularly." He rolled his eyes skyward and reached to pick up the biography. "All right, let's hear more about this pesky Lutheran pastor. Why does it have to be so difficult?"

Karen flexed her wrist, smiled, and tapped the purple strands into place. Weaving, like life, called for patience.

Chapter Twenty-Four

Tuesday, March 28

The smell of fresh coffee greeted Cecil as he walked into the just-opened bistro. Only a few other customers were present. He spotted William at a booth near the door, a mug of coffee cradled in both hands. Unshaven, rumpled, he looked decidedly grumpy. But then, getting called out by the cops before dawn because your business had been broken into could do that to a man.

Cecil slid into the booth. "What happened? Is the Anonicelli safe?"

"Hell, I don't know. Police crawling all over. They wouldn't even let me look around after I shut the alarms off and showed them how to access the surveillance footage."

Cecil ordered coffee. The waitress obliged his request of a to-go cup—he didn't want to have to leave it and go off to a crime scene.

"Glad this place finally opened up. I was dying for hot coffee." William paused to take a swallow. "They almost caught the guy. They said when the first cop got there, the back door was open, and the guard was lying on the ground unconscious. A white car was peeling out of the lot next door."

Cecil held the cup in his hands, inhaled the heady aroma, and relished the first swallow spreading its heat within. "What time was this?" A call to Tuttle was in order as soon as he had a bit of privacy.

"Just after four thirty. The police called me a bit after."

"Where was the guard, Keller?"

"Off Mondays and Tuesdays. Had a sub. Guard's car alarm went off. He opened the back door and stepped outside. Got hit with pepper spray and knocked out with a blow to the head. Didn't see a thing. He was sitting up, kind of groggy, talking to police when I got there. They took him to the hospital by ambulance."

"Was anything taken?"

"Don't know yet. Dammit, I hate waiting. They say they'll go in with me after they're through gathering evidence."

"How long did it take the police to arrive?"

"Six minutes from when the alarm first hit the police department."

Cecil looked up as a man carrying a zippered notebook came in, saw William, and came over.

"Mr. Adams," said the man, showing his identification. "We met once before. Lieutenant Schultz, Santa Fe PD."

"Lieutenant, this is Cecil Dupre. He installed our security system. I called him to meet me here."

Cecil nodded. Local cop. Lieutenant yet. Wondered if he was just marking time until he retired. Wondered if the locals would get lucky and actually discover something.

Schultz's handshake was firm. "Glad you're here. I have questions for you."

"Coffee?" asked William.

Schultz grimaced. "I'd love it but can't take time. The crime scene investigators were just finishing as I left. Mr. Adams, I'd like you both to walk through the gallery with us."

◆ ❖ ◆

Cecil followed William and Schultz into the gallery through the back door, past the yellow tape strung around the area.

"Let me know if you see anything out of place or missing," said Schultz.

Cecil saw nothing disturbed in the fishbowl, the gift shop, or the Near Room.

As they went into the Middle Room, Schultz said, "The video showed the intruder standing motionless for more than a minute in front of the Anonicelli. Then he shook the bars, turned, grabbed a small painting from across the room, and ran like hell. Can you explain that?"

William let out a sound of dismay and strode toward the blue alcove. "Is the Anonicelli okay?"

The lady looked out serenely from behind her bars.

Schultz pointed into the Far Room at a blank spot where a small painting had hung.

"That's what he took?" William's voice showed incredulity.

The detective's look questioned him.

"Portrait of an old Navajo. Nice enough, nothing special. Deceased artist. Not a name people know."

Schultz made a note. "Do you have a photo of it?"

"Otto can get it for you," replied William. "Why take that? Did you look for fingerprints?"

"Video showed him wearing gloves. No point."

"Lieutenant," said Cecil, "what did the video show of the thief?"

"Dressed completely in black, ski mask too."

Good. Tuttle should at least be able to compare that with footage from the other robbed galleries. "Do you mind if I check something out on the Anonicelli security?" asked Cecil.

"Go ahead."

Even as Cecil uncovered the keypad and raised the grille, he noted the little tracking device he'd attached to the Anonicelli frame still in place. Re-Didion had to have gone through his routine because he was lying under the metal plate.

Cecil grinned at William. "The burglar watched Re-Didion, iris scans and all. Then he tried to grab the droid through the grille. That's the only way the droid could end up under the trap door. I hope the thief's worried."

"I think you can explain to me," said Schultz, "what the hell made him just stand there?"

Cecil shrugged. He didn't feel inclined to tell this local cop about Re-Didion. Why bother? The outcome wouldn't change. However, he would ask Tuttle if the other three Anonicelli thefts had involved trial runs before a more sophisticated approach was attempted. The actions of this thief indicated it wasn't Guy Roquet. Guy knew about Re-Didion.

He caught the detective watching him and William. Schultz was gauging their reactions. Grudgingly, Cecil knew he'd have done the same.

"Isn't it unusual to have a grille arrangement like this in a gallery?" asked Schultz.

Cecil nodded. "It was installed decades ago by the former owner. We upgraded it and added more security that alerted the police. I'm thinking that's what saved the Anonicelli. I don't think they had a clue there'd be a grille."

William sighed. "This is a damned inconvenience."

"It won't take long to put things back in order, William," said Cecil. "I'll check out your system before I— Sorry, Lieutenant. Have you released the scene yet so William can get started?"

The detective raised one of his eyebrows. "I believe we have all we need except for the photo—from Otto, is it?"

Cecil smiled inside. He knew Schultz was not satisfied with his explanation of Re-Didion. It would give the man a puzzle to gnaw on.

CHAPTER TWENTY-FIVE

Sunday, April 2

Winter didn't want to relinquish its hold. Clouds passed overhead, and the early afternoon air held a dampness. It was the kind of day one expected to see a few snowflakes drifting down.

The guests for Karen's birthday celebration were starting to arrive. Hearing car doors slamming, Karen looked out from her studio window to see Sam, Farah, and Leyla, along with their Airedale, Scherzo.

Karen and Dom went out to welcome them. She hugged her arms, appreciating the warmth of her birthday-present top of smoky-slate-blue softness. Another car pulled up full of redheads—Hoot and Melody Stewart, their son, Matti, and their daughter, Bonnie. Hoot worked for the National Forest Service in Pecos. He and his family had been well and truly adopted into the Circle Sleuths.

Escaping the chilled air, they soon filled the hallway with birthday greetings and happy chatter. Twitch and Shadow came racing to greet their littermate, Scherzo, with enthusiastic barking. Quixote joined in.

"I would love to see how your tapestry is coming," said Farah. "May we take a look?"

Karen turned into her studio. "I'm only about a quarter of the way up. The picture and the colors are starting to take shape. I've done just enough for it to start rolling around the cloth bar."

Karen led the way to the large loom, and gently moved the attached butterfly skeins, laying them across the warp threads so her guests could see the finished part. Their appreciative comments filled her with pleasure.

"How do judges figure prizes with so many different mediums?" asked Sam.

"The way they phrase it, if you're accepted into the exhibit, you are a winner," said Karen. "From the sixty winners, the judges will choose a theme prize and first, second, and third prizes."

"When's your deadline?" asked Farah.

Karen drew her brows together, gauging the amount she'd done compared with what seemed like a mammoth task ahead. Lately her weaving had a slow-motion nightmare quality, as if she were mired in molasses. "The end of June. I've scheduled three months for the actual weaving. This is one month's worth. I suppose you could say I'm behind, but it usually goes faster at the end. I'd like to be done weaving by June, because I need time to take it off the loom and finish it."

She relaxed her right wrist and massaged it gently. She was shocked, really, by not being further along. A little niggle of worry surfaced inside.

Anton's voice called from the doorway. "Everyone is here. Maria says the buffet is ready. Mom, tradition says you go first."

Karen led the way down the long hall to the family room where more birthday greetings and hugs awaited her. While she'd been showing off her tapestry to the Martinezes and the Stewarts, Anton had welcomed Cliff and Lou McCreath, and Pete and Akiko Schultz. All had been among the original Circle Sleuths, a group formed almost two years ago to solve the mystery of Krista's kidnapping. Cliff and Lou now had a nine-month-old son, Dougie.

Dulcie and her son, Santos, were here too. They still hadn't met everyone, but Karen had no doubt they'd fit in well.

As the hall opened up to the family room, Karen paused. Something in the room seemed different, out of place. It wasn't just that large package, which had mysteriously appeared on the coffee table.

The cushy loveseat, which usually sat near the wall opposite the kitchen, wasn't there. Why? Now a single dainty chair, with spindly legs and a Scandinavian-embroidered seat cover, sat in that spot. For some reason someone had moved it from a guest room. Had something happened to the loveseat?

No, there it was, across the room. Whatever.

Some of her favorite dishes awaited her as her birthday buffet supper. Grilled salmon, roasted asparagus, mashed potatoes, and more side dishes.

Karen started the buffet line and settled in to eat in the family room. She and Dom carried their plates to one of the sectional couches near a coffee table. Akiko followed them, but Pete headed for that dainty chair. What an odd choice. He was only an inch or so taller than Karen and probably didn't weigh more than a physically fit hundred and sixty pounds, but even so, the chair creaked audibly when he sat.

Krista called out to Leyla, "I win."

Anton asked, "What game are you playing?"

"We had a bet," said Krista. "Pete always sits in the loveseat. Leyla thought it was because it was more comfortable. I said it was because of where it was. Just now he chose the place, even though we changed the chair."

Pete leaned back gingerly, as though shifting to get comfortable, but not trusting the chair. "Why did you think I would still choose this spot, Krista?"

"It's what you always do," she replied. "From there, you can see the back door and the front door."

"Hah! Rule of survival number three," said Pete. "Always be aware of your surroundings."

"How many rules are there?" asked Krista.

"Ten," said Pete, with no hesitation.

"There are eleven on my rules list," said Sam as he added salmon to his plate.

"Oh? What's your eleventh?" asked Pete.

"One's chances of survival are better if you follow Pete's example."

The crowd laughed.

"But you disappointed me by breaking an important rule," said Sam. "Don't act in a predictable manner. Vary your routine."

"Excellent point, Sam. I have erred."

Krista added a bit of butter to her mashed potatoes. "What are the other rules?"

"What do you think?" asked Pete.

"Are these in a police manual?" asked Leyla, helping herself to the asparagus. "Is Dad's list the same as yours?"

"This is my personal list."

"That means we have three out of ten already," Krista whispered something in Leyla's ear. They both giggled.

"I may be sorry I asked," said Karen, "but what's the third one?"

"Always know where your next cup of coffee is coming from," called Krista.

"The kids have you pegged, Pete," said Karen.

Pete raised his coffee mug and took a sip. "Absolutely right! You guys are good."

"Can we guess the rest?" asked Leyla.

"You're welcome to try," said Pete.

"Somebody should write these down," said Anton, "and save them for posterity. Never know when they might become important."

"If you give me the little notebook from the desk," said Skyla, "I will." Then a surprised look crossed her face, and she put her hand over her stomach, rubbing it gently.

"Is Junior kicking?" asked Anton, as he handed her the notebook and a pen.

"Our baby just scored a field goal."

"Do you know if it's a boy?" asked Cliff.

Anton shook his head. "Our due date is mid-May. We'll know then."

Skyla jotted down the first three rules. "Any ideas for the rest?"

"I got one," said Leyla. "Dad always says to keep in shape, eat healthy, and exercise."

Sam nodded.

"Don't swear," said Santos.

Sam and Pete began laughing.

Santos was indignant. "Hey, it's what you always tell our basketball team."

Dom chuckled. "How are you going to get out of that one?"

"We're talking police here," said Sam. "You'd take away half our vocabulary."

"Can you imagine Pete without his German swear words?" asked Anton.

"Maybe it's not a survival rule, but on another list," said Karen, "It was a good thought, Santos."

"Ever the diplomat." Pete's gray eyes twinkled.

"I have a good survival one," said Dom. "Never leave home without chocolate."

Karen flicked her hand at his arm. "Get serious."

"It's on my list," said Dom. "Seriously."

Karen rolled her eyes, but she noticed Santos perked up at the laughter directed at Dom. "One he's mentioned to me is treat everyone fairly."

"Good one, Karen," said Pete.

"Don't let the trail go cold," said Anton.

"Be observant. Don't let yourself be distracted," said Krista.

Lou paused in feeding little Dougie mooshed-up salmon from her plate. "Both of those are good. I know another one that Dad holds dear. Never underestimate your opponent."

Karen's gaze swept the room. The quiet showed thoughtful faces.

"I'm not a cop," said Diego, "but I think a good survival rule would be to know when to retreat."

"And call for backup," added Cliff.

"How many do we have now?" asked Karen.

Skyla counted. "I've written nine."

"I'll give you the last one," said Pete. "It's an attitude, really, but its importance is often overlooked. Don't give up. Think positively. You will survive."

"I hope we never need to resort to your survival rules," said Melody. "Keep safe, everybody."

Pete laughed. "Good habits make a difference no matter what your profession."

◆ ❖ ◆

Voices raised in a chorus of "Happy Birthday" made Karen turn to see Anton carrying in a sheet cake. He placed it on the table in front of her.

"Make your wish, Gramma," called Krista.

The chocolate icing was decorated with piped-frosting flowers and lit candles shaped like a five and a seven. What would she wish for? One of her wishes had already been set aside—temporarily she hoped—when Dom had given her the sweater. While she loved it, she'd been hoping for an engagement ring. Did second marriages call for one? She didn't know how people felt.

Another wish pressed in—getting her tapestry done on time. She blew out the two flames. If only it were that easy.

Karen looked around her family room with satisfaction. The Circle Sleuths had turned out in full force for her birthday. They all claimed responsibility for what rested within the gaily wrapped box. She was sure she knew what was inside—a Pueblo Native American storyteller.

Traditionally, the central figure of a pottery storyteller had an open mouth to tell stories or sing. Listening children surrounded the teller and often climbed on its back. The first storyteller was created to honor a grandfather—one who passed on Pueblo tradition, experiences, and the values of his culture.

About ten months ago, the group had all chipped in to give Dom one. His was large, about fourteen inches high. They kidded that he was their storyteller, who kept them grounded in history. At the time they threatened to get one for her. They'd said she was the keeper of the community, by opening up her home for them, by her welcoming attitude, and by extending contagious kindness.

With anticipation, she began unwrapping the gift. She lifted the lid and scooped out handfuls of cornstarch packing pellets, uncovering the head of the storyteller, dark hair smoothed back into a bun, and the first of the smaller figures clinging to its shoulders.

When enough of the storyteller showed, she started to raise the sculpture, then changed her mind. She caught Anton's eye.

"My wrist is bothering me. Can you lift it out?"

Anton dug down, grasped the base, and lifted the statue from cascading cornstarch puffs. He set the storyteller on the table, and Krista helped pick up a few stray white puffs.

Karen blinked with emotion. Even though she'd known, how awesome to see all the little ones with open mouths. A blanket covered the storyteller's shoulders. Small figures peeked out from its folds; more found a place to cuddle where it draped over the base. This figure matched Dom's in size. She checked the base for the signature. As she suspected, it had been custom made by the same Cochiti Pueblo artist they'd found to make his.

"So many little ones." The storyteller had her left arm bent, holding one child next to her heart. She caught Dom's gaze. "Is this you?"

He nodded, and she laughed delightedly. There was even a black-and-white dog next to that figure, its mouth open in a wee howl.

Four-year-old Bonnie nudged between the coffee table and Karen, peeking mischievously through her red hair, and pointing to a grouping of four, one of whom had a papoose on its back. "That's us." She touched the papoose with a tiny finger. "That's our baby, but he's not borned yet."

Hoot, sitting nearby, picked up Bonnie and put her on his lap. Melody beckoned their son, Matti, closer so he could see. One by one the families came forward and pointed out their figures and named the little black-and-tan canines frolicking among the singing crowd attached to the storyteller.

There was a commotion at her feet as nine-month-old Dougie crawled past on a quest to capture an escaped puff. His dad, Cliff, picked him up and swooped him high in the air.

Karen caught the look of naked longing on Sam's face as Dougie laughed in delight. Even though Sam had adopted Leyla, he still had no baby of his own on the way. Then his look was hidden, his smile was back.

Lou picked up the pellet. "Dougie's a speed demon on all fours. One minute he'll be quietly playing with a toy, and the next thing you know, he's across the room getting into trouble."

Finally, there was only one unclaimed figure left on her storyteller. It clutched a tiny white bear with red hearts on its feet. Karen touched the figure gently. "Who?"

"That's Adoncia," said Dom. "I had the artist add her. She stands for all the random acts of kindness we do, even though we will never know how they turn out. We do them because that's who we are."

The tears did roll down her face then. She squeezed Dom's hand. Her eyes went from the storyteller to the faces around her. Every one of those lives, so precious, so beautiful. What a wonderful gift.

◆ ❖ ◆

As their guests admired Karen's storyteller, Anton's cell phone pinged a series of soft notes. He excused himself, refilled his coffee mug, and went to the ranch office. His phone pinged again as he watched a magnificent buck sail over some rabbitbrush.

Dom came quietly into the office with Pete and Sam close on his heels. "I recognize that ping sequence. Truman again?"

"Truman?" asked Pete. "Who's he? Everything okay?"

"Fine. Truman is what Dom named the big buck we see all the time. You know—buck stops here? Look." Anton angled his chair back from the monitors so they could see the deer moving along. "You're aware we have security cameras at the gate and other locations. This footage is from my newest play-toy."

"Where's it set up?" asked Pete.

"Remember where our driveway comes to the top of the ridge and curves back, where you can see the house?"

Pete nodded. "Doesn't wildlife set it off all the time? How do you wade through all that footage?"

"I heard about this camera with artificial intelligence. It recognizes bipeds. When it sees a two-legged critter, it alerts my phone with a distinctive series of pings."

"You're amazing," said Sam. "Do you just have the one?"

Anton shook his head. "There's one on our riding trail, and one on the high spot on our east boundary where those dirtbags were spying on us a couple years ago."

"Why haven't I heard about this technology?" asked Pete.

Anton turned back to his monitors. "Ask Cecil Dupre, the security systems guy. I learned about them from him."

"I hope your days of needing to track down creeps here are over," said Pete.

"I hope," said Anton, "now that I have the cameras, we'll never need them."

CHAPTER TWENTY-SIX

Monday, April 3

After the first two days of cold, blustery April, the weather improved enough for Cecil and Tuttle to meet outside in the sunshine at the Starbucks on Cerrillos Road. Since most customers preferred the inside warmth, the chill allowed them to speak privately.

"Did Schultz show you the police report on the Anonicelli attempt?" Cecil savored the heat of his brew.

Tuttle nodded. "Yeah. First officer on scene called in the white Subaru leaving and for backup while he tended to the guard. Second officer came moments later, searched for the vehicle. No sign."

"How about the black-clad figure?"

"Subject even had black makeup around the eyes. No clue even as to race."

"Weight? Height?"

"I'd guess, five-nine. Pushing two hundred pounds. Average."

"William told me the guard is fine. What did they—"

"Hit him with a rock from the landscaping from the gallery next door where the getaway car was parked. Subaru Outback with a covered license."

Cecil snorted. "Were there trial—"

"No trial runs on the Anonicelli thefts we're investigating." The agent warmed his hands around his cup.

"How about comparisons—"

"You're a lucky bastard, Dupre, getting footage of him. Our suspect's been adept at avoiding cameras. Anything on that sculptor, Jimenez?"

"You going to interrupt me again?"

Tuttle threw back his head and laughed. "Maybe."

Cecil rolled his eyes. "Short of asking Jimenez point blank where his money came from, nothing. He's well connected in the art world. He's never expressed interest in old paintings."

Tuttle drained his cup. "If he were, would he advertise it? Keep in touch."

Pete finished an interview on another case and eased into the traffic on Cerrillos, heading back to the station. He pulled into the Starbucks drive-through, his mind going back to the meeting that morning with Tuttle.

He got his coffee and exited past the outside seating area, glancing over at the familiar scene.

Speak of the devil! Agent Tuttle. Pete slowed. And who should be next to him? Cecil Dupre. How did they know each other? Was Tuttle quizzing suspects?

Didn't look like an interview. More like old friends, laughing and relaxed.

The driver behind him tapped his horn. Pete waved apologetically and drove back onto Cerrillos.

What was that meeting about?

For crimes like this Anonicelli business, very few folks got a free pass of innocence without Pete's considered scrutiny, especially if they were strangers to him. He and his detectives had already checked on Adams and the gallery employees. Hadn't ruled any in or out completely.

Curious, when he got back to his office, Pete ran Cecil Dupre through the system. With the results displayed on his screen, he leaned back, propped his feet on his desk, and steepled his fingers. Graduate of University of Maryland in Criminal Justice. Master's degree in art history from Sotheby's Institute of Art in New York. FBI Academy at Quantico and part of the FBI Art Crime Team. He'd left about a decade ago and begun his security systems business, specializing in art galleries and museums.

Now it made sense. The ease in Tuttle's company. The ability to home in on significant facts. Above all, that certain cockiness Dupre shared with Tuttle and all of the FBI agents he'd ever met.

Did he have questions? *Ja.* He learned Dupre's wife and son had been murdered around the time he left the FBI. Had that prompted him to quit? Pete wondered how that scene played out—the worst nightmare of an officer. But Dupre kept to himself, a classic workaholic—businesslike, well-regarded, and successful.

He lowered his feet to the floor and closed down his computer. Even though he was not immune to tribal conflicts among law enforcement agencies, one would hope they were all working on the same God-damned side, and he was a firm believer in working together to keep justice. He'd head toward the business park where Dupre Tech was located and clear the air with Dupre.

Might even make him squirm first.

Too bad this conversation was on Dupre's turf, thought Pete, looking around the organized clutter of Dupre's office and at the man leaning comfortably back at his desk. This was no fancy showplace, but a space where work happened.

A large glass interior window looked out into a room full of drafting tables, desks holding unrolled plans, computers, and electronic gadgets in various stages of assembly. This was not unlike his own office overlooking the bullpen.

Dupre's attitude was wearing on Pete. He'd answered Pete's questions about the Anonicelli attempt with a touch of insolence—not contempt for the law, but like he viewed the whole thing with annoying amusement. If Pete were correct, that was his way of avoiding anyone getting too close to him. His gut said Dupre had nothing to do with the theft. Pete was ready to move on to the cooperation stage.

"Enough, Dupre," Pete said. "We're both wasting our time."

"Excuse me? You mean you finally believe I had nothing to do with the gallery burglary?"

"No, I mean I saw you this morning at Starbucks." He closed his portfolio. "With Tuttle."

"Took you long enough." An irritatingly superior smile appeared on Cecil's face.

Pete leaned forward. "There may be a few gaps in my knowledge, but yes. I know you used to be a member of the FBI Art Crime Team, and they pressed you into service recently because of the Anonicelli thefts."

"Regrettably, yes."

Pete allowed a hint of his anger to show in his voice. "While we're playing games, this Anonicelli thief is still on the loose. What does concern me is if you and I and Tuttle can't work together, it will take us longer to catch this scumbag."

Cecil leaned back and crossed his ankle over his knee.

Pete sighed. "Look. We can share what we know. Even more importantly, share questions and ideas. Cooperation means we'll get there faster and possibly with fewer bodies along the way. Let that sink in."

"Where is it written that I have to share anything with you? I quit chasing bad guys. Go see Tuttle."

"I asked him about you. Gave him the same speech. He's keen on seeking information but not on sharing it."

Cecil chuckled. "I'd like to have heard that conversation."

"All three of us took the same God-damned oath. Even if you quit, I respect your experience and training. I'm even inclined to like you as a person, though maybe not much this minute."

Cecil laughed; the sarcasm gone. "Same here."

"I want to hear more about the MO of the first three thefts," said Pete. "Tuttle told me some, but I'm sure you have your own ideas."

"Whoever the guy is, he gains the confidence of one or more employees to get inside help. Perhaps he was able to spot weaknesses and exploit them to his advantage."

Pete nodded. "Tuttle said Guy Roquet had been in all the target cities."

"I doubt it was Roquet who was responsible for this theft." Cecil told him about his being present for the Re-Didion demo. "I was curious where Guy was though, so I asked Otto for a copy of his schedule. Supposedly he's in Phoenix now."

"Are you confident Adams has nothing to do with this?" asked Pete.

"Yes. Doesn't fit with anything I know of him. In ten years, I've always seen him as honest."

"How about Roquet?"

Cecil hesitated. "I've known him that long too."

"Has he always come across as honest?"

Dupre took his time in answering. "William is too trusting."

"Why so reluctant to give an opinion of Roquet?"

"Do you own a terrier?"

"Huh?" Pete grinned. "As a matter of fact, several. Airedales."

"Figures. Your tenacity. People often own dogs that reflect their personalities."

"So why aren't you telling me about Roquet?"

Cecil sighed. "It's only instinct—no facts to back it up. I don't like him. That may be unfair to him. That's all I'm saying."

Pete rubbed his upper lip between two knuckles. "Works for me."

Cecil's chair creaked as he leaned forward. His face took on an almost pleading look.

"I'd just as soon you didn't mention anything to William about my FBI background or that I once had a family. He doesn't know. I'm not happy about it, but …"

Pete gestured toward him with an open hand. "Your personal reasons are yours. He won't hear it from me. Thanks for your help. I mean that."

As Pete drove away, his last image of Dupre stayed with him. He'd been sitting, eyes downcast, a look of pain on his face. Whatever memories were on his mind, they weren't resting easy.

Chapter Twenty-Seven

Wednesday, April 12

Purity Gold had fallen into the habit of eating with Bruno at the Hog Bristle Bistro at least once a week before his shift at the Swift & Adams Gallery. She'd learned more than she wanted about his younger siblings, his parents, and their ranch. Who cared if cows had their own personalities, let alone their own names? Bruno was sweet, and there was no doubt he admired her, but …

Only half-listening to his current tale of looking for a rowdy bull named Black Bart, she looked past Bruno into the bar area. Who was here tonight? The only familiar face was that dark moody sculptor, eating by himself as usual. He was back, after being gone for several weeks. He wasn't bad looking, brown skin, strong and muscular, but honestly, he gave her the creeps. Once when she'd smiled at him, he just scowled. Very unfriendly. Always watching.

The sound of Bruno's voice told her he'd come to the end of the story. "That's nice. Has your gallery picked up any new artists lately?"

"Didn't much notice. Sometimes they get paintings I like. They had one with cattle in a background that looked like home. But the artist put lots of bluebonnets where the cattle were grazing. That's wrong."

"Why? Bluebonnets are pretty. They'd be nice in a boring grassland."

"They don't belong there. They're poison to cows. Their calves might have birth defects—things like crooked legs and cleft palates. We had to put down a calf—"

Purity put her hand over his. "Bruno, that's gross."

"Sorry, I forget you're so soft-hearted." He looked at his watch. "Gotta go. I'll walk you to your car."

After Purity drove away, she only went around the block to park in a different spot before she went into the bar. Another drink, that's what she needed. She wasn't in the mood to spend the evening alone. She passed by the sculptor and sat at the long bar. Nursing a drink for an hour or so while waiting for someone interesting was a skill she'd perfected.

She perked up when a young man came in. He was ordinary looking, yet something about him appealed to her. He was often here, but they'd never met.

"Hey, Ruben, how ya doing?" The bartender brought his order and stayed to chat.

In the bar mirror, Purity watched as they joked back and forth before Ruben made the brief rounds, talking to others. Maybe he'd say a few words to her too. She got another cosmopolitan and slowly sipped, but the man settled at someone else's table.

May as well go home. She felt grumpy as she got into her car. She turned the key in the ignition. The car only made an odd noise. A vulgar word left her lips as she got out. Now what?

Then Ruben came out. She flicked open a button on her blouse. He came over.

"Trouble?"

"My car won't start. It was fine earlier."

"Get in and unlatch the hood."

Purity got in and looked up at him. "How do I do that?"

He reached in to show her. When he drew his hand back, his fingers brushed along her leg. Damn! She should have tried this car-won't-start thing before.

Ruben lifted the hood and bent over the engine. She had no clue what he was doing.

"Try starting it now."

Nothing. He fussed some more.

"Try it again."

It purred to life. She got out as he wiped his fingers on his jeans.

"Thank you." She reached out, sort of accidentally touching his arm.

"Ruben is my name. And yours?"

"Purity. Purity Gold."

Ruben tucked a strand of hair behind her ear. "Lovely name for a lovely girl. You know, I should follow you home. Make sure your car doesn't conk out again. Don't you think?"

"Oh yes, I'd be so grateful. Really grateful." She blinked once slowly with her thick eyelashes.

He smiled. The most sexy smile.

He ran a finger from her collarbone downward, pulling it away just as he reached the point where her heart raced. "I have a bottle of wine in my car. When we get to your place, we could get better acquainted."

No need to put on an act. The smile stretching her face was the real thing.

♦ ❖ ♦

Purity lay on the rumpled black polyester sheets, admiring the contours of the man dozing beside her in the light of her lava lamp. They'd killed his bottle of wine. He was so easy to talk with and loved her paintings—gushed about them.

He knew art. Told her about his cousin in Tampa who had a gallery. He mentioned other galleries, talked about their managers and how he would help them choose art for their exhibits.

Certainly he could help get her into any number of good galleries. That's what he did, helped people out. It gave meaning to his life.

Such a refreshing change from guys always wanting to talk about themselves. A perfect man, right down to being great in bed and making it good for her, which didn't often happen.

She'd worried what he would think of her body. Her bedroom lighting was romantic, a description she liked better than dim. Without underwires and spandex, perky got saggy and pillowy. But he hadn't complained, just made her feel special.

Ruben stirred and stretched. He hissed in a breath.

Her laugh was low. "What's wrong? Did I wear you out?"

"I helped some elderly friends move this morning. Did all the heavy lifting."

"That's nice."

"Do you have any ibuprofen?"

"In the bathroom. I'll get it."

"No, I have to get up anyway." He sat up and looked back at her. "We're not done yet."

She hoped Bruno hadn't left any obvious traces of his presence in her bathroom, but it was too late now. The sounds of a flush, water running, and the creaky door of the medicine cabinet reached her ears. Soon Ruben was back.

He left about four, after saying he hoped to see her again and that it was his lucky day when her car broke down.

Pulling his pillow into her arms and hugging it, she inhaled deeply. The faint scent of sex made her smile. She drifted into a dreamworld, parading on Ruben's arm—a world where she was someone, and everyone who had laughed at her wore the green eyes of jealousy.

Chapter Twenty-Eight

Tuesday, April 18

Karen sucked in a breath and cradled her wrist closely. The warp threads below caught the butterfly skein as it dropped from her tingly fingers. Catching her lower lip between her teeth, she rubbed her wrist, rocking slightly back and forth on her weaving bench, and willed the pain to subside.

Uff da. It was too early. The past few days the gnawing, achy crescendo of pain had waited until at least afternoon. Seldom did her wrist feel good enough anymore to forget about—even bothering her at night—always niggling on the edge of her consciousness.

She didn't need this—she'd no time for weakness. She couldn't afford to fall behind, but damn it, she was. April was more than half gone, and with it, more than half of her scheduled weaving time.

After the tapestry was done, she'd go through the hassle of doctor's appointments. She pushed away the idea she might be developing carpal tunnel syndrome, that she'd need surgery. She worried that it wouldn't go as planned, and she'd lose dexterity or range of motion.

Just let her get through this. Then she'd deal with those fears.

She picked up the bluey-purple skein, awkwardly trying with her left hand the movements that her right knew by heart.

◆ ❖ ◆

Outside the Bjornson family room was a portal, a covered porch. Anton, on a break from getting the nursery ready to welcome their baby, headed there now, stepping out onto the flagstone pavers. He breathed in the fresh spring air. It would be warm today. Not a cloud in the sky, and already it was in the sixties. He held his cup of coffee securely as Twitch and Shadow brushed past him to chase away a jay who had dared invade their back yard.

The weather had been decent enough to put out their chairs with colorful cushions. Dom was already outside, sitting on the wicker loveseat with Quixote nestled against him. The dog looked up but didn't budge as Anton approached. Dom seemed lost in another world. He looked tired, as if each of his seventy years lay heavily upon him.

Anton settled in a chair across from him and took a refreshing swallow of coffee. "You okay, Dom?"

Dom nodded. "It hurts to see Karen like this. I want to fix things, but I'm helpless against what bothers her."

"She's always been hard on herself, but I've never seen her driven to this degree."

"She's frustrated. Powerless to change a world too big to control."

"Is there anything we can do?"

"I've tried to get her to go away for a while, but she won't consider it. Says there's not enough time."

"A few minutes ago, when I looked into the studio," said Anton, "she was sitting at her loom, not working. There was no music on. She was slumped over, rubbing her wrist. I asked her if she'd injured it. All I got was a no. What's with that?"

"It's been bothering her. More and more. Maybe a repetitive-strain injury acting up?"

"Years ago, she went through that." Anton propped his feet up on the cushioned hassock. "I'll pick up one of those elastic wrist braces for her. Lord knows she won't stop and get one for herself."

"I've even thought of tricking her, to get her away. But at what cost?" Dom's eyes were troubled. "If I kept her from finishing on time … I don't even want to consider it."

"What could bring back her energy? All that excitement she had when she began is gone." Anton sipped his coffee.

"If only …"

"If only what?"

"What if she heard people tell their stories, what if they could bring back that inspiration? I have some teacher friends, but they're in El Paso." Dom's voice trailed off, and he seemed to drift away again. "Maybe … Would they do it? Could they?"

"Dom? You're muttering to yourself."

"Sorry, I was scheming. She needs to hear immigrant voices and listen to their stories." Dom leaned forward in his chair, now looking energetic as if there was something he could actually do. "Maybe my friends could arrange for Karen to hear those folks."

"Take a trip to the wall," said Anton.

"Huh? The wall?"

"The border. To El Paso where your friends live. Let Mom see that struggle for herself. That would light a fire under her."

"Wouldn't work. It'd take too long to drive there, meet people, hear their experiences, visit the wall, and drive back. Not to mention exhausting."

"Remember Glenn, my helicopter pilot friend?"

Dom's eyebrows lifted. "You're not serious?"

"I am. He could fly you and Mom there. Take maybe a couple of hours. If you can stay with your friends, I'll make the travel arrangements. Could you do what you need in a weekend?"

"Would you come?"

Anton shook his head. "Skyla's due in a couple weeks. I need to be here."

"Karen would never consent to be gone that long. Damned Norwegian stubbornness."

Anton grinned. "I'm another stubborn Norwegian. Would it be easier if Mom were presented with a fait accompli? Don't tell her what's going on? Just take her? Maria could pack her bag, and I could sneak it onto the helicopter. Let's get our plans made. Try for this weekend."

"You realize what could happen if I trick her? Her anger can be formidable."

"Maybe I could do it. I'm family. She's stuck with me. It'd be hard for a while, but she'd get over it."

Dom rubbed the bridge of his nose. When he looked up, his face showed all the misery he must be feeling. "This is something Karen and I have to work out. I hate conflict. I can't believe I'm even considering your idea."

Anton watched conflicting emotions flit across Dom's face.

He was muttering again. "It's tempting. If we're to build something solid." Dom looked into Anton's eyes. "I feel like I'm on the cusp. I love your mother, but if this goes wrong, it may end what we have."

"Or it could be the move that brings you even closer."

"I'm afraid." Dom shook his head. "No, I can't risk it."

"It's ironic. About a year ago, we were sitting in this same spot. Remember? I was miserable, toying with the engagement ring I'd gotten for Skyla. At that point it was a toss-up that she'd ever wear it. You could let things slide, Dom. Avoid the conflict. Keep what you have."

"But she would still be in pain. And the next challenge … Uff da. It would be worse."

Anton chuckled. "That's the first time I've heard you say uff da."

"It's what happens when you hang around with Norwegians." Dom heaved a big sigh and sat up straighter. "God help me. See if Glenn is available. I'll call my friends."

Chapter Twenty-Nine

Friday, April 21

Karen frowned in concentration as she dealt with a change of colors in an area which butted up to the statue. The shadows in the greenish verdigris figure contrasted with the adjacent section that transformed from deep red to a luminous gold. It required several different blended skeins to accomplish that gradient.

She looked up as Dom came into the studio.

"Karen, I want to take you to some friends' house for dinner tonight. Would you be able to leave soon?"

"Good grief, Dom, it's not even two o'clock." She checked the skein number and guided the butterfly of blended dark red yarn behind several warp threads to the front of the tapestry again.

"It's Friday. Anton's driving. He wants to avoid the traffic."

"Where do they live?" She dropped the butterfly skein and shook her right hand. Sometimes that relieved the tingling.

"It's a surprise. Please, say yes."

She sighed. He did look excited. Maybe she would indulge him this time—she'd been saying no a lot lately. "Do I know these folks?"

"Don't think so. Herb and Yolanda Nelson. He's a history professor I worked with. You'll enjoy them."

"All right." She looked down at the clothes she'd thrown on this morning. "Uff da. I'll need to shower and change."

"Casual is fine," said Dom. "Anton'll be back in about fifteen minutes, give or take."

"You could have given me more warning."

"Do your best."

◆ ❖ ◆

So far, so good, thought Dom as they got into Anton's car. Now if they could get her onto the helicopter.

"Mom, I got something for you." Anton handed her a plastic bag emblazoned with a red bullseye.

Karen took the package out of the bag with a small sound of appreciation. A black elastic brace for her aching wrist. She put it on, adjusted the Velcro fastenings, and flexed her fingers. "I looked for my old one, but I couldn't find it. Thanks, that was sweet of you."

After they'd driven about a mile, Anton turned onto a road in an undeveloped subdivision, which looked toward the Santa Fe Opera House. It was a beautiful day with billowy clouds sending shadows chasing up and down blue-green mountains.

At the end of one street, in a turn-around spot, sat a helicopter. Anton parked nearby and opened his mother's door. As she got out, he said, "Your chauffeur awaits."

Her eyes widened. "A little surprise? Why a helicopter?"

"It'll save time," Dom said.

Karen turned to the smiling pilot walking toward them with his hand outstretched.

"Remember me, Mrs. B?"

"Glenn, Anton's college roommate. Good to see you again."

"Dom wanted you to arrive in style." Glenn took her hand to help her step up into the helicopter. Dom sat across from her.

She ran her hand over the plush seats. "I've never been in a helicopter this fancy."

"It's an Augusta Power Elite. My favorite bird. I do executive charter flights. You'll find it's fairly quiet."

Karen glanced back at Anton, still standing on the road. "Why is no one telling me where we're going?"

"Mom, please don't be mad. Dom is doing the right thing."

Dom cringed inside. Anton's words weren't what he wanted Karen to be thinking about before they even left the ground.

"Mad? You think I'm going to be mad?" Her head whipped to Dom. "What's going on?"

Anton stepped back quickly toward his car and saluted the pilot. "Take good care of them."

The pilot nodded, closed the passenger door, and climbed into the cockpit. The rotor blades began and soon they were aloft.

Dom looked down at Anton, growing smaller and finally disappearing from sight. The first time he'd flown in this helicopter, he'd gotten butterflies from the motion. This time he was more worried about the growing anger of the woman sitting across from him.

Karen glared at Dom. "Why does Anton think I'll be mad? And why haven't you told me where they live? This better be important enough for me to lose hours of work."

"You'll enjoy meeting the Nelsons. It'll be worthwhile. Trust me."

"Why do we need to fly? Tell me."

"Like I said, flying saves time. Herb has arranged for you to hear some stories."

"Stories?"

"I'm hoping this is what you need. I'm aware time is short, and that you resent being away from your weaving. You need to stop using your wrist for a few days to allow some healing."

Karen jerked away from the seatback. "A few days! Dom, I don't have that luxury. Take me home. Now."

"I'm sorry. I can't."

"You can, and you will."

Dom leaned back in his seat, shaking his head.

"If you do this to me, I may never speak to you again. You can't kidnap me! Where do your friends live anyway?"

"El Paso."

"Texas? My God, Dom. I thought he taught with you here."

"He did, but he's at the University of Texas El Paso now."

"You lied to me!"

"I didn't."

"You damn well misled me."

"The Nelsons have the same passion you have for making a difference."

"What right—"

"Karen, you can't keep on the way you've been."

"But I can't stop. The deadline—"

Dom's voice sharpened in his frustration. "You won't make that deadline in the state you're in. You've slowed to a snail's pace. You need a break."

"And now you're a doctor?"

Dom ignored her sarcasm. "When we started spending time together, I loved watching you weave. The joy you got as your vision came to life and grew. You were relaxed, music flowed around you, and your fingers flew. Now you sit in silence. You're driven, and the joy is gone. It breaks my heart to see you like this."

"I hurt. I'm afraid. Please, I'm begging you, take me home."

"Monday morning I'll—"

"Monday! That's insane."

"Maria packed for you. Anton gave our bags to Glenn earlier."

"Anton got it wrong. I'm way past mad. I'm furious!" Karen's nostrils flared. "Maria too? The lot of you are traitors. When we get back, they can help you pack your things. You won't be welcome at my house anymore."

Dom ran a hand through his hair and closed his eyes. *Madre de Dios.* His throat ached, and he felt like he was shrinking inside. He'd feared this would rip her from his life.

"If that's what it takes to see you well and happy again, I'll go," said Dom. "But, my heart, don't you see? What makes you *you*. I don't see it anymore."

Karen tilted her head up. That Norwegian stubbornness showed in the set of her chin.

"Damn it, Karen. I'm not your enemy. Why can't you be reasonable?"

Uh, oh. Why had he said that? Her jaw muscles flexed as her teeth clenched.

"I'll be civil to your friend and his wife." She bit each word off. "They aren't part of this. I thought I knew you. I thought I could trust you. Yet you see yourself in charge, making decisions for me. How can I marry someone who will treat me that way? I thought I loved you, but now I wonder if I even know you." She put her hands up to her ears. "It's crumbling all around me."

He started to say something.

"Don't you tell me it was for my own good. In fact, don't talk to me. I don't even know you." Karen jerked back in her seat and turned her head away from him.

Dom swallowed against the lump in his throat, felt hollowness deep inside. He leaned back and stared out the window. He only half saw the green, oasis-like *bosque* unfolding as the helicopter began to follow the Rio Grande, sun glinting off the water.

Karen and Dom were met by Herb and Yolanda Nelson at the El Paso airport. Glenn confirmed the return arrangements for Monday, then the helicopter lifted off and disappeared into the distance. Now Karen was stuck. Committed to the care of these strangers.

The Nelsons, cheery and welcoming, didn't comment on their guests not speaking to each other. She could imagine how annoying it must be to have such company thrust upon them with such little notice.

Yolanda seemed energetic and outgoing. She wore her dark-blonde hair in a collar-length bob. Karen relaxed some at her ready smile, which brought laugh lines to her deep-set eyes.

It was obvious that there was a genuine friendship between Herb and Dom when their handshake ended in a mutual hug, and both wore big smiles. Herb was in his mid-thirties with an easy-going manner, wavy brown hair, beard, and mustache. His light blue eyes were too penetrating for her mood at the moment.

She got into the back of the car with Yolanda. As they left the airport, she looked out the window, studying the dry El Paso landscape.

Home for the Nelsons was a two-story stucco house with a tile roof in a newish development. Looking in one direction Karen saw a dry, eroded mountainside dotted with brush under a relentless blue sky. In the other direction, houses and urban development sloped downward where the blue faded out in a brown haze.

How can they stand it? wondered Karen. Then she saw the desert willow, with orchid-like flowers of lavender streaked with purple, gracing the simple rock-scaped yard. Near the covered walkway, a squat, dwarvish statue, looking for all the world like a fantasy creature turned to stone, held a lantern lighting the way to the door. The Nelsons had made their own impression on this environment and evidently saw life with a sense of humor.

Inside, the living room was dominated by a grand piano. A bookcase nearby overflowed with music and books. Karen glanced at the open sheet music on the piano.

Yolanda noted her interest. "I don't know what Dom told you about us. Both of us are professors at the University. Herb, of course, teaches history, and I teach music. Let me show you to your room."

Yolanda led the way upstairs and into a pleasant room with pale sage-green walls. She waved her hand past the bed at the cluttered desk and more stuffed bookshelves. "Our guest rooms double as our studies. I hope you don't mind." She pointed toward an open door. "Bathroom's there. You don't have to share it with anybody."

Herb came in with her suitcase before going into the room across the hall. She heard him and Dom talking. Thank God she wasn't expected to share a bedroom with Dom. This was awkward enough.

Karen became aware of Yolanda still standing there. "You're very kind. Thank you."

Yolanda smiled. "Come down when you're ready." She closed the door as she left.

◆ ❖ ◆

Karen did not want to be here. Did not want to make conversation with strangers.

She unzipped her suitcase. What had Maria packed? On the very top was a sketch drawn by Krista with a note. "Hi, Gramma, I hope you're feeling better. Have fun in El Paso with Grampa. Love and Kisses, Krista."

Anger filled her. Had they even drawn her grandchild into the betrayal?

But then the sketch captured her attention. Skyla sat in the family room with Anton kneeling in front of her, his hand curved over her belly. How had her granddaughter managed to capture his expression, the wonder he felt? What talent Krista had!

She looked at the outfits Maria had packed. A powder blue top, soft and casual. Jeans, a sweatshirt, shorts. And one of her favorite outfits—an in-your-face raspberry skirt and top with a blue undertone, which kept it in her color palette. More clothes that could be dressed up or down. Whatever the next two days would bring, Maria had chosen well.

At the bottom were her favorite flannel pajamas. The most unsexy, comfortable night clothes she owned, just a few steps away from rag-bag status. They spoke of home and a time where she could just be—no artifice, no deadlines, no pressure. She sat on the bed, holding the pajamas to her, and let the tears flow.

CHAPTER THIRTY

Saturday, April 22

The next morning, Karen deliberately waited until she was sure Dom and Herb had left. Last night after dinner, Herb said he wanted to take Dom to his university office in the morning. She could sleep in, if she wanted, a suggestion she accepted quickly.

When she heard them drive away, she ventured downstairs, following the smells of coffee, bacon, and hot cinnamon buns. Yolanda sat working on papers at the breakfast nook. Wooden-slat blinds over the windows were open to let in the sun.

Yolanda smiled. "Good morning. Sleep well?"

"Yes, thanks." Karen sat. It was all she could do to be polite.

Yolanda set a cup of coffee in front of her. "Breakfast?"

"Don't go to any trouble for—"

"You don't have to pretend with me," said Yolanda. "Dom told us why you two are here this weekend. I'd be furious, too, dragged off against my will and plunged into a nest of strangers. I'm not going to pry. I want you to know you're welcome."

Karen raised her chin. "I'm not very good company at the moment. I'd much rather be at home weaving. I know Dom is a friend of your husband's, but right now, he's not a friend of mine."

"I hear you. We have this super bakery not far from here. Their cinnamon rolls are to die for. Bacon? Eggs?"

"Yes, please."

Yolanda soon set a plate in front of Karen with bacon, eggs, and a decadent-looking roll with a pat of butter melting into its cinnamon swirls. Then she got another roll for herself.

Karen finished her breakfast, leaving the roll to the last. She tore off a piece and popped it into her mouth. Mmm. Spicy, buttery goodness. "You're right about these." She licked a drip of butter from her fingers and uncurled another strip.

"Dom said you're working on a tapestry with an immigration theme."

Karen set down the bit of roll. "I'm playing with the themes of light and darkness, of walls and bridges, of people working together. The deadline is too soon." She swallowed against the ache in her throat. "This tapestry is supposed to be a way for my light to shine, for me to make a difference in this messed-up world."

"How did it all start?" asked Yolanda.

Karen told her about the contest and the exhibit tour.

"Since Herb and I moved here, we've been caught up in the immigration thing. You can't avoid it in El Paso, not if you have a heart. The stories, well, you'll hear some of them today."

"I don't want to do this. I'm sorry. I can't deal with more problems."

"Listen to me." Yolanda cradled her cup in both hands. "You see, like you I have voices inside me that need to be heard. I understand why you're driven, that it controls your very being. I feel that too. When I got into my composition, I couldn't eat, sleep. I barely managed to teach my classes, and even that time away from my vision I resented bitterly."

Karen nodded, intrigued despite herself. "Voices? You mean through your music?"

"I'm a composer. I've never tackled anything of this magnitude. When I finally started, it just flowed. It left me in tears many times. I was moved, and I took that as a good sign. But now, I'm frightened. What if no one else hears the story I need to share? Tomorrow is the test."

"Tomorrow?"

"The debut of my creation, the concert. I've been rehearsing with the choir and orchestra for months. I think I'm feeling what you will feel when your tapestry is done and you surrender that piece of you, that chunk of your life to the judges. I'm a nervous wreck."

"My God, Yolanda. Tomorrow? Dom foisted us upon you in the middle of your big moment?"

"It helps keep my mind off it. I'm ready, but second thoughts about other ways I could have written it drive me crazy."

"When is your concert?"

"Afternoon. Three o'clock."

Karen saw the strain in Yolanda that she had earlier blamed on their untimely, unwanted visit. She reached out to cover Yolanda's hands with her own. She felt their coldness.

"You're hurting too," Karen said in wonder. "The waiting. The butterflies. Tell me about your music." She gripped Yolanda's hands tighter. "I need to hear. I need to know that our art can make a difference."

"I wanted people to feel what an asylum seeker feels, so strongly that they get off their butts and do something. How could my music do that?"

Karen let go Yolanda's hands and sat back. "Go on."

"Finally, I decided to focus on one personal story. And yet it's everyone's story. It could happen anywhere in the world. One family forced to leave their home in Central America, to journey a thousand miles through danger and tedium with their faith in God and a hope for a better future. It's a journey with pain no one should have to go through. I don't even know that it has a happy ending, because the story doesn't end when they get to our border. You know you must point them toward hope. Strangers in a strange land, looking for a place to belong in a world that doesn't want them."

"You said choir and orchestra. What kind of music?"

"Traditional classical mostly. It has some elements of the Mass. My lyric sources range from modern poetry to scripture. I didn't follow any prescribed formula. I let the story tell me what it needed. One of my recurring musical themes is from a lullaby, popular in Mexico."

"Instinct." Karen picked up her coffee. "Scary, but when it works, it's serendipity. Will I be welcome at the concert? If your journey has been anything like mine, I understand why you're scared."

"I was hoping you'd want to come. Afterwards, there's a reception. And then Herb has invited people to the house—for either a celebration or a postmortem."

"I'd venture to say your orchestra and choir would already have given you feedback."

"But are they saying what they're really thinking?" Yolanda chewed the last bite of her roll. "Composing is a solitary art, but the performing brings together a community of folks. Music is a language that connects."

"Weaving is solitary. The support from friends and family is great, but hearing what the outside world says—that's huge."

Yolanda's expression grew wary. "We'll be deserting you this afternoon for our dress rehearsal, but we've arranged for a friend from the university to take you and Dom around. We met through the Lutheran Church hospitality center where we volunteer."

Karen humphed, reminded of Dom, the interfering old busybody.

Yolanda rushed on. "I know what you're thinking. But several times when I hit a snag, I went where we've asked Ted to take you. To see the wall, to speak with immigrants. It put it all in perspective for me."

"You're saying, grow up and take your medicine like a big girl?"

Yolanda sat back, a surprised look on her face. "I wouldn't have phrased it quite that bluntly, but yes. But big girls have the option of saying no. You could always plead fatigue, stay here, and spend the afternoon napping."

Karen held the young woman's gaze for a time before looking down. Then Yolanda went back to her papers. Karen refilled her coffee mug, helped herself to the cream from the fridge, and sat, thinking.

She adjusted one of the Velcro straps on her wrist brace and flexed her fingers. No pain. She felt a rush of gratitude for her son's thoughtfulness. Why hadn't she taken the time to get another brace when she couldn't find her old one? Sometimes she could be her own worst enemy. It was time to grow up, to take care of herself.

"I do want to visit the wall," she said quietly. "Have you told this Ted what he's getting into with us?"

Yolanda made a note with her red pen and then pushed the papers aside. "Yes. He's cool with it."

"You're amazing."

"I hope you find what I did."

CHAPTER THIRTY-ONE

After lunch, their tour guide arrived.

"Hi, I'm Ted," he announced. He raised his orange and white UTEP baseball cap in a brief salute, showing a balding pate with short gray hair on the sides. "I teach political science."

Karen wondered about the story behind his T-shirt stating HUGS NOT WALLS. Maybe she'd ask him later. It didn't seem to be the thing one asked immediately.

After wishing Yolanda luck on her dress rehearsal, Ted led the way to his car, a burgundy compact SUV. Karen got in front, Dom in back.

"I'm glad you want to see for yourselves what life in this border town is like," said Ted.

As they sped along the freeway, Karen caught glimpses of the cleared dry area along the river and the fences separating the two countries. The Rio Grande here surprised her. "I expected to see the river higher. It's smaller here than in Albuquerque."

Ted chuckled. "It's dry now. Water gets diverted into canals, and most of our rain comes in late summer and early fall."

After negotiating the freeway exit to drive through an older neighborhood of small homes and businesses, Ted parked near a colorful mural. Behind a row of buildings, a tall chain-link fence stretched.

"First we'll see the old downtown border fence." Ted led them toward the barrier.

Dom smiled. "I've heard that the first wall was proposed here more than one hundred years ago to keep Chinese immigrants from coming across the border."

"Chinese?" said Karen. Surprise made her forget she wasn't talking to Dom. "Here?"

"Yes," answered Ted. "At first, they were welcomed as cheap labor to build railroads, but sentiment and politics changed. The reasons for that wall might sound familiar. The Chinese would take our jobs and bring in drugs."

"Uff da. A hundred years ago." Despite her earlier resistance to this trip, Karen suddenly knew she wanted to have photos from it to look back upon. "Is it okay if I take pictures?"

"Sure," said Ted. "Just use your judgment when it comes to people. Some might not appreciate it."

Ted took off his glasses and polished them with a fold of his T-shirt. "Beyond this fence near the bend of the river is where 'Hugs Not Walls' happens."

"I was going to ask you about your shirt," said Karen.

"It's from an event we had at the end of January. Another is planned for October. Permitting is a hassle. We have to work with a host of bureaucracies."

"That's a challenge," said Dom.

Ted laughed. "We had four hundred families last time. They line up on both sides of the border behind the fences and wait. Some haven't seen each other for decades. It's all coordinated. The families have been registered and are given a number. An airhorn blows, they come through the gates, walk down ramps to the river and wait for their number to be called to meet their families. Then three tear-stained minutes later, the airhorn blows again and they have to leave to make way for the next families."

"Only three minutes? After being separated for so long?" asked Karen.

"Just enough time to hug, to cry, and maybe take a couple of quick pictures. Even so, the Border Network had to turn away hundreds of families this year. Four hundred families are all you can fit in the five hours allowed."

"I bet it's well controlled," said Dom.

"All the U.S. family members wear blue T-shirts; the Mexicans wear white. Many who came wrapped their feet in trash bags to wade through the water. It was about ankle deep this January."

"My God. Three minutes," said Karen. The vision of the high, sloping concrete canyon, the lines of blue mingling with lines of white, reflected and distorted in the shallow river filled her artist's eye. Three minutes washed in tears of joy and pain, ending with the blast of an airhorn, repeated again and again in a macabre dance.

"Couldn't they do it more often?" she asked.

"We're lucky to get it twice a year. Next, I want to show you the Lutheran hospitality house where Herb, Yolanda, and I volunteer. It's only one of a number of faith-based organizations here in El Paso."

◆ ❖ ◆

Inside the busy facility, Ted gave them a brief tour, then excused himself to check on arrangements in an upstairs office. Karen wondered, because of the layout, if this building had once been a school.

Dom struck up a conversation in Spanish with a family waiting to speak to a volunteer. Karen wandered back towards the entrance where immigrants were greeted, and their needs determined. While volunteers talked to the adults, kids were given paper and crayons. Their work was tacked up on a wall, showing Karen a glimpse of what the children had been through on their long journeys.

A young mother with a girl about Krista's age caught her attention as they looked through boxes of donated shoes. Bruises darkened the girl's thin arms and face. She found shoes that fit, put them on, deposited her old ones in a box to be discarded, and left.

Karen went to the box and picked up the shoes. Once they had been running shoes. The laces were frayed, broken, and reknotted. Holes big enough to let the toes show on each foot. Tread worn away. One shoe was separating from its sole. With each step the sole would have yawned away from the top like crocodile jaws. How many miles had she trudged in these?

What story did the child's bruises tell? Karen wondered as she took a photo of the shoes. What would be the impact on her life? How long before she would find a place where she felt safe, could go to school, and learn to play again?

The more she heard, the more Karen realized what the immigrants were up against. They weren't wanted anywhere. They were caught up in a game designed to make them fail. She thought back to when Krista was little, and they'd played "Chutes and Ladders." The immigration game was a system constructed with far more chutes to set them back rather than ladders allowing them to move forward.

But this was no child's pastime. Being sent back in the immigration game meant separation from loved ones, detention, or sliding back to the violence and death they'd tried to escape.

It made her appreciate the faith-based support groups. But most people who tried to seek asylum at this border never made it to the hospitality houses in El Paso. They were turned away at the border, sent back to wait, given empty promises, or just treated as inhuman, sometimes with deadly consequences.

Ted returned to introduce them to some volunteers. He engaged them in conversation with a few immigrants, translating so Karen could ask questions and hear why they came to the U.S. While Ted and Dom were helping a man trying to make sense of a form he'd been given at the border, Karen wandered outside to sit on one of the benches lining the shady portal. She snapped more pictures.

A tall, thin woman with straight, mousey-brown hair hanging to her shoulders approached a volunteer sitting on the next bench. She was plainly dressed. Her only jewelry was a filigreed crucifix hanging around her neck. "Hello, I'm Sister Mary Catherine. My job requires that I drive to Albuquerque several times a month, and tomorrow's one of my trips. I usually check to see if there's anyone who needs to go that way. It saves them bus fare, and I'm glad for the company."

The volunteer smiled. "I don't know of anyone, but I'll ask. Someone told me about your offering rides. I'm glad to meet you."

What a kind thing to do, thought Karen. She stood as Ted and Dom came toward her. Their itinerary had one more trip to a different spot along the wall before going back to the Nelsons.

◆ ❖ ◆

At the end of their afternoon, Karen put her hand on the wall in front of her, feeling the roughness and heat of the iron slats. She was looking into Mexico—here just a dry inhospitable expanse of scrub brush. Rust-covered, steel-plate rectangles topped the fence, forming a garish orange ribbon, stretching to distant mountains, scarring the landscape along with the dirt patrol road. Brush and weeds as far as the eye could see.

Ted had brought them to a border location west of El Paso near where Texas ran into New Mexico. At this particular point, the fence built to deter people crossing from Mexico became a fence that would only stop vehicles.

Previously, she'd laid the blame on the current administration, but what she'd seen this afternoon told her the problem had plagued leaders of both sides for decades. There was not the political will to do the soul-searching and comprehensive work to deal with immigration issues.

Was there any hope?

A breeze lifted a strand of hair from her face, then ventured past her to stir up an eddy of dust and grit.

Ted stood leaning against the car, patiently waiting for them, a bottle of water in his hand.

Karen had been moved by the folks he'd had them meet. Moved by those providing food, medical and legal aid, shoes, and water. Life-giving water.

Yes, there was hope. Ted had stopped at a few places where folks had scrawled graffiti on the wall. Hope even in those messages. One brought a wry laugh from her. MR. PRESIDENT, TEAR DOWN THIS WALL. R. REAGAN.

Another sobered her, playing again and again in her head. I WAS A STRANGER, AND YOU WELCOMED ME.

She blinked her eyes and looked in the direction Ted was facing. Dom stood several yards away, his hands resting against the barrier.

Alone. His head was bowed, his eyes shut.

Alone.

She didn't feel anger anymore, just a deep sadness.

Chapter Thirty-Two

Sunday, April 23

Karen didn't know what to expect from this concert. She resolved to listen carefully and to be encouraging. Even though she'd known Yolanda for only a few hours, they'd become friends.

A church, not far from the university campus, was the concert setting. Because they'd had to arrive early for the flurry of last-minute details and the choral warmup, Karen had wandered outside to enjoy the sunshine.

The church was built in Mission Revival style with a tiled roof and light-colored stucco sides. A cloister, a covered walkway on one side of the sanctuary with arches and columns, bordered a courtyard with benches, planters, colorful succulents, and a few shade trees.

She found a place to sit and watch. Her loom seemed a world away.

The people she'd met yesterday were on her mind. Stories from the news were one thing. Listening to real people, seeing their faces, and feeling their emotions was quite another. Witnessing the volunteers in action was uplifting.

The idea of random acts of kindness, something she'd always believed in, was taking on a whole new dimension in her mind. Her previous ideas seemed like play-acting against the real need she'd seen yesterday. Need that would continue until enough people cared to make changes in the system. The insight intrigued her. Who would have thought that it was an act of kindness to inspire people to open their eyes?

People started to arrive, so she went inside and stood in the narthex, looking down the long aisle into the high-arched sanctuary. An array of organ pipes and tall, narrow stained-glass windows flanked a carved-wood Celtic cross at the center.

She and Dom had ridden with their hosts, but she had no idea where Dom was. They hadn't spoken more than a few words to each other since they left Santa Fe. She sometimes felt his eyes on her but tried to pretend he wasn't there. Her anger had been replaced with numbness as far as he was concerned.

Finally, Karen ventured down the center aisle and sat in a pew near enough to watch Yolanda conduct. The instrumentalists filtered in and found their chairs, arranged on the lower, broad steps of the carpeted chancel. The pleasant din of a tuning orchestra began.

She spotted Dom several rows back, talking with Ted. She knew Dom had seen her—she was anything but invisible in her raspberry outfit that complemented her blonde looks and gave her confidence.

Karen turned her attention to the program in her hand. She scanned Yolanda's brief notes, describing the musical progress from movement to movement. This was the story of one family's journey to asylum, though countless variations could be found the world over.

The choir filed in to stand behind the orchestra. Yolanda strode out, bowed, and stepped onto the podium. She wore a feminine version of a tux, the all black relieved by a crisp, white wing-tip shirt.

Karen settled back in her seat, captivated from the first notes of the musical story unfolding. A theme based on a joyful, Central American folk song began with the panpipes, then was tugged back and forth between singers and instruments.

A second motif, reminiscent of the catchy lullaby tune, *"Esta Niña Linda,"* wove itself seamlessly into the chanting of the community of the faithful, ending with the *"Kyrie."*

The mood darkened in the next movement. The chorus and instruments became increasingly driven and intense. Finally, percussion and brass exploded in an ominous swirl of sound. Fragments of the previous gentler motifs were tossed about in the tumult, only to be eaten up by an aura of anguish and aggression.

Fascinated, Karen saw Yolanda almost in a dance with singers and instrumentalists, becoming one with them. Strings and woodwinds joined the fray, their colors mirroring the travelers' grief and sadness with sobs and wailing glissandos.

Now the journey settled down, moving into a dirge-like steady beat of the unfolding trek. A hymnlike tune wafted quietly above, carried by the rich colors of the English horn and a throaty alto flute injecting a note of hope in the midst of danger.

Soon both dark music and the program notes introduced inevitable tragedy. The youngest child fell ill. The mother, sung by a contralto soloist, cried a sorrowful reprise of the lullaby. The motif was doubled by the lower choral voices, until all moved together into a gentle *"Pie Jesu,"* a song of reassurance. The program note said they journeyed on, leaving behind a small grave.

In the respite that followed, Karen could almost feel the warm sun and see the refreshing water flowing over rocks as she listened to the chuffing breath of pan flutes. The trilling and piping of a tiny ocarina let her see a playful songbird rising and falling on the breeze. Then a hawk called. Muffled sticks played on a gong gave a metallic threat. The intensity grew to a clash out of which the beat kept on relentlessly, the peace shattered as they fled again. The pulsing somber cellos and bass made her heart beat with terror. Then the tension fell and gave way to the sounds of night—mournful howls of the distant coyotes as two muffled saxophones called to each other from opposite sides of the orchestra.

The main theme resurfaced as the sojourners reached the border. Cellos picked up the theme, playing it with a rich, somber vibrato, which made Karen want to weep. That hymn of faith was tugged back and forth by patriotic tunes, all with an uneasy edge and chords that refused to resolve, proclaiming peace and home had not yet been achieved.

It ended with a glimmer of hope, tempered with a question. The work resolved with an *"Agnus Dei,"* O Lamb of God. The closing text, *"Dona nobis Pacem,"* Grant us Thy Peace. These last words, sung first by the mother who had lost her child, then repeated by a reassuring choir.

As the last notes faded, Karen felt she had been on this journey. She had felt the terror, the long tedium, the grief, and the uncertainty that lay ahead. She felt the hope and knew within the community of the faithful the seekers would find a home again.

As Karen rose with the others in a standing ovation, she felt tears sliding down her cheeks. Yolanda, too, was a weaver, but instead of alpaca yarn and color, she wove voices and sound, bringing them all together in harmony.

What a gift! Exhilarating. Inspiring.

Humbling.

For a fleeting instant Karen was even a little jealous, then the emotions of the music swept over her again, moving her. The world needed both their talents.

Chapter Thirty-Three

At the post-concert reception, while mingling with the musicians, Karen found her eyes straying to Dom, noticing his fatigue, the strain evident even beyond his easy chatter with others.

Back at the Nelsons' home, the friends Herb had invited provided a potluck meal. After Dom ate, he excused himself quite early. Whether to sleep or to escape, she didn't know. She stayed with the guests for a while longer, then retired herself. The sun set, but twilight lingered.

This weekend had really thrown her into the air. Her relationship with Dom was definitely at a crossroads. Being shanghaied, kidnapped, tricked into this trip, whatever you call it, still made her angry. And though Dom owned the biggest blame, her own son bore considerable responsibility.

Dom had ridden roughshod over her feelings, but even so she would not have wanted to miss this experience with the wall, the concert, and to meet another artist dealing with the same yearning she felt. Yolanda was a kindred spirit, a new friend she treasured. One who provided a glimmer of hope.

That didn't make Dom's actions okay. She was shaken, still wondering if marriage between them would be advisable.

Was she a fool?

She got ready for bed, turned out the light and sat there in the darkness. Tears threatened. What if she broke it off with Dom?

Dom had such an impact on their lives. If he left, everyone would lose. She didn't want to imagine the emptiness and pain.

She thought of home, of Anton and Skyla, Krista, and the baby soon to arrive. Maria and Diego.

She thought of how awkward it would be with Sam, Farah, and Leyla. She cherished being Leyla's gramma. Well, great-grandmother really. Having Sam and Farah as her grandchildren. That brought a rueful smile to her lips. The relationships would be forever altered.

Somehow her tapestry had taken on a dark side, coming between her and those who loved her. The most beautiful tapestry in the world was no more than a pile of threads without love. How could she have worked so hard on a thing of light and found herself in such darkness?

Karen slipped on her robe over her pajamas and opened her door. This rift couldn't go on.

The sounds from below told her that a couple guests remained. No light showed beneath Dom's door.

Disappointment warred with relief.

Well, disappointment mostly. Morning was a long way off and would bring others to intrude on something that was theirs alone to work out.

Would he be asleep? Should she wake him?

Then Dom's door swung open. Looking tired and miserable, he was in pajamas and scuff slippers, his hair rooster-tailed like he'd been tossing and turning. In the dim, ambient light from downstairs, her eyes met and held his.

"I was coming to see you." Dom swallowed. "To apologize. I was hoping we could talk."

"Okay." She went into her room and turned on her bedside light. She leaned her pillows against the headboard, got in and pulled the covers up. It was chilly enough so they felt good.

Dom came in, closed the door, and hesitated. She waved him toward Yolanda's desk chair.

He sat, ran a hand through his hair, and cleared his throat. "I should never have brought you here after you said no."

"No, you shouldn't have."

"But I wanted to fix things, to give you a break, to help you find your joy again."

"Why didn't you just ask me?"

"I tried. I got noes and your saying not enough time."

"I told you before I began that I get obsessed with a project. You knew that."

"Obsession." Dom huffed. "I was thinking that meant task oriented. I didn't know it meant your going into a self-destructive mode."

"Maybe this time I got a little carried away." Karen looked down, wiggling the fingers of her right hand and smoothing the black brace coming out of her robe sleeve. "Dom, I know you meant well, and as it turned out, it has been very special to me. But you might have tried harder to convince me."

"Would you have come? If I said I wanted to take you to El Paso for the weekend to see the wall, and hear immigrant stories firsthand?"

Karen tilted her chin in the air. "We'll never know, will we? You took the choice away from me."

"I'm sorry." Dom propped his elbow on the chair arm and rubbed the bridge of his nose. "I shouldn't have tricked you. I dread the emptiness ahead if I have to leave you. I don't want to."

"You scared me."

"What? No."

"You and Anton both. You decided you knew what was best for me. You ignored what I said and what I felt. And that hurts. I need to be able to trust you. I need to know that when I say no, you will hear me. I need to know that if we have a problem, we can work it out together. None of this you and Anton playing the big strong men, knowing what is best for the little woman. Pat her on the head and decide for her."

Just saying it out loud made her anger seethe again. "That's bull."

"But you were glad you came?" Dom hugged his arms and drew his knees tightly together.

"Yes, it was valuable—the wall, Yolanda, her concert. It means a lot to know other artists are working, using their art to make an impact."

She noticed a smile begin on his lips and sat up straight. "The ends do not justify the means, Domingo. It doesn't make what you did okay. You took the power away from me. What about the next time you feel you know better? We are entering a time of life where health issues may come up. Who's in charge here? Is this an equal partnership or not? What if I did that to you?"

Dom searched her eyes. "I would hate it." He shivered. "And I can see … how down the road, it might lead to resentment." Another shudder ran over his shoulders. "Hang on a minute. Let me grab the blanket off my bed."

"Oh, for God's sake. Get under the covers. You'll be turning blue."

He moved with alacrity.

Karen sent him a warning glance. "Don't get any ideas. It's hard to carry on a conversation with someone whose teeth are chattering."

Dom tucked the blanket around his shoulders. They still weren't touching anywhere, but nearness was a warmth too.

"Karen, I really am sorry. You're right to be angry with me. I shouldn't have done what I did. As a preview of how we'd solve problems as a married couple, I guess I blew it."

"Completely."

"Can you forgive me? I want to make it up to you. But I … Do you still want me to leave when we get back?"

"Yes. And no."

He raised an eyebrow. "What does that mean?"

"I think it means maybe we need a little space. I haven't been easy to live with this past month. I realize that."

Karen appreciated the fact he didn't comment. "You were right about my not taking care of myself and right about taking breaks. I want time to process all this. Maybe rebuild a little trust. I thought I knew you, Dom, and this shook me."

"I do love you, Karen. I don't want to imagine life without you. Many times this weekend I found myself wondering what you were thinking. About little things like that dwarf with the lantern in the yard. About big things, if you and Yolanda talked about her music. If there was any similarity in designing a tapestry and composing a musical score. About your feelings at the wall."

"Talk to me now. I wondered much the same about you." Karen turned her body slightly toward Dom so she could watch his face.

They talked long into the night, circling back to raw feelings every now and again. They talked about hopes, dreams, about Ted and his inspiring work at the center. They wondered about the Sleuths and how they would have reacted to the wall, to the concert. He told her more about his friendship with Herb and Yolanda.

A clock downstairs chimed three, startling them. They laughed, and Dom reached out a hand to cover hers under the covers. Without even thinking, she jerked away. As she did, something within her rebelled.

He began drawing his hand back. She stopped him by hooking her pinkie over his. He froze, then squeezed her little finger between two of his—the slightest pressure, acknowledging her touch—then stilled.

Such a small innocuous contact, but the gulf, still real, had been bridged. The warmth went all the way to her heart and remained. Skin to skin—two beings in touch.

A promise.

They would try again.

Chapter Thirty-Four

Monday, April 24

Now back from El Paso, Karen had to put her resolutions into action. It would be hard; she knew how easy it would be to drift back into the habits that got her into this situation in the first place.

Both she and Dom had raw emotions on the helicopter ride home. He'd reluctantly agreed about the space, maybe a few nights apart. She had time to deal with the lingering doubt, fears, and anger, and what lay ahead. They agreed they wanted to be together, needed to be. They still planned to marry, but what changes had this experience made in their togetherness?

She went back to her tapestry, putting into practice things she and Dom had talked about. She took breaks, one walking out to see her alpacas and talking with Diego. He showed her the basketball hoop and the half court that he, Anton, and Sam had set up.

"Santos loves it. He's a good kid." Diego chuckled. "Anton told me it wouldn't hurt Krista and Leyla to experience something Santos excelled at either. The physical exercise would do them all good." Then he coughed.

The sound, which had nothing to do with clearing the throat, brought her gaze to his. "Exercise. Are you hinting I'd benefit from some, like riding?"

Diego's eyes twinkled. "What a good idea."

Karen made a point of getting up early enough to have breakfast with her son before he left for work. She spoke to him about riding rough shod over her feelings. "You erred. Don't go there again."

"But Mom—"

"There are better ways of working out problems. I know you and Dom meant well, but ends do not justify the means. Just because you *can* do it, doesn't mean you *should*."

On another break, she was surprised to see Skyla in the kitchen. "Why aren't you at work?"

Skyla grinned. "I've started my maternity leave."

Karen picked up some baby-sized overalls that were lying on the counter. "These are adorable. I bet Krista picked them out—the fabric is covered with puppies."

"Krista *made* them." Skyla's voice was filled with pride.

"What?"

"Maria has been teaching Krista how to sew. Aren't they great?"

Karen smoothed the colorful fabric, running her fingers over the seams. "Uff da. Very impressive. I've missed out on so much while I've been holed up with my tapestry. I've been so blind. I'm sorry."

Skyla put a hand over hers. "Anton told me about his conniving with Dom. I thought it was just a surprise. I'd no idea they tricked you and took you against your will. I would have been so angry."

"Did he also tell you I reamed him out for his part in it?"

Skyla chuckled. "He did. I have to thank you. He needs reminding sometimes."

Karen laughed and hugged her daughter-in-law. "You're welcome."

♦ ❖ ♦

Later, Karen watched with a critical eye as Dulcie began threading the weft yarn through the open shed of the warp. It was frustrating to sit back and let someone else work on her tapestry. She rubbed her wrist, frowned, and tried to relax.

"Just a bit more bubbling," she cautioned. "That color section is wide there."

Dulcie obediently adjusted the amount of weft thread and tapped it down with her fork.

Karen kept an eye on the distance between the warp threads to make sure they remained even.

"I have watched you," said Dulcie, "but you're so fast. I turn and go the other way with the weft in this spot. I don't want any lice. Am I doing it the way you would?"

Why did her wrist have to play up now? Karen knew she was making Dulcie nervous, watching her like a hawk. The color was even; no white warp bits showed, avoiding the dreaded faux pas weavers call lice.

"You did good," said Karen. Would this work? Would it save time to have Dulcie physically do what she itched to do herself? As she watched Dulcie gain confidence, she had to admit progress was steady. She relaxed a little.

Maybe she could make butterfly skeins, or would that aggravate her wrist? She tried one but stopped with a bit-off expletive.

Dulcie faltered and looked up.

"It's not you. It's me. I hate doing nothing."

"It must be hard. Can you tell me about El Paso? I've been there many times. That was the road my husband and I used when we visited family. I got very familiar with that long boring drive."

After telling Dulcie what they'd seen, Karen was surprised to find how much progress had been made that day. She flexed her wrist. It felt better. She'd try weaving again after dinner.

Dulcie started a new color, listening carefully as Karen guided her through this step. When the color was well underway, she spoke again. "Tell me about Niemöller. Before this tapestry, I'd never heard of him."

"Niemöller went along with the nationalism, the anti-Semitism, and what he saw Hitler trying to do." Karen related as best she could what Dom had told her of Hitler's rise to power. "It was only when Hitler interfered in what Niemöller considered the church's business that he spoke out against him."

"You mean he was okay with how the Jews were treated?"

"He was a complicated man. He wasn't that concerned at first about what was going on. Then he spent years in concentration camps, some at Dachau."

"Dachau! I've heard of that. How awful."

"Dom read to me about a turning point for Niemöller. After the war, he took his wife to see where he'd been at Dachau. Near the entry, a sign stated that during 1933 to 1945 over two hundred thousand people were cremated there. The dates jolted his conscience."

"But he was in prison. What could he have done?"

"For eight of those years, yes. But the first four, while Hitler was rounding up his opposition and getting a grip on power, Niemöller had done nothing. He felt guilt and shame, thinking Germans should take responsibility for what they had allowed to happen. He was torn, seeing the need to rebuild the country and boost the morale of a people left in poverty. Many people wanted the Germans punished. His understanding and the quote were a long time in coming."

"Thanks, Karen. His words are important. I can hardly wait to see all the art together."

"God willing, one of them will be this tapestry."

Chapter Thirty-Five

Tuesday, May 9

The phone rang, jangling Pete's concentration on the police reports he was reading. "Lieutenant Schultz."

"You're the detective working that burglary at the Swift and Adams Gallery, right?"

"Who's asking?" Pete rolled his chair back from his desk. This was a surprise. Finally a lead?

"Sorry. Joaquin Jimenez. I'm a sculptor."

Pete knew that name and had admired his bronzes. "What can I do for you?"

"The painting that was stolen? I think I've found it."

"You think?"

"It was in my garden shed. I don't often go in there. But I saw this thing, wrapped in newspaper on the shelf. I didn't open it all the way—only enough to see what it was. I thought I'd better call you."

Pete got the address and asked another detective, Cheveyo Loloma, to provide backup. Loloma was a good man. Quiet, more than competent, he didn't miss much. Before Pete left, he sent a photo of the stolen painting to his phone.

◆ ❖ ◆

Under gray skies, Pete and Loloma arrived at Jimenez's place on Canyon Road. They turned on their bodycams and got out of their car. The wiry, muscular man was waiting outside, wearing an anorak. His handshake was firm, his eyes direct. Bypassing the open-by-appointment-only studio in front, Jimenez led them down a side path and through a wooden gate. The path opened to a small, shady backyard surrounded by adobe walls. A matching gate was set into the back wall.

Pete noticed the windows of the living quarters looked out upon a portal with a few utilitarian chairs and a worktable. A budding lilac bush spilled over the walls and loomed above narrow beds with daffodils and hyacinths. The canales draining the roof dripped water near where lily of the valley bloomed, scenting the air. A raised circular yin-yang shape made up the focal point of the small yard—half of it formed into a shallow pool, pattered by intermittent raindrops, and half a base where a sculpture of two children danced for all time, captured in bronze.

Jimenez opened the wooden door of an adobe-style shed, pointed to the wrapped object on a lower shelf, and stepped back. A portion of the painting, wispy white hair over the red headband of the old Navajo, showed where the newspaper was torn away.

Pete snapped photos on his phone and looked around the small space before putting on his gloves and stepping inside. Cobwebs in the tiny window. Bags of potting soil, assorted trowels, pruning shears, and other tools. Labeled boxes of seasonal stuff. Rakes, hoes, snow shovel, and brooms standing in a corner. Dusty. Dry. While not recently swept, there were no tracks on the floor. More organized than a hundred similar sheds.

With his pen, Pete lifted back the newspaper. Certainly looked like the painting on his phone.

"When were you last in here?" asked Loloma.

Jimenez waved at the boxes of votive candles and a tub of sand. "After Christmas when I put away the farolito makings."

"Do you keep the shed locked?" asked Pete.

"No."

Loloma filled in the information on a large brown evidence bag. Then he slipped the painting, still in its newspaper, inside and sealed the bag.

"What made you think this was the stolen painting?" asked Pete.

"I'm in and out of William's gallery almost daily when I'm in town. I know the art he carries."

"Where were you on March twenty-eighth?"

"Last couple of weeks in March and the first week of April, I was on an east coast tour. I can give you my itinerary if you need it."

Loloma protected his paper container under his rain jacket. He took a last look around.

"We'll take the itinerary," said Pete. "Thanks for your call."

"No problem." Jimenez shut the door. "I'll get the itinerary for you."

Pete gestured toward the back gate. "Mind if we take a look?"

At Jimenez's shrug, Pete opened the gate and peered out. He took more photos. No houses in back, just an open area with trees and brush growing along what looked like a small ditch, but was actually the Santa Fe River. Beyond lay East Alameda Street. Anyone could have entered without being noticed.

Back at the office, Pete called Cecil. "Just had an odd thing happen. We recovered the painting that was stolen from Adams's gallery on March 28. I'd like your take on this. Are you up for coffee?"

"Have you seen the weather forecast?"

Pete glanced through the big windows at the fast-moving, dark gray clouds. "Looks like good coffee weather to me. The Starbucks on Cerrillos?"

"I'm not sitting outside in this."

"If it's raining too hard for you, we can come back here or sit in my car. Your choice."

Cecil's sigh came over the speaker. "You're buying."

Inside Starbucks, it was warm, noisy, and steamy. People were lingering, hoping for a break in the rain.

Pete motioned to Cecil's cup with its lid full of whipped cream. "What the hell did you call that?"

"Cinnamon dolce latte. I figured since you were buying, I'd splurge."

"We'll have to run for it," said Pete as he shouldered open the door.

When they were settled in his car, Pete told Cecil about the call from Jimenez. "What do you think?"

"Jimenez is an odd duck. Closed off, except when you get him going about art. He has a security system, not mine, but I know he's got one. Garden shed?" Cecil licked the whipped cream off his lid. "Shit. Anybody could have put it there."

"Planted?"

"What was the date on the newspaper?"

"April first," replied Pete. "Could have been wrapped around it any time. I checked his schedule. He was where he said he was."

"Who has a grudge against him? Shit, look at that." An employee outside struggled to cinch the umbrellas, one of which threatened lift-off.

"Look how dark it is off to the south. What put the idea of a grudge in your head, Dupre?"

"Right after Tuttle dragged me into this case, Jimenez came onto our radar. He's been in all three locations where Anonicellis have been stolen."

"And?" asked Pete.

"Tuttle wondered how a young sculptor could afford to live on Canyon Road. I haven't been able to find out."

They traded ideas back and forth. Then the skies opened up, drumming rain on the roof. Cars sent sheets of water flying from puddles pooled by the curb. Pete's radio warned of a severe weather alert.

"No kidding," said Cecil. "Bjornson and I were going to meet this afternoon and fly drones. I think we'll wait." Lightning forked across the sky, followed almost immediately by the loud rumble of thunder. "Definitely wait."

Pete smiled. "Anton Bjornson? He said you helped him with his security cameras."

"We've flown drones quite a few times since then. How do you know him?"

"We met after Anton's daughter was kidnapped."

"He mentioned the kidnapping." Cecil looked down with a frown.

What was Cecil thinking? About his own family? Pete hadn't forgotten the unanswered questions from his check on Cecil's past.

"I don't think I've ever met another family like the Bjornsons. They're so damn … Can't think of the word. Hallmarky. That's it. They all get along. The world isn't like that."

"But it is, Dupre. There are good people out there. Maybe they're the glue that holds the fabric of our society together. The law deals daily with scum. Why shouldn't there be those on the opposite end of the spectrum?"

Cecil slurped the last of his latte, still frowning.

Pete looked at the man, fiddling with his cup. Normally he wouldn't share personal things, but he could read between the lines enough to know there was something going on, a hollowness that needed filling. "My wife, Akiko, and I count Karen and Dom among our closest friends. They're genuine. When I'm down, I can spend time with them and come back ready to deal with the cesspit again."

Cecil drew his brows together. "Why would a gal settle for an old man like that? She'll end up a widow again. Why put herself through that pain?"

"They're good for each other," said Pete, tipping his head to get the last drops of brew.

Cecil scowled. "Is this when you tell me about the rainbow?"

Pete choked, then laughed. "Hadn't thought of it and don't see one."

"Not coming down as heavy now. I'll take the cups. Thanks, Schultz."

CHAPTER THIRTY-SIX

Thursday, May 18

Early in the morning, Anton carefully cradled his three-day-old son in one arm and quietly closed his bedroom doors behind him with a soft click. These carved doors, based on those of Edoras in *The Lord of the Rings*, had always reminded him of his responsibility for his family. Now, even more so.

Twitch brushed past him. As they passed Krista's room, Twitch's littermate joined him in a race for the stairs. Anton followed them silently along the hall. Skyla needed a few hours of unbroken sleep away from the demands of their babe.

He carefully descended the stairs, holding onto the railing. As he entered the family room, the aroma told him the coffeemaker had completed its timed task. He went to the counter dividing the kitchen and family room to pour himself some coffee. Awkwardly, with one hand, he added a splash of milk, and let the dogs out. Then he sat on the sofa in the family room.

Light fell upon little Lucas cradled in Anton's arm. After a few swallows of coffee, Anton set down his cup and just sat, looking into his son's face. Wee hiccups and soft infant sounds came from the squirming, swaddled body—so precious. Unfocused baby eyes opened, seemed to look past him, squinted, and opened again.

"You've brought such joy to your mommy and me. I'd wanted to marry again, to have more children, but I had no idea how much I would love you both." He leaned forward to get a few more sips of coffee. He put down the cup and gently smoothed his fingers over Lucas's pale, wispy hair. So soft. So fragile a life.

He stroked the baby gently, marveling at the miracle he held. The hiccups ceased, the kicking inside the swaddling stilled against his hand. Gradually lashes came to rest against soft cheeks in slumber.

"Good morning." At the sound of his grandmother's voice Lucas's eyes opened again, blinking against the call of sleep.

Anton looked up and smiled. "Morning, Mom. Isn't he amazing?"

Smiling, Karen bent over them, touched the baby gently, then caressed her son's stubbly cheek. "Really amazing. Both of you." She went to the counter to pour her coffee.

Krista came downstairs, let in the dogs, and plopped down beside her father, cuddling close to watch the baby. "Was I ever that tiny?"

Anton chuckled. "Morning, sweetie. You were even a wee bit tinier. You were seven pounds when you were born. Lucas is eight."

"Anton was eight pounds when he was born," Karen brought the coffee pot and refilled Anton's cup.

"Thanks, Mom."

"I like having a brother." Krista smoothed the baby's hair. "Does he see my hand? His eyes are all over the place."

"He can't focus yet. He'll begin to in a few weeks."

She giggled. "He went cross-eyed just now. Can I hold him?"

"Watch how I'm putting him in your arms, so his head is supported." Anton placed the baby in Krista's eager hold.

"Lucas Edvar Bjornson," said Karen.

The way her voice relished each syllable touched him. He'd known she'd be over the moon with happiness.

"When you told me his name—I still get teary-eyed. Lucas. Bringer of Light. A beautiful name. And Edvar after his grandfather."

Fluttering lids closed again, and the baby slept.

Anton looked up as Dom came in with the newspaper and got his coffee.

"Good morning," Dom said. "I can see I have to wait in line for my turn to hold Lucas." Quixote, Dom's border collie, padded in after him and sniffed Lucas cautiously. "Dare I name him as my grandson?"

Anton smiled. "We'd be honored to have him call you Grandpa." Then he laughed. "What do you suppose Sam will say?"

"My oldest grandson is fine with it. We talked about it already."

Twitch ran in from the kitchen and jostled his way between Quixote and the baby. The border collie backed away and lay down on the hearth rug, stretching out with a doggie sigh.

"Uff da, Twitch," said Krista, pushing his head away from the baby. "Leave it. Your beard is all drippy." Twitch maneuvered the curious Shadow away, and they both lay down by Quixote.

"We should plan a get-together for the Circle Sleuths to welcome Lucas," said Karen.

"Goodie!" said Krista. "Leyla and I have been wondering. When are we going to celebrate Dom's birthday?"

"It's okay with us if they happen together," said Anton. "How about Memorial Day, the twenty-ninth? Is that okay, Dom?"

"Certainly. One celebration here would be easier on your mom too. Less time away from her weaving."

Karen frowned. "I can spare the time for two celebrations. These are important."

"You'll still have two, Karen," said Dom. "Remember my daughter snagged my actual birthday on the thirtieth for our family dinner."

Anton raised his brow as Karen wiped her face free of expression. Dolores was still cool to the idea that her father was in love again.

"Daddy! He spit up." Krista's voice was worried. "Did I do something wrong?"

"No, sweetie. Babies do that. Let me—" Anton caught Karen's wistful expression. "Let your gramma take him." He watched the careful transition to Karen's arms. "You'd better eat your breakfast, Krista. The school bus will be here soon."

Karen couldn't look away from the tiny person cradled in her arms. She whispered, "Lucas Edvar." She blinked to clear the moisture from her eyes. "Edvar should be here."

Dom's hand gently covered hers where it rested on the swaddling blanket. "I believe he is. He lives on in this family."

She searched his eyes. He understood. His Isabel, too, would always be a part of him. How lucky they were to have found each other after such losses. She brushed her grandson's soft cheek.

It had been more than three weeks since El Paso. Her *Tapestry of Light* was progressing steadily. It had been privy to many conversations she and Dom had had. In some ways, she knew him even better than before their dust-up. Their living arrangements were almost back to what they had been. Thursday nights though, he always spent in town. As far as she could tell, Dom's special time with Dolores had yielded no movement toward accepting Karen.

Karen certainly wasn't looking forward to the birthday dinner Dolores was hosting for Dom. She enjoyed the rest of the family, but Dolores had a way of inviting disaster.

Chapter Thirty-Seven

Wednesday, May 31

Walls. Bridges.

Karen slid onto her loom bench, automatically straightening the butterfly skeins resting on the completed portion of her tapestry. Dom's birthday dinner had been monumentally disastrous even on a Dolores standard. Her heart ached to see Dom so discouraged.

She pressed a foot treadle and passed the blended blue hues into the shed of warp threads that opened. Frowning, she tapped the weft into place with her fork. The images she was weaving fit hand in hand with her experiences of their recent celebrations. Walls—especially those built with fear, prejudice, and hate. Bridges that soared over, connected, brought together the best in people so they could work together and solve problems.

What a contrast between Dom's two birthday celebrations.

Monday night, the Circle Sleuths had gathered at the Bjornsons' home. Easy going, pleasant. Small conversations about trivialities that ebbed and flowed as the crowd shifted, catching up on everyone's lives. Big conversations as they talked about ideas that mattered to them as a community.

Lots of laughter, generations interacting with each other. Music, both singing and instrumental, ending with Sam's playing on his guitar, "Asturias" by Isaac Albéniz, a piece he'd recently mastered. An evening full of happiness and warmth.

And then Tuesday night. She hadn't wanted to go. But Dom wanted her with him. "For my sake," he'd said. "She's my only child. Both of you are part of my family."

She said no more but went.

The evening at Dolores's started out fine. More formal. Sparkling silver and china. Gorgeous flowers. Everyone minding their Ps and Qs. Karen could understand why Sam always called his mother, Mother. She wasn't the mom sort.

Dolores's birthday celebration for Dom was staged for family only. Dolores and her husband, Frank. She and Dom. Sam with Farah and Leyla. The youngest of Sam's three sisters and his two brothers filled the rest of the table. Dolores had seated Karen and Dom as far from each other as possible. Karen hadn't minded that. Frank and Leyla were good company.

Karen tapped down another strand of color.

Dolores was not a bridge builder. She wasn't reaching out. She was more into poking with petty grievances. Last night, she poked where it really hurt.

That scene halfway through dinner had been forever burned into Karen's memory with the barbed comment from Dolores to Sam.

"Thank goodness you and Farah haven't had children. They'd be half-Arab."

Dolores's words exploded overhead like an unexpected firecracker, stunning the audience.

Sam's face had turned white. His chair toppled behind him with a crash as he stood.

"How dare you!" He held out his hands to Farah and Leyla. "I will not allow you to poison my wife and my daughter with your words. God willing, we will have many children, but you will not see them!"

Tears sparkled in Farah's eyes as she took Sam's hand. The three hurried from the room.

"Well, how rude—"

"Dolores!" Frank stood, snatching his napkin as it slid from his lap. He flung it onto the table, overturning his wine glass. A blood-red stain spread across the snowy-white linen.

"My tablecloth! Look what you've—"

"That's enough." Frank's words cut. "Everyone is excused." He followed after Sam.

Karen stood, her eyes on Dom. His remaining grandchildren melted away from the room. Dom stood next to his daughter.

He shook his head and walked slowly to Karen, putting his arm around her waist, and speaking in a near whisper. "Let's go home."

She bit her lip, remembering the pain on his face as they left the wreckage of his birthday celebration.

Karen knew Sam would remain in touch with his other family members, but the bridge with his mother, precariously rebuilt after his decision to marry Farah, was now in shambles.

Sam desperately wanted children. He and his grandfather had always been able to talk with each other about things that mattered. Karen knew they'd had conversations about children. Since Farah already had a child, Sam was convinced the fault lay with him.

Her heart ached for the young couple. But it hadn't been that long – some couples took longer to conceive than others. They shouldn't even be thinking "fault" for God's sake. She wished she could tell them to just relax, to give it more time.

Walls. Bridges.

Could Karen be a bridge? How? Did she dare?

What if she did nothing? Didn't speak up?

She looked up from her loom to Niemöller's quote hanging nearby.

I didn't speak up, because…

Because what? It wasn't her place?

But if she really believed in what she was doing?

Damn it! Maybe she was a self-righteous busybody. She'd been called that before. But doing nothing, letting those she loved remain in pain? Impossible.

How about a compromise? If the opportunity arose, she'd take it?

Couldn't she put this off until her tapestry was done?

Karen wove in more strands of a white-yellow blend in an area where the light source shone against the darkness.

That would mean the divide would remain between Sam and his mother, would let Sam and Farah suffer more, would let Dom be hurt and distanced from his only child.

No. It couldn't wait until the tapestry was done.

She'd told herself she would take breaks for the sake of her wrist. And now for those she loved.

Take a break, Karen.

CHAPTER THIRTY-EIGHT

Saturday, June 3

Several days later, Karen was checking out the early crop of summer vegetables at the Santa Fe Farmers' Market when she bumped into someone. She looked up, startled, an apology on her lips, to see Dolores. She froze, conflicting thoughts racing through her mind. Was this the opportunity to bring healing? One voice in her head screamed no, another sighed in resignation. Get it over with.

Before she could form any words, Dolores spoke.

"Could we talk about Dad?" Dolores motioned with her hand. "There's a new coffee place across the street."

Dolores sounded surprisingly cordial. Karen nodded.

Locals and tourists were taking advantage of the fine weather and sitting in the coffeeshop's outside area, filling the air with an undulating hum of chatter and laughter. They carried their lattes out to join them. Several yards away across a walkway lay the tracks of the Rail Runner Express, the commuter train that ran between Santa Fe and Albuquerque.

"Mmm, delicious," said Karen as she tasted her coffee. "I'm glad you invited me to talk. Dom has been feeling down since his birthday."

"Why? What's wrong?" Dolores looked innocent.

Karen raised her eyebrows. Was the woman completely oblivious to the hurt she'd caused?

Maybe not. With shaking hands, Dolores took a quick sip of coffee and splashed it on her chin. Not the move of an at-ease person. Uff da. Maybe she should jump right in and have it out with her.

Karen leaned toward Dolores and spoke quietly. "Isn't it obvious after what you said to Sam and Farah? Dom loves Farah and has always been pleased Sam married her. Why is pure Spanish ancestry so important to you?"

"You wouldn't understand."

"Help me. Ancestors aren't what makes a good or bad person."

Dolores didn't respond, but her color grew higher.

"Isn't it more important how people treat each other?" asked Karen.

A train came nearer with the insistent *clang-clang* of its warning system. The white locomotive with its red and gold roadrunner was followed by two white cars with their swooping red and gold suggestions of the feathered body of the iconic bird.

"It's you who are making Dad unhappy. He's wishing he never got involved with you."

"What?"

"You think you found a sugar daddy." Dolores's voice was raised over the *da click, da click* as the wheels of the short train passed over the rail joints.

Karen set down her cup to clatter in its saucer. "I beg your pardon. I misunderstood because of the train."

"You heard me. All you want is a sugar daddy."

Her voice was too loud for the sudden quiet of the train now moving away. The people at the next table looked over at them and snickered.

"That's an insult to him and to me. I am not interested in Dom because of his money."

"My father will never marry you, no matter how much you claw your little gold-digger fingers into him."

"Oh, for God's sake." Karen struggled to keep her voice low. "You know I don't need money."

"Some people never get enough. I don't want your greed taking our rightful inheritance from my children."

"Well, we agree on something. I'm not excited about you getting any of Anton's either. Dolores, this is silly. Dom and I are working all this out with prenuptial agreements. You have no cause to worry."

Dolores narrowed her eyes. "He's just having a late mid-life crisis, but now he's coming to his senses, praise be to God. Dad feels sorry for you now."

"Sorry for me?"

"He was talking with Nita and me after Mass a few weeks ago. Or didn't you know he's been going to Mass with his old friend, Nita, every Thursday since February. Ever since he found out she's a widow. They're the same age, you know, and have always been very close."

"He goes to church with you on Thursdays."

Dolores sat back with a sly smile. "Is that what he told you? The old fox. Sometimes they invite me, yes, but I don't like to intrude on their time together."

Karen pushed aside her unfinished latte. "I don't believe a word you're saying."

"Maybe you should ask him how his dinner was at the Blue Goose last Thursday. They were there. I ran into them when they were eating dessert—sharing some decadent chocolate concoction."

Karen rose from her chair and picked up her purse. "How you can lie with a straight face, I will never know. I'm sorry I tried to help."

She'd known what Dolores was like. Remembered the lies she'd told Farah to stop her from seeing Sam. But damn, what if there was some truth to it all?

Another commuter train came closer.

"Help, you say." Dolores laughed. "You're the one who needs help. You're pathetic." Her voice grew almost to a shout. "Leave my father alone."

The *clang, clang, clang* wasn't enough to drown out Dolores's words.

Now the center of unwelcome attention, Karen's face burned. She left, sending one last look at the smug expression Dolores wore.

Somehow, Karen made it to her car without stumbling, even though her eyes were filled with tears. That smugness was etched in her memory, convincing her she'd been set up by Dolores. Such a poisonous person.

Dom would never behave in that way.

Would he?

No. Dolores knew just what buttons to push.

But the chocolate dessert?

Karen stuck her needle into the fabric and set aside the rod pocket she was making for the back of her tapestry as Dom came into her studio. It didn't seem the right moment to be wielding a sharp instrument. Her head was screaming. *Who was Nita? Why had he never mentioned her?* Uncertainties rose to the surface, feelings she thought had been put to rest after El Paso.

Dom didn't look happy either. "What did you say to Dolores this afternoon? She called me in tears."

"I know you've been upset ever since your birthday dinner, so I—"

"She said you began haranguing her about ancestors and calling her a liar." He scowled. "I told you I would talk to her."

"Well, you hadn't, and I thought, when we ran into each other at the market, it would be a good opportunity."

"How do you know I hadn't talked with her? I was easing into it. Then you had to go and interfere."

This was not fair. She stood and faced him. "Was it interference when I offered my home and support for Sam and Farah when your daughter caused the rift between them? Was it interference when I stood up for little Adoncia when that brat threw hot cocoa all over them? You praised me for those actions."

"Those were different."

"Were they? Was it interference when you took me to El Paso?" She sent an exasperated glance skyward. "I don't like seeing you, Sam, or Farah in pain. I wanted to fix it if I could, so I said yes when Dolores invited me for coffee." Why couldn't he thank her for trying? Maybe Nita, whoever she was, could do better.

"Now we're back to square one," said Dom. "I have to go see her."

"Fine, see her then. And go see your daughter too." Karen turned her back on him, muffling a sob.

Dom put his hand on her shoulder.

She jerked away violently, her arms wrapping around her middle.

She listened as his footsteps receded on the tile floor. Then to the sounds of his car door shutting, the start of his engine coming to life, then fading away to nothing. To emptiness.

She sank into a chair, hunched in silent misery.

Had to see who? Dolores?

Or Nita?

Chapter Thirty-Nine

As Dom drove back into the city, he was not pleased with himself or with Dolores. The whole damn thing was so irritating—why was there so much tension between Dolores and Karen? The twenty-minute drive gave him time to cool down, to look at things rationally.

Had he heard Karen right? "Go see her. Go see your daughter too."

Too? What did that mean?

Just before Dolores had hung up from her tearful phone call earlier, she'd said, "Dad, don't believe those lies she'll tell you. Karen just wants to drive a wedge between you and me."

Who was driving the wedge?

On the Thursday before his birthday, in growing anger Dom realized he'd been set up by Dolores. Preferring to believe Dolores's innocent reasons for Nita's presence on Thursdays, he'd been ignoring signs and hadn't confronted his daughter. He should have put his foot down at the beginning. God, would he ever learn?

Dolores had said Karen had started this latest confrontation. How could he believe her? Dolores, with her controlling ways, owned that wedge. He loved his only child. When she was little, he could send her to the corner until she was ready to apologize. Not anymore. Since Isabel died, her manipulation had gotten worse. Frank had to be a saint to put up with her.

He hated conflict. He only became a peacemaker when the conflict became intolerable. God knows, peacemaking wasn't something he enjoyed.

Karen, true to herself, had not tried to blame anyone else. She'd seen people in pain and tried to help. It's how she was programed; she was being truthful. Now she was hurting.

What of their growth since El Paso? Had that been destroyed?

"Hi, Frank. Is Dolores in?" Dom stepped into his daughter's home. Though this dwelling didn't have the old world feel of his ancestral one, it was traditional. Dolores loved to entertain, and her house would have fit nicely into *Sunset* magazine articles on Southwestern décor.

"Welcome." His son-in-law shut the door, still holding a book in his hand with a finger holding his place.

"You don't look surprised to see me."

"I'm not." Frank smiled. "I hoped you'd come and help mend fences." He squeezed Dom's shoulder. "She's in the den. Go on through. I was just going to make cocoa. Want some?"

"You know me and chocolate."

"I'll bring it, then make myself scarce."

"You're a good man, Frank."

As Dom walked into the den, Dolores put down her needlework and smiled. "Dad, why are you in town tonight?"

"I thought I'd stop by and see how you were feeling. You were upset earlier."

Dolores's expression changed. She'd always been able to quickly don a poor-me look.

"What did she tell you?"

"Last February, you said you wanted some father-daughter time, so we started meeting on Thursdays. Then Nita started coming to Mass with us. Lately, you began inviting her to join us for dinner. Where's the special time you wanted?"

Dolores smiled. "She's a lovely person, isn't she?"

He shrugged.

"She reminds me of Mom."

Dom squeezed his eyes shut momentarily. *Don't get angry. Watch what you say.* "If I wanted to marry again, she's the type of woman you'd choose for me?"

"Yes. She's your age. That Bjornson woman is way too young for you. It's unseemly."

"Nita is several years older than me."

"Well, women live longer than men. She'd be perfect for you. She doesn't have kids."

"In other words, there would be no rivals for your inheritance?"

"What?"

"Perhaps you thought that if we married, she could move into the old place with me."

Dolores sat up straighter. "What would be wrong with that? I grew up in that house. It has been in the Baca family for generations. You want to move out and go live on that—" Her lips twisted as though she had tasted something unpleasant. "Bjornson ranch. I'm being pushed out!"

With her voice still echoing in the small room, Frank came in carrying mugs of hot chocolate and handed one to each. Then he retreated and shut the door.

"I'm leaving the old place to Sam, your son. How is that pushing you out?"

"You don't understand. It's not home anymore. I don't feel welcome."

"Welcome! Now why would that be? When what you said at dinner was so vile? I couldn't believe those words came from my daughter's mouth!"

Dolores rattled on, running right over his rebuke. "Farah's changing everything—giving away my mother's things."

"Offering Isabel's china to you for your daughters is not what I'd call giving away her things. You owe Sam and Farah an apology, and they aren't the only ones."

"I don't want Farah to have the antique bed. I love that bed."

"Whoa. When the time is right, that bed will go to Sam, or another child of yours. More generations of our family, your grandchildren, will be conceived in that bed. But until then, that bed is moving with me. My wife and I will be sleeping in that bed."

Dolores's face flooded with color. "That's obscene. You're too old—"

Dom raised an eyebrow. "Don't. Go. There."

A tear snaked down Dolores's cheek and fell to darken a spot on her shirt.

"Dolores, can't you see? Karen and I both had wonderful marriages. We grieved when our mates died. Now we have found love again, and we are happy."

"But now you have her. You won't love me anymore."

"Don't be silly. You're my child." He reached out to gently raise her chin. "Dolores, honey, can't you be happy for us?"

"But Nita—"

Dom let go her chin and sat back. "Yes, Nita. Let's talk about her. We had an interesting conversation after you abandoned us at the Basilica—"

"I didn't abandon you. Something important came up."

"You lied to us, *abandoned* us, and sent us to the Blue Goose where you'd made reservations."

Dolores said nothing.

"Nita said you told her I'd finally reached the point where I wanted companionship again after my loss, and she was at that same place. Then she invited me to her house."

Dolores looked down and fiddled with her mug.

"Talk about awkward. It was apparent that you had been manipulating us all along."

Dom paused to drink a few swallows of cocoa. Still Dolores didn't look up. "I asked her if she knew I was engaged and said she would understand why I must decline her invitation."

Now Dolores raised her eyes in a glare.

"Nita was taken aback. She didn't think you knew about my engagement. The poor woman was put in an embarrassing situation since she was led to believe I welcomed her interest. You also owe Nita an apology."

"What did Karen say about Nita?"

"She didn't mention the name at all."

"Mother of spit." Dolores ground out the epithet from her teen years.

Dom felt his cool sliding away. "Grow up, Dolores. Your question tells me that you told Karen all about Nita and me going to Mass together. You told her we went out to dinner every week, didn't you? I doubt that you made it sound so innocent."

Her glare turned sullen.

Dom got to his feet and set his mug on the end table. "You deliberately—" If he stayed any longer, he'd be yelling. He quietly closed the door behind him and leaned against it.

Frank stood down the hall, his face questioning. Dom shook his head.

Suddenly the door jolted against his back as something hit it. The sound of crockery crashing on the tile made him jump.

Frank looked heavenward. "Thanks for trying, Dad. I'll see you out."

Soon after, Dom let himself into the Baca ancestral home through the outside door of his suite. The not-quite-full moon gave enough light to navigate the shadows of this familiar space.

He reached out to a bedpost feeling the cool smoothness. Leaning his head against it, he sighed.

Quiet. Darkness.

Emptiness.

God, he was tired. Tired of the in-between. Caught between his daughter and Karen. Tired of being accommodating and of not being able to put his feet up and do as he damn well pleased. Tired of suitcases, of living between two places where always what he wanted was at the other. Tired of being torn between his church and Karen. Tired of having to make peace because he couldn't tolerate conflict.

Just tired.

Why did it have to be so difficult?

CHAPTER FORTY

Wednesday, June 7

Dom knew he should call Karen. Yet here it was Wednesday. Still procrastinating.

He'd been busy, or at least playing with busy. Going to Sunday Mass with Sam and his family, going out to dinner. Napping. Holing up in his room pretending to work on his novel, but the muse hadn't been there.

He wondered how Karen's tapestry was coming. Wanted to be with her, to celebrate its completion. Surely that must be soon. Then that became an excuse. If he stayed away, she could concentrate on her work with the looming deadline. She wouldn't want the distraction, or so he convinced himself.

He reached out in the night, only to find the cool smoothness of empty sheets instead of Karen.

He missed the Bjornson dinner table. Sure, he enjoyed eating with Sam, Farah, and Leyla, but he also missed holding baby Lucas. Missed Skyla, Anton. Missed Krista, even though Leyla delighted him. Missed the solid, comforting presence of Diego and Maria. Envying their closeness, wondering if they too felt the pressure of the outside world encroaching on their private lives. He knew they were lovers. More power to them.

And God above, he missed Karen. Missed seeing her at her loom, watching those deft fingers create beauty, missing their conversations about Niemöller, about things that mattered. Could missing be a physical pain? He felt it.

His phone rang. He looked eagerly at the number, hoping it might be her, but it wasn't. He let it ring.

This procrastination had to stop. He knew better, knew that a straightforward conversation could go a long way toward clearing the air and making things right.

Yet he couldn't make his feet move in her direction.

How could he have screwed up so badly? Hadn't he learned anything after El Paso? He'd have to tell her how he'd been manipulated by Dolores, tell her about Nita. He'd have to apologize. Again. He wasn't looking forward to it.

He got on Highway 84 and drove toward the ranch, intending to go see Karen, but found himself passing the turnoff, driving through Española, heading toward Abiquiú. Then he spotted the signs for the Ohura Lavender Farm. He turned off the highway and found the farm nestled in a bend of the Rio Chama. The lavender was beginning to bloom. He stood by his car, eyes closed, feeling the warmth of the sun, the caress of the lavender-scented breeze. The fragrance put him back in Karen's studio.

He wandered among the rows of plants and finally into the gift shop. He selected a lavender wand, touched the delicate blooms. Spotting tiny baskets woven from lavender stems, he picked one, small enough to cuddle in the palm of his hand, opened its lid, and inhaled. He moved to set it down but thought Karen would love it. It, too, had to go home with him.

He headed back to Santa Fe, the dry, herby scent filling his car, bringing calm. The thought of gifting Karen with that wand brought hope. He'd keep his purchases for a while, their scent a reminder of her presence. He'd know when the time was right.

Soon.

♦ ❖ ♦

That night after dinner, Sam appeared at the open door of his grandfather's study. "*Lito*, I was just about to take Scherzo for a walk. Are you and Quixote up for joining us?"

Dom pushed back from his computer and looked at Quixote. Upon hearing the word *walk*, Quixote cocked his head at Dom and looked hopeful.

"Quixote says we are."

Twilight had fallen on the quaint old Santa Fe neighborhood. Walking here meant narrow streets, a variety of adobe walls and coyote fences made of upright saplings wired together.

"How's Karen's tapestry coming?" asked Sam. "Will she make the deadline?"

"Haven't seen her since Saturday. Sorry I haven't told you what's going on." Dom walked on. "Karen and your mother had words about the dinner fiasco. It made it worse."

Sam paused so Scherzo could sniff a rabbitbrush shrub. "I'm certain that's what Mother intended. *Lito*, can I speak frankly?"

Dom smiled at the treasured, affectionate name for grandfather. It was special between them and often signaled important conversations. "Sure. You know you can."

"Remember when I was dithering about staying on the police force or quitting and going to grad school?"

Dom shot him a glance. "You're not having second thoughts?"

"No. I like being a detective. You said something that helped then."

They walked toward the next streetlight.

"It always stuck in my mind," said Sam. "You were talking about Mother and told me that I have a tendency to keep the peace, but at too high a cost."

"I remember."

"You reminded me of the oath I had taken, that the problem wouldn't go away until I faced Mother head on. You told me that I wasn't being honest with myself and that I'd forgotten my courage. At first, I was offended."

Dom was silent.

"But you were right. I thought maybe you could use that same advice now."

"Are you telling me that I lack courage? She's the one who owes the apologies and not only to you and Farah."

Sam shook his head. "Mother's not the point. It's you and Karen I'm talking about. I know I'm not privy to your conversations, but I know you're both in pain."

Sam stopped and sat on the edge of a low adobe wall outside a darkened business. Dom sat next to him. Scherzo walked through a bed of marigolds, filling the night air with a pungent scent.

"Scherzo, come. Sit." The Airedale came back to Sam and sat by Quixote.

"*Lito*, I know you love Karen. I truly believe your marriage would be the best thing and make you both happy. If I'm wrong, you can tell me to take a flying leap, but I think you're the one holding back from marriage, and it's because of Mother. You want to make peace with both her and Karen. The cost is too high. Peace with Mother comes at the expense of the years you will have with Karen."

Dom stiffened. A touch of belligerence surfaced.

Sam forged ahead. "You told me back then to have courage, to stop wallowing."

Dom snorted. "I wouldn't have said wallowing."

"You did say it. I remember it clearly. I got all stubborn. Maybe that's how you feel now. But it was sound advice. Seize that courage, *Lito*. Get a ring on Karen's finger and make her my grandmother in truth. That's what I wanted to say."

Dom stood up. "It's chilly when we stop walking."

He was annoyed, but as they continued, he felt a great rush of love for this grandson he'd mentored as he was growing up. Sam's words were worth thinking about.

Maybe he had needed a little kick in the pants.

CHAPTER FORTY-ONE

Friday, June 9

Sounds of a ball being dribbled, voices from older and younger, and the bonk of the ball off the backboard told Karen of a pickup basketball game in progress outside her studio. The midafternoon sun shone through the clerestory windows. A bright day, a good day.

It lacked one thing to make it perfect. Dom. Would somebody have thought to tell him her tapestry was almost done? That they would be celebrating?

If he knew, would he come?

Karen shot Dulcie a look of excitement as she drew the loom beater bar toward her, pushing the last of the actual design into evenness. She looked along the expanse of wool, checking to make sure nothing had been overlooked. The last several rows would be her header, invisible when the finished tapestry was hemmed. She did the first header row, then relinquished her spot on the loom bench to Dulcie who started the second.

Dulcie's eyes shone. "Almost there."

"I'll be right back." Karen hurried into the kitchen to find Maria. "We've started the header. Let everyone know. Party time coming up."

Maria gave her a wide smile. "Great! The champagne's on ice."

Karen went back to the studio. Just a few rows more and it would be finished.

Little by little, the gathering grew around the large loom. Skyla came first with Lucas, snug in a carrier against her chest. Krista, Leyla, Santos, Diego, Sam, and Anton came in from the outside, flushed and sweaty from the basketball court.

Karen smiled at them, glancing beyond to see if Dom might have come.

The doorway was empty.

She ducked her head to hide her disappointment, concentrating on her work.

Then Maria came with a large tray of cheeses, fruit, and crackers. Farah followed, rolling the serving cart with the champagne and a bottle of sparkling apple juice for the kids. In their wake were three Airedales—and Quixote!

Karen's eyes swept the doorway again, and there was Dom, his eyes alight.

"Do you want me to finish?" Dulcie's quiet voice prodded Karen from her time-stood-still moment.

Her face grew warm. "Uff da, no, I've got it."

Soon the beater bar pressed against the weft threads one last time. Karen slid off the bench and met Dulcie's hug. "We did it. And on time!"

Everybody wanted hugs. She was whisked from one embrace to the next.

Dom took her in his arms. "Congratulations."

Then Leyla tugged her away. "Cut it free! Let us see."

"I can hardly wait," cried Krista.

Anton opened the champagne with a satisfying *pop*.

Now was the moment.

There was no going back to fix anything after the tapestry had been cut loose. It was like cutting an umbilical cord. From now on the tapestry would take on a life of its own. Karen loosened the tension on the warp threads with a screeching of gears.

With scissors poised in her hand, she looked around at the happy, expectant faces. "Here goes!" She severed the first warp threads about six inches from the top of the tapestry. Steadily she cut across the width. When the last warps had fallen away, she and Dulcie manipulated the bulky tapestry. With more screeching of gears, they exposed the bottom end. She handed the scissors to her helper. Dulcie selected a spot on the warp threads and glanced at her.

Karen gave her smile of approval, and Dulcie severed the threads until the jumbled fabric fell into their arms. They laid it across a large table, smoothed it out, and stepped back.

"Wow. Seeing the whole thing. Wow." Dom's voice was reverent.

It was amazing, seeing the expanse of the entire design. Though she'd seen each and every thread until it rolled under the cloth bar, she'd never seen the total, seen how the design flowed, the colors blended. Wow, indeed.

"Your painting," said Skyla, "didn't prepare me for how beautiful it would be. I'm in awe."

"Can I touch it?" asked Santos.

At her nod, he turned over a corner to see the backside. It was a kaleidoscope of tangled, colored yarn ends. "It's all furry," he said. "Will it stay like that?"

"It's not done yet. Some of the ends will need to be stitched in; some will be cut much shorter. It needs to be hemmed, steamed, and have a pocket for the hanging rod sewn on. It needs to be photographed. Dulcie and I still have work to do," said Karen, "but for today, we have done enough. We have reached a milestone."

"A huge milestone." Anton handed glasses of champagne to her and Dulcie.

When everyone had their glasses, Karen raised hers. "*Skål* to the *Tapestry of Light*."

Following the custom, they raised their glasses, met each other's eyes, and nodded. At the end of this routine, Karen's eyes finally moved to Dom's. They held joy, excitement, and warmth. He nodded with a slight tilt of his head, and a smile that seemed to be for her alone. At least she wanted it to be.

Then Karen drank, the bubbles tickling her nose. Everyone began talking at once.

Santos lowered his glass of sparkling juice. "Skole. What does that mean?"

"It's a toast, Scandinavian style," said Skyla. "Like cheers, congratulations, and good health all rolled into one."

They sat, pondered the beauty of the weaving, and dug into the cheeses and crackers.

"Don't fill up too much," cautioned Anton. "Sam brought take'n'bake pizzas. Maria has a huge salad to go with them."

Karen's gaze was drawn back to her work. What did Dom think of his first cutting ceremony? Would he stay, or go back with Sam? She was glad he'd come.

These folks all loved her art and seemed impressed. Dulcie was radiant. But how would the judges react? Maybe they wouldn't see the connection to Niemöller. Maybe she could have come up with a more original design than the Statue of Liberty. Maybe she should have used different colors.

Shoulda, coulda, woulda. The cutting ceremony was final. It would have to do. And deep down inside, she felt a glow.

Her eyes sought out Dom's again across the crowd. He winked and his smile for her widened.

She raised her glass toward the tapestry, nodded and drank. She said nothing aloud, but her thoughts centered on her creation.

To my Tapestry of Light. May it speak for me and make this world of ours a little brighter.

Late that evening, Dom rested against the couch cushions in the Bjornson family room. He and Karen still hadn't had the opportunity to talk alone, but damn, it felt good to be back. The guests had left for home and most of the family had gone off to bed. Quixote snoozed at his feet.

Anton was in the kitchen, readying the coffee pot and starting the timer for the next morning. He set the alarms and turned out the kitchen light.

"Night, Dom."

"Goodnight."

Karen had slipped away while Dom had been catching up with everyone. Where to? She wouldn't have gone to bed without saying anything.

Then he knew where she'd be.

The light was on in her studio. She sat on a stool overlooking the completed tapestry, touching the fibers here, brushing a color there, smoothing out a bump, quietly taking it in.

He came up beside her. There were tears on her cheeks, but no sign of stress or sadness. She smiled at him. Sliding his arm around her waist, he joined her in looking. Enjoying the luminosity of the kneeling statue's torch, the tension in the giant's reach toward the little girl, the struggle of that movement toward hope.

"Exquisite," he murmured.

She slid off her stool into his arms.

He touched her cheek. "Karen, I'm sorry." His fingers drifted down over her shoulder, idly stroking the softness of her sweater.

"I need to tell you about Nita."

Her body stiffened, and a wary look settled on her face.

He was right. Dolores had made mischief. "She's a friend of Dolores's—"

"Of Dolores!" Her eyes, wide with surprise, found his.

"Yes. I'm sorry. Dolores lied and tried her best to separate you and me." He told her how he'd been manipulated and set up at the Blue Goose.

"You haven't known her for a long time?"

"Never met her before Dolores brought her along to Mass."

"Dolores was so convincing about the two of you," whispered Karen.

"What did she tell you?"

Karen looked down. "You're going to think I'm silly. It was what she said about the chocolate dessert that hurt the most."

He tipped up her chin. "My family and friends know I love chocolate, but with you, and only you, chocolate carries— How do I say it? A turn on, a seductive memory."

"Only me, huh?"

"Only you." He cupped her cheek gently. "I'm sorry I spurned the gift of your reaching out to Dolores. I tried too. It hurts. My only child."

"Dom, what are you saying?"

"I'm saying I don't have enough years left, but all of them are yours. I've missed you. You make my life whole."

"I've missed you too."

"It's good to be home."

"Home?"

"Home. Where you are."

The sticky wickets still waited but were fading. Like her tapestry, there was more to do, but it would wait for the morrow.

Her hand, fingers outstretched, glided over his chest. Her eyes began to smolder, before her lashes lowered. Their kiss grew from gentle to hot, open-mouthed. Her hand slid into his hair; her body pressed against his.

Tonight was for celebrating.

His breathing quickened as the tapestry blurred into the background, and Karen's responsiveness grew.

He tugged, and she followed eagerly. With Quixote padding silently behind, Karen's hand brushed against the light switch as they left the studio.

◆ ❖ ◆

The instant darkness soon gave way to moonlight. It gleamed through the clerestory windows, found the tapestry lying quietly, its figures in shadow, and the fibers relaxing at last after months of tension.

Chapter Forty-Two

Thursday, June 15

What was wrong with him, wondered Cecil. Anton had called to rearrange their plans for flying drones that afternoon. He was watching the baby while his wife and Krista were off shopping.

Cecil heard himself saying he'd come anyway. He and Anton had become friends, though he was still leery of all that Bjornson Hallmarky stuff.

What drew him to this family like a moth to flame? He'd avoided being around children, except Algie, since his own son died. Now Cecil was asking for pain—visiting a proud father with a new son. Would he end up running again?

Anton, with his son in a carrier strapped across his front, met him at the door, and invited him up to his study in his suite. There, two computers sat side by side on a built-in desk. A bassinet had been rolled nearby. Anton laid the baby down and took off the carrier. From a small refrigerator, he produced a pitcher of lemonade—just the thing on a stinking hot afternoon.

Cecil had been in this study earlier but had never come through Anton's suite. They'd accessed it before by a staircase from Anton's workshop in the garage below. There was a door off the landing at the top of the stairs which went out onto the roof. Anton had said he often flew his drones from there.

They talked about the small glitches and the solutions Anton had worked out with the AI system cameras. Cecil lost himself in the gadget talk, and the time flew.

"That technology is amazing." Anton picked up Lucas, who'd begun to fuss. "I can't tell you how awful it was when Krista was kidnapped. Playing with this technology is fun, but important too. I'll do anything to keep my family safe."

"If I can ask," said Cecil, "what happened to Krista's mother?"

Anton's eyes shut briefly. "She was murdered." He swallowed and looked toward several framed photos on a bookshelf.

Cecil was shocked into silence. His own gaze found among the photos a young woman who reminded him of Krista. Then the investigator within asked, "Did—did they ever catch who did it?"

"Yes, but not before they tried to wipe out the rest of us. That's one reason Mom made this place into a sanctuary for friends who've found themselves in danger. I try to keep it as secure as possible." He cradled his son against his chest.

Cecil heard words tumbling from his mouth. "My wife—" He swallowed against the ache in his throat and closed his eyes. He hadn't been able to keep them safe.

Cecil heard deep shuddering sighs, knew they came from him, felt the pain all over again. He knew Anton was looking at him, could feel it in the electricity of the moment.

"Do you want to tell me?" asked Anton. "Or not, that's okay."

My wife. Had Cecil actually said those words aloud? He pushed against the memories, unable, unwilling to speak of the horror. He sensed Anton would understand, but—

Anton's soft voice broke into his thoughts. "When Sonja was killed, I moved back here with my parents. Krista was only four. I threw myself into my business—all the energy and creativity I could muster. I recognize that same drive in you."

At that Cecil opened his eyes. Anton wasn't looking at him at all, but at his son. His voice went on.

"Then I discovered success wasn't enough. I wanted to live again, to be with someone. That need grew. So did the fear of being hurt again. It was hard. Damned hard."

The baby hiccupped. Cecil watched Anton's hand span his son's back and rub gently. Memory flooded him—holding his own son, the bonding. Fleeting images from those five short years of his son's life.

What he wouldn't give to hold him again. He looked up to make eye contact with Anton.

What insight had made Anton say those words? Was it because he'd been there?

Cecil broke the contact and cleared his throat. "How sharp are the images from your overlook camera? Got any stills? I'd like to see them."

"Sure."

"We need the best damn images we can get if there's ever a need to identify an intruder."

CHAPTER FORTY-THREE

Sunday, June 18

This was huge.

Dom sat beside Karen, head bowed, in the sanctuary of the church where he'd belonged all his life. And his family—for generations beyond memory. He'd had his first communion, had been married, his daughter had been baptized, and his grandchildren as well—all in this place. When Isabel died, he'd found comfort here. For a lifetime, this had been home.

He loved the words of ritual and prayer. The responses came automatically to his lips. He loved the traditions —the glorious music, the chants. The pomp, the vestments, and the pageantry. The smoky incense that drifted in the ornate vastness of soaring architecture.

He should have been filled with gladness. Instead, he saw this day with the eyes of an outsider. He was out of step, technically unwelcome at his Lord's table. Living with Karen, outside of marriage.

She'd come with him today, knowing he was troubled and needed her. His hand stole into her lap to cover her fingers. Her response was immediate, turning her hand to grasp his.

Karen, who welcomed friends so warmly to her home, gave safety and sanctuary to those in danger, and provided a place where love, laughter, and music filled hearts. He had chosen her—this loving woman, generous in acts of kindness, passionate about making a difference, and inspirational for family and friends to make the world a better place.

He was not in a state of grace.

His being was steeped in history. His faith, his family, his very profession. He, more than most, knew the transgressions of mankind as they passed from age to age. Moments of despicable cowardice and greed, moments of inspiring sacrifice and generosity. His own ancestors, in the name of the church, had participated in cruelty, racism, acts of damnation, but also acts of redemption.

Had each of his forebears throughout those generations come to such crossroads, where heart-rending choices lay before them?

This had been building within, troubling him for a long time.

Change was a hallmark of life. He'd never looked for love again nor expected it would find him. Now, with a sense of doom, he felt that nothing would ever be the same. As others rose and moved forward down the center aisle, he stayed seated in his pew.

At the front, the priest pressed wafer after wafer into raised, cupped hands. Softly the ongoing refrain echoed back. "The body of Christ … the body of Christ … the body of Christ."

Dom spoke into Karen's ear. "Come with me." He caught her startled look and knew she was aware of the strain he felt.

They left down the side aisle. The nave stretched forever under the vaulted ceiling. He doubted anyone even noticed their leaving. Many left after receiving the host.

By this time, tears of grief were running silently down his face. They went out through the wooden double doors into the sunshine. He tucked Karen's hand in his and kept walking to the plaza a block away. He found a bench, sat, and Karen settled beside him.

He started to speak, but it was too soon. Swallowing against the lump in his throat, he blinked away the wetness, and squeezed her hand. Her other hand covered his, gently soothing it. Her knees angled close, her warmth a comfort.

He tried again. The words came. "I've just left behind something precious to me. Or maybe it was gone long ago, and I just now—" He struggled with the words. "Gained the strength to see."

She waited in silence.

He smiled wistfully. "As I walked out of that church, a lifetime of memories flooded me. But it doesn't fit anymore. I'm not the same person I was when I belonged there."

He raised his hand to trace her face, looking deeply into her still-troubled eyes. "And it hurts."

"Dom." Her voice was a whispered cry. She turned into his arms, holding him to her. He dropped his chin to rest against her head and closed his eyes. A breeze lifted a wisp of her hair to tickle his skin.

The sun warmed him but brought no sense of peace or healing. The distant sounds of children laughing, voices chattering crowded back into his consciousness. Life still moved on.

In bittersweetness, the Cathedral Basilica bells tolled their familiar peal.

A new hour.

What would it bring?

CHAPTER FORTY-FOUR

Monday afternoon, June 19

"Get a ring on her finger and make her my grandmother in truth." Sam's words echoed in Dom's head.

Fallout lay ahead from yesterday's painful leave-taking from church, but the choice had been made. He would find a way to work it out.

The other sticky wicket? He was resigned to the fact Dolores might never come around. He loved her, but he could not allow her prejudice to stop him from choosing love. Together, he and Karen were better people, enriching, not diminishing each other's lives.

He'd researched custom jewelers and found one he was excited to work with. He wanted to surprise Karen, but it was critical that the ring he chose appealed to her and worked with her lifestyle. Both Isabel and Karen had worn diamond engagement rings. He wanted something different. A sapphire, blue like her eyes. She was outdoors a lot, riding, and working with her animals. Something simple, not fussy. Like him, she was more into symbolism than bling. A design holding a hint of history appealed.

Now, as Karen and Dulcie worked on the final tapestry steps in the studio, Dom sat at the kitchen counter, checking the internet for old Norse and Viking designs. They often used Celtic knots—not surprising since the Vikings had roamed the seas around Britain and had intermingled with its inhabitants in both blood and culture.

Maria puttered about in the kitchen. She passed behind him to pick up stray mugs from the family room, carrying them back to the dishwasher. Then she faced him across the counter with a shy smile. "I like the direction you're going. Whatever you choose, smooth is important. She won't wear it if it snags on her weaving."

Startled, he met her amused eyes. "You won't say—"

"Of course not. It just makes me glad."

He grinned. "I could use your help. I need to get the size right."

CHAPTER FORTY-FIVE

Wednesday, June 28

Karen checked and rechecked the contents of her entry for the Niemöller competition, looking at the guidelines. She proofread her bio and the required statement about her art and its vision for change. She double-checked the jpegs of the tapestry, the closeups of detail, and her entry-fee payment.

Then, with a deep breath, she hit SEND on her computer.

It was gone, wending its way through cyberspace.

Done! Two days before the deadline. By July 14, the list of finalists would be announced. Once you were a finalist, you were in. Just before the exhibit opened to the public, the judges would award the prizes.

Sixteen more days of being on tenterhooks.

She glanced at the time—not even ten o'clock yet. She and Krista planned to pick up Leyla. Maybe they'd do something special to mark this occasion and stop by the Hog Bristle Bistro before coming back to the ranch.

They walked into the bistro before the lunchtime crush. The smiling hostess indicated they could sit where they liked. Karen spotted a dark-haired teenager sitting by himself, working on his computer. Algie Adams. She guided the girls to an empty table next to his. He didn't look up from the graphics on his screen.

Karen looked at the menu, tempted by one of their signature appetizers. Why not? This was a celebration! In a moment of decadent indulgence, she ordered the bacon pastry twists to share with the girls. Puff pastry, sprinkled with shredded cheddar cheese and twisted around bacon strips. Baked until the pastry was golden and the bacon crispy. To die for! The girls ordered peach smoothies, and she added coffee for herself.

The girls were quiet, focused on Algie's computer screen. They whispered now and then when the art transformed as new layers were added.

Karen saw Algie's posture change when he realized he was being watched. He hit minimize on his screen, and his work disappeared.

"Aww," said Krista.

He glared at her.

Krista reddened. "I'm sorry, but what you were doing was really cool. How did you learn to do that?"

Still frowning, he looked at Karen.

She saw the flicker of recognition in his eyes. "I'm sorry they bothered you, but I'm not sorry they had a chance to see what you can do. I'm Karen Bjornson. We talked at the school art show."

"You were with that white-haired guy. You're different. I've never seen old people holding hands before."

"Rather refreshing, isn't it?" She held his gaze for a moment before motioning to the girls. "My granddaughters, Krista and Leyla."

Karen noticed the girls grinning at each other. Uff da. Was this her first public acknowledgment that she considered both her granddaughters?

She knew his father called him Algie, a nickname she didn't like. "I know your last name is Adams, but what do you like to be called?"

Algie's eyes widened. After a few seconds' pause, he said, "Uh, Grayson. Call me Grayson."

Was he leaving the old Algie behind? Good for him.

"Hi," said Leyla. "Was yours the digital painting of the guy by a crumbly castle?"

Grayson nodded.

"I liked the way you did him," said Krista. "What program did you use?"

"We draw and paint too," volunteered Leyla.

"Good. You should learn to do all the stuff with brushes and pencils. There's no better way to learn."

Karen smiled as she noticed Grayson was not immune to feminine adulation, even from twelve-year-olds.

Krista persisted. "Gramma uses Photoshop sometimes in her designs. Is that what you're using? I've never seen her do all the stuff you were doing."

"That's because I don't know how," said Karen. "I've barely scraped the surface of what Photoshop can do."

"I used Photoshop and Illustrator. They're part of the Adobe Creative Suite."

"That's what Lou uses," said Leyla. "She's our teacher for drawing and watercolor. She illustrates kids' books."

"It's a good tool," said Grayson.

"How did you learn digital art?" asked Krista.

Grayson shrugged. "I've met some folks who are good at it. We got a little in school. Mostly I look at how-to videos on YouTube and play around. I wish I could have a good teacher."

"Do you take any art classes outside high school?" asked Karen.

"Sure. Oil painting." He grimaced. "My teacher wouldn't be caught dead doing anything digital."

"Why?" asked Leyla.

"Would I be correct in thinking when your teacher went to school, digital painting didn't even exist, and they look down their nose at it because it intimidates them?" asked Karen.

Grayson chuckled. "For an old person, you're good."

Karen smiled. "I'll take that as a compliment. Are you learning anything worthwhile from your oil teacher?"

"Yeah. I just don't tell my dad that what I'm learning helps in my digital art too. Traditional art is a good foundation. There's no substitute really."

Karen's smile grew broader. "For a teenager, you're good."

Grayson laughed out loud. "Thanks. I'll take that as a compliment."

He's a delight, thought Karen. In small ways he reminded her of Vidar, her nephew, abandoned by his mother, and resented by his father. A lost soul. Not that Grayson was neglected—he appeared well-cared for physically—but emotionally? If she guessed right, his father had never been able to resolve his grief over the loss of his wife. She wished William could see his son's talent.

"If I wanted a good digital-art teacher," asked Karen, "is there a local one you would recommend?"

"This guy, Costain. I've gone to several of his gallery demonstrations. He's good. When he finishes talking to you, you're dying to go home and try. Then he shows you another new thing, and you're off again. He does traditional stuff too."

"Are there things you can still learn from him, or have you already reached his level?" asked Karen. A devious plan began in her head.

"I wish," said Grayson. "I'd love to take classes from him."

"Might you be interested in sharing what you can do with a couple of twelve-year-old girls?" asked Karen. "Or are you too busy to teach beginners?"

The two girls exchanged delighted expressions.

Grayson looked surprised. "Me? Teach? I'm only fifteen. And my dad would never give the go-ahead for anything with digital art."

"If you were interested, I would arrange it with him." Karen cleared her throat. "We dinosaurs might speak the same language."

Grayson flushed. He met her eyes and finally nodded. "I may be interested—after I've seen what they can do."

"We'll put together our portfolios to show you, Grayson," said Krista, adding in a biting tone, "but it's only fair if we see more of your work."

"Yes, maybe we can do better," said Leyla, arching her brows.

Karen coughed to disguise her laughter. She hadn't known Leyla had it in her to be a mimic. That was a perfect Dolores impression.

Then Krista laughed. "Really, it'd be fun. It's cool, what you do."

CHAPTER FORTY-SIX

Thursday, June 29

Early the next morning, Karen and Dom rode horseback on the trail around the edge of the Bjornson ranch. The terrain varied from wider stretches through piñon and juniper to places where they had to pick their way single file through arroyos and rocky outcrops. The higher portions gave marvelous views of the Sangre de Cristos.

She'd been pleased to discover Dom was a capable, experienced rider, but it made sense. His son-in-law bred, raised, and trained Andalusians. The horse Dom rode was a steady dapple-gray that Frank had gifted to Dom.

The digital-art-class scheme she'd outlined the night before filled her mind. She'd set two goals. Krista's birthday was in June, and Leyla's in July. They'd had their parties, of course, but she'd told them that she'd be giving them their gift after her entry was turned in.

The other goal was to give Grayson the chance to receive the instruction he desperately wanted.

As they rode on a wider section of the trail, she told Dom about their meeting with Grayson and her plan. She thought he'd be as excited as she was, but the idea hung in the air too long before his response came.

"Grayson?"

"He asked us to call him that."

Dom held back for a moment as the piñons crowded the trail. "Well, as a birthday present, the girls would like nothing better, but …" A frown played with his eyebrows.

"But?"

"Why do you have to involve Al—Grayson? His father won't be pleased."

"He's part of the reason I want to do this. Dom, I'm surprised by your reluctance. It's important for young artists to get support and encouragement."

"He's not your child. You know how William feels. You're interfering."

Uff da. They were back to that.

The trail narrowed again. Karen nudged her mount ahead, thinking about her motives. Maybe if she'd been able to support Vidar more, to bolster his confidence. But he was gone. She couldn't make it up to him. For Vidar, it was too late.

She stopped when the trail widened and patted her mare's neck. Karen felt the sweat trickling down her face. Another hot one, already in the eighties, and the day had just begun.

When Dom came alongside, she responded. "I could do nothing, because Grayson is not my own, or I could at least try to make a difference, to help him reach his dreams."

Dom sighed. "You're going to go ahead and do it, no matter what I say, aren't you?"

"I think I am. I'd rather you stood by me in this."

"May I go along when you talk with William?"

"I would like that. Do you want to be there when I talk with Farah and Sam?"

He smiled. "I always like to be with you."

How was she to respond to that? His words took the sting out of it, but a niggle remained in her mind. She was independent, used to doing what she thought best. She liked it that way.

◆ ❖ ◆

Karen ran the plans by the girls' parents. They thought it was a great idea.

Next, she researched Costain. Satisfied, she went to Lou McCreath. As she'd thought, Lou was interested in improving her skills and could use what this man had to teach.

Then she set out to talk to Costain at the gallery where his work was shown before offering him a custom-made class. He would split his time between two young beginners and Karen, and two experienced artists—Lou and Grayson—who were eager to move to the next level.

Costain rubbed his walrus mustache. "Adams? The one whose father owns a gallery?"

"Grayson said he's been to your demonstrations."

"Talented lad. I'd like the chance to work with him. Glad his dad is open to it."

Karen felt her cheeks redden. "Getting his permission is next on my list."

Costain's deep-set eyes twinkled. "Getting your ducks in a row?"

"You might say that."

He looked at her for a few seconds, then nodded. "You'll work it out. I'll be there."

The remaining details were quickly set. She left their meeting inspired.

The class location? A cinch. Her studio. Internet, tables, space, art supplies were all there. Birthday presents for Krista and Leyla would take the shape of the programs and computer hardware they'd need to participate.

They'd hold classes on Wednesdays and Fridays until school began mid-August. Then they'd re-evaluate. Costain would come on Wednesdays, but Lou and Grayson would be there both days to help the beginners as they practiced.

In her approach to William, she didn't plan on making a big deal about Costain and that they would all be learning from him, just that Grayson would be helping by sharing his skills, which were far above theirs. She tried to think of all the objections William might raise. He'd probably want to bring his son out for the first class. Karen could assure him that Grayson would have rides to and from. No problem there.

With everything lined up, Karen and Dom stopped by the Swift & Adams Gallery to ask if William was available for coffee. The three of them went across the street to the bistro.

After their first sips, Karen plunged forth. "William, would it be okay with you if your son gave our granddaughters lessons using his skill in digital art? They are very interested and have been taking drawing and painting classes. I want them to be acquainted with digital art. Your son does fine work."

William set down his coffee. "Wherever did you see anything of his?"

"At the school district art show in March. Since then, we've run into him here at the bistro, and he's showed us more. Both Dom and I were impressed."

"I didn't go to that show. We had words when I found out what he wanted to enter. Why would you want your granddaughters to learn that? I want better for my son."

"But will you give him permission?"

William's jaw flexed. Karen thought he'd say no, but he settled back in his chair and picked up his coffee again.

"William, your son has extraordinary talent. His skill is marketable in today's world, and he's excited about it." She looked toward Dom. Why had he wanted to be there? He hadn't said a word.

Karen reached a hand toward William and rested it on the table. "Our granddaughters met your son here at the bistro. He was doing art on his computer. One thing impressed me. He said, 'Learn to do traditional art first. There's no better foundation than using real brushes and real paints.' "

"He said that?" asked William. "That was my son talking?"

"Yes. So can he come out to our ranch and show the girls how to do what he does?"

"I don't want it interfering with his oil painting." William stirred his coffee. "Why does this mean so much to you?"

"When I entered the Niemöller competition, I wanted a way for my light to shine. I'm learning that others have dreams, and when I support them, together light shines brighter."

"Damn. Hoist with mine own petard." William looked down. The silence stretched as he swallowed once and then again.

When he raised his eyes to Karen's, she saw a haunted look.

"You and Gloria would have been great friends. Yes, he can help your granddaughters." He looked at his watch. "I have an appointment."

Karen wanted to set this in motion before her plan had time to unravel. "I noticed your son was at the gallery. Can we talk to him now?"

William's brows drew together. He hesitated. "I'll send him over."

While they waited, her thoughts centered on this young man, who'd lost his mother so young.

Grayson came in, excited. They told him about his father's permission.

"Wow. Really?"

They went over the schedule and plans for the class.

"There's one thing I'm curious about before we go," said Karen. "Months ago when we were in the gallery, I saw a young man rushing out. I learned later that was you. When we left, the head of the borzoi statue was dripping with spit. What was that all about?"

Grayson's face reddened as he looked down. "I was angry with Dad. He was putting down digital art again. It's amazing you got him to go along with this class."

"Did you spit on the dog to get back at your father?" asked Dom.

Grayson nodded. "It was stupid. I loved that dog."

"What happened to him?" asked Karen. She had to listen carefully to catch his hesitant voice.

"After Mom died, Dad wouldn't talk about her. I would talk to Swift. He'd listen and lick my face. I never meant to kill him." Grayson ducked his head.

"You don't have to tell me," said Karen. "I'm sorry—"

"It's okay," said Grayson. "I was walking him. I didn't see the damn cat. I'll never forget that awful feeling—he jerked the leash away and chased the cat. I was powerless. The car hit Swift. The sounds … he died in my arms. I'd failed again. I had to tell my dad. It was horrible."

"That would have been extremely hard," said Dom.

"What comfort did your father give you?"

"Comfort? It was my fault. He just looked at me. Turned away, like he couldn't stand the sight of me. I wish I could make it up to him. But I never could."

"Grayson, how can you say it was your fault? Borzois are powerful animals with a strong instinct to chase prey. Even a grown man couldn't have stopped him. You were only what? Eight? It was an unfortunate accident."

"But he still died, and my dad lost someone else he loved. Because of— I have to go now."

Grayson stood. His eyes swam with tears as they met hers. "Do you still want me to do the class?"

"Definitely." Karen smiled. "Wednesday, July 12. Everything has been worked out. We're all looking forward to it. Costain too. He had good things to say about you."

Grayson blinked, and a smile crinkled his eyes again. "What did Dad say about him?"

"Ah, well," Karen said, "maybe I neglected to tell him about Costain."

Grayson laughed. "Sneaky."

"I'll take that as a compliment," she said.

CHAPTER FORTY-SEVEN

Sunday, July 9

What would Pete and Akiko think of her tapestry? Karen had invited them to lunch at the ranch. Their reaction was crucial to her. If they found it meaningful, then she would have accomplished something important.

After they ate, she watched as they turned into her studio and faced the hanging tapestry. At first there was only silence. Then she saw Akiko's hand slide around Pete's back. He put his arm over her shoulders.

"I knew it would be inspiring," said Pete. "I'm in awe."

"Beautiful doesn't even come close," said Akiko.

Pete gently touched one of Karen's favorite details in the lower right-hand corner, which had initially given her such grief. The foam on the roiling sea with its Munchian scream merged into darkening colors and was lost in despair. "This feels powerful to me. All the terrors forcing one to flee are caught up in this."

"That statue—that it could kneel down and reach out to a small child." Akiko turned to Karen with tears in her eyes. "It glows with hope."

"Hope, yes," said Pete, "but it also calls out somehow."

"It raises a challenge," said Dom. "Or maybe gives a jab to the conscience. I've felt that too."

Karen looked at them in surprise. Dom had never said that to her.

Pete nodded. "Something's changing in our world. I feel more urgency now."

"I see the challenge. The story is only beginning," said Akiko.

"That isn't just rhetoric for you, is it?" said Dom.

"Something's emerging." Her dark eyes were apprehensive.

"Maybe it begins again for each generation." said Pete. "Our memories are short."

"True," Akiko said, "underneath it's stirring, like lava. It's frightening—it has to come out somehow."

Karen looked at her work again with new perspective. "The light. It can be dimmed, quenched."

"But also rekindled," said Dom.

Pete's gray eyes were thoughtful. "Is this tapestry a wake-up call?"

Akiko's finger traced the short distance from the outstretched hand to the little girl. "When do you hear it's been accepted?"

"July fourteenth," said Karen.

"Not to worry," said Pete. "The judges will love it."

"But Adams said there'd been over five hundred entries," said Karen. "Only sixty will get in."

"Yours will be one of them," said Pete. "It's magnificent."

Karen smiled. Her work had spoken to these friends. Maybe the judges would find it appealing. "Shall we go back to the family room?"

Pete answered by snagging some chairs. "I want more time with this tapestry before it gets whisked away. How's your novel coming, Dom?"

"Slow. It was easier to write nonfiction. Haven't even found the story I want to tell. Now I've fallen down the Niemöller rabbit hole and discovered more possibilities."

"How so?" asked Akiko.

"In Germany, Hitler was the central power, sucking up the spotlight. But in all the reading I've been doing on Niemöller, I've seen an intriguing phenomenon. Turn your eyes away from that central figure to the little people around him. They jockey for position on shifting sands of power. Perhaps they know better, but they allow themselves to be seduced, caught up in a slide from decency. Good intelligent people. How did it happen? That's where I see a story."

"Are you looking to set it during the Second World War?" asked Pete.

"Could be any time, even a fantasy."

Pete nodded. "I read fantasy. What's important to me is the character. How they overcome obstacles and change inside. Tolkien sure did it well."

"Think how Martin Luther or Niemöller faced their choices. Things could so easily have gone the other way. All that conflict and emotion."

"You know what I think?" asked Akiko.

"What?" asked Dom.

"I think you're looking for a place to let your voice be heard—only coming from a sweep through history."

Pete waved at the tapestry. "You and Karen have even more in common than you were aware of."

◆ ❖ ◆

In her sitting room later that evening, Karen looked up from her sketchbook. Dom was on the loveseat with a book in his hand but hadn't turned a page for a while.

"What are you thinking?" she asked.

"What Akiko and Pete said. It reminded me of a fellow I knew who spent time in a concentration camp."

"In Germany?"

"A Japanese camp. Same one that was portrayed in the movie, *The Bridge Over the River Kwai*. I met him when I was at Princeton, at grad school. Ernest Gordon, a Scotsman. He was the dean of the chapel there. Through my years of teaching, I often thought about him, his gentleness, his dedication to helping students. The questions he posed for us. How can we take care of each other? How can we live in peace? I hear you echoing many of his thoughts about community."

"How did you meet him?"

"The library, where I spent a lot of time, stands next to the Princeton University Chapel." He smiled at her. "The word chapel conjures up something small, but this was a huge Gothic cathedral. One day I ventured inside and was blown away. I felt like I'd been transported to some medieval European city. Huge stained-glass windows showed a vast array of towering figures in literature, poetry, church history, and the Bible. The space was bathed in color and light. Certainly, God must be present."

"I would love that."

He closed his eyes. She felt he was back there.

"I dropped by frequently, and I met Gordon. He'd fought in the Second World War, been in that Japanese prison camp, barely survived, and gone on to study theology."

Dom raised his head. His eyes were dark and intense. "He made me see things differently, lifted me out of my narrow perspective on history. Grad school was a mountaintop experience."

"Mountaintop?"

"Special. Elusive. Rare. Occasionally I've felt it with my faculty peers, not often, but enough to treasure the moments when they come. Friendships like those of Herb and Yolanda. People with whom I could explore ideas, deeply held beliefs, and faith." He smiled. "People like you who listen, who offer insights that make me think. Does that make sense?"

"I love that part of you. Your mind, your ideas, your thoughts about things that matter."

"I've felt it with Pete and Akiko."

He stuck a bookmark in his book and closed it. "I haven't always found that feeling in church. What you said about communion. As a Catholic, I've been thinking it always had more to do with our relationship to God, the vertical aspect, the state of grace between me and God."

She doodled a series of circles. This religion thing still wasn't resolved. It brought him pain, though his mood seemed lighter tonight.

Dom set his book aside. "Your idea was more the horizontal aspect of it, what it means in relation to others. Maybe it needs both. I haven't always felt it—not the feeling of God-with-us, the God of love that Gordon talked about. I'd like to." His voice took on a wistful tone. "The time feels right. If you and I were open, could we look together for that in a community of faith?"

Karen set her sketchbook aside and came to sit beside him. "Yes. I would love to." She took one of his hands in hers. "But, Dom, are you sure? That day in the park. You were in such pain."

"The pain I felt wasn't only because of us. It's been festering inside me for a long time. That Sunday, I felt like it was all or nothing. Now I'm thinking it's less about leaving a church and more about aligning myself with a community that makes a difference, doing God's work together. God can't be captured like a bird to put into a gilded cage. Nobody has all the answers. I can go back to the Basilica, drink in all the positive force that it has been in my life. But I can embrace new experiences also."

His arms slid around her. "It's time to put this particular sticky wicket behind us."

A weight seemed to lift away from her. She caught a deep breath and let the rush of feeling flow over her.

CHAPTER FORTY-EIGHT

Wednesday, July 12

As William drove his son through a largely undeveloped area northwest of Santa Fe, he wondered how he'd been talked into letting Algie give digital art lessons. After his son had expressed an interest in UNM with their digital art program, William had started plans for an eighth gallery and moving to a new city. Get his son out of proximity with his stubborn proclivity to a medium William despised.

He'd chosen Boston. He made a mental note to remind Guy again about the big CD. Guy should arrive in Santa Fe this week and be there until about August 1. William would need those funds to find the right property. There many good opportunities for a traditional art education in Boston—shouldn't be hard to excite Algie about those. Though moving was a hassle, this one had good purpose. The sooner they were away from Santa Fe, the happier he'd be. He glanced over at his son. Algie would adjust. He was young.

William checked his GPS, read the Bjornson name on a mailbox, and drove through an open gate under a high, adobe arch.

When he first heard Karen lived on a ranch, he'd expected a practical, mundane layout with square corrals on flat land. Upon learning where the ranch was, flat disappeared from his mind.

He'd looked at this pricy Monte Sereno Drive area when he first came to Santa Fe.

William slowed his car as he reached a high point on the Bjornson driveway. The two-story home below was huge and sprawling, a fine example of adobe-like southwestern architecture. The ranch buildings were spread out nearby.

"It makes me want to paint," said Algie as they surveyed the panorama. "Look at the way colors change on the land as the clouds move overhead."

William drove on, soon coming to a large corral with several horses. One, a dapple-gray with charcoal mane and tail, tossed his head and moved into a playful, reaching gait, almost like he was showing off remnants of a routine learned long ago.

"Someday I want to come early," said Algie. "I'd love to get reference photos of that gray."

Karen and Dom were waiting and invited William and Algie inside to a spacious studio with several looms, spinning wheels, and cubbyholes filled with rainbow colors of spooled yarn. Two young girls were seated with their laptops at tables arranged for the class. A young woman with silky blue-black hair chatted with a blond man.

Karen introduced them. "Lou McCreath—she illustrates children's books. My granddaughters, Krista and Leyla. My son, Anton. Both Lou and Anton are on the schedule as your son's drivers."

William looked up into the blue eyes of the man, so much like his mother's.

"I've been in your gallery several times," said Anton. "I'm the one who will be driving Grayson home today."

"Grayson?"

Algie's face flushed. "They asked what I want to be called. I said Grayson. I've been pond scum long enough."

The last was muttered almost under his son's breath. Funny, he hadn't heard that allusion for a while. "Grayson. Your mother always preferred that name. I'll try, but habits are hard to break."

William turned to Leyla. "I met your father a few days ago. He looked familiar, and now I see why." He spoke to Dom. "Would that be your son?"

Dom raised an eyebrow. "Grandson."

"I see. He stopped by to introduce himself as one of the drivers for Al—er Grayson."

"We'll get set up here," said Karen. "Thank you for bringing Grayson."

William followed Anton and Dom out.

"Went by some nice-looking horses as we drove in," he said to Anton. "I was especially taken by the gray. Do you and your mother ride?"

"Yes, my whole family does. Do you?"

"Sorry, city-born and bred."

Then a car drove up and parked. Another student? Then William recognized Costain.

Dom introduced them.

"We've met." William sucked in a breath as Costain followed Dom into the studio. He'd seen his work. Some paintings, which were not bad, and—

Damn. Digital art.

This was not what he wanted for his son. While he'd known Algie was here to teach digital art, it seemed there was more going on—actual encouragement for Algie to delve deeper into what William despised.

William began to think he'd been had. Leaving Anton with no explanation, he wheeled abruptly and went inside.

His son looked at him with a guilty look, and he was positive of it.

Karen got up from her computer and came over to him.

He shot an annoyed look at her. "You never said anything about Costain being part of your scheme."

Her eyes met his. "Yes, isn't it wonderful that he can be here occasionally? We'll rely on Grayson the rest of the time."

Should he pull the plug on this underhanded scheme?

"You are a devious woman, Karen Bjornson. I—"

Karen flashed him a brilliant smile. "Thank you. I'll take that as a compliment."

His son chuckled. William frowned, uncertain why his son's reaction annoyed him so.

Karen's head was held high, her eyes steady on his. He closed his mouth without finishing his sentence. He remembered that look. Gloria had perfected it.

He turned and left. This afternoon had been an eye-opener in more ways than one.

When he got back to the gallery, he'd call his realtor in Boston and push him to accelerate the process.

CHAPTER FORTY-NINE

Friday, July 14

In her studio at nine o'clock in the morning, Karen checked her email for the umpteenth time. This time, the long-awaited results had arrived! She read the message once, twice to make sure, and squealed in delight.

Dom looked up from his computer, where he was working on his novel, and smiled broadly as she tugged him to his feet for a hug. "My tapestry is in!" she said.

"Congratulations, my love. When do you deliver it?"

She went back to her email to read the instructions, which followed the brief, congratulatory news. "I can bring it in today."

"Let's deliver it, then celebrate over lunch."

"Great."

She danced out to the family room to tell Maria, Skyla, and Krista. She phoned Anton at work and then found Diego. Dulcie deserved to be among the first to know, so she texted her. Her exuberant high spilled over into happy texts to Pete and Akiko.

Karen looked one last time at her creation, touched her fingers to her lips and then to the little girl, and the giant verdigris torch bearer.

She checked to make sure the linen signature piece was securely attached on the back. Then she carefully rolled it, tucked the protective coverings over the ornate finials on the hanging rod and slid the whole thing into the duffle-like canvas bag she'd made to protect her work as it traveled.

Vaya con Dios!

◆ ❖ ◆

Karen carefully maneuvered the bag with its shoulder sling through the gallery doors as Dom held them. Would anyone else be delivering theirs already? Would she know any of them?

Rather than Otto Griffin at the front desk, Karen found a tall woman with gray-streaked dark hair and the posture and bearing a queen would envy. William had said something about one of his employees who handled all the special exhibits. This must be she, Adelle Gupta. She was accepting a large flat parcel from another winner, who glowed with excitement.

After Karen relinquished her tapestry, she spotted Joaquin Jimenez talking with the winner who'd had the flat parcel. He beckoned Karen and Dom over with a smile.

"You made it too?" Karen asked. "Isn't it a wonderful feeling?"

"It is. Have you met Linda Kapaun?" Joaquin introduced them. "Karen weaves art tapestries. Linda does calligraphy and illuminated manuscripts."

Linda's eyes sparkled. "Good to meet you."

Karen responded to the open friendliness. "This is such a great day. I'm looking forward to meeting all the finalists and seeing all the art together."

"Sixty different interpretations," said Joaquin.

"Would Niemöller be pleased?" asked Linda.

"If it makes people think, I believe so," said Dom. "Now the world awaits."

◆ ❖ ◆

"Vicky, wait up!" Dulcie called to her friend in Spanish as she saw her getting into her yellow car at Lemon Élan after their day's work. "I'm so glad I caught you. Been a long time."

"How's your weaving project?"

"We're done. Got the news this morning. It's a winner! The exhibit opens on August fifth. I can hardly wait."

"Great. Let me know. I'll come see it too."

"How are things going for you?"

Vicky's face fell. "You were right about Rafa. He's gotten worse. Last night he invited a bunch of guys over and they got drunk again. From what I overheard … They scare me. But if I say anything …"

"Do you want to stay with Santos and me for a few days?"

"No. Rafa's into payback. That pack of javelinas he hangs around with are worse. I couldn't bring this danger to you or Santos."

"Vicky, what are you going to do?"

Vicky sighed. "You know, I used to be afraid they'd attract the attention of ICE. Now, I'd be glad. He should be deported. I'd move away then. I don't trust him to leave me alone if he thought I snitched. He'd sneak over the border again and come looking for me. I could be a housekeeper in another state."

"You won't disappear without telling me where you're going?"

"Never, *amiga*."

CHAPTER FIFTY

Monday, July 17

Guy Roquet yawned as he sat at a table in the fishbowl working on the payroll quarterlies. The numbers on his laptop pixelated, danced, and wouldn't come out right. What had been child's play last year now took him twice as long. What wouldn't he give for a good night's sleep?

He'd taken to drinking in the evenings, which worked for a while, but lately that had changed. Even when sleep came, it was fitful. He'd wake up about one o'clock, worrying, tossing, turning. Lying there, reviewing options, none of them good. All because of his own stupidity and that moron of a stockbroker. He never should have trusted him.

Payroll, employee taxes, workman's comp. Expense accounts, petty cash, and travel. What could be diverted for a while and not be missed? What could be siphoned off little by little? How long would it take to make up that certificate of deposit? It had been sitting there for several years, rolling over and over. Guy still listed it as an asset on William's balance sheet.

But it wasn't there.

He'd wracked his brain, searching for ways to make it up.

William came in with a jaunty step. "Just think, Guy, less than three weeks to the Niemöller Gala."

He sat by Guy at the table. "I'm glad I caught you alone. I've been wanting to talk with you."

Guy sucked in a breath. Had William noticed anything? After all, his boss had majored in business. He knew his way around QuickBooks even though he preferred spending his time dealing with art and artists.

"Now that Santa Fe is doing splendidly, I'm thinking about an eighth location. Boston."

Guy exhaled. William moved slowly and meticulously when it came to researching locations. He still had time.

"Algie's thinking about UNM, but I can change his mind. He chose them because of their digital art program. I'll get him into a college with the best teachers for fine arts, the best for painting."

"You haven't even been open a year here," said Guy.

"But it's going well." William stood. "I'll move quickly on this before Algie gets stubborn. I've already done my research. The big CD will be fine for a down payment on a property. It comes due at the end of August, doesn't it? Don't roll it over. I want the funds available."

William went to his office door and looked back at him. "You don't look too good, Guy. Feeling okay?"

"Something at lunch didn't agree with me. The big CD? Fine. I'll be okay."

William's brows drew together. Then he shrugged and went into the inner sanctum.

What the hell was Guy to do if he couldn't pay back the CD? He'd already found ways to raise a significant amount of cash, but not enough. After all, he had a life to live too. What did William need the money for?

Maybe there was an alternative. One he'd fantasized about.

Otto came into the fishbowl doing his god-awful humming. He made some photocopies and left. Just shut up already. Or learn to carry a tune. Guy scowled. Serve him right if some fancy bookkeeping made it seem like Otto had been pilfering cash.

Guy paused.

Now there was an idea. Might consider adding that to his plan.

Giving up on finishing the quarterlies, he shut down his computer. Otto was in the gift store, talking to the clerk there. Guy slipped into the Middle Room and stopped in front of the Anonicelli. If he only knew a collector who had the wherewithal and the wish to own this painting. Surely he knew a sucker for old masters who wouldn't ask too many questions. He'd just have to pin the blame on someone.

On the other hand, anything involving such a well-known painting would be difficult. He'd be better off with several pieces of lesser-known art.

He pulled out the art asset list he'd compiled. He was getting tired of the life he was living, kowtowing to William, doing his bidding, yessir, no sir, anything you wish, sir. Disappearing was looking very attractive.

Guy began to feel better, seeing that there actually was not only a way out of this mess he'd made, but a way to a whole better life where he could be someone.

CHAPTER FIFTY-ONE

Wednesday, July 19

Grayson waited outside his two-story home in the shade of the tile roof extending over the front entryway. His computer case was slung over his shoulder with everything he'd need for their third digital art class at the Bjornson ranch. It was Wednesday—a Costain day. Cool.

Karen was driving today, and Krista was in the front passenger seat. She started to get out.

"No, I can sit in back." From there, Grayson could people-watch. He'd been doing a lot of that lately, since his oils teacher had challenged him to paint what was there, not just what he expected was there.

As they drove along the four-lane Highway 285, he told them about Mrs. Oaks and her challenge. They understood. All of them were artists—peers. Awesome.

"What else are you working on in your oil painting, Grayson?" asked Karen.

"Putting expression into a painting."

"How did she help?"

"I showed her photos of Mom's portraits. They showed emotion, but I had no idea how to get that. I could have learned so much from Mom." He paused, then cleared his throat. "What school will you be going to this year, Krista?"

"Milagro. I've always been at Carlos Gilbert. A new one's kind of scary," said Krista. "The middle school art I saw at the show was so much better than our grade school stuff."

"Yours was good too, Krista," said Karen.

"The dog being all curves was a nice contrast to its background," said Grayson. "I remember that one."

"Really?"

"It had an Airedale. Who else would have painted that?" His voice was teasing. "But the reason I remember, is the dog's mouth was open. Much easier to draw it closed and not worry about teeth and tongue. That's another reason you'll get better. You're not satisfied to stick with easy stuff."

The smile she threw over her shoulder warmed him. Like the compliment made her day.

"Remember your fourth-grade entry, Krista?" asked Karen.

Krista giggled. "Pretty funky. That was before I started taking lessons from Lou."

Karen glanced at Krista. "When you are finishing seventh grade, some sixth grader is going to look at yours and ask how you got to be so good."

Krista grinned. "Like you're always saying—work hard and practice. Thanks, Gramma. That helps."

"Here's an idea," said Grayson. "Keep your work from year to year. Look back, and you'll be amazed."

Krista twisted around in her seat to look at him. "Did you save your art?"

"Only a little bit. Since we moved so often, a lot of things got thrown away. I've never stayed at one school more than two years."

Then he chuckled. "When I was little, I had a book about a bunny. In the front and back, there were blank pages. I took crayons and filled those pages with my own bunnies. My dad yelled at me, but Mom said, 'The pages were blank. What were they for, if not for drawing?' "

Karen laughed. "I can so relate to that." She slowed for the turn onto her drive and pressed the gate-opener clipped to the car's visor.

His mom had treasured that book with his bunnies. Had his dad kept it?

As Grayson looked from Karen to Krista, a sudden hot feeling burst through him. Crap! Was he jealous of their easy back-and-forth talking? How they talked out problems, and it helped?

Couldn't be jealousy. Except he did feel a huge hole where his mom used to be. He remembered her touch, her silly pet names for him when she wasn't calling him Grayson. Funny how Karen calling him Grayson reminded him of his mom, and a warm long-ago feeling.

Was that love? He'd never questioned it. Just knew it'd be there— Until it wasn't.

He missed that feeling, craved it.

Chapter Fifty-Two

Wednesday, July 26

"Mmm, I smell lavender," said Karen.

Dom sat beside her on the loveseat in her sitting room. "I picked up a little something for you a while back." He handed her a gift bag with blue tissue poking out. "It's time I gave it to you."

"Mmm. My favorite scent." Karen pulled out a lavender wand, held it to her nose and breathed in.

"There's something else," he said.

He sounded curiously eager, almost boyish. She took out a tissue-covered roundish object and unwrapped it.

"How sweet, a covered basket woven of lavender. Ohura Farms. You were lucky to find one."

She lifted the lid. More tissue. "Something's inside." She unfolded the paper and lifted out a square velvet box. "Dom!"

With shaking fingers, she tipped back the lid. Through tears she saw a beautiful ring with a large round sapphire set in a bezel of Celtic knots. She ran a finger over the smoothness of the ring. "It's perfect," she whispered. Her eyes flew to his. "Absolutely perfect."

He took it and positioned it by her finger. "Will you marry me and be my love? Will you have me, sticky wickets, wrinkles, and all?"

"Yes, Dom. Oh, yes."

He slid the ring onto her finger and smiled when it fit perfectly. Holding the hand with her ring against his heart, his other hand slid along her cheek into her hair. His eyes shone with happiness. Their lips met in a kiss.

She snuggled closer, gazed at her hand lying across his palm, reveling in the radiance of this long-awaited moment.

"We should have a special dinner for both our families," said Karen. "Soon. Something simple."

"Dolores too?"

Karen closed her eyes briefly. "If you think she or your family is ready for that?"

"Not unless she apologizes to Sam and Farah."

Karen put out her hand to caress his cheek. "And to you. We'll celebrate with those who do come."

Chapter Fifty-Three

Tuesday, August 1

Frustrated, William pressed END on his phone. Guy still wasn't answering. Why?

William's realtor had called this morning. A property they'd been eyeing, a perfect location in Boston for his eighth gallery, was available. If William wanted to hold it until he could fly back and inspect it, he needed to come up with earnest money, and soon after, a down payment.

Adelle knocked on the door of the inner sanctum. He looked up.

"William, I need to talk with you—"

"What about?" He spoke sharply.

Her eyebrows rose. "The Hoogstra collection is—"

"Not now. I'm right in the middle of something."

"But—"

"Not now." William punched in the number for his bank as the click of her heels retreated through the fishbowl. Her back was rigid. Damn. All he needed was her anger.

He listened to the rings. It was already afternoon in Boston. He wanted to get this done today. Since he couldn't reach Guy, William called the bank himself to transfer it.

There was some confusion, causing him to work his way up the chain of command. Finally he talked to the manager, who said that CD didn't exist. It had been withdrawn after Christmas.

"Impossible!" William insisted. "It shows on our gallery balance sheet for July. I told my financial director I wanted it available. He said it didn't mature until August this year, till now."

"It matured at the end of December, sir, and that's when you withdrew it."

"Obviously, you are looking at the wrong one. This is the $500,000 one." He rattled off the account number again.

The number matched.

But the CD wasn't there.

"Who authorized the withdrawal?" William demanded.

"Guy Roquet signed for it. He is authorized to handle the transactions for you. Am I not correct?"

"Yes, he is. I'll check with him and get back to you."

William hung up in defeat.

It had to be a misunderstanding. Guy had assured him all was well.

The phone rang. It was the manager of his New York gallery wanting to speak to Guy. It was payday, but the checks weren't there yet—unusual—they always arrived promptly on the first and the fifteenth. Where was Guy?

William began to get a sick feeling in his stomach.

Cecil stopped by the gallery to talk with Otto. It was the first of the month, and he wanted to make sure Otto had changed the security passwords. Otto was busy with a customer, so Cecil walked back to talk to William.

Through the glass of the inner sanctum, Cecil saw William sitting at his desk, head in hands. Cecil knocked.

William raised his head. His face was pale and distraught. After what seemed an inordinately long pause, Cecil heard him say come in.

"Something wrong?" asked Cecil.

"Have I been robbed?"

"Robbed? What happened, William?"

"My CD—my bank said it was withdrawn. Last December. Yet …" He held out a balance sheet and pointed a shaking finger at a circled item. "It should still be there. Guy said it didn't mature until August, but the bank said last December. I told Guy not to let it roll over. I wanted to use the money. But they said …"

Cecil looked at the sheet. His eyes widened at the amount. He knew his friend was well off, but having the luxury of that much cash sitting there shocked him. "Where's Guy?"

"He was here last night working late. His schedule says he's in Santa Fe till the end of the month when he goes to L.A. But he's not answering his phone. I don't understand. Guy's been my friend for over ten years. Even before Gloria died. There must be a mistake."

Shit. Cecil wasn't at all shocked, half expecting someday Guy would act stupid. Likely Guy and the money were gone. William would be devastated.

"William, it doesn't sound good that you can't reach him under these circumstances. Do you want my advice?"

William nodded.

"I think you should call the police—"

"No!" William burst out. "He's a friend."

"Time may be important here. Maybe something happened to him. If he's okay, you can apologize for overreacting."

"Hell." William looked defeated. "Who would I call?"

"That Santa Fe PD detective, Schultz. He's a good man. I'll call him for you, if you want."

"Guy is going to be pissed, but I can see, speed might help. Tell him to get right over here."

As Cecil opened the door to go back into the fishbowl, Adelle Gupta practically tore it from his grasp. What riled her?

"Mr. Adams—"

"Can't you see this is not a good time?"

"But—"

William shouted, "Not now!"

She slammed the inner sanctum door hard enough to make the panes rattle and strode by Cecil, leaving him alone in the fishbowl. What had her knickers in a knot?

William's problem took priority. Cecil called Schultz.

◆ ❖ ◆

While they waited for Schultz, Cecil got hot strong tea and cookies from the bistro for William. Tonight, it would be scotch, but now, tea. As he was carrying them back to the office, he heard Schultz come in and Otto's interception.

"Lieutenant. There's something I need to tell you."

"I'll talk with you after my meeting with Mr. Adams."

Otto looked dismayed but nodded.

Cecil took Schultz into the inner sanctum and shut the door against Otto's curious ears.

William's color picked up a bit after he started the tea and cookies. William had just told the story of the missing CD and the payroll snafu when the office door swung open, and Adelle barged in.

William's eyes filled with anger as he rose. "Ms Gupta, we are—"

The woman, whom Cecil had always seen as the embodiment of graciousness, had sparks in her eyes. "Mr. Adams, I don't want to interrupt your tea party, but I must talk to you."

"This better be important," said William.

"The Hoogstra paintings of Canyon de Chelly were in storage in this gallery. I need to ship them to Phoenix for the exhibit, which will be opening there soon. They were here yesterday morning. I saw them with my own eyes. Now they're missing."

Cecil sucked in a breath. Holy shit. Guy! Had he stolen the paintings too?

"Otto probably—"

"Otto doesn't know anything about them. Did you move them?"

"No. Look around—"

"Read my lips. They are NOT in this building."

Before Cecil's eyes, Schultz took charge. "We will speak quietly. Mr. Adams, perhaps Ms Gupta could join us? This may shed light on our, ahem, tea party conversation. I would like to hear about these paintings. How much is this collection worth?"

Cecil grabbed a chair from the fishbowl for Adelle and shut the door again. William looked stunned and slowly sank into his seat.

"About a quarter million dollars," said William. "You don't think—"

"What is happening?" asked Gupta.

"May I?" Schultz looked at William, who nodded. He turned to Adelle. "I'm Lieutenant Schultz, Santa Fe PD. Mr. Adams has just made some upsetting discoveries. Cecil suggested he call me in to see what we can learn. It seems a large amount of money is unaccounted for. Mr. Roquet is not answering his phone. The payroll is not done, and now some valuable art is missing."

Adelle's mouth dropped. "Sweet Lucifer, are you saying Guy stole—"

"Nothing of the kind. He isn't answering his phone, which can happen for many reasons. We would like to speak to him ASAP."

Cecil watched the verbal ping-pong flying. He admired Schultz's skill in handling the emotional tension.

"I'm sorry, William," said Adelle. "I had no idea."

William looked gobsmacked. "What the hell do we do now? The Gala Reception for the Niemöller exhibit is Friday." He looked toward Schultz.

The voice of the detective was reassuring. "Mr. Adams, I'm sure it's not the first time you've faced daunting odds. You will organize what needs to be done and start chipping away at it."

William straightened and drew a notepad toward him.

"As far as the police are concerned," said Schultz, "we will put out a BOLO, a be-on-look-out, for Roquet. He's not accused, he's a person of interest. Has he been attacked, kidnapped, or done a bunk? We don't know. I will bring in officers to check his residence in Santa Fe and look for his vehicle. I'll need information from you to do that."

Cecil studied his friend, sitting behind the desk. Bewildered. Lost. This betrayal hadn't really hit William yet. He was probably hoping Guy had an accident or another benevolent reason would explain his absence. Inside Cecil, the truth was becoming obvious.

Schultz was patiently prodding William. "You will want to contact all your galleries and tell them you haven't been able to reach Roquet and you're worried. Have them tell you immediately if he shows up. Find out if their payroll checks have arrived. Check with your banks—not only about the payrolls, but about any company cards Roquet may be using."

William made notes from Schultz's advice.

"I'm going to bring in Detective Sergeant Ruiz to help. She can talk with you about hiring a forensic auditor. Knowing the extent of any damage is crucial."

"William, I can make sure the Gala runs smoothly," said Adelle. "I'll meet the judges when they fly in tomorrow."

"Oh, God, the judges." William wilted again. "And the press. I don't want press involved."

Cecil chimed in. "You were going to be closed on Thursday anyway to set up the exhibit. Closing a day earlier would appear natural. Would that make it easier?"

William nodded.

"I just had a thought," said Adelle. "That art asset sheet Guy wanted to do? We should compare that to my records and have the managers do a quick inventory of what's in their storage. If the Hoogstras are missing, perhaps other art has disappeared as well."

The gracious, efficient Adelle was back, and Cecil approved. Quite a trooper.

Pete caught their attention. "Mr. Adams, tell me about these paintings in storage."

"I keep an eye out for estate sales or museums shedding some of their collections. Art and antique dealers alert me to opportunities. That's how I came by the Anonicelli. Adelle works this art into exhibits. I'd say each gallery has in storage up to ten works waiting for the right opportunities to showcase them."

"William," Adelle said, "I can compare those lists."

"I'll change the passwords and update your system," said Cecil. Maybe now wasn't the time to say it, but he'd see the managers at the other locations did the same.

"One more suggestion," said Pete. "It may be good to at least temporarily block access to Mr. Roquet to all your assets."

William nodded. "Yes, you may be right."

The meeting broke up and everyone started their appointed tasks. Cecil pulled the blinds in the fishbowl. The gallery was still open, and they didn't need curious eyes watching.

Cecil sat in the fishbowl and methodically began the changes in the passwords. Pete had retrieved his laptop from his car and was typing away.

Otto came in, puzzlement on his pudgy face. "Why did you pull the blinds? What happened?"

Cecil filled him in, at least what he thought William would share.

"Oh, my. Can I talk to you now, Lieutenant?"

Schultz looked up.

"After they tried to steal my lady, Cecil had us change passwords every month. I updated them in my special file. This morning, it wasn't where it should have been. And the copier was on all night. I never do that."

"Your special file? This morning?"

Otto bit his lip. Then he pointed at a file drawer. "Aunt Mary was stuck into the middle of another file!"

Schultz closed his eyes briefly. "Aunt Mary?"

Cecil almost laughed aloud. Somehow, Schultz kept his voice patient.

"Yes, the file where I keep all my passwords and security codes."

Otto opened the file drawer. "See? I didn't touch it yet."

There, stuck in the middle of a fat file with records and receipts from a painter, stood a folder at an angle. Its top was bent where it had been closed in the drawer.

"This may be important. We'll dust it for prints. Good work, Griffin."

The monitors under the shuttered windows showed a family entering the gallery. Otto scurried up front again, leaving Pete and Cecil alone.

"I notified Tuttle," said Pete. "At first, he sounded alarmed, then the tone of his voice changed. For Tuttle, it sounded like excitement, but then, never having heard Tuttle and excitement uttered in the same breath, I wasn't sure."

Cecil grinned. "I know his mind. He's cooking up an idea. That's good."

Pete went back to his laptop.

Cecil began entering changes, going back and forth between his phone and the security panels. He looked up from his phone to see a trim, official-looking woman, carrying a computer case, walk into the fishbowl. About five years older than himself, her demeanor spoke law enforcement to him. Schultz introduced her as Sergeant Elena Ruiz and took her into William's office.

A patrol officer with an evidence bag came in. Cecil noticed Pete wave at him from the inner sanctum and point to Cecil. Cecil showed him the drawer, Aunt Mary, and the file was taken away.

Algie came in, flushed and sweaty from riding his bike. He hung up his helmet. "Whatcha doing, Uncle Cecil?"

"Something has happened to Guy. He's not answering his phone. We're taking precautions to avoid any unauthorized access."

"Wow. Change everything? Can I help?"

"Yes." Cecil glanced at Algie. "Otto's going to be stressed. Can you fix a new cheat sheet for him? None of the gallery payrolls were done, and your dad has to transfer funds and do them. He's really worried about Guy."

"Who are the people with Dad in the inner sanctum?"

"Police. Don't tell anyone about this, Algie. Your dad doesn't want Guy's absence leaked to the press." Cecil humphed. Good luck with that, since there was a BOLO out.

"It's almost closing time," said Algie. "Will everybody stay late?"

"It may be a long night here."

"I can get takeout for everybody at the bistro and pick it up at six. Would that help?"

"Great."

Cecil and Algie created a cheat sheet for Otto. Then they took it to him, making sure he understood the new changes. The sign went on the door saying the gallery would be closed to set up the new exhibit, which would open to the public on Saturday, August fifth.

At six, Algie, Otto, and Cecil went across the street to pick up the food. "Otto, will all this muck up our plan for Friday?"

"Nothing to worry about, Algie. It's under control. After all, Guy didn't have anything to do with our plans."

Cecil smiled at them. Such a good kid. William should be proud.

CHAPTER FIFTY-FOUR

Friday, August 4

The private Gala Reception for the exhibit based on the "First They Came" quote by Martin Niemöller was finally here. Artists and guests, invited dignitaries, and the press would attend that evening.

Karen's excitement grew as Anton's car pulled near the gallery to drop them off before the official opening at five o'clock. "I've been to many receptions," she said to Dom, "but this feels special. A point like no other in my career."

Dom smiled. "I'm glad for you. Have any of the others held your light this high?"

She chuckled, delighted at his metaphor. "Not even close." She brushed a stray hair from her trusty little black dress. Actually, it wasn't black—which did terrible things to her complexion—but a smoky navy. Whenever she wore it, she tried to make it look different. Tonight, she'd added a loosely draped, cobweb-felted scarf of alpaca and silk, using the colors from her tapestry—cool marine tones merging into colors of light.

Artists had been encouraged to arrive early. There was no way Canyon Road parking could accommodate this many visitors in an already crowded tourist season, so Anton had volunteered as their chauffeur. She and Dom got out, invitations in hand, to join the line moving toward the door.

Just as Karen got to the head of the line, a courier in uniform brushed past her, carrying a package from a chocolate company. He cut in front of her to speak to the woman at the desk.

"Excuse me, delivery requiring the manager's signature."

Otto signed for the package and set it down near the cash register in the gift shop area.

Karen and Dom showed their invitations and received their programs. She donned a nametag with elegant calligraphy proclaiming her as an exhibiting artist. Then they moved into the bustling showroom.

"Look," she said, "there's the governor talking with William."

"Impressive crowd," said Dom.

"Oh, this must be Linda's." Karen stopped in front of an easel, transfixed by what appeared at first to be a medieval, illuminated-manuscript page. A purple rosette and ribbon on the gilded frame proclaimed it the winner of the Niemöller Theme Prize.

Niemöller's quote was done in calligraphy on a two-by three-foot sheet of vellum. Each line of the quote had an ornately decorated capital letter and one defining miniature scene. Some initials were raised and adorned with gold leaf. The colorful border around the text overflowed with twining leaves, flowers, and animals.

"Look at the detail and how the message stands out so clearly."

"Exquisite," said Dom. "She's paraphrased the quote for 2017 in her calligraphy. I like the interpretation. But the illustrations and the illuminated capital for each stanza, they could be medieval."

"The themes!" said Karen. "In her paraphrase, she has the first stanza saying they were coming for immigrants."

"Then those who worshipped differently, and finally, those who didn't look like me."

Karen soaked in the total effect. "Nothing, not a flourish is wasted. I could look at this forever and still not take it all in."

Linda Kapaun stood nearby, her face aglow. "I'm glad you like it."

"Like doesn't say it. I'm impressed. Congratulations."

Karen turned next to a set of bronze sculptures perched atop waist-high pedestals near the archway into the Middle Room. Standing next to them, Joaquin Jimenez talked animatedly to a reporter. He, too, had captured a prize—the blue ribbon.

His set of bronzes depicted a dreadlocked Black youth, shielding an injured man. The youth, resolute, strong, held up a hand to ward off blows, his body cradling the man protectively. In a twist of what the viewer might expect, the injured was a White police officer lying, eyes closed. Two Black attackers, postures filled with rage—one with knotted fists and the other brandishing a knife—formed the other statue in the set. The title was a simple, *He Is My Brother*. The tension, the emotion on the faces, and the action were everything she had come to expect of Joaquin's work.

"Congratulations, Joaquin. A stunning job."

"Congratulations to you too."

Karen held out her hand with its ring. "Yes, Dom and I—"

Joaquin laughed. "I see, but that wasn't what I meant. Look at the program."

Karen lifted the thick booklet. Her hand shook as she fumbled with her reading glasses, hung by a leash under the folds of her scarf. A few pages in, she spotted the list of prize winners. Second prize had gone to Marcus Red Feather for an acrylic, *The Bystanders*. Third prize to Karen Bjornson, *Tapestry of Light*. Three other artists were listed with honorable mentions.

Joaquin chuckled at the jaw-dropped expression she knew she wore and waved her toward the Middle Room through the milling crowd of visitors.

She turned the corner and feasted her eyes. A spotlight enhanced her vivid colors and the light from the giant statue reaching for the hand of the little girl, clutching her bear. A yellow ribbon hung near a lower corner.

Tears formed in her eyes. Dom slipped his arm around her waist, and she sagged toward him.

"Your light shines," he whispered.

Might her voice truly be heard through her tapestry?

Might it make a difference?

"You will want to see the rest before the crush gets too heavy," suggested Joaquin. "People will be pelting you with questions and comments, and you won't be able to get away then."

Karen nodded and turned to an acrylic painting adorned with a red ribbon. A man in his twenties stood next to it, his slender height exaggerated by a stiffly erect, eight-inch-high Mohawk of robin's egg blue emerging from otherwise jet-black hair. His chosen theme was bullies and bystanders. The painter's innate drama extended to his art with bold brush strokes and strong color.

Karen found herself drawn to his work, which somehow managed, despite its energetic in-your-face approach, to contain an appealing sensitivity. Five figures stood out in *The Bystanders*. The gloating, self-important visage of the bully and the agony of the bullied figure were well done. What struck Karen were the expressions on the bystanders clustered near the bully. None of them were impassive. Where would they bestow their allegiance? Would one of them reach out to stop the bully? Do something about being trapped in the middle, in the tension of indecision? She got the sense this artist had worked through his own pain to become confident in his own skin, yet he still reached out to those caught in struggle.

She smiled at him, and he smiled back. She walked on, eventually finding all three honorable mentions—another acrylic, an oil, and a watercolor.

In the Near Room, the quiet melodies of a hammered dulcimer began. She accepted a glass of white wine from a uniformed waiter. All three showrooms had long tables loaded with crackers and cheeses, bite-sized fruit, and tempting hors d'oeuvres. Guests milled around them.

As she and Dom moved through the exhibit, she knew she'd have to come again to take it all in. Paintings, pastels, and colored pencil. More 3D art. Several photographs, memorable and poignant. Some artists had submitted work in media one normally didn't see in art shows—an art quilt, a wood carving, and two intarsia pieces.

She appreciated that several of the artists were in their late teens or early twenties. What a jump-start this would be for their careers. She was delighted to see Gordon Bard, a long-time fixture of Santa Fe's art world. He had to be ninety, bent and wizened, but still painting in oils, still with a bright twinkle in his eyes. He had earned this honor over a lifetime.

Artists had used many images and themes in their interpretation of Niemöller's words: Who is my neighbor? Standing up against the bullies. Races working side by side in common purpose. Different faiths working together.

Images inspired by Matthew 25. "I was hungry, I was thirsty. I was a stranger."

Civil rights, women's rights, gay rights. Freedom of the press. Even climate change.

Acceptance, Diversity, Inclusiveness.

As she and Dom circled back to Linda's illuminated manuscript, she had no quarrel with the judges' choices. She was glad that a medium, which might be excluded from many shows "because it was only illustrative" had seized the Niemöller Prize.

The woman, playing the hammered dulcimer, had yielded her spot to a classical guitarist. As she walked by the works of art, he began playing the familiar "Malagueña."

By the time Karen had followed the exhibit from beginning to end, she was moved to tears. Such a gift to witness this outpouring of creativity honoring Niemöller's statement. No work on its own would be nearly as effective. She felt a surge of gratitude to William and his late wife for their vision. This indeed was a light on a hill, a voice ringing out with strength. One could not overlook this. How awesome to be a part of it.

There was nothing comfortable about this show. Certainly, the works were of excellent quality. One could go through and dispassionately remark on the quality of the brushstrokes, the use of light and darkness, and how the compositions drew the eye. But the collective human anguish as the subjects in each work of art faced choices—caught in moments of time, tension, and conflict—gave birth to a theme she found powerful in its resonance. Courage in the face of adversity, and the knowledge that each viewer bore a responsibility to forestall a terrible end.

The guitarist began the haunting theme from *Schindler's List*. The yearning, lyrical music wove itself into her mind with the images which surrounded her.

She didn't feel alone anymore, didn't feel caught in a constant barrage of indifference and hate.

"I wish Herb and Yolanda could be here," said Dom. "They would love this."

"Yolanda would know exactly what I'm feeling right now."

"And Dulcie."

Karen smiled. "I wish they'd let us bring more than one guest, but she had to work. She'll actually be here later tonight. This gallery is on her cleaning schedule. Not the same experience we're having, but she will see it."

Hope filled Karen. This was an artist's dream to be uplifted, surrounded by those who cared deeply, inspired by their common humanity. Awed by their creativity.

Art as a catalyst for change.

"Let go of me!"

The shrill voice intruded into the elegance of the evening, shattering Karen's mood. The guitarist faltered mid-tune and stopped. Polite conversations broke off as attention was drawn toward the interruption at the front of the Near Room.

A blonde, wearing an orange-and-purple floral print top over tight black leggings, yanked away from the agitated security guard. She pulled a framed abstract painting from her tote bag. Purple curves cut through bright orange and yellow blobs. "My work is beautiful. Better than anything here. I should be in this show. Your judges are fake. They wouldn't know change if they fell over it."

The guard, his hands outstretched, tried to shepherd her to the door. Adelle and Otto hastened to control the situation.

"Good God." Joaquin, standing near Karen, looked disgustedly at the unfolding scene. "It's that nutcase again."

"Stop that!" screeched the woman, shaking off the hand of the guard and swinging her painting at him. Her loose top slipped off one pale shoulder. "Touch me again, and I'll call the cops."

"Please do, ma'am."

Karen heard the guard's voice and caught the nervous chuckles from the crowd. The woman was escorted out, the doors closing on her raucous voice. A feeling of pity mixed with surprise at the woman's lack of etiquette moved through her.

"You know her, Joaquin?"

"By reputation only. Calls herself Purity Gold. All inflated ego and no talent. Even if she has legitimately entered this competition, no judge would take her seriously."

"I've never heard of her before."

"She hangs around the fringes of the art world." He turned back to the reporter he'd been talking with, who appeared to have caught the incident on video.

The guitarist picked up again. His eyes closed and he seemed to drift back into a musical world of his own making. The hum of conversation picked up as people resumed milling about.

Karen met and talked with the judges. She found a moment to thank William. Karen was a little puzzled by his demeanor. He looked tired, but more than that. Strained. She'd have thought he'd be euphoric at what she saw as a smashing success.

Before seven, attendance thinned. Karen circled back to her tapestry. Without the crowd in the way, she stood and took it all in. The yellow rosette added a sunny burst to an already perfect day.

Dom found her and pulled out his phone. "Stand next to it. This is such a special moment; you'll want a picture."

Anton called to let them know he was outside. She was eager to tell him about her prize. He, Skyla, and Krista planned to see the exhibit tomorrow. She could hardly wait to hear their reactions.

Chapter Fifty-Five

Dulcie arrived early to look at the exhibit. She parked her lemon-yellow car behind the gallery, next to a dark-colored SUV with an open hatchback. Bruno's rattletrap pickup was next to it.

Nice warm night. Her yellow polo shirt would be enough. Tossing her black jacket back into the car, she put the car keys into the pocket of her black jeans. Her phone went into a hip pocket in case Santos called. This last week or so, the phone had been giving her grief—it wouldn't keep a charge. After finishing with the noisy vacuum cleaner, she'd plug it in. She'd started carrying the charger in her purse.

Who did the SUV belong to? The caterers?

The back door was ajar. She put her basket of cleaning supplies on the utility cart in the hall and set her purse on the kitchen counter. Couldn't be the caterers' vehicle. They were gone, having done a decent job tidying the kitchen.

Hearing male voices, she wondered who might be talking to Bruno. He was so sweet in a brotherly way. She took a metal serving tray from the cupboard near the kitchen door to collect stray glasses.

How exciting it would be to see the Niemöller exhibit displayed. How thrilling that Karen's tapestry had been chosen. Karen would tell her all about who had been at the reception and what they said.

The voices were coming from the Middle Room. Funny, neither sounded like Bruno. She glanced toward the front. No, he was slumped in his chair, as far as she could see, asleep. He'd confessed he sometimes napped on duty.

On soundless crepe soles, she moved toward the voices.

"Got it?"

"Yeah, here's the tape."

She peeked around the corner into the room where much of the Niemöller exhibit was displayed. Two men were strapping duct tape around a long roll covered with a black garbage bag. The wall next to them was bare. A large carton sat nearby, part of a bronze statue sticking out the top. Framed art lay scattered next to a smaller carton containing more frames.

She sucked in a breath. One of the guys was familiar. What was his name?

She flicked another glance at the taped-up roll. *Madre de Dios!* That finial sticking out of the black plastic was on Karen's tapestry rod! The tray slipped from her fingers and clattered to the floor.

The men spun around, saw her, and dropped the tapestry. The older of the two lunged toward her. "Shit," he yelled. "You said no one would be here."

Dulcie ran toward the back, screaming, "Bruno! Wake up!"

He didn't move.

Racing through the Near Room, she jerked the stanchions lined against the walls, knocking them over behind her. Her pursuer went down in a tangle of fat red velvet ropes. Without stopping, she shoved the cart holding her cleaning supplies careening toward him. She pulled her keys from her pocket and ran out to her car, starting it as he burst through the door. He slammed the hatchback down and jumped into the SUV driver's seat.

Dulcie pulled onto Canyon Road with tires squealing. Oh, God. He followed. She turned left off the narrow one-way street, seeking a main drag. The SUV stayed right on her tail.

Madre de Dios!

The Canyon Road area of Santa Fe was old. Lots of tiny, narrow lanes, high walls, and practically devoid of nightlife. These dark streets felt like traps. Get to a well-lit, busy area. Surely that would make the man stop chasing her.

The police station was at least six miles away, maybe more.

Going home was a no-no—it would be stupid to let them know where she lived, and it would put Santos in danger.

She blew through a stop sign. The SUV followed, swerving wildly as another car with the right of way slammed on its brakes and set its horn blaring. She sped on.

Ahead was a busy intersection. The light was green, but she slowed. The SUV came closer. The light turned yellow ahead, but still she dawdled before pressing hard on the accelerator, shooting through the last of the yellow, and turning left. Her jacket slid to the floor.

The SUV was stuck behind her at the red light. With more cars around her, she turned again. Ahead was an apartment complex. She drove in and parked in the shadow of a large pickup, turning off her lights, and getting her distinctive car out of sight.

Her heartbeat slowed to a less frantic pace. No sign of the SUV. Maybe she'd lost him.

The house where Vicky lived was nearby.

Think! Put on your jacket. Black was better than the bright shirt with its logo. Reaching down to retrieve her jacket, she suddenly froze. Her purse! It was still in the gallery in plain sight. Her driver's license with her address. Santos was home by himself!

Dulcie pulled out her phone and called him.

"Hi, Mom,"

"Santos, listen. Two men were robbing the gallery. One's chasing me. Don't answer the door unless you know it's me. Call Sergeant Martinez."

"Mom, where are you?"

"I'm near Vicky's. I'll call the police—" She looked at the phone in her hand. "Santos, you still there?"

The phone had gone dead.

Where was that SUV? She pulled out of the parking lot, suspicious of every car that shared the street, and carefully drove several blocks to her friend's home.

Dulcie parked and ran past a white van in the driveway.

Vicky's front door was wide-open, and Dulcie heard her yelling inside in English, "You no right. You no come in!"

What was going on? Had she arrived in the midst of a fight with her boyfriend?

Too late Dulcie noticed a man behind her. She screamed as he grabbed her arms. Another man appeared in front of her.

She broke away and ran. Someone tackled her from behind, slamming her into the ground. Rough hands forced cuffs onto her wrists. Dazed, she struggled before they threw her into the van. Men in black shoved Vicky and several more in after her. The doors slammed shut, and the van started moving.

CHAPTER FIFTY-SIX

Sam Martinez's cell phone rang insistently. He reached for it, struggling through the fog of sleep. The clock said ten-fifteen.

"Martinez," he answered.

"Coach, it's Santos." The boy's voice shook. "Somebody's chasing Mom."

Sam sat up in alarm. "Santos, what's going on?"

"Mom called me from the gallery where Karen's tapestry is. Something bad happened. Told me not to let anybody in unless I knew it was her. Said I should call you."

"When did she call?"

"Just now. She sounded scared, 'n then her phone cut out, 'n then I remembered the survival rule. Don't let the trail grow cold."

"Good. Is she driving her little yellow car?"

"Yes."

"Listen, I'm going to put you on hold. I'll call dispatch, have them check the gallery, and send a patrol car to your apartment. Don't hang up."

Behind him, Farah turned on the light and sat up. As he spoke with dispatch, he threw on the clothes he'd laid out before he went to bed.

Then he talked to Santos again. "I'm on my way." He hung up, finished dressing, and double-checked his vest and gun.

Farah reached out to him. "Santos?"

"He's alone and scared. I'll see that he's okay." He leaned over to give Farah a kiss as her arms went around him. "Love you. Go back to sleep, sweetheart."

"Love you too," she said. "Be safe."

He felt her arms sliding away as he stood, then he touched her cheek, seeing the love and worry in her eyes. He closed the door quietly, already focusing on Santos and what he might find.

♦ ❖ ♦

Sam glanced across the tidy Rodriguez apartment at the clock. Eleven-fifteen. Santos, chewing worriedly on his lip, sat on the couch, stroking the purring, pumpkin-colored cat. No news of his mother's whereabouts. With every sound of a passing car, the boy froze, listening, looking at the door expectantly. Then he would sigh, and resume petting the cat.

Sam's phone rang. Pete again. He excused himself and stepped outside. "What's happening?"

"The security guard's in the hospital. Still unconscious. Vitals aren't good; listed as critical. They're testing him for drugs."

"Attempted murder?" asked Sam.

"Wouldn't surprise me. The manager, Griffin, has calmed down a little. One of the stolen pieces is *Lady in White*, by that seventeenth-century painter. *Scheisse*, we knew it was targeted, and they still got it."

Sam whistled.

"The gallery owner, Adams, arrived a while ago. It seems the thieves managed to disarm the security system somehow."

"Inside job?"

"We'll look at that. They also stole art from the competition. Adams was in a state of denial and said the exhibit opens tomorrow. I told him it's not going to happen. It's a crime scene."

"Any word on Dulcie?" asked Sam.

"No sign. I'm anxious to talk to her when she shows up. We have a BOLO out for her and her car. Get a suitable photo of her from Santos to add to it. Meanwhile, have you given thought to where Santos should stay tonight? She's in danger and possibly her son as well. They could try to snatch him to get to her."

"He knows everybody at the Bjornsons' place. How about I take him there for the night?"

"Have you talked with Karen?"

"I'll call her."

Sam hung up and called Karen. Immediately she said Santos would be welcome. He could tell them what was going on when they arrived.

◆ ❖ ◆

Sam looked at the obstinate boy.

"I'm not going anywhere without Tuffy."

"Cats are okay being alone overnight."

Santos wheeled and went to his room, coming back with the cat carrier. "If I have to go, he's coming too."

While Santos collected what he thought Tuffy would need—food, litterbox, treats, toys—Sam wrote a note for Dulcie with a PD number to call.

Santos added a postscript to the note before placing it on the center of the counter, anchored by a gaudy orange-and-turquoise ceramic horned toad. Only then did Santos collect his toothbrush and clothes for the next day.

Sam knew he was procrastinating—hoping his mother would be home before they had to leave. "Got your cell phone?"

"Yeah, by the cat carrier," said Santos.

"Charger?"

Santos disappeared into his bedroom and came back with his charger and a duffle bag. He got grocery sacks for the cat's belongings.

Then it came time for Tuffy to go in the carrier. Suspicious, the cat ran and hid under the bed. Sam reached under, grabbed him, and hauled Tuffy out. Suddenly Sam dropped the cat, who sped away, knocking over Santos's pile of belongings near the duffle.

"Damn—" Sam bit off the words he didn't want Santos to hear as he looked at the long scratches on the back of his hand. Sam glared at the cat, who stood all bristly on the back of the couch. He went to the sink, rinsed off the blood, and patted the scratches dry.

Tuffy, now sweet as could be, let his master shut him in the carrier. Santos threw his stuff into the duffle bag and zipped it shut. Then they left.

♦ ❖ ♦

At the Bjornsons' home, Sam parked by Karen's studio where Karen and Dom waited. Santos fetched Tuffy, who was meowing unhappily, and followed them in, down the long hall and through to the family room. Santos set the carrier down.

Sam began telling what happened. Loud barking drowned him out as Twitch skidded to a stop in front of the carrier.

Santos, his eyes large, grabbed it up high, and yelled. "Get away! Don't you hurt him."

Sam caught Twitch by his collar and pulled him back. Piercing barks hurt his ears. Another noisy dog came running. Karen grabbed Shadow as the dog raced past her.

Krista flew down the stairs in her pajamas, her hair flying. "Shadow, leave it." Her voice was firm. "Quiet!" She took her dog from Karen.

Sam heard running steps in the hall above and Anton came downstairs wearing only jeans. Twitch still scrabbled to get away from Sam. His barking hadn't ceased.

In the carrier, at his fierce tomcat best, Tuffy added to the caterwauling. Anton opened the sliding glass door and shoved Twitch out. Krista sent Shadow after. Anton slid the door shut on the din. Two Airedales stood on their hind legs, front paws against the glass.

Santos set the carrier down. Tuffy, every hair standing on end, looked huge in his small cage. His puffed-out tail lashed back and forth. He hissed loudly.

Maria appeared in the hall with Diego right behind her. "What's wrong? We saw Sam's car and heard—"

"Santos?" cried Diego, "Why—"

"I don't want to be here. Those horrible dogs will kill Tuffy. And I need to find my mom." The eleven-year-old's bravado had vanished.

Diego opened his arms wide, and Santos rushed to hide his face against the man's chest.

"Sam, what happened?" asked Anton.

Sam told them, censoring what he divulged. "Karen said to bring Santos here."

"I'm not staying. Tuffy's not safe here."

"Karen," said Diego, "the boy and Tuffy are welcome to spend the night in my spare bedroom."

Karen nodded.

Diego eased Santos away and looked into his eyes. "There are no dogs in my house. You can let Tuffy out of his carrier there. He won't come to any harm. Okay?"

Santos finally nodded and wiped his eyes on his sleeve. He picked up the carrier and followed Diego and Maria down the hall.

"I'll bring your things," Sam called after them.

"How about coffee before you leave?" asked Anton. "And some antibiotic? That hand looks nasty."

"I'd say Tuffy won that battle," said Dom.

Sam examined his oozing, angry-looking scratches. "If Twitch ever does come face to face with that cat, it won't be the cat crying 'Poor me.' "

CHAPTER FIFTY-SEVEN

Saturday, August 5

As the forensics team wrapped up their investigation at the gallery, Pete called Cecil to meet him there. He walked him through the gallery and gave him selected highlights of what they knew. He watched as Cecil's frustration and puzzlement grew. Interesting. This man had all the knowledge to pull this off. Technically he was a suspect.

"Shit. No sign of forced entry and the whole damn system is off. You say no signal went to the police station?"

"Nothing."

"How in the hell?" Cecil strode over to the blue alcove, empty now of the lady. The grille was raised and hidden, just like it would be when the gallery was open. "Is it okay if I check to see if the droid moved?"

"Forensics is done. Go ahead."

Re-Didion was still at his starting point. "How—" Cecil sputtered with exasperation. "Guy wouldn't have been able to do this. We figured he copied Otto's file, but since he scarpered, we changed everything."

"Can't be too many with the knowledge to disarm the system. Can you account for your whereabouts last night?"

"Home. Went to bed about eleven." His eyes flashed to Pete's. "Alone. Your damned five-thirty call woke me up."

"Who else could have disarmed the system?"

"William. Otto. He goes through it every day when he opens. Though I suppose someone could have used his cheat sheet."

Pete made a mental note to ask Otto where he kept that sheet. "How about the part-time guard? Or Gupta?"

"Neither could disarm the art security."

"Don't leave town, Dupre."

Cecil's troubled eyes met his. "You're right to say that. I won't. I just don't understand."

◆ ❖ ◆

By seven a.m., Pete Schultz was back in the detectives' bullpen. He passed by Loloma's cubicle. There was something of a cat-like quality to this quiet, muscular man. He'd seen him leap from this customary stillness into athletic agility.

"Loloma?"

Loloma raised his head. His Hopi heritage showed in his high cheekbones, perceptive deep-set eyes, and straight black hair cut in regulation police length. He nodded, almost imperceptibly.

Then Pete noticed the folded waxed paper lying on Loloma's desk. A few blue flakes of Hopi piki bread remained. "I'm sorry. We pulled you away from something important."

Loloma broke his stillness with a slight shrug. "My sister insisted, even though it will be hours until they share it."

Pete waited. Loloma would share his thoughts only if he wished, and in his own time.

"It's my sister's granddaughter's naming ceremony. Giving me piki is her way of saying she understands why I cannot be there, that I must walk in two worlds."

Pete thought back to the long conversations they'd had over the years about the pulls between cultures. He briefly grasped Loloma's shoulder. "As I recall, this is her way of giving you wisdom and strength for walking in our world?"

Loloma's somber features broke into a broad smile. "You remembered."

Long-ago lessons from the Japanese man who became his father in-law filled Pete's mind. It seemed right. Facing Loloma, he bent his body slightly from the hips. His eyes lowered. "Thank you for walking with us."

Pete straightened and went into his office, where a wall of windows looked out upon the bullpen. He set his portfolio on the round table and turned to his one-cupper coffee machine. Fortified, he sat.

Sergeant Ruiz was the first to join him. On call last night, she'd worked with him at the gallery scene. Pete reached back to his desk and picked up a stack of papers.

"Ruiz, here is what I have so far of all the potential witnesses."

She chuckled as she took the stack. "I knew this was coming when I saw Griffin give it to you."

Pushing fifty, Ruiz was next in line after him in seniority. She had a nose for sniffing out white-collar crimes. She'd be handy in this case involving dignitaries and gallery owners. She'd been on the Santa Fe scene long enough to deal comfortably with artists who made up a huge portion of the population.

Sam Martinez came in with Loloma to take their places.

Pete set his mug down and opened his binder. "Last night a private reception was held at the Swift and Adams Gallery on Canyon Road for an exhibit, which was to open today. Not long after, a burglary occurred. Loloma, could you jot these times down on the white board?"

Loloma nodded and rolled the board closer to him.

"At eight p.m., Otto Griffin, the manager, left, the last to leave after the event. At the same time, the security guard, Bruno Keller, arrived."

"Did they see each other?" asked Sam.

Pete nodded. "They spoke. The cleaning woman, Dulcie Rodriguez, arrived at nine forty-five. She allegedly interrupted two men burglarizing the place. The thieves got away with a seventeenth-century painting by Anonicelli, valued at more than a million."

Ruiz frowned. "Guy Roquet is still on the loose— embezzlement and more. Wouldn't surprise me if he was involved in this. Does that FBI agent investigating the Anonicelli thefts know?"

Pete took a hefty swallow of coffee. "I left a message for Agent Tuttle. The thieves also took art from the exhibit."

Pete and Sam told the other detectives what they knew about Dulcie Rodriguez and her son.

Sam concluded by telling about Dulcie's aborted call to her son.

Loloma finished his note on the board. "It could be that the thieves got to her."

"She's an eyewitness," said Pete. "It concerns me that she hasn't gone home or contacted her son. Martinez, I'd like you to focus on finding her. It's possible she could be missing because she had something to do with the burglary."

Sam jerked forward. "Hang on, Pete. There's no way in hell she would do that and let her boy suffer."

Ah! Pete had expected this reaction. While Sam had kept his relationship with Santos on a proper professional basis, he knew Sam cared greatly about the direction the boy's life was headed. This was a good reminder to enter this investigation with an open mind.

Pete held up a hand. "It's unlikely, I agree, but nevertheless you will remember it. The value of the stolen art is a powerful motive, and she does have a key to the place. Flag her credit cards and bank accounts for activity. Get what you need from her home."

Sam nodded and settled back.

Pete picked up the narrative again. "Within minutes of Sam's notifying dispatch, things started to get strange. Otto Griffin, the gallery manager, called 911 about the burglary. He said the bartender from the bistro across the street had called him at home to tell him there was something going on at the gallery and he should come right away and check it out."

"What time did Griffin get the call?" Loloma poised his marker at the whiteboard.

"A few minutes after ten," said Pete.

Ruiz jumped in. "After Griffin told us that, I checked with the bistro. Neither the bartender nor other staff had noticed anything, nor had they made phone calls. The bartender claimed he didn't know the name of the manager, let alone have his home phone number."

"Could Griffin have been in on the burglary and lied, making up that story to save his butt?" asked Sam.

"Can't rule that out," said Pete, "but I got a little ahead of myself. Let me tick off the sequence of arrivals for you." He touched his thumb. "When patrol got there, the lights were on, back door open, security system off." He touched his next finger. "Guard unconscious at his desk, alive, but vital signs were weak."

Pete kept ticking off arrivals. "Patrol called an ambulance and said Griffin arrived five minutes later. Ruiz and I got there when the ambulance did. The manager, Griffin, called the owner at ten-fifteen. The owner, Adams, arrived at ten-thirty."

Pete's cell phone rang. "Schultz." As he listened, his eyes closed briefly. "I'm sorry to hear that."

He hung up. "*Scheisse.*" He paused, then looked around at the expectant faces. "Bruno Keller just died. There will be an autopsy, of course, but his blood and urine tests showed a lethal amount of a prescription sleeping medication and alcohol in his system. Now it's a homicide investigation."

"Homicide?" asked Loloma. "Or stupid behavior on the guard's part?"

"There were two cups from the bistro on the desk by Keller," said Ruiz. "One had dregs enough so toxicology can analyze it. One cup had lipstick on it."

"Could Rodriguez be mistaken? Could she have seen a man and a woman?"

"Don't know at this point," said Ruiz. "The wastebasket next to where the guard sat was empty except for a chocolate box, which had held six truffles. All six wrappers were in the trash. I'm curious what those truffles contained. Forensics has the packaging. Griffin said the guard was a chocoholic and that a courier had delivered the box during the reception. It was addressed to Keller with an attached thank-you tag."

Sam looked up from his notes. "Who did the courier work for?"

"Griffin didn't recall," answered Pete.

Ruiz sat back. "Griffin told the guard about the gift on the desk. He said the guard was fine then—wasn't acting unusual at all."

Loloma capped his marker. "The cups, the box and the wrappers still being there make it appear that Griffin might be telling the truth."

Pete nodded. "I interviewed Griffin briefly when I got there, then set him to getting the staff and guest lists. It's a logistical challenge. Well over two hundred people were there last night."

"How about the gallery owner?" asked Sam. "Where was he during all this?"

Pete circled the name in his notes. "Adams said he left when the reception ended, about seven p.m., and took Adelle Gupta, the woman in charge of the exhibits, and the judges to their hotel. They had drinks and talked until eight. Then Adams went home, watched TV, and fell asleep."

Sam scribbled a note. "I don't suppose anyone could corroborate the owner's alibi?"

"Adams said his son was home, but he was in his room, and the door was shut. They didn't make contact."

"The security system," said Sam. "It has to have been sabotaged or disarmed. What company?"

"Dupre Security Systems," said Pete. "I had Cecil Dupre meet me at the crime scene this morning. Ex FBI, though that information doesn't go beyond us. Ruiz and I have been working with him on the Guy Roquet investigation."

Pete turned to Loloma. "I want you to follow up with forensics on the chocolates and the bistro cups. Find out all you can about Keller.

"Ruiz, you and I will interview the judges and Ms Gupta before they leave town. After that, we'll talk with Griffin."

"Got it. And then the artists whose work was stolen?" asked Ruiz.

Pete swallowed the last of his coffee. "Yes, I've asked for that information to remain quiet. I want to see their reactions when they learn of it."

Pete's phone rang and he looked at the number. "Hang on. It's Tuttle." After a brief conversation, he hung up and said, "He's flying in. I'm meeting with him this afternoon."

He put his notebook away and eyed his team. "We'll touch base at four p.m. back here."

CHAPTER FIFTY-EIGHT

As Sam left the detectives' meeting, Santos called him.

"I can't find my phone. Diego and me are going to my apartment. Can you meet us there?"

"I'm on my way there now," said Sam.

When Sam got to the apartment complex, he spoke with the patrolman, who had seen nothing unusual while he was there during the night.

As Sam finished talking to him, Diego arrived.

Santos jumped out of Diego's truck and ran to Sam. "Have you found Mom yet?"

"Afraid not," Sam responded. "Did your phone show up?"

Diego shook his head. "We looked all over before Santos called you."

"I bet Tuffy knocked it onto the floor after you grabbed him," said Santos.

In the apartment, they looked around where the cat had knocked over the pile. Nothing.

"Let me call your number," said Sam. "Did you leave your phone on?"

"Yeah, I thought Mom might call again."

Sam called the number but heard no ringing in the apartment or outside. "When was it last charged?"

Santos's shoulders slumped in defeat. "Yesterday."

"Was patrol here the whole night?" asked Diego.

"On and off. He responded to several calls during his shift."

Santos ran to the counter and pointed to where their note lay. "Look!" he said, wide eyed. "Somebody's been in here. I left the horny toad on top of the note. It's what Mom and I always do. Did you guys move it?"

The toad was a good two feet away from the note. Sam shook his head and glanced at Diego.

"Didn't go near it," said Diego.

Sam touched Santos's shoulder. "I saw you put it there. We'll check it for prints. Right now, pretend you're a detective like me. Look for anything that's not right."

Santos scanned the rooms. Then his face grew angry. "They took some pictures."

Sam pulled a notebook from his pocket. "Tell me. I'll report your phone stolen too."

"One of me in my basketball uniform. One of my mom and dad. My favorite picture of him. I want it back."

"Diego, can you help Santos pack more things in case he has to stay with you longer?" asked Sam.

While they packed, Sam bagged the horny toad, stowed it in his car, then checked with the manager of the apartment complex. Security cameras? No. Sam looked but could find no sign of forced entry.

Diego and Santos had finished when Sam came back. "Santos, I need you to find another good picture of your mom to help look for her. And recent bank statements and bills from her credit cards. We'll flag those accounts. If she or someone else uses them, it may help find her."

A little before eleven-thirty, Saturday morning, Karen and Dom walked into the police department. She felt a weird combination of eagerness to find out what was going on and apprehension that she wasn't going to like what she'd hear. Sam hadn't told them much.

This morning, she and the other exhibit artists had received an altogether unsatisfying email from William Adams, saying the exhibit was postponed and the gallery temporarily closed. The police were investigating an incident that happened there last night. No specifics given.

Dom gave their names to the officer at the window, and they sat to wait. Karen tapped her foot impatiently.

Soon they were ushered into a small, second-story room with a window overlooking the street. The furnishings were simple—a table and several chairs. Pete rose as they came in.

"Have you found Dulcie yet?" asked Karen.

"Unfortunately, no," said Pete. "We have a BOLO out for her. I put Sam in charge of the search."

Karen studied Pete's tired face. She couldn't detect that he was holding things back. Just concern.

"Tell me what you observed at the reception last night," said Pete as they sat.

Karen tried to put Dulcie's image out of her head and focus on the gala. "It was special to me. The impact of all that art focused on the quote was very moving."

"Did you hear any unusual or confrontational exchanges?" asked Pete.

"It was cordial," said Dom. "Lots of praise for Adams."

"Anything out of the ordinary?"

"Nothing until a ditzy artist crashed the reception," said Karen.

Interest sparked Pete's expression. "Tell me about that."

"I was talking to Joaquin Jimenez, the sculptor, when she burst in," said Karen. "He said her name was Purity Gold. She made a big stink about her work not being accepted. The reporter standing near us recorded it all on her phone."

"Did you catch the reporter's name?"

Karen shook her head. "She was from the *New Mexican*, and her article was in today's paper."

"I'll contact her." Pete made a note.

"What did happen last night, Pete?" asked Dom.

"Sam told you there was a burglary?"

Karen nodded.

Pete handed her a piece of paper. On it were eight names, all artists from the exhibit, her own name among them. She looked at Pete curiously. "This looks to be a list of winners, though I don't—" She stopped, afraid of what he was going to say. "What was taken?"

"The burglars took the entries from those artists."

Karen's mouth dropped open. She blinked several times.

"No!" She swallowed. "No. Pete, people have to see this exhibit. They can't take it."

Pete's eyes were troubled, but he didn't take back the words.

Karen blinked again. "My tapestry," she whispered. "My God, no."

Dom put his hand over hers.

"All that work. The time. The pain." Her eyes teared up. "Why? Why the contest pieces? Really valuable paintings hang in that gallery. Why my tapestry?"

"Karen, I'm so sorry."

Karen's eyes met Pete's. He'd taken a personal interest in this work; it meant hope to him too.

"They took only one of the Jimenez pair of bronzes—the man protecting the policeman," said Pete. "You may remember a painting by a seventeenth-century artist, Anonicelli? It's gone too."

"William had that painting well-protected," said Karen.

"Evidently not well enough," said Pete. "It's a curious combination of items to take. Muddies the motive. Money? A grudge against Adams? Someone whose work was rejected so they wanted to spoil it for everybody?"

"Pete, not my tapestry." Karen bit her lip.

Pete's expression grew somber. "The security guard, Keller, died this morning. It's now a homicide investigation."

"Jesus," said Dom. "Dulcie?"

Karen looked at him in shock. "Dulcie!" She stretched her hand across the table to cover Pete's wrist. "If they killed Bruno … What if they caught her?"

◆ ❖ ◆

Pete watched as Otto Griffin came cautiously into the interrogation room. He was curious to see if the man's story remained consistent.

He explained the routine and asked him to go over his actions after the last gala guest left.

"I closed out the register in the gift shop."

"What can you see from there?"

"The front entrance, all the art displayed in what we call the Near Room. The caterers were cleaning up. I couldn't see in the kitchen, of course, but I could hear them. Quite a jovial group."

"What time did the caterers leave?"

"At seven-thirty. The head guy checked with me. I went back to lock the door."

Pete glanced at his notes. "I understand you have a cheat sheet for the security system. Has anyone had access to that?"

"No. It's been in my wallet ever since Cecil gave it to me. No one even knows it's there."

"Is it there now?"

Otto pulled his wallet from his pocket, found the sheet, and showed it to Pete.

"Does anyone besides you and Adams have the codes?"

"The security guards, of course. And Cecil. Have you found Guy yet?"

"Not yet. What happened after the caterers left and you locked up?"

"I put the money away, said good night to my lady and left. It was seven forty-five."

"Your lady?"

Otto flushed. "You might think it's strange, but I feel a personal relationship with the *Lady in White*. I talk to her quite often. That's no crime, is it?"

"No, Mr. Griffin, it's not."

"Are we through?"

"Not quite. You said chocolates had been left for the guard?"

"They were delivered by courier shortly after the reception began. I signed for them. Thought it was strange, but also a very thoughtful thing to do."

"What courier company? Did you see their vehicle?"

"I didn't. I couldn't tell you the name of the company. Before I left, I put them on my desk where I knew Bruno'd find them, plus I told him. He came as I was leaving."

"What was the first indication you had that something was wrong?"

"Someone from the bistro called me at home. Said there was something weird going on." Otto frowned.

"Your cell phone or your home phone?" Pete's pen was poised to make a note.

"Home phone. Land line. I'm trying to figure that out. I didn't think they knew me. Anyhow, I came back to find police swarming around, and Keller in the ambulance. How is he?"

Pete studied the open, inquisitive face. No hint of fear or apprehension. "He died this morning."

Otto's mouth opened in shock. "Died? But he's so young! He seemed fine last night. Oh, my. Did he have a heart attack or something?"

"There will be an autopsy, Mr. Griffin. We'll know in good time."

"Oh, my."

CHAPTER FIFTY-NINE

Karen turned off the music playing in the car. How could she listen to "Lark Ascending" when her mind was filled with gnawing worry over Dulcie? When the young guard lay dead, and her precious tapestry stolen? The dancing, soaring notes of the violin seemed wrong for the moment, or maybe they were too right, their poignant sadness too overwhelming.

"Damn it," she burst out.

Dom flicked a glance at her before turning back to his driving. Cerrillos Road was clogged with tourists. "My love?"

"I can't believe it. My tapestry. But I shouldn't be thinking about my art when Dulcie's life is in danger. The thieves must have caught up to her."

"Not necessarily," said Dom. "And I do understand your feelings. You lived and breathed that tapestry for months."

Images of Dulcie as they worked together streamed through Karen's mind. Dulcie's lip-biting concentration as she threaded the warps through the heddles. Her graceful movements as she blended the butterfly skeins. The mischievous light in her eyes as she told of Tuffy's antics with leftover yarn.

"This hurt so many," said Dom as he slowed for a light.

"Certainly did." Karen thought back to her euphoric experience, seeing the exhibit as a whole. Tears came to her eyes. "How dare they? To rob people of hope. To take Bruno's life. And Dulcie."

Dom's cell phone rang.

"That's Herb Nelson's number." He pressed the button to answer it through the car speakers.

"Hey, Dom, we stopped by the gallery to see the exhibit. Why is it a crime scene?"

Karen sat up straight. "You're here? Now? In Santa Fe?"

"Yes, we wanted to surprise you. We're at the Hog Bristle Bistro."

"We'll meet you there shortly," said Dom, switching lanes.

"But what happened?" Yolanda's voice came through the speaker.

"Long story. Tell you when we get there," said Karen. "It'll be wonderful to see you."

After welcoming hugs, the four sat in the outdoor dining area of the bistro, sipping their coffee. The corkscrew willow growing next to the low adobe enclosure sent tortured patterns of shade to dapple their table and the flagstones below.

All had ordered the green-chile cheeseburgers, a Bistro specialty. The invitation to stay at the ranch had been extended to the Nelsons and accepted. Karen and Dom told them about the thefts, Dulcie's disappearance, and the guard's death.

Karen sagged in her seat as their explanations ended. Her glance strayed to the yellow crime-scene tape across the street. Tourists wandered by, some stopping and pointing to the tape.

Last night's gala had been charged with positive energy. Guests should be enjoying the exhibit right now, rather than speculating on what happened.

"It just feels wrong," she choked out. "I can't sit idly by and wait for others to find Dulcie."

"The whole Niemöller exhibit emphasized the danger of indifference," said Dom.

A curled willow leaf drifted down to rest in front of Karen. She picked it up, her fingers straightening the pliable green smoothness. "When someone goes missing, the first forty-eight hours are the most critical."

"I'm going to call Sam," said Dom.

The waitress brought their burgers.

"Sam, can you use volunteers in your search?"

Dom's face lightened as he listened. "Her car? That's good news, isn't it? Why the frustration in your voice?"

Everyone went quiet.

"Where was it found?" asked Dom.

Karen crossed her fingers.

"Sure, I understand. Call us back when you can."

Dom tucked his phone back in his pocket. "Dulcie's friend, Vicky, lives off Calle Polvorienta. Both Dulcie's and Vicky's cleaning company cars were there, but no one was home. Sam's not getting much cooperation from the residents."

"As I recall," said Yolanda, "that neighborhood is mostly Spanish speaking."

"I can understand why some are reluctant to say anything," said Herb. "Why draw attention to themselves?"

Yolanda licked a bit of melted cheddar from the side of her bun. "I know Santa Fe is a sanctuary city, but trust is still a problem. Could we put up fliers and talk to folks? Does Sam have any printed?"

"I'll ask when he calls back."

Fifteen minutes passed until Dom's phone rang. He listened, holding up a hand to forestall their questions. "Sam, remember Herb and Yolanda? They'll help us go door-to-door with your fliers."

He smiled at the Nelsons. "A patrolman will meet us with fliers in an hour by the apartment where Dulcie's car is."

The Calle Polvorienta neighborhood was a palette of browns and tans broken up by dusty juniper bushes. The two-story apartment complex claimed unimaginative landscaping and a sun-drenched playground.

Soon they were armed with fliers and a map of where Sam believed they should concentrate. They split into pairs to work. Karen was frustrated by her poor Spanish, but Herb was fluent.

Each door they knocked at brought the same frustrating answer. No one had seen Dulcie. Finally, they came to a lower-floor apartment. Mexican pottery held vibrant red geraniums. Karen knocked, and a short, middle-aged woman answered. Her body turned slightly away from them, her shoulders rounded, almost like she felt the need to protect herself. Herb gave their spiel in Spanish. The woman shook her head.

They were running out of people to ask. Karen bit her lip in frustration. She stabbed her finger at Dulcie's photo and pleaded. "Please help. She's in danger. She has a little boy." Karen made no effort to wipe away the tear, which was sliding down her cheek.

Then Herb pointed at the yellow cars across the street. "Her car is there."

The woman answered in a hesitant voice.

Herb translated. "One of those cars belongs to the lady who lives there."

Karen answered quickly. "Vicky? Dulcie works with her. Where can I find Vicky? No one answered the door."

The woman asked a question.

Herb answered her, then translated. "We're just volunteers. Dulcie is a friend of ours."

"No ICE?"

Karen blurted out, "No! Please, the child needs his mother. His father was a soldier, killed in Iraq."

The woman made a face when Herb translated. She dropped her head, allowing a long black braid streaked with gray to fall over her shoulder.

The woman's voice began slowly. Karen turned to Herb for the English.

"ICE was here last night. She turned out her lights, locked her door and watched through curtains. She doesn't trust ICE. She heard yelling, doors slamming. They grabbed everyone in the house and took them away."

The woman spoke again.

"She doesn't care what they say," said Herb. "It isn't right to take mother from child."

The woman clasped her hands together and spoke.

"She wants to be certain we don't tell anyone she talked to us. She's got to live here, and she's not a snitch. I told her we wouldn't."

"*Gracias*," said Karen.

The woman smiled. "*Vaya con Dios.*"

They finished knocking on all the doors. Karen looked back at the woman's apartment, smiling as a curtain twitched into place.

When they were all back in the car, Dom called Sam to give him an update.

"An ICE raid," said Sam. "Figures. I guess I'm off to Albuquerque. Thanks, guys."

"Albuquerque?" asked Karen.

"The first stop when ICE pulls anything in Santa Fe."

"I know why you just can't call," said Herb.

They heard Sam's chuckle over the speaker. "It's harder for them to blow me off when I'm in their face. If I impress upon them that Dulcie's a citizen, that should make them a little more cooperative."

CHAPTER SIXTY

Sunday, August 6

"Come to the police station."

The request—no, the order—rattled Purity. They wanted to question her about the events at the Swift & Adams Gallery on Friday evening. The more she thought about it, the faster the butterflies swarmed in her gut.

She still got teary-eyed about poor Bruno. The news on television had been skimpy. She couldn't believe it. What did they do to him?

Such a sweetie. Now they'd never be married. Of course, he hadn't asked her, but he could have done. Would have done. Maybe. She'd never have been able to tolerate even a week at the back of beyond where they talked cows all the time.

Early Saturday morning, Ruben had showed up at her door with a duffle bag. He said they were painting the inside of his apartment, and could he leave some things with her? Then he went off to be with a friend who was going through chemo and couldn't be alone. So helpful.

She supposed that the police wanted to talk about her crashing the reception. What good would that do them? They couldn't know she'd been there later. How would they find out? She'd never watched cop shows to learn how they did stuff.

The police station was an alien world. Beige building in a brown landscape. Beige outside, beige inside. Walls covered with official-looking notices, and don't do this, don't do that. Uniformed officers separated from real people by glass. Butt-ugly hard chairs. They could have used art to liven up the place.

She gave her name to somebody behind a window and settled herself on a hard chair to wait. Soon they came to get her, taking her down a long hall, turning several times, going through more doors to a dinky gray room.

Two people rose when she was ushered into the room. One was an older man with receding grayish hair and ramrod upright posture. The other was a fit-looking woman with her dark hair skinned back. She wore almost no makeup. Why would a woman be a policeman?

"Ms Gold. I'm Lieutenant Schultz." The man motioned to the woman. "This is Detective Sergeant Ruiz."

They sat, and he said some stuff about recording, and she wasn't under arrest, but suddenly, looking into the man's hard gray eyes, Purity froze. He knew about the painting she'd hung at the gallery. Did they think she had something to do with the robbery?

She thought about running but had no idea how to get out of this place. She moved restlessly on her chair. It creaked. Her hands were wet. She wiped them on her leggings. She moistened her dry lips.

The lady cop left and came back with a bottle of water for her. She took a sip and relaxed some. The lady might be okay. Purity decided to look at her rather than the man.

The man started the questions. "On Friday night, there was a private reception at the Swift and Adams Gallery. You came uninvited. Can you tell us why?"

Purity told him about the contest, about how her entry must have been overlooked, because it was obviously better than what won. She came to convince the judges they'd made a mistake, and then, of course, they would include her in the show.

She glared at the man whose questions forced her to tell him she'd been thrown out. "That rent-a-cop grabbed hold of me. Assaulted me. I should have had him arrested."

"Can you tell us what you did for the rest of the evening?"

"I went to the bistro across the street, had a drink, and then went home."

"You didn't go back to the gallery?"

"Why would I do that? Everyone was gone." She wished this man would back off. She would rather talk with the woman.

"Not everyone," said the man. "Your friend, Bruno Keller, was there."

"My friend? Yes, I knew Bruno. But he was working. No, I went home."

"Ms Gold, we need the truth to find out who killed Bruno Keller."

"What happened? Did those men hit him over the head or something?"

"What men would those be?"

"Uh, the ones who stole the art. It was on TV."

"What made you assume the thieves were men?"

Purity was annoyed. He was trying to trick her. "Whatever. Men, women, gorillas—had to be somebody. And now poor Bruno's gone." A fat tear rolled down her cheek.

"Did you receive any calls while you were in the bistro that night? Answer carefully."

"I don't think so." Why didn't they ask her about her painting? What were they waiting for?

"Ms Gold, Keller's phone showed that he called you at ten minutes after eight. About ten minutes later, his phone showed an incoming call from you."

"Oh, now I remember."

"Did you go back to the gallery after the reception?"

"No. I told you that already."

"We found two coffee cups. One had lipstick. The cups will have fingerprints. We can prove you were there."

"Well, of course, I was. Just forgot for a moment. Bruno called me. He said he was sleepy and asked me to bring him some coffee, so I did—one for him, one for me."

"What kind of coffee?"

"Uh, I guess it must have been Irish coffee. Bruno likes it with double whiskey."

"So you and he sat there and drank the coffee?"

"I wandered around, looking at the art. When I came back Bruno was still sleepy. I gave him my coffee. I hadn't drunk much of it."

"When did you leave?"

"Not long after that. Bruno fell asleep. He was snoring, so I left."

"You didn't see anyone else?"

"No."

"What time was it when you left?"

"About eight-thirty." Should she tell them about the two guys?

"Think carefully. Did you let anyone else into the gallery?"

"No. I didn't let those guys in." Oops. Purity closed her eyes.

"Those guys?"

"Uh, when I was on my way out, I heard someone at the back door. I didn't want to get Bruno in trouble, so I hid in the kitchen. First one came in. He went up front – or as near as I could tell from what I heard. Then he came back and said, 'It's okay. He's asleep. Alarm's not even set.' Then the other came in, and they both went into the middle room. I got the hell out of there."

"Can you describe the men?"

"Never saw them."

"How about their voices?"

"Nothing special. One only said a few words." Purity frowned. The voice sounded familiar, but why tell the cops that when she didn't know who it was?

"Then what did you do?"

"I went home."

The detective stabbed her with those all-seeing gray eyes.

"Okay. I didn't want to get into trouble." Purity looked toward the lady cop. "Did those men kill Bruno? Did they shoot him?"

"Are you acquainted with Guy Roquet?" This time it was the lady cop asking.

"Who?"

"Guy Roquet. Maybe you met him at the Hog Bristle Bistro?"

"Never heard of him."

The woman kept on. "Ms Gold, before you leave, we need to have you fingerprinted. Since we know you were in the gallery, it will eliminate yours from others at the scene."

"What happens if I don't want to be fingerprinted?"

"Perhaps they would issue a warrant for your arrest."

Purity rolled her eyes. "I guess I'll let them."

"Ms Gold," said the man, "we will want to talk with you again."

Purity couldn't stand it anymore. "It's about my painting, isn't it? You wondered how it got there. What have you done with it?"

"Your painting?"

"I hung it while Bruno was drinking his coffee. I took some boring landscape off the wall and put it on the floor. I hung mine so when all the people came for the exhibit they'd see it, see how wonderful it was."

"Tell me about this painting."

"It's an abstract acrylic, in a fourteen-by-sixteen frame. Wonderful colors—purple, orange, yellow. Lots of swoopy lines. It's very avant-garde."

"Ms Gold, I don't remember seeing a painting of that description."

Purity spat out a crude word. "They stole my painting too?" She rolled her eyes. "The thieves had better taste than those frigging judges. My beautiful painting's worth thousands of dollars."

Pete settled back in his rolling chair after Purity had been escorted away, still free for the moment. He shook his head. "What a ditz."

Ruiz laughed. "What about the painting of hers? Is there a kernel of truth in her tale, or was that pure fantasy?"

Pete tapped his portfolio with his pen. "There was a landscape leaning against the wall in the Far Room, and an empty space on the wall where it had been."

"So it could have been the truth. We didn't know about it—it just came rolling out of her mouth." Ruiz stood and picked up her notes. "Do you suppose she realizes her Irish coffees contributed to Keller's death?"

"The amount of prescription medication probably would have been enough by itself. But was the drug in the chocolates or the coffee? Either Purity Gold is innocent or extremely clever. I'd say high on our suspect list, but she couldn't have done it alone."

CHAPTER SIXTY-ONE

In Books and Bearclaws, Krista and Leyla sat on low stools in the area where middle-grade fiction gave way to young-adult books. Santos hunkered down nearby, perusing several sports-hero books he'd pulled from the shelves. Krista reached for a mystery with a cover she didn't recognize.

A man's quiet voice from the other side of the bookshelves caught her attention. "Hang on a minute. Too many to overhear."

Krista opened her eyes wide in curiosity. Overhear what? She looked up to see a tan, tweedy-looking flat cap on brown wavy hair on the other side of the bank of shelves. Couldn't see his face, but he spoke again.

"Okay, I'm in the kids' section. Nobody here. I can talk now."

She grabbed Leyla's arm and pantomimed for her to remain silent, but her attention was focused on the man. His hand, showing the cuff of a tan leather jacket, reached up to tug the brim of the cap.

"What have you heard? Have they found that damn cleaning lady yet?"

Santos's head whipped around; his eyes opened wide. Both Krista and Leyla gave him the be-quiet sign.

"You're okay as long as she doesn't go near the cops." The hat and the voice moved along the shelf away from them, toward a display of picture books. The voice dropped; the words became indistinguishable.

In a few seconds, the man would cross an open aisle. Would Krista see his face?

He was speaking louder now, sounding more annoyed. "Don't worry about it. Calm down, and don't call me again."

He ended the call and pivoted, his footsteps receding back into the coffee area. Krista peeked around the shelves. The man in the tan flat cap picked up his cup from a table near where her dad was sitting and turned toward the door. Krista motioned for the other two to stay put. She rounded the bookshelf and put the book she was carrying on the other side. Then she picked up some freebie bookmarks from a display and came back.

"Did you get a good look at him?" whispered Santos.

Krista shook her head and whispered back, "No. He turned away, and now he's leaving."

"How can we find out who he is?" whispered Leyla.

Krista handed Leyla a bookmark. "Take this, go to the barista, and say the guy in the tan leather jacket dropped it. Ask him if he knows his name. Ask him if he can give it to him next time he comes in."

"Why wait?" asked Santos. "Let's go after him."

As he moved to follow, Krista grabbed his wrist. "No, we don't want him to know about us. It's not a good idea to meet him."

"Why me?" asked Leyla.

"Santos can't. It's his mom that's missing. The guy might know what Santos looks like. And it was my gramma's tapestry that was stolen. He might know who I am. He doesn't have any reason to think you are connected to the case."

"The case?" asked Leyla.

"Yeah. We're going to find out what happened to Santos's mom. It must have been her he was talking about."

"Do you really think we can?" Santos wore an eager expression.

"We've learned about solving mysteries," said Krista. "Cliff's books are good teachers." She pulled a couple of his books from the shelf and showed them to Santos. "I have them all if you want to read them."

"You know the guy who wrote these?"

"Silly, so do you. He was at our house on Gramma's birthday."

"Who do you suppose that man was talking to on the phone?" asked Leyla.

Santos looked worried. "When Mom called me that night, she said she saw two people. What if one of them was this guy?"

"He must be," said Krista.

"Did he murder the guard?" Leyla's voice was filled with horror. "Should we tell Dad? Or Pete?"

"Let's see what we can find out first," said Krista. "I'll use the dropped bookmark story and ask my dad if he knows who the guy was."

"I wish my mom would come home. What if—"

Leyla reached out to touch Santos's arm. "We'll find her." She marched off toward the barista.

Krista went to her dad's table and set the bookmark in front of him. "The guy who was sitting at the table next to you dropped this. Do you know who it was?"

Anton shook his head. "Didn't pay him any attention. He can get that freebie anytime."

"I'll put it back." Krista returned to the kids' area.

Leyla came up, her face alight. "It worked. The barista says he's a nice guy. I got his first name anyway. It's Ruben!"

Krista raised her hands in a high five to Leyla, then to Santos. "Super. Wouldn't it be great if we could catch the bad guys and find Santos's mom and the stolen art?"

Chapter Sixty-Two

Why didn't his mother come home?

Tears threatened as Santos let himself into the pen where the male alpacas were kept. As he turned to latch the gate, he saw Coach Martinez enter the big house with Diego and Maria.

His coach had come after everyone had eaten dinner. He took Santos aside and talked to him. Told him about her being picked up by ICE and taken to El Paso. Santos appreciated that—talking with him first because it was his mother who was missing. He'd treated him like he was important, not just a kid.

He'd hoped for good news, but there wasn't much, leaving him with a hollow ache inside.

The alpacas crowded around, sniffing him for treats. They soon lost interest in his empty hands and wandered away. Only Thunderbump stayed, smelling his hair, tickling his skin with velvety lips, and nuzzling his cheeks where the tears ran.

This was so hard.

If his dad were here, he'd have driven down to El Paso and found her. He'd never missed his father more than right this minute. His fingers pushed into Thunderbump's fleecy topknot, and stroked down his long, cloud-gray neck, sinking into the downy softness. The yearling leaned into him.

"I want my mommy, my daddy," Santos whispered.

All was quiet, except for Thunderbump's comforting humming.

♦ ❖ ♦

Karen and Dom waited in the family room with Maria, Diego, Herb, and Yolanda for Sam to finish talking with Santos. When Sam joined them, Karen poured him a mug of coffee. Then she sat on the edge of her seat, anxious to hear from a police perspective how the search for Dulcie was coming and learn of ways she might help Santos.

Diego's eyes focused on Sam. "How's Santos doing?"

Sam cradled his mug. "He's trying hard to keep it together."

"He's been worrying about his phone," said Diego. "He's sure his mother is trying to call him."

"How does it work with stolen cell phones, Sam?" asked Karen. "I could buy him a new one."

"But he'd need his old number so Dulcie could call him," said Diego.

"Could I get him one with his old number?" asked Karen.

"It's not that simple," said Sam. "He's a minor. The carrier contract would be in Dulcie's name. I've been thinking, you as one of Dulcie's employers, and I, as the policeman who recommended he stay with you, and Santos should go downtown. The three of us should clarify all this with the Children, Youth, and Families Department and maybe a judge about a temporary guardianship, or whatever they want to call it. Then with their support, we'll go to the phone carrier, get a new phone, and impress upon them that it's important to have his old number so his mother can reach him."

Karen nodded. "I'd be—"

"Wait," interrupted Diego, "I want to be there too. He's living in my home. He and I have spent a lot of time together since Dulcie has been working here. I care about that boy, even though we're not related by blood. I don't want to be left out of this." Passion and conviction rang in his words, strengthening the plea.

Karen met Diego's eyes. "You're right to ask. I think you should come."

Sam nodded. "I'm glad you spoke up. The CYFD looks at kinship. Their definition goes beyond blood to other bonds and relationships."

"That's settled," said Karen. "Sam, let us know where and when. We'll be there."

"You must be trying to track the thief's location by pinging his cell phone," said Dom. "Have you had any luck?"

"None. Could be turned off, but I'm guessing that early on, he got what information he wanted from it and then ditched it."

"You haven't told us yet what you found out about the ICE raid," said Dom.

Sam sighed. "I was hopeful at first. ICE did take her to Albuquerque. For some reason, she had no identification, so they fingerprinted her and sent her to El Paso with the others. They got the results of the prints there, proving she was a citizen. They released her about noon yesterday and dropped her off in El Paso in an area full of immigrant-hospitality centers. At that time, we didn't even know ICE had been involved."

"Yolanda and I volunteer at one of those hospitality centers," said Herb.

"How about the BOLO?" asked Dom. "Wouldn't ICE have seen that?"

"They should have," said Sam. "To be fair, they're probably overwhelmed with a flood of alerts every day. Damned frustrating bureaucracy to work with. I got in touch with the El Paso PD about the BOLO. They only contacted the bus stations because she couldn't fly without identification."

Maria looked puzzled. "No identification? Where was her purse? Would she have money or credit cards?"

"Her purse is tan leather," said Karen, "with a shoulder strap."

"She'd bring it inside the gallery, not leave it in the car," said Maria. "Probably put it on a counter."

Dom shook his head. "If so, there's a good chance the thieves took it."

Karen shot a glance at him. She didn't like the sound of that.

Sam slapped his knee. The noise brought her eyes back to him.

"That's why! She called her son first. Didn't want him to let anyone else in but her. I wondered why she thought they'd know where she lived unless they knew each other. That must be how the thief got her address and her keys. That's how he could get in and steal Santos's phone."

"Maybe she's been trying to call Santos," said Karen, "but the thieves are getting those calls."

"If that phone was on, we would have tracked him down," said Sam.

"Did her friend, Vicky, make it back okay?" asked Karen.

"Yes," said Sam. "Vicky, who has a green card, was still being held when they released Dulcie. She has no idea where she could be."

"My God," said Karen, "this just gets worse and worse."

"Herb," said Dom, "you let people use the phones at the centers. She could have called the police from there. Why didn't she?"

"It can be crazy on Saturdays. Often the phones are busy, and lines of folks are waiting," said Yolanda."

"Have you contacted the hospitality centers in El Paso?" Herb asked.

"I'll follow up on that," said Sam, "though the El Paso PD said they would."

"We're going back tomorrow morning," said Herb. "It'd be worth a shot to visit the centers personally."

"Great," said Sam. "Face-to-face is better."

"I suppose it's possible she could get a ride with someone," said Yolanda.

Karen sat back, thinking of when they'd toured the center. Busy, crowded. Desperate, hopeful people. Volunteers doing their best. Get a ride. The memory of someone doing good deeds niggled at her. She pulled out her phone and began scrolling through photos.

"What are you looking for?" asked Dom.

"While I was waiting for you and Ted outside the center, I took lots of pictures. I overheard a nun saying she made trips to Albuquerque a couple times a week. She offered rides to women traveling alone. I wondered if by chance I'd gotten a picture of her."

Maria looked hopeful. "Do you suppose Dulcie met up with her or some other kind soul?"

"She called herself Sister Mary something. Mary Catherine."

Dom shut his eyes. "Hundreds of nuns have that name! How—"

"Aha! Here's her photo," said Karen. She handed her phone to Sam.

"Can you send this shot to me?" asked Sam, passing the phone on to Yolanda.

Yolanda enlarged the photo with her fingers. "To us too. Somebody we work with might remember her. Interesting crucifix she's wearing."

"The cross might indicate what order she's from," said Dom.

"It makes sense for Dulcie to approach a nun," said Maria. "For a woman traveling alone, it would be a godsend. You can't be too careful these days."

The small group became quiet, Karen wondering what could have happened that kept Dulcie from coming home.

Into the silence, Sam spoke. "Karen, Dom, what are you going to do about your engagement dinner tomorrow night?"

Karen's jaw dropped. "Oh, my God! I totally forgot."

"Me too," said Dom. "How can we—"

Karen reached out a hand to Dom. "We'll have to postpone it. A celebration when Dulcie's missing? Oh, Dom."

His hand squeezed hers. His face filled with sorrow, resignation. The room became quiet again.

"For better, for worse." Sam's thumbs had been busy on his phone. "I hadn't forgotten. In fact, I hope we do have your dinner."

Karen studied Sam's face. "But Santos?"

Diego leaned forward in his chair. "What he needs more than anything right now is someone to stand with him and help him through it."

"A family." Dom's soft voice. "Marriage isn't just for happy times. This dinner won't be the same, but Sam has a good point."

Karen's eyes flew to Dom's. The feeling seemed to come from her toes, flooding through her being. "I love you so much. You always surprise me."

He smiled at her before turning to Maria. "Maria? What do you think?"

"If Sam and Diego can make it right with Santos, I'm all for it. We can adjust."

Anton came into the family room, followed by Skyla. "Sam texted me. A family meeting. What's up?"

They explained their thoughts to them.

Anton's first question was to Dom. "What do you feel your daughter would say?"

Dom's jaw worked. "I—I don't know that she'd come in any case."

"But the food? Isn't that short notice?" asked Karen.

"I hadn't forgotten the dinner," said Maria. "I was just waiting to see how it played out. Karen, I know you love sauerbraten. Well, the meat, enough for twenty, has been marinating since Thursday. I figured if we didn't use it for the engagement dinner, we'd eat it anyway."

"Maria, you are absolutely amazing," said Karen.

"My dad was wondering if he could bring chocolate silk pies," said Sam. "He wants to contribute something. He's highly in favor of this match."

Anton nodded briefly. "That's settled. We will have the dinner, but may I suggest a change?"

Karen looked at her son.

"We'll use the dining room," he said. "Maria and Diego eat with us when we use the breakfast room, but they've generally declined when it's a more formal dining room occasion. Santos won't feel supported unless he's part of the group at that table," said Anton. "I want this to be a sit-down meal with everyone, including Maria, Diego, and Santos."

"Oh, but we couldn't—" Maria bit her lip.

"Certainly you can, Maria," said Dom. "Anton's right. It makes a statement to Santos."

"I agree," said Karen.

"Me too," said Krista from a stool at the kitchen counter.

Karen turned to her in surprise. "I didn't know you were here."

Krista shrugged. "Dad knocked on my door when he went past. Said there was a family meeting. I'm family."

Chapter Sixty-Three

Monday, August 7

Just after eight a.m., Ruben parked some distance away from Purity's apartment, but with a good view of her front door and car. Now he wanted her out of the way so he could box up the Anonicelli and send it to the buyer. She'd bought his story about his apartment being painted and his needing to stash his duffle with her. He called her number.

"Purity, my friend's daughter is visiting him, so I'm free for a while. Could you meet me at the bistro for breakfast?"

Purity's voice was enthusiastic. "Ooh, yes. I'll leave right away."

He waited until she left, then let himself into her apartment.

He'd never met the buyer, only knew he lived in Florida. His orders had been to ship each Anonicelli to a courier, part of the buyer's trusted entourage. As soon as Ruben got the rest of his money, he'd disappear into another life. He already had a disguise and persona in place.

Ruben had been in Purity's apartment often enough to know where she kept everything. In her workroom he found the packing materials he needed. Helping himself to her scissors, he cut bubble wrap to fit a carton. From a card in his wallet, he copied the name and address of the courier onto a shipping label.

He retrieved his duffle from the closet where he'd stashed it and pressed the sequence of numbers on the combination lock.

He'd take one last look at the art someone was paying him five hundred thousand dollars for—half down, and half when they had it. The buyer had become increasingly impatient. Now he and his goons could get off his back and send him the rest of his money.

He pulled the duct tape from the fleecy blanket material he'd wrapped around the painting at the gallery and unfolded the fabric.

What the—

Blobby, garish colors of purple, orange and yellow emerged from the soft black material. This was not the lady, but Purity's garbage.

Frantically Ruben looked at the other two paintings in the duffle. Where was the Anonicelli? He'd put it between those two paintings himself.

That bitch! How had she gotten into his bag to switch it? Where would she have hidden it?

In a panic, he started on the closet, rummaging through everything. He flipped through her paintings, yanked things out of drawers, heaped things in piles.

Having torn apart her workroom, he moved to her bedroom, alarmed at the time on her bedside clock. She would be back soon. He pulled things from the closet, letting them fall where they would.

Then Ruben heard the front door open and charged into her living room to confront Purity. "Where is my painting? What have you done with it?"

"You said to meet you at the bistro. Why are you here?"

"I said I'd meet you here and take you to the bistro. You never listen." The lie rolled smoothly off his tongue. "You took it. Where is it?"

"That's not what you said." Purity's face grew red.

Ruben grabbed her shoulders and shook. "Don't play innocent with me."

"Stop it." Purity pulled away. "What the hell's gotten into you?"

"Where's the Anonicelli?" he roared.

"I don't even know what a nonny chelly is."

Ruben pushed open the door of her studio, slamming it against the wall. Crunching over her paintings on the floor, he grabbed his duffle and shook it at her. "It was in my bag. Where is it? Tell me now, bitch, or you'll be sorry."

Purity stood in the doorway, her mouth hanging open as she looked at the shambles. She bent and picked up a painting, cradling the canvas with swoopy lines in its splintered frame to her chest.

"My painting, my beautiful painting." Her voice was high-pitched and thready. "How did you get this? I hung it in the gallery."

He threw his duffle against a wall where it slid to the floor. "Where is the Anonicelli from the gallery?"

"I've never seen you like this." She looked bewildered. "From the gallery—"

Her mouth dropped again, and her eyes grew huge.

"You're the thief!" Her expression changed. "I'll tell."

"That would be incredibly stupid—incriminating yourself. Your sleeping pills killed your precious guard. They'll have you for murder. Now where is my painting?"

"You killed Bruno?" Her eyes narrowed.

With a harsh, wailing *ooooh*, Purity snatched up the scissors. Raising them high, she lunged toward him. Her cry rose to a piercing screech.

He grabbed her wrist and wrenched the scissors away. "Stop it, you vicious little harpy!"

She snatched up her palette knife, swinging at him again and again. He put up his arms in defense. One blow connected, and the point of the knife sank into his cheek. Blood ran down his face.

Still, she kept at him. He backhanded her and knocked the pointy metal tool out of her hand. It flew across the room to clatter on the floor. She came at him again, face distorted in anger, fingernails outstretched, raking his skin.

Ruben ducked away and lashed out with the scissors he still held, hitting her in the neck. Blood sprayed. He blinked to clear the red film from his eyes.

Her expression changed from anger to horror. He let go of the scissors, and she crumpled to the floor, her eyes wide open. Red pulsed around the scissors to pool beside her.

Damn! Now what? Blood all over him. Everywhere! His stomach heaved.

Rushing to the kitchen away from the sight, Ruben washed off his face and hands. He swore as the water hit his torn cheek, then pressed a cloth against the wound to stop the bleeding.

Don't panic. Think. Erase the evidence of his being there.

But first—find the Anonicelli. He finished tearing the place apart with no luck.

The growing urgency to leave finally overtook his need to search for the Anonicelli. He went back to the workroom, sidestepped the body with its wide, unseeing eyes, grabbed his duffle, and emptied it out. He retrieved several articles of his from the bedroom and bathroom. Her purse went into his bag. Didn't have time to look through it now.

Stripping off his bloody shirt and stuffing it in his bag, he looked down at his T-shirt. That would never do. He ripped it off, put it on again with the back to the front, and put his jacket on over it. It felt weird, but the blood didn't show. *Calm down, you fool.*

It was time to take the duffle to his car, come back, and methodically erase the last traces of his presence.

As he stowed the duffle in his hatchback, a white car with government plates, and two cop cars turned into the drive. Heart racing, trying to appear casual, Ruben got in and drove away.

Rage seethed as the rearview mirror showed several police officers moving toward Purity's door.

There was nothing worse than effing loose ends, and this was all unraveling before his eyes.

◆ ❖ ◆

Pete, search warrant in hand, arrived at Purity Gold's apartment complex. With him were Ruiz and four patrol officers. Gold was a person of interest based on evidence relevant to the theft of paintings from the gallery and the murder of the guard. Purity's prints had been on the landscape painting leaning against the wall in the gallery. She admitted being there.

Perhaps if they arrested her for the gallery burglary and the murder of Bruno Keller, she would squeal on her accomplices.

Near her apartment door, Pete froze and put out his hand to stop the others. He pointed to the sidewalk. Reddish marks and partial shoeprints in the same red. He and Ruiz put on gloves.

"Looks wet."

Pete went to the door, turned the knob, and it swung open, showing things thrown around. "Ms Gold, are you there? It's Lieutenant Schultz, police."

Silence.

"Anyone here?" called Ruiz.

Pete pulled his gun and stepped carefully to avoid treading on anything. The place had been ransacked. He motioned Ruiz to the kitchen and the rooms on the right. The coat closet door to his left was open. Carefully he determined no one was hiding there. His eyes swept the living room and looked into the workroom.

"*Heilige scheisse!*" He stepped carefully in and put his fingers on Purity's wrist. He shook his head as Ruiz peeked in the door.

"All the rooms are a mess. I didn't see anyone else."

"Take a good look at this room, and we'll leave it for forensics." He gestured toward the painting near the body. "Purple, orange, swooping lines. And look. Is that another weapon there?" He pointed to a palette knife lying by the wall. Red covered the point and splattered the floor near it.

Carefully they went outside. "Call dispatch. Tell them we need the medical examiner. Secure the scene."

A patrolman pointed down the sidewalk where the red spots petered out. Staying on the grass, others were looking for any signs along the walk.

Pete nodded. "Include that area. Olson, you and Perez go around back. Whoever killed her hasn't been gone long. Hell of a struggle."

He motioned to one of the officers. "Gonzales, find the apartment manager and see if they have surveillance cameras. Get the videos if they have them."

His prime suspect dead. "*Scheisse,*" he muttered. Well, they'd known there was more than one person involved. Was it Roquet or someone else?

Back to the drawing board.

CHAPTER SIXTY-FOUR

Where's the Anonicelli?

After he drove away from Purity's, Ruben parked in a strip mall to collect his thoughts.

If Purity had taken it, Ruben would have found it. If by a slim chance he'd missed it, he assumed the police would discover the painting when they went through her apartment looking for evidence. They would search her car, too, which he never had a chance to do.

He hated not being in control.

Take a deep breath. All was not yet lost.

There were other places it could be. He remembered wrapping it between two other paintings of the same size and putting all three into a box. Algie didn't have anything in his hands when he dropped him off Friday night. When Ruben got to Otto's, he'd taken those wrapped paintings out of the box, put them in his duffle, and locked it. Then he stashed everything else at Otto's.

What were the two paintings he'd grabbed to protect the Anonicelli? He hadn't even looked—it was only important they were the right size. Were they the ones that ended up in his duffle? He damn well hadn't taken Purity's crap.

She had to have switched them. How else would hers have ended up in his bag?

So where was the Anonicelli now?

How could Purity, who didn't have a brain in her head, have managed to screw things up?

There was another piece of that blanket material he used for wrapping. He thought he remembered putting it over the sculpture in the box, but maybe they'd used it to wrap something else, and that's what ended up in his bag. He'd been in a hurry, rattled by the cleaning lady.

The stash at Otto's hadn't been found yet. The Anonicelli could still be there.

Think. While he was chasing the cleaning lady, Algie, that slimy pond scum, was still filling boxes. When he got back, the boxes were all by the back door ready to load. It had to be at Otto's.

Tomorrow morning after the little turd of a manager had gone to work, he'd check out the stash. But before that, a visit to Algie seemed in order. Kid needed an iron fist to keep him in line.

Later that afternoon, Ruben drove slowly by where William and Algie lived. They sure didn't make it easy to keep tabs on a house in this area. Houses weren't lined up along streets, one after another. Rather they were plunked along ridges on lots chosen for views. And cars parked here with drivers inside looked altogether conspicuous. On the other hand, all that brushy growth gave privacy to watchers as well as inhabitants.

No car in the drive of the two-story, Mediterranean-style house. That meant William wasn't home yet. Good. Algie would probably be there alone. Ruben had never worked with somebody so young, and he'd never do it again. That phone call yesterday at the bookstore —Algie full of panic at hearing about the guard's death—should never have happened.

Couldn't trust him. Ruben was tempted to tighten the screws on Algie even more. It was best for Algie to take his own life. That would wrap up loose ends, except—

Just possibly the kid knew where the Anonicelli was. Until Ruben had recovered it, the kid was worth more to Ruben alive.

The people Ruben had been housesitting for were due back in the country soon. He had to wrap this up.

◆ ❖ ◆

Algie curled up against the headboard on his bed. He couldn't eat, couldn't sleep. He started a new digital painting, just messing around at first, but then it became personal—an expression of his own feelings. The image wound up making him feel more isolated and afraid. Walls seemed to be caving in on him, and he couldn't see any way out of the mess he'd made.

How could he have been so stupid? Ruben's lies played again and again in his head:

"Otto, Bruno, and I have a plan for making things right with your dad. Your face is too easy to read. It's best if you don't know the details."

"Your dad will be so grateful to you for solving this and recovering the art. Don't sweat the details. It'll be fine."

"Otto knows the art will be at his home. Bruno plans to take a sleeping pill, so he won't get in trouble."

Yeah, right. He'd wanted to believe Ruben so badly, that he hadn't allowed himself to think it through. Everything Ruben said was a lie.

Algie felt sick ever since he found the Anonicelli wrapped in that black material. With the force of a lightning bolt, he knew he'd been duped. Duped into believing this guy actually wanted to help him make things right with his dad. Hah! Ruben was only out for himself—a million-dollar heist—and Algie had made it so easy for him.

He'd been stunned, only rousing himself enough to hide the Anonicelli before Ruben returned, barely making it. He'd brought the art they were stealing to the backdoor while Ruben was off chasing the cleaning lady. And what had he done to her? Could he trust what Ruben said about her getting away?

This time, he'd really let his dad down. One could argue the deaths of his mother and Swift were accidents. This Algie had done deliberately. Nothing could make this better. Nothing he did was right. Everything he touched ended in disaster.

And then Bruno died. Every time Algie closed his eyes, he saw him. The cleaning woman's brown eyes haunted him too.

Ruben said no one would get hurt.

Algie couldn't go back. No do-overs.

Death was final.

◆ ❖ ◆

The doorbell rang when Algie was upstairs in his studio, painting—or trying to—for his class. He jumped at the sound. Who was going to be there? A policeman to cart him off to jail?

He slid his phone into his shirt pocket and crept down the front stairs into the living room. At the front door, he looked through the peephole.

It was Ruben, not the police.

He couldn't say which he preferred.

"I know you're there, Algie. Open the door."

He didn't trust Ruben at all. Algie pulled out his phone, activated the recording app Cecil had shown him, and put it back.

"Algie, open the damn door. You'll regret it if you don't."

He swung the door open and stepped back.

Ruben barged in, looking wild. Ugly wounds marred his face. "Where's the Anonicelli?"

"The Anonicelli? We took exhibit pieces."

"You fool. I need that painting. It was in the boxes with the others."

"You put the art at Otto's. Or did you lie about that too?"

"Don't get smart. You're the only one who could have taken it." Ruben stepped closer, fists clenched at his side. His features twisted into a snarl.

Algie moved backward, his heart pounding. He held up a defensive hand. Fear must have shown in his face because Ruben got nastier.

"You *should* fear me. If you don't give me that painting and keep your mouth shut, I can kill your father and make it look like you were the one who did it and stole the art."

"I don't know where—"

Ruben's threats slammed into his head.

Algie's voice cracked. "K-kill my dad?"

"You know those prescription sleeping pills your old man takes? Those pills were used in the chocolates that killed the guard?"

His dad took sleeping pills? First he'd heard of it. "You're lying."

"You really should set your security system when you go bike riding." Ruben's lips formed an evil smile. "It was your fault the guard died. You'll be arrested for murder, they'll try you as an adult, and you'll spend the rest of your life in prison."

Algie began breathing faster.

"And I will disappear." Ruben snapped his fingers. "Poof. Everything will point to you." He stabbed a finger at Algie's chest. "Your only hope is to come up with that Anonicelli and be quick about it."

"I don't know where it is."

"What do you have to live for? Your dad will always hate you. You'll never get out of prison. And you know what happens to young prisoners stuck in a cell all day, *all night* with some sex-starved maniac? You'll wish you were dead. That's what you have to look forward to unless you give me my painting."

"But—"

"If I don't get it soon, your old man will die. The cops will think you killed him. I can make that happen. You know I can."

CHAPTER SIXTY-FIVE

Karen's wishes for their engagement dinner were simple. What she really wanted was for Dulcie to be found safe and come home. If she couldn't have that, she wanted to support Santos and help him through this tough time. For herself? To strengthen the ties between the two families and for Dom to find joy even if his daughter would not come. How would this work? Had they been foolish not to postpone the dinner?

Fifteen people crowded around the big dining room table on Monday evening. Sixteen, if one counted Lucas, sleeping in his bassinet near his parents. She and Dom sat at the head of the table.

The sauerbraten, spaetzle, red cabbage, and asparagus were hits.

"What are the little crumbly things in the gravy?" asked Santos.

"Smashed-up gingersnaps," replied Maria.

"Gingersnaps!" exclaimed Sam. "Farah, get her recipe. This is so good."

"I like it," said Santos, turning to Maria. "Can you show Mom how to make it when she comes home?"

Maria smiled. "Sure. Be happy to."

At the end of the main course, Anton led off with the first toast. Then Sam. Frank gave a moving tribute and bevy of good wishes to them both. He didn't mention Dolores, but Karen could see the tiredness, the strain in his demeanor. It had to hurt that Dolores remained estranged from family.

Then it was Karen's turn. She stood, gathering her thoughts while moving to each dear face. "Thank you for being here, for gathering as our family. Thank you to the Martinezes, who welcomed me and who share Dom with me. Thank you to the Bjornson household for the welcome you have given Dom. We pledge to be and do our best for this extended family. *Skål*."

Dom rose. "Speaking from my heart. We grieve that everyone is not here, especially Dulcie. This is a sad time, an upsetting time in our lives, full of pain. Things aren't going like they should. They are broken. Yet marriage is not just for the happy times, not just for when we can feast and dance. Marriage is for the times when you hold someone who is crying, because of grief, loss, sickness, and pain. It is when you can say to the people you love and care about, we are here for you. It is for better or worse."

Then he drew Karen up to stand next to him. "And so, Karen and I chose to go ahead with this dinner. We hold you close, and we do believe hope is also with us and joy will come. Things don't always turn out the way we wish, but we face our future together. God willing, it will be a better day tomorrow." He raised his glass. "*Skål*."

Karen knew she would remember Dom's words forever.

Around the table there was a lot of raising of the glasses, nodding, meeting of the eyes. Solemn faces, young and old, drinking to the toast. As Karen's gaze went to Dom, not a shred of doubt remained in her mind.

Their marriage was meant to be.

Whatever the future brought, they would work it out.

CHAPTER SIXTY-SIX

Tuesday, August 8

Ruben picked the lock on Otto's backdoor. The idiot didn't even have a deadbolt—child's play for him. After he entered, he checked quickly, looking for any sign that Otto might have found the stash.

Ruben sneered at Otto's utilitarian taste in décor. He doubted anything had been modernized since the place was built. In the living room, several oil portraits hung on the walls. Otto's interests were obvious in the massive bookshelf crammed with art books. An easy chair, a floor lamp, an ancient, uncomfortable-looking couch, and a bulky older model TV completed the dreary room. Stodgy, predictable, just like Otto.

As Ruben went into the spare room, he heard voices at the front door.

What? He'd seen Otto leave. Otto should be at work. Ruben went to the window and was surprised when it slid open quietly.

Otto's voice came from the hall. "I'm glad you could help me out, Cecil. It's probably just nerves, but ever since the night of the robbery, I had the feeling that somebody had been in my house."

"This should make you feel safer," came another voice. "After I finish your installation, anybody breaks in, it rings at the police station."

Who was Cecil?

Otto was putting in a security system?

Ruben sat on the windowsill, swung his legs over, and dropped to the ground. He ran out the back gate and around the block to his car across the street. Too close for comfort. Why wasn't the fool at work?

Cecil followed Otto into his entryway, half-listening to his drone-like voice.

"I've nothing valuable except for art books. Nothing that would excite a thief."

"I'll put the panel near the door so it's convenient." Cecil's well-trained eyes swept the hall and the living room.

Otto started toward the kitchen with the bag he was carrying. "What—" He stopped and frowned. "That's odd. I never open that door. I'm sure it was shut when I left."

Cecil passed Otto and peered into a dusty, neglected room. The curtains at the window fluttered gently in the breeze. The screen leaned against the wall. Senses alert, he crossed to the window and looked out. The back gate was ajar. The ground-cover rocks below the window had been disturbed and part of a lavender plant was crushed, filling the air with fragrant scent.

He looked back at the frowning Otto. "We surprised someone who broke in. They left through this window."

"You're kidding." Otto braced one hand against the door frame. "I was only gone a few minutes." He held up the bag with its convenience store logo. "Hadn't even gone back inside before you pulled up."

"Look around. See if anything is missing."

"Nothing missing here." He opened the closet. "Egad. It's even fuller than I remember. After my mother died, I put her things here. I should go through them, but I don't want to. I hate sorting through what was so important to her."

"I can help you check the usual spots thieves target. Then I'll bring in my tools and get started."

Cecil welcomed this unexpected opportunity to check out the home of a gallery staff member. He'd use the excuse of the intruder to have Otto search with him.

Otto was guileless; they'd check any safe or gun cabinet that Otto might own and have a look at the contents of the medicine cabinet. Would he find a sleeping medication like the one given to the guard?

The timing of this break-in alarmed Cecil. Why now, just after a million-dollar painting had been stolen? Was Otto's jovial innocence an act? What secrets did the man hide?

Ruben managed to drive away without calling attention to himself. That little bore had just screwed things up royally. Just let Otto cross the street ahead of him. Nothing would give Ruben more pleasure than grinding the little man into the ground under his car.

A security system! This should have been so simple. Now what?

He went through all that had happened since he and Algie had stolen the art. The bitch said she'd hung that painting in the gallery. He didn't know when or how. Could Algie have switched the Anonicelli for Purity's purple shit while Ruben was chasing the cleaning lady? Who knew where it was by now? Had he sold it? What a devious brat!

His phone rang—the Florida number. Should he answer it? Listen to more threats of what they'd do to him if he didn't send the painting soon? He didn't need that. He decided to ignore it.

When Algie went to bed last night, he'd been exhausted, but sleep didn't come. He lay staring into the dark, worrying about this mess he'd created. He gave up after midnight and got up to work on his digital painting. The picture emerging from the shadows of his mind captured the fear and the agony. The darkness frightened him.

No one else had seen it, yet he wanted someone to. More than any other painting he'd ever done. Maybe if someone saw it, he could be connected again.

He printed out a copy and put it in his computer case.

Who would understand?

He felt so alone, knew anger waited close by to explode over him. It was all his fault.

He managed to grab a few hours of fitful sleep before he was awakened by his dad getting ready to go to work. When his dad left, Algie opted to get out of the house.

First, Algie put several little tricks from the internet into action. He taped threads over doors and drawer edges in such a way that if someone tried to open them, he'd be able to tell. In his bathroom, he arranged the toothpaste tube, deodorant, comb in a precise pattern and then recorded it on his phone so he could tell if they'd been moved. Then he rigged the medicine cabinet door to let him know if it'd been opened. He smiled grimly when it worked and reset the trap. He did the same in his dad's bathroom. While there, he checked the contents of the cabinet. No sleeping pills. No prescriptions at all, except for allergies. Most likely Ruben had lied about the pills.

Unless Ruben had taken the whole bottle? Surely his dad would have missed that. He'd have asked Algie about it since he got blamed for everything anyway.

When his dad had looked for a place to live in Santa Fe, he'd avoided those quaint, close-together homes in the historic part. Instead, he'd purchased one in a northeast neighborhood off Bishops Lodge Road. A twenty-minute ride on his mountain bike could bring Algie to his dad's gallery. His dad had accommodated Algie's method of transportation by putting a bike rack on his car.

After setting the alarm and attaching one last thread/tape combo high up on the front door, Algie began biking downtown.

Bishops Lodge Road was two lanes here with an uneven gravel shoulder. As he pedaled along feeling vulnerable, unease grew. Scowling at the heavier than normal tourist traffic, he stopped to check the map on his phone. Traveling on side roads might take longer, but he wasn't in a rush. He put the phone back in his pocket and pulled back onto the berm, looking over his shoulder at the oncoming traffic.

Suddenly a dark SUV swerved onto the shoulder to within inches of his handlebars. Algie corrected to the right, careened along the rutted gravel surface, and landed tangled in a tough stand of scratchy rabbitbrush.

He looked down the road. Holy crap. Ruben. Had to be, speeding away. Dust rose from the shoulder where the SUV had deliberately left the road surface. To hurt him? Or just scare the hell out of him?

A car coming from the other direction stopped. The driver yelled at Algie. "Hey, kid, you all right? That crazy moron almost killed you."

Algie wrenched his bicycle from the woody shrub. "Okay, thanks."

"You sure?"

Algie nodded. He adjusted his helmet and the Velcro on his fingerless biking gloves. The car drove away.

The pungent scent of rabbitbrush filled the air. He looked over his bicycle, pulled some stems and leaves from the spokes, breathing a sigh of relief it wasn't damaged.

He hadn't fared as well. Still, scratches and bruises from brush were better than road rash and eating gravel. As he bent his knee, he sucked in a breath. A thin rivulet of blood ran down his shin. Why hadn't he worn long pants?

Stagecoach Road was just ahead. He'd go that way, maybe even cut across country where a car couldn't follow.

With a sigh of relief, he made it to the gallery, racked the bike on his father's car, and headed to the restroom to clean up. No point in telling anyone what happened, but now he was even more determined to keep an eye out for ways Ruben might harm him or his dad. He knew Ruben had another vehicle besides the SUV, but he didn't know what. That meant Algie could never rest easy. All vehicles were suspect.

Otto was in a chatty mood, telling him about his new security system and the intruder at his house. Crap! Algie knew who it must have been. He hoped all the art was still at Otto's.

How the hell was he ever going to get out of this mess?

CHAPTER SIXTY-SEVEN

In his office after lunch on Thursday, Pete received an alert from Forensics signaling the preliminary report on the Purity Gold crime scene was ready. He pulled a notepad toward him and opened the document.

Going first to the section dealing with the art, he checked the photos of the two paintings found in the apartment, which were not done by Gold, against what had been stolen from Swift and Adams. A match. The connection to the burglary was confirmed.

Next was the photo he'd requested of the damaged purple-and-orange painting. He compared it with the video from the Santa Fe New Mexican reporter. It certainly looked like the one Gold was waving around. He'd have someone ask Griffin and others who were nearby at the time if they recognized it. A close examination by forensics would clinch it. He made notes.

Pete leaned back in his chair. Why hadn't police seen that Purity Gold was in the gallery later that night when she claimed she hung the painting there? Evidently, though Keller was already impaired, he'd turned off the cameras, still lucid enough to know that letting Purity be seen wasn't a good idea.

The weapons drew Pete's attention next. The scissors, as the murder weapon, were first. Getting prints from scissors was never easy. He flicked to the preliminary autopsy report on Gold. She had type O blood.

The palette knife was also listed. "That's interesting," Pete muttered. "The knife also had blood on it, but type A—not

Gold's." He read on. Gold had fought her assailant, raking them with her nails. Tissue had been recovered from under her fingernails. "When we do find that bastard, we have DNA to bolster our case."

Another fact held high interest. Forensics found a bottle of a prescription sleeping aid, zolpidem, in her medicine cabinet. Keller had had a high level of that category of drug in his system.

Pete skimmed ahead. "*Ach du Lieber!*"

It looked like someone, maybe Purity, was getting ready to ship a package before the struggle. Under Gold's body, they discovered a shipping label addressed to someone in Florida.

He leaned back again with a smile. Tuttle was going to be ecstatic to get this report. He remembered Tuttle talking about some dodgy collector living in Florida but lacking any evidence to nail him.

What had they planned to ship? The Anonicelli?

He looked at the measurements listed for the carton and then back at the information on the Anonicelli. The painting would have fit.

Since it wasn't in the apartment, had it been taken by whoever killed Gold?

Whoever killed her was still looking for something afterwards. Stuff had been thrown on top of bloody shoeprints.

A crime scene told you a lot if you knew how to read the evidence. But what wasn't there, that you expected, also spoke volumes. They'd found a number of purses, but none that appeared to be in use. No wallet, no ID, no cellphone, implying that her killer had taken those.

He sat at his desk in thought, forming his index fingers into a steeple. Gold was involved at some level, but there was at least one other individual. Likely she'd been used by the mastermind of the whole operation. That would fit the MO. Adams and Griffin didn't look likely. Roquet? Prime suspect at this point. Someone not on their radar yet? Who?

His phone rang. It was Agent Tuttle. Pete gave him a brief overview of the forensics report and arranged to send it to him. "But that's not why you called. What's up?"

"Ever since Roquet disappeared a week ago, I've been pulling strings."

"Have you located him?"

"I want you and some of your folks to join us for a sting operation tonight at the Santa Fe Airport. Roquet's going to come to us."

Pete's feet hit the floor and he stood up. He noticed Loloma in the bullpen and motioned for him to come in. He made notes as Tuttle explained the plan. When he hung up, Pete grinned broadly at Loloma. "If this works, I may have to raise my opinion of the FBI a notch. Agent Tuttle has set up a sting operation to net Roquet. We will join him at the Santa Fe Airport at six tonight."

CHAPTER SIXTY-EIGHT

Hot gusty winds whipped across the parking lot and runways of the Santa Fe Airport, threatening to dry Pete's skin to leather. As he got out of the car near the terminal, the light jacket he wore seemed ridiculous now but hid the fact that he was packing. Its warmth would feel good at sunset a few hours away.

Loloma parked nearby. He looked comfortable with his bolo tie, loose sports jacket, boots, and black Stetson.

A flight was arriving at the public terminal, bringing a flurry of activity to the small airport. Pete and Loloma turned instead toward the Jet Center, used for private pilots and aircraft, where they were to meet Tuttle and another agent. They walked along the chain-link fence, separating the public area from the restricted apron.

Inside the Center, the AC felt good. The lodge-like main room had seating grouped around bright area rugs. Pete recognized the two plainclothes SFPD officers he'd co-opted. They'd arrived earlier in their black-and-whites and parked them near the public terminal. One was busy on his phone, the other reading in a fat leather armchair. They would already have been briefed.

Agent Tuttle appeared. As he turned to lead them into an office for their briefing, Pete rolled his eyes. The back of Tuttle's navy-blue jacket was emblazoned FBI in huge yellow letters. So much for incognito. As Tuttle faced them, the requisite reflective sunglasses peeked out from a breast pocket. Pete sincerely hoped, as the hour drew near, Tuttle would blend in better.

The office was small and spartan. An aerial view of the airport, maps, and framed licenses hung on the wall. A wood table, a couple of computers, a copier, and several wood chairs completed the furnishings.

"Ever since the Anonicelli has been targeted here," began Tuttle, "Roquet attracted our attention. Then in July, we noticed that he met several times with a fence-slash-art collector, a little fish who has been on our radar a long time. It suited us to leave this collector alone and watch. It doesn't hurt that he knows we know and knows what will happen if we decide to stop him. He has proven valuable in the past for our catching bigger fish."

"Does this collector have a name?" asked Loloma.

"Yeah." Tuttle's head bobbed several times. "But I'm not sharing his real name. I'll call him Slimeball. And to make a long story short, we leaned on him."

Pete shook his head, stifling his own grin.

"We told him to contact Roquet and tell him he had a collector who was willing to pay cash, no questions asked, for a collection of paintings by three Arizona artists. We named Hoogstra and two others."

"Why three artists, when it's the Hoogstras we need?" asked Pete.

"Somewhat less coincidental sounding." Tuttle scratched his nose. "Slimeball thought it sounded more legit. Anyway, we wanted him to get Roquet to Santa Fe with the art. The collector would fly in on a helicopter at a particular time, make the sale and fly away again. I gave Slimeball till last night to convince Roquet." He smiled. "So far, it's worked like a charm. You'll be able to hear most of the transaction, by the way. Slimeball is wearing a wire. The collector with the cash is an agent. There are two other agents in the Jet Center."

"Is the pilot an agent?" asked Pete.

"No, a local. Glenn somebody. He's worked with us several times. The plan," said Tuttle, "is that I'll do the arrest, charge him with knowingly selling stolen property. Other charges will be pending. Then I'll remand him to the custody of the Santa Fe PD."

The other agent left. At seven, Pete and Loloma followed Tuttle out the apron door and to a van parked on the runway side of the chain-link fence. The agent with whom they'd been briefed was in the driver's seat. A tech sat in front with the communication equipment, listening. The van was hidden from the entrance into the Jet Center by a maintenance vehicle.

The New Mexico sky showed one of its signature sunsets. Brilliant color painted the clouds over the distant Jemez Mountains.

The tech spoke to Tuttle, "They've arrived." She turned up the volume on the receiver so they could all hear the voice of the wired slimeball now in the Jet Center. Anticipation grew in the van as they listened to the unseen players.

"The buyer is flying in on a helicopter," said Slimeball's voice. "We can watch out this window."

The sound of luggage wheels marked their progress across the textured wood-like floor and over the rug to the window.

"Are you sure he's going to show? I feel very conspicuous with this huge suitcase." Roquet's voice.

"Will you quit fidgitin' and relax? You're making me nervous. There. Lights. Looks like a chopper."

"Can we wait outside? Too many people in here."

The new sound of wheels on cement told Pete they'd gone outside. They'd called it right about the helicopter. Pete watched as it landed and rolled to a nearby parking spot angled away from the Jet Center. After the rotors ceased, the pilot got out and opened the passenger door. The lights were on inside, showing off the posh interior. The single passenger climbed out and stretched. His silhouette against the lit interior showed a big man, not fat, but broad and muscular. He waved the pilot toward the Center.

"That's our signal," said Slimeball. "Come on."

Then Pete saw Roquet come in view, trundling the suitcase across the macadam. He heard him exchange a few pleasantries at the helicopter door. Then the agent/collector went in, hogging the seat facing the rear, and leaving the two smaller men to heft the suitcase up through the door and squeeze in past it. He heard Roquet gushing about the art, heard the man's complaint that they didn't have paintings by all three of the artists he'd been seeking. Guy named a price and they haggled. Pete heard the frustration in Roquet's voice change to desperation, and finally, as a deal was reached, to relief.

As the negotiations came to an end, the tech turned down the volume. Tuttle would still hear it on his earpiece. Pete, Loloma, Tuttle and the other agent got silently out of the van and approached the helicopter from the rear. They walked to the tail but stayed out of sight of the passenger door.

Slimeball and Roquet climbed out.

Then Tuttle stepped out and shouted, "FBI. Down on the ground!"

Roquet screeched and took off running.

The idiot! Pete and the others surrounded the pair, guns drawn. More armed police materialized out of the twilight. As they appeared, the little bean counter seemed to wilt, dropping to his knees, then to the ground.

Officers cuffed them both. Tuttle rattled off the charges and the familiar words of Miranda. Roquet glared at the slimeball lying next to him on the ground. "How did they find out? You fool."

The officers dragged the accountant to his feet. A search of his pockets yielded keys to a rental car, his passport, and a notebook full of details and account numbers. A one-way ticket to Barcelona, which began with a red-eye flight from

Albuquerque late that night, gave a moment's pause to Pete. Thank God for Tuttle's sting.

Roquet was bundled into a squad car to be taken to jail and booked. The only thing he said, over and over, was that he wanted to talk to his lawyer.

They retrieved Roquet's rental car and his luggage. Pete was looking forward to the report of its contents. The FBI gave Slimeball his thirty pieces of silver and escorted him away.

Pete invited Tuttle to his office where Cecil would meet them.

CHAPTER SIXTY-NINE

Later, Pete and Tuttle gathered in Pete's office at the round table to share with Cecil how the sting had succeeded.

Pete set his papers on his desk. "Thanks for your help, Tuttle. Just in the nick of time. Guy Roquet would have been a lot harder to nab if he'd used that ticket in his pocket to Barcelona."

"Probably on his way to Andorra," said Cecil.

"Andorra?" asked Pete.

"No extradition treaty with the U.S."

"What're the chances Roquet knows where the Anonicelli is?" asked Tuttle.

Pete got to his feet and popped a pod into his coffee maker. "He's lawyered up. Anyone want coffee?"

Tuttle shook his head. "Too late for caffeine. It's going to take a while to sort out all the cash and what appeared to be offshore account numbers in that little book. Should be a way of tracing it, even if he's unloaded it already."

"Never too late for caffeine," said Pete. "And my day's not done yet. I have to see Adams."

"Would it be okay if I were there when you tell William about the arrest, Schultz?" asked Cecil.

"When are you going to tell him about your past?" asked Pete.

Cecil rubbed the back of his neck. "Now doesn't seem right. He's just been betrayed big time."

"And you think it's going to get less awkward as this unfolds?"

Cecil scowled at Pete. "I'm not ready."

Pete raised an eyebrow. Cecil's scowl darkened.

"Why isn't that tracking gizmo of yours working, Cecil?" asked Tuttle.

Pete's ears perked up. "What gizmo? You still holding out on me, Dupre?"

Cecil grimaced. "I don't know what the hell's going on. I put a tracking device on the Anonicelli. I'd have let you know if it worked but haven't heard a peep. Faulty device? Bad batteries?"

"Did Roquet know you put the gizmo there?"

"No," said Cecil. "I suppose he could have spotted it and destroyed it. If it just broke off, it should still be sending signals."

Pete stood and stretched. "These twelve-hour days have got to stop. Tuttle and I need to touch base on the interrogation schedule for Roquet, but then I'm going to head over to Adams's place. Dupre, if you want to just happen to be there, you might want to get going now."

Cecil pushed back his chair. "Thanks, Schultz. Appreciate the heads up. See you."

◆ ❖ ◆

At the Adams' home, Algie was back to viewing himself as pond scum. His dad had been in a foul mood, ever since Guy had fled with a large amount of money.

Now this so-called plan of Ruben's had blown up in Algie's face, making things infinitely worse. How could he ever make this right?

The safest thing to do was to stay out of his dad's way.

Later that night, their doorbell rang. His dad answered, and Algie heard Cecil's voice. His dad started in ranting about Guy again. They settled with their scotches downstairs in the living room facing the fireplace, their backs to the staircase leading up to the balcony.

Ever since they'd moved to Santa Fe, Algie had found this balcony a handy place to eavesdrop on grownups' conversations. He'd nip up the back staircase, the wrought-iron circular one near his bedroom, and sit leaning against the wall in the upstairs hall. The sound of voices below carried well.

The doorbell rang again. Lieutenant Schultz, the policeman Algie'd met the day Guy disappeared, came in. He didn't have to listen very hard, for they were loud.

Guy had been arrested just in time, caught in a sting, selling art belonging to the gallery. They still didn't know the whereabouts of the Anonicelli, and Guy wasn't talking.

Algie was stunned. Crap, they thought Guy stole the Anonicelli? Had Ruben been conniving with Guy too? Algie didn't understand the money part, but his dad's anger came through clearly.

"How dare he betray me? I trusted him as a friend."

"You have," said Cecil.

"Nothing's worse than betrayal by a friend or family member. A Judas. No place hot enough in hell to throw him. No punishment too great. Unforgiveable." His father's voice rang hot and bitter.

Stifling a sob, Algie scrambled away from the wall, slung himself down the round staircase and into his bedroom. He collapsed on the bed and curled into a fetal position. His father's angry words reverberated.

Unforgiveable. Unforgiveable. Unforgiveable.

Chapter Seventy

It was Sam's turn to drive the kids to their digital art class. He cast a brief glance at Grayson in the passenger seat and then at the rearview mirror. In the back seat, his daughter's expression was animated as she chatted with Grayson about today's art lesson.

Sam frowned and checked his mirror again. "I wonder if someone's following us. There's been a white Subaru keeping pace since we left Grayson's house."

"Go around the block and see if they do the same thing," said Leyla.

Sam nodded his approval. "Good thinking. Trouble is, out in the country there's no block to go around."

Sam focused on his driving, then noticed the sudden quiet. He looked at Grayson. He'd slumped down in his seat and was gripping the arm rest with white knuckles, no less. Sam took in the pale skin and the clenching jaw muscles. Good grief, the kid was strung as tight as one of his guitar strings.

"Grayson, do you know anyone who owns a white Subaru?"

"N-n …" Grayson coughed to clear his throat. "No."

Sam turned in the ranch driveway and stopped in front of the wrought-iron gate set into the adobe wall. He watched the Subaru go past. It must be more than someone's being lost or just exploring the area. There wasn't much past the Bjornson Ranch on this road, and the pavement soon gave way to gravel.

"Let me open the gate," said Leyla. She jumped out, pressed the code, and got back in. Sam drove through, and the gate closed smoothly behind them.

"Thanks." The guy following them, if he really was, bothered Sam.

What was it that caused Grayson to be so tense?

He'd give Anton a call, and if possible, he'd come back tonight, check out the surveillance videos, and see if this guy swung back again. Anton should be aware of him too. The thought of some guy being in a position to show an inordinate amount of interest in a teenage boy or acting creepy around his or Anton's daughters made his skin crawl.

As their art class ended, Karen saved the digital painting she'd done and closed the Adobe program, pleased with the day's progress. Costain had already gone. The girls and Lou were in the hallway, talking with Dom.

Grayson putzed nearby, taking extreme care in collecting his notes and putting them in order.

Finally, Dom called goodbye to Lou and Leyla and came into the studio. "Feels good in here with the air on."

"Uff da," she said. "It'll be hot tomorrow too."

"Hello, Mr. Baca," said Grayson. "How are you today?"

She glanced at the teen. His greeting was too polite, too enthusiastic. Something must be on his mind—he was not good at hiding his feelings.

Finally, Grayson was ready to go, his computer case slung over his shoulder. Lou and the girls were now outside. Still, the teen showed no inclination to hurry out to Lou's car for his ride home.

Suddenly, he set down his things, zipped open the case, and handed a print to her. "What do you think?"

She held it so Dom could see.

The print showed a young man standing against a mottled background of blues—not serene restful tones, but tortured, mixed with purples, and browns. He was moving unwillingly toward what looked to be an entrance to a deeper cave, painted in dark, murky tones. His posture spoke of pain and despair. He looked over his shoulder toward the light source—one hand stretched back, palm out, as if to push against the terror stalking him.

While much of the painting was out of focus, almost abstract, her gaze was drawn to the face, done in great detail, and to the man's eye that held pure terror.

She studied the painting, her mind torn between awe and alarm. The quality of the work was excellent, but the feeling it evoked! This painting was deeply personal. She couldn't find words.

Dom broke the silence. "This is amazing. Very emotional."

"Your composition, the shadows, the expression. It's powerful." Karen tore her eyes away from the painting and met Grayson's.

Emotions flitted over his face. Defiance. Wistfulness—a pleading.

"Grayson, is this you?" she asked.

Grayson didn't answer immediately but zipped up his computer case. "How could it be me?" He cleared his throat. "It's not even from this world. Somebody wanted me to do a book cover for them."

Karen held out the painting to him. She knew the cover story was not true.

"Keep it," he said. "I don't care. I can print another." He turned and almost broke into a run going out.

Karen and Dom looked at each other.

"What just happened?" asked Dom. "His things were all packed up, then he pulled that out."

"You thought it strange as well."

"A cry for help?"

"So dark, so filled with pain." Karen looked at the print, her hand at her throat, stroking it absently. "What is he going through?"

"Something disturbing is going on," said Dom.

"How do you mean disturbing?" Karen searched his face. "You mean it isn't a good idea to have him around the girls?"

"That's not it. Sam talked to me when he dropped him off today. Said at first Grayson was over-polite, you know how people are around policemen. Yet as they got closer to the ranch, he seemed almost relieved. More natural."

"They don't know each other well yet."

"Sam noticed a car following them. He asked Grayson if he knew anyone who drove a white Subaru. Grayson said no, but his behavior changed, enough to make Sam alert, to make him wonder if someone was stalking the boy. He planned to talk to Anton about our security camera footage—just to be safe."

"Good. I hope he does." Karen picked at a loose thread on her shirt hem. "Grayson made an odd comment to me earlier. Said he liked it here. It was peaceful. And *safe*."

"Safe?"

"Should I say something to William?"

"Absolutely not."

Karen was surprised at his quick decisiveness. "Why not?"

"First, he's not your child. William might see it as interfering. You already annoyed him by lining up Costain as his teacher. Second, we don't know what is going on in Grayson's life. Who or what he fears? What he needs to be safe *from*."

"You're right. I won't say anything," said Karen.

"We'll keep our eyes and ears open," said Dom. "If we believe it will help Grayson, we'll say something."

Karen looked again at the print. Felt the terror. Heard the plea.

◆ ❖ ◆

When Sam returned to the ranch that evening, he followed Anton into the ranch office.

"Start the playback just before two o'clock," said Sam. "That's when I got here."

"You want the gate camera?" asked Anton. "Or the overlook?"

Sam pulled his notepad closer. "Gate first. Then the other."

Anton nodded, skipped to the desired time at the gate, and started the playback.

After a few seconds, Sam pointed. "There! That's us arriving."

The recording showed Sam turning in, Leyla opening the gate, and a white Subaru driving slowly past.

"He may return," said Anton. "They often do when they reach the end of the paved road."

Sure enough, the white car returned. But rather than driving past, it stopped in the turnaround. A man wearing a flat cap got out, studied the mailboxes like he was reading the names, then reached back into his car and got a pair of binoculars.

"What the hell's he doing? Do you recognize him?"

Sam frowned and shook his head.

"He parked at a weird angle. Can't see his license plate."

The man looked at the closed gate and walked to the side, out of camera range. A minute or so later, he appeared on the other side of the gate and began walking along the drive.

"Hello. How'd he get inside?"

Anton scowled. "A ways into the brush, the fence becomes barbed wire. Easy to get through."

When the figure walked out of range, Anton switched to the overlook camera. A few minutes later, the man entered the frame. There he stopped in the shade and raised the binoculars, looking toward the houses.

"Uff da. I don't like this at all." Anton made a few mouse clicks, and the screen split— one image with the man, and the other pointing toward the ranch buildings.

This camera looked down upon the parking area outside Karen's studio. It caught the edge of the alpaca pen by the barn and the duplex. It showed Sam and his passengers talking to Santos and Diego. Karen, Dom, and Krista came from the studio. The man watched intently.

All went inside except Santos, who stayed to pet a small gray alpaca. Still the man watched. Only when Santos disappeared did the man lower his binoculars.

As though he'd seen enough, the man turned and jogged out of camera range. Then he appeared on the other side of the gate and drove off. The cameras caught Sam arriving at the gate. The turnaround spot was empty when he passed through.

Sam sat back in his chair. "I'd like a copy of this footage. Our tech might be able to enhance it and get good stills of the guy."

"Holy hell, Sam, what is this all about?"

"He followed us from town. Who was he interested in? Grayson? The girls? Stalking a cop?"

Anton copied the footage to a flash drive. "Yet he seemed very interested in Santos. Does that mean anything? Was he casing our place? Looking to kidnap a child for ransom?"

Sam shook his head. "You, I, and William have wealth. Son of a gun. I wish I knew. You might warn your family, Anton. What we just saw scares me."

Chapter Seventy-One

Thursday, August 10

Dom picked up his mail at his old house on Thursday morning, and then drove to his daughter's home. He rang the bell and waited. God above, he wished he didn't have to make this visit. It was quiet inside. Frank said she'd be home.

He rang again. This time he heard movement.

Dolores opened the door. She wore a sun hat and gardening gloves. Dirt smudged one cheek.

"Come on through. I'm transplanting mums."

He followed her through the silent house, and across their portal, well-appointed for entertaining.

"I'm almost finished." She knelt down and added more potting soil to some yellow mums.

It was lovely here. Flagstone pavers extended beyond the cover of the portal to make pathways wandering among manicured beds of Russian sage.

The sound of falling water drew him to a wall with a fountain. Painted Spanish tiles with birds and flowers formed a backdrop for the basin, from which water overflowed into a small pool below. The pool was bordered by curved ledges of a comfortable height for sitting. He sat and scooped a leaf out of the water.

After a while, Dolores came over to sit on the other side of the pool ledge. "What's on your mind, Dad? You look too serious."

Dom's eyes traced her face. His only child. God above, she showed no signs of upset by the rift she'd caused. How had it come to this? His support must lie with his grandson and with Karen.

He cleared his throat. "I thought by now that you would have come to realize what you have done and that you would have apologized to Sam and Farah."

No sign of yielding, of warmth. No flicker of emotion at hearing her son's name. How could her rigidity become more important than her own family? Yet nothing, when his own heart was breaking.

"We missed you at our dinner Monday."

Dolores set her teeth and her nostrils flared.

"Given the fact that life is somber and unsettled, it was still moving. Karen and I will be married in October."

"I will nev—"

Dom held up a hand. "We want you to be part of our lives. When you are ready, we will welcome you."

Her voice burst hot and angry. "How could you choose her over me?"

He stood. The tears in his eyes blurred her image. The whisper seemed to be torn from his throat. "My daughter. The choice is entirely yours."

She turned away, and he left, his heart a deep ache.

When Dom got back to the ranch, Karen was waiting. His eyes met hers, and he shook his head. Then she was in his arms, standing with him, holding him, murmuring words of comfort.

At dinner they let him be. Accepting. Drawing him in at his own pace. Drawing him back to life. He was tired, he realized, but home.

As Dom and Karen were relaxing in her suite later, he looked at his ringing phone. "It's Herb."

Karen looked up from her sketchbook. "Hope he's got better news than they did Tuesday."

"Glad we got you," said Herb. "Today some volunteers recognized the pictures."

Dom put the phone on speaker. "I could use good news. Tell us."

"Someone remembered Dulcie in her yellow shirt on Saturday. They gave her the standard—a tote bag with a sandwich, fruit, and a couple bottles of water. They said she wanted to use a phone, but they were all busy. She was definitely at our hospitality center."

"Was she okay?"

"They didn't notice anything wrong," said Yolanda.

Herb's voice chimed in. "Then, even better news. Another volunteer looked at the pictures and said she overheard Dulcie talking to the sister about getting a ride. Sister Mary said she'd be glad to take her to the police station after she made her delivery in Albuquerque. Said she was on a tight schedule, so they couldn't wait in El Paso for a phone. Dulcie said that was fine. The sooner she got home, the better."

"I got contact information from both volunteers," said Yolanda. "Your cop friend, Sam, can talk to them if he wants. I'll email them to you."

"Excellent," said Dom. "Did either of them see what kind of car Sister Mary drove?

"Like me," said Yolanda, "they weren't good at cars. It was blue."

Karen stood and paced after Dom hung up. "So long ago. This is Thursday!"

"Two women traveling alone? What do you suppose happened?" Dom pressed Sam's number. "At least Sam'll have leads to follow."

When Sam answered, Dom put it on speaker phone.

"This is a puzzle," said Sam. "I've been contacting the churches in the Albuquerque area, and I sent them the photos. No one has ever heard of a Sister Mary Catherine—at least in relation to that photo. None of them knew about any deliveries or knew of any employee who fit her description."

"What churches have you tried?" asked Karen. "Just the Catholic ones?"

"Started there but did most of the main line ones and the mega churches. Not all. I'll keep trying."

"I've been looking online for that filigreed cross she was wearing," said Dom.

"Me too," said Sam. "Haven't found any order with crosses like that. I also contacted the state police about any accidents or incidents on routes leading back to Albuquerque. Checked all the hospitals. Nothing."

Dom rubbed his forehead. "Is there something you aren't telling us, Sam?"

"It's just that people have seen and talked to this nun, but none of the El Paso churches or humanitarian organizations know anything about her. They can find no record of employment for her and no reason for a job like hers. There's something foul about the character of Sister Mary Catherine."

Chapter Seventy-Two

Thursday, August 10

What was that sound?

Diego left his study and walked silently into the dark hallway leading to the bedrooms in his duplex. As he stood outside Santos's room, he heard it—long shuddering intakes of breath, followed by quiet sobs.

Diego's heart ached. He felt helpless against the boy's grief. First losing his father, now his mother. She should have been back. A week tomorrow. Not knowing, imagining all kinds of disasters.

He stood in the dim light. He didn't have the answers the boy needed so desperately, had no great gift of words that would bring comfort. He crossed to the open door between his half of the duplex and Maria's. Maybe with her mothering instinct, she would know the right thing to do.

Maria was sitting on her couch, knitting.

"I need your help," said Diego. "Santos is crying. I don't know what to do."

The needles flashed until she came to the end of a row. "Of course I'll come."

He took her hand as she rose and dropped a light kiss on her knuckles. He loved this warm, generous woman. She never hesitated when someone needed her.

Diego led her back and knocked on Santos's door. "*Mijo*, it's Diego. Can Maria and I come in?"

The sobs stopped. "Yes."

The light from the hallway showed the boy sitting up, wiping his eyes on his pajama sleeve. Tuffy rose from where he'd been cuddled next to him and stretched. Maria pulled the chair closer, and Diego sat on the edge of the bed.

Santos sniffed. "Have you heard anything?"

"No," said Diego, "I heard you crying—"

"I'm sorry," blurted Santos.

"It's okay. There are times men need to cry."

"Sometimes it helps to talk," said Maria. "Things that worry us don't seem as bad when somebody listens."

"I want Mom back. I worry about her, 'n if somebody's hurt her." Santos wiped his eyes.

Diego gently brushed the hair back from the boy's forehead. "Santos, I won't lie to you. I'm worried too. But don't give up hope. She would move heaven and earth to get back to you. I'm certain of that. She loves you."

Santos looked down, picking at the satin border of his blanket. "But what—what happens if she doesn't come back?" He sniffed again.

Maria handed him some tissues. He blew his nose.

"What's going to happen to me?" he cried, wadding the tissues.

Diego put his hand over the boy's. "*Mijo*, don't let that worry you. This is your home for as long as you need it—even forever."

Santos's eyes searched his. Diego looked steadily back. Suddenly the boy lurched forward and threw his arms around him. They rocked back and forth, Diego's hand awkwardly patting the boy's back.

The promises he'd made. Could he make them come true if Dulcie never came home? Did he have the right?

◆ ❖ ◆

Not long after, Diego and Maria left Santos to sleep but kept the door to the hall open. When Diego checked later, Santos was truly asleep. Tuffy raised his head, twitched the very tip of his tail, then curled against Santos and closed his eyes. Diego heard his rumbling purr.

He got two fleecy shirts, slipped one on and offered the other to Maria. "Come to the swing with me?"

She nodded, settled the warmth of the shirt over her shoulders and took his hand.

Diego squeezed it. "Thank you. You helped a lot."

They climbed the stairs to the deck of the barn where the swing seat hung. Diego got the pillows from their spot inside the loft door. He treasured these pillows covered with Peruvian fabric—a gift last Christmas from Maria. He sat close, his arm around her. His foot set the swing gently swaying.

"He's a good kid, Maria. Bright, willing. My heart goes out to him. He's good with animals. He needs a dad, a man to show him how to behave. I didn't know what to say to him. All I could do was to hold him as he cried."

"That was all he needed, to know you cared."

Maria leaned her head against him and took his hand, gently rubbing his fingers. Her touch felt so good.

She looked up at him. "What will happen if Dulcie doesn't come back?"

"Was I right to tell him what I did? It frightens me that he might end up in foster care. I've seen too many kids get lost in the system. I don't want that for Santos."

"Are you saying you'd like to keep him? To make that temporary guardianship permanent?"

"I'd like nothing better, but what are the chances with CYFD? I'm single and almost old enough to be his grandfather."

"If we don't find out what happened to his mother, would he like to live with you?"

"I believe so, *querida*. Except for missing his mother, he's happy here."

"Diego, if you are serious, let's do something about it. CYFD wouldn't have a problem with a married couple, even if they are older. Especially if there is already a relationship—that kinship thing Sam was talking about."

He turned to look at her and moved his hand to caress her cheek. "What are you saying?"

"You know there is no one else for me but you. We have been sharing our lives for years and have become close. Neither of us saw the need to do anything about it before. But if we want to increase our chances to take care of Santos and give him a home where he is loved, I believe we need to be married. He deserves that."

"I'd like nothing better than to have him be truly ours. Do you want to raise a child?"

"A son with you because we chose him? Love him? I would be proud to."

"And if, God willing, his mother comes back? What if we married, then she came home? Would we regret our marriage?"

"If she comes home, we will be happy for Santos. We will be to him grandparents, or *tía* and *tío*. And we will gain a sister to love. Dulcie has seen too much pain. She needs a family."

"I've never thought to have another child. But my daughter lives so far away, and I missed much of her childhood." He set the swing moving again. "Could we do it?"

"How could CYFD say anything but yes? You're a man to respect. You have a good job, a home. You have friends of standing. Resources. And if I'm not mistaken, you'd be happy to pass your skills on to set Santos up for the same success you have."

Diego cupped his hand on her cheek, his rough, calloused fingers gentle against her skin. "*Mi vida.*" His dark eyes searched hers. "It pleases me. Love has crept up on us. Somehow when we weren't looking, it became as important as breathing. This is not for Santos. This is for us."

Maria nodded; her lips trembled.

"Maria, will you be my wife?"

"Yes, with all my heart."

His arms slid around her to hold her close. A miracle, slowly, silently, softly blooming into such goodness.

Chapter Seventy-Three

Friday, August 11

Santos slumped back on the couch in Diego's living room. Daytime was better than night when worries ganged up on him.

This morning he'd been invited to go shopping with Maria and Diego. The ranch supply store with all the pet food and small critters had sounded fun, but in the end, he decided against it.

For the time being he was on his own—didn't happen that often at the ranch. The digital art class had begun in the studio and would go for a couple of hours. Dom was around, probably reading. Anton was somewhere in the big house with the baby.

His sneakered foot kicked repeatedly against the leg of the coffee table, which held Cliff's mysteries. Krista had lent him the books, but he wasn't in the mood to read. He couldn't sit still with tension curling inside. All he could think about was his mother, but there was nothing he could do.

His cell phone rang, and he pulled it from his pocket. Could it be Mom? It was a strange number! "Hello?"

"Santos?"

His excitement deflated. A man's voice. "Yeah. Who's calling?"

"I'm so glad you answered. I need to talk to you. My name is Ruben. Er, Ruben Smith. We can rescue your mother."

Wow! Rescue his mom? Santos jumped up. "You know where she is?"

"Yes. She's being held captive by a couple of thugs. They don't know I'm an undercover officer and have infiltrated their gang. I've spoken to her. But she doesn't trust me and won't leave. If you were with me, she'd know I was on her side. We could get her out of there."

"You mean rescue her and that nun?"

"Ah, yes, Nunn. Mr. Nunn is one of them. Not a good person. You are willing to help, aren't you?"

"Oh, gosh. Sure." Hope rose high.

"Listen, you can't let anyone know. They said they'd kill her. If they see a cop anywhere near the place, you'll never see your mother alive again."

"How far away is it?"

"Far away?"

"You know, where the nun took her."

"Oh, Nunn's not there anymore. They've moved her back to Santa Fe."

"They?"

"Look, kid, I hope you're not dumb enough to think Nunn was working alone? I said gang."

"Sorry. When can we go?"

"I can be at the end of your driveway by the big gate in twenty minutes. Remember, don't tell anyone."

"Okay!" He figured it would take him fifteen minutes to walk to the gate. "I'm on my way."

Quickly, Santos scribbled a note for Diego. As he wrote, Tuffy wound around his legs with a motor-like purr.

He anchored the note with a drinking glass on the table, chucked Tuffy under his chin, and went running out the door, slamming the screen behind him.

Chapter Seventy-Four

Karen wondered what kind of a mood Grayson would be in for their class on Friday. She was still troubled by the dark painting he'd shared with them Wednesday. How would he function as their teacher? Costain wasn't scheduled for Fridays.

After some initial stiffness, Grayson relaxed as the girls shared their excitement about their art. By the time he answered all their questions, he seemed in tune with his work.

Gathered around tables in her studio, Grayson sat in the middle, she and Krista on his left and Leyla and Lou on his right. Their laptops showed screens open to Adobe Illustrator workspaces upon which they'd each created their own drawings of a partly open door.

Krista hovered her cursor over the panel of tools. "I like doors. There's always a mystery about what's on the other side."

Her granddaughter constantly surprised her—how many twelve-year-olds would come out with an intriguing thought like that?

"Remember to start a new layer for each step," said Grayson. "It's easier to correct a mistake."

As he leaned forward to point to Krista's screen, his dark hair fell over his eyes. He finger-combed it back before grinning at Krista. "That's right. You got it."

Karen stifled the urge to chuckle. No need to remind the girls to pay attention to their teacher. Both Krista and Leyla were very aware of this teen who had so much going for him.

"It won't let me select it," complained Leyla, looking up from her computer. "How come?"

Grayson swiveled to Leyla on his other side. "What layer are you on?"

"Oh, that's why. I keep forgetting."

Grayson smiled. "Soon it'll be automatic. I forgot, too, when I first started. We're all going to try—"

Karen's cell phone rang. "Sorry. It's Diego. I'd better take it."

Diego's first request was about Quixote's dog food. Then he wanted to ask Santos about the cat food Tuffy ate. Karen turned to Krista. "Can you and Leyla go find Santos? Diego has a question for him, but he's not answering the phone. I just saw him out the window a bit ago."

The girls left. Lou asked Grayson a more advanced question. Karen listened, phone in hand. Both question and answer were Greek to her. Grayson was remarkably patient with their different levels of experience.

A commotion outside caused her to look up in alarm.

"Help!" Leyla bellowed. "Everybody. Help, help!" She burst through the open studio door, her eyes wide, a piece of paper in her hand.

Karen stood. "What's wrong?"

"Santos has gone to meet Ruben. To rescue his mom." Leyla paused to catch a breath.

Dom came rushing in with a book from wherever he'd been reading. "What's the matter?"

Anton was right on his heels, his baby in his arms. Lou went to take the baby, cuddling the little one against her shoulder.

Leyla's words tumbled over each other. "Krista took off on her bike to stop him."

"Who's Ruben?"

"Ruben?" echoed Anton.

"Here!" Leyla thrust the note at Anton. "You've got to stop him."

Anton read the note aloud.

Mom's alive! I'm going to help Ruben rescue her.
He said not to call the cops or they will kill her.
He's meeting me at the gate.
Santos

Diego's voice sounded urgent, but unintelligible from the forgotten phone in her hand. Karen put it back to her ear. "Diego, you'd better come home at once."

Karen hung up. "Call 911. Anton, come, I've got my car keys."

◆ ❖ ◆

Karen peeled out of her parking spot and headed down the driveway. She must make it to the gate before Santos reached the man. Who knew how long this Ruben would need to get there?

A quick glance in the mirror showed dust billowing in the wake of her car. She hit a pothole and winced.

Anton grasped the handle above the passenger seat window. "Uff da, Mom! Slow down. It won't help if we skid off the road."

Ahead Karen saw her granddaughter pedaling furiously. She was alarmed at the distance she'd already traveled toward the gate. Would they be too late?

Anton rolled down his window. "Stop for her."

Karen shot him a look.

"I'm not leaving my daughter out here alone with a kidnapper on the loose."

She drove just past Krista and stopped.

"Leave your bike," Anton called out the window. "Get in. Hurry."

Krista was quick to obey. Sweat rolled down her face, leaving behind rivulets on her dusty cheeks.

Karen sped off in a spurt of gravel, soon coming to the low spot near the gate. She spotted Santos not far ahead. He looked over his shoulder and took off running.

Karen braked to a stop just past him. Krista and Anton threw open their doors and got out.

"Santos, stop," yelled Krista.

Santos veered off the road and into the brush as Anton sprinted after him.

"No, get away!" The boy evaded Anton's grasp and darted back to the road.

Movement on the other side of the gate caught Karen's eyes. A white car swerved to a stop in the turnaround, facing the direction toward town. The driver got out, raised his arms, and pointed something toward Anton.

"A gun!"

Karen saw a flash and heard a shot. She needed to get the car between Anton and the gunman! She jerked ahead, yelling, "Get in! Now!"

Anton caught Santos and struggled with the kicking boy.

"Let me go!"

Krista scrambled into the front.

Karen saw Ruben turning his gun toward the car.

"Get down," she screamed. She hunkered over Krista in the front, eyes focused on the space between the seats, allowing her to see Anton's ongoing struggle.

Anton shoved Santos in. Santos scrambled across the back seat and opened the other door. Anton pulled him back and yanked the doors shut. "Damn it! Stop kicking."

More shots came. Karen squeezed her eyes shut when she heard the thunk of a bullet hitting the car. Then another sounded, followed by a tinkling sound. A whimper left her mouth.

She heard a car door slam and an engine rev. She raised her head, peering over the dashboard to see the man fishtailing away from the gate.

Karen sat up. "Did he hit anyone? My God, my windshield." A round hole had appeared near the top of the glass. The window was spiderwebbed, and little cubes of glass lay scattered.

Her head whipped around to look at Anton.

"We're okay, Mom," said Anton, keeping a hand on the boy's arm.

Santos stopped his struggling and subsided into bitter tears. "Why'd you stop me? My mom needs me!"

Shaky and in a state of disbelief, Karen turned and made it back up the drive to park outside the studio. As they got out, her heart ached at Santos's defeated and hollow-eyed expression.

◆ ❖ ◆

Karen led the way into the studio, where alarm surrounded them. She glanced back to see Anton, his hand securely wrapped around Santos's wrist. The boy dragged his feet and tried unsuccessfully to pry Anton's fingers from his arm. Krista followed behind.

Karen had seen that look on her son before. Santos didn't have a hope of getting away. Red marks from being kicked showed on Anton's legs below his shorts.

Santos heaped blame on them. "I could've saved my mom. I hate you!" He sank into a chair, sobbing. Anton let go of him.

Santos edged off the chair and moved toward the door.

Anton grasped his shoulder. "Don't even think it." Santos angrily subsided back in his seat. Then Anton sat in front of Karen's laptop screen, which showed the real time security-camera action at the gate.

For the moment the gate was quiet, but in her studio, a hubbub of voices arose.

"We were watching on the monitor," said Leyla.

"Lou called 911," said Dom.

Karen sat next to Dom and looked at Grayson. He was tense, his jaw muscles flexing.

"I called Dad. He's coming," said Leyla. "Grayson positively yelled when we saw the gun. Dom had to hold him from running after you. Then we saw Ruben shooting. We were all scared."

"Santos," said Karen, "we need answers. Who's Ruben?"

Santos glared at her. "He's an undercover agent. Ruben Smith. He knows where they're keeping Mom." His voice rose, and he stood. "I don't know where she is, and you chased him away. You ruined everything."

"Santos, sit down."

Karen's firm voice got his attention. He sat abruptly on the edge of the chair.

"How did this Ruben get in touch with you?" she asked.

"He called me on my cell phone."

"Is it the same Ruben we heard in the bookstore?" asked Krista.

Karen looked at her granddaughter. "Ruben? Bookstore?"

Krista rolled her eyes. "We overheard this guy talking about the cleaning lady and she'd better not call the cops."

Karen heard a slight moan. Grayson's face was sickly white. She faced Krista. "When was this?"

"Sunday," said Leyla. "Krista thought of a way to find his name using bookmarks. It worked. The barista told us his name was Ruben."

"Why didn't you tell me about this Ruben dude before?" asked Anton.

"We were going to see what we could find out first." Then Krista glared at Santos, her arms akimbo. "Santos, use your brain. If this guy was an undercover officer, why did he shoot at us?"

Santos rubbed his sleeve across his dirty, tear-streaked face. "I don't know. He said they were going to kill her."

"You *do* know. You just don't *want* to believe it. He's lying. I don't think he knows where your mother is at all."

Santos screamed, "He does know!"

"Good guys don't act like he does," yelled Leyla.

Anton turned from the computer. "Listen to me, all three of you. This is not a game. You are not to go around playing detective. If you hear something, tell an adult. Better yet, a cop. Tell Sam or Pete. Do you hear me?"

Sam strode in. Leyla ran to his arms. His eyes swept the others over her head. "Is everyone okay? Anyone hurt? Those are bullet holes in the car."

Anton's voice was urgent. "Did they catch him?"

"Not yet. Patrol cars are searching. We'll want to see this new footage ASAP. What the hell happened?"

Anton started to fill him in when Diego and Maria burst in.

Diego rushed to Santos and enfolded him in a hug. "Thank God, they got you in time, *mijo*."

Maria knelt in front of Santos. "We were so frightened." Santos went to her for another hug.

As Karen watched, Pete walked in, his eyes seeming to take in the whole picture, resting briefly on Santos, on his daughter, Lou, holding little Lucas, and then meeting Karen's own eyes.

Dom reached out to him. "Did they catch him yet?"

"There's a BOLO out. It includes his picture from Wednesday's footage."

Karen rose and went to where Lou stood with an increasingly fractious baby. She took his squirmy warmth in her arms, bending her head to his, and rubbing his back.

She raised her head as Twitch, Shadow, and Quixote ran in, full of canine exuberance. The Airedales competed in greeting everyone, running back and forth, barking in their excitement. Even the placid border collie had lots to say. Skyla entered the studio, wearing her park service uniform.

"What on earth is going on?" Her voice barely penetrated the din. "There are police cars all over."

Skyla's frantic gaze focused on Lucas in Karen's arms. The baby had begun to cry again as the noise and confusion grew. Skyla took him from his grandmother.

Karen put her hands over her ears. The chaos in the room rose another notch. Everybody, it seemed, was talking. God, she needed a whistle to call time out.

"*Ach du Lieber Gott*! Shut UP!" Pete's parade-volume shout brought total silence.

CHAPTER SEVENTY-FIVE

In the hush following the shout, Karen swung to face Pete. Lucas, startled into silence, refilled his lungs to send his baby wail into the breach.

"We're not going to solve anything with this crowd," said Pete.

"Do you need Krista and Leyla?" asked Skyla.

Pete's expression was grateful. "Later, not right now."

"Girls, bring the dogs. Come with me." Skyla led a small parade from the studio.

Pete started issuing orders. "Diego, you and Maria take Santos over to your house. Sam, go with them."

Diego nodded and led them out, his arm around Santos's shoulders.

"Dad, is it okay if I leave?" said Lou. "Grayson, ready to go?"

Karen saw the tension increase on Grayson's face. He shook his head. He still hadn't said a word.

"We'll see that he gets home, Lou," said Karen. "You—"

Pete interrupted. "I'd rather talk to everyone before they leave. You too, Lou."

Lou gathered her things. "Then I'll be with Skyla and the girls."

"Anton," said Pete, "I'd like to get your surveillance video from today and hear your story first. Can we go to your office? Then I'll come back here to talk to Karen, Dom, and Algie, isn't it? William's son?"

"He prefers his real name, Grayson," said Karen.

Pete nodded and followed Anton out of the room.

The studio was quiet.

Dust motes danced in the afternoon sun streaming through the windows.

Grayson shut down his computer and collected his things. His movements were slow and jerky as though he were in a daze.

"This is Friday. Bound to be traffic," said Dom. "Should we call your dad and tell him you'll be late?"

Grayson switched off his mouse and tucked it into his computer bag. "He—" He cleared his throat. "He won't even know. He's going out tonight."

"When do you expect him home?"

"He has opera tickets."

"It's Handel's *Alcina* tonight," said Karen. "He'll be lucky to get home by midnight."

"Well, then," said Dom. "He won't worry."

Grayson made no move to get up. He sat, eyes downcast. His body began to rock slightly.

The silence stretched.

Karen flicked a glance at Dom, then spoke softly. "Grayson, what's wrong? Can you tell us?"

Silence.

"Grayson?"

"He'll find me. Don't wanna go home."

"Who will find you?"

No answer.

"Your dad?" asked Dom quietly.

No answer.

Karen put her hand over the teen's. "Grayson, who will find you?" His hand felt cold. "You're afraid, aren't you? The painting you showed us?"

He nodded.

"It's gotten too big to handle by yourself, hasn't it?"

He nodded again and kept on rocking.

"Is it your dad you are frightened of?" asked Dom.

"No." There was a long pause. "Ruben. He'll find me."

His answer startled Karen. "Why would Ruben be looking for you?"

She kept her eyes on Grayson's face. His eyes scrunched, and tears emerged. He still rocked back and forth, but now shuddering sighs threatened to turn into sobs.

"I— I stole it. The art from the gallery."

Karen's sudden intake of breath was echoed by Dom's. In disbelief she listened to Grayson's soft words.

"Ruben's bad. My dad will never forgive me. It keeps getting worse. Ruben twists you into his lies. There's no escape."

"You feel trapped?" Dom's voice was gentle.

Grayson raised a hand to wipe his eyes. "My life is over. It doesn't matter anymore. But now he's after Santos. I can't let Ruben destroy him too."

"Grayson," said Karen, "if Ruben has done something evil, I think you should tell someone who can stop him. You know Pete's a policeman. Would you like to talk to him?"

Grayson nodded, hunched over, hugging his arms.

"I can't go on. It hurts so bad. I wish I was dead."

Grayson began sobbing—quiet sobs of anguish.

Karen felt her eyes brimming. She picked up her phone and texted Pete, "Come to the studio. Urgent." Her throat ached as she watched the boy, wracked with pain.

Dom rested a hand on the boy's shoulder. "Grayson, maybe we can help."

Seconds later, Pete grabbed onto the door frame and almost skidded into the room in his haste. Karen pointed to a chair near where they were sitting. Pete came in and sat.

"Tell us what happened, son," said Dom. "You're safe here."

"Dad thinks it was my fault my mom was on that plane. My fault the car hit Swift. Ruben said he could help." Grayson swallowed.

Karen saw Pete's eyes widen. He pressed a button on the body cam he wore.

"Ruben? Help? How?" asked Pete.

"I just wanted to make things right. With my dad." Grayson drew a shuddering breath. "But I couldn't."

Karen saw Anton peek into the studio. She shook her head at him. He backed out and closed the door.

"Ruben said he had a plan. It would make … my dad see me as a hero. It'd fix things."

"His plan?" prompted Pete.

"Ruben said he felt sorry for me. For how my dad treated me. He said he, Otto, and Bruno had come up with this idea. We would take some of the exhibit pieces from the gallery and—"

Pete interrupted with his hand touching Grayson's wrist. "Hold on, son. There's something you need to know before you say anything more. I'm a police officer. I need to inform you of your rights. Your father—"

"You don't understand." Grayson's voice rose in volume. "I can't wait for my father to get here. You have to stop Ruben. Anyway, it doesn't matter about me. I screwed up. But he said he'd hurt my dad. Now he's after Santos."

"But you—"

"I know all about that Miranda stuff." He shouted at Pete, "Listen to me. I need to tell you this. Now!"

Pete's voice was firm. "I hear you, first I will state your rights. I don't have a choice." When he was through, he said, "I must also tell you this is being recorded—"

"Good! I want it to be. Now you listen."

Pete sat back, and Grayson's voice continued, sometimes hesitant and choked with tears. "Ruben said no one would get hurt. The guard would take a sleeping pill, so he wouldn't get in trouble. We planned to hide the art in a safe place. Then I would somehow discover it somewhere. My dad would be happy. But it was all lies."

He wiped his eyes. "I was stupid to believe him. I wanted it to work, so I didn't think it through. Ruben said it was better if I didn't know the details."

Karen handed a couple of tissues to Grayson, and he blew his nose.

"God, I just want to die."

"What happened that night?" asked Pete.

"At first, it went just like he said. Bruno was sleeping. Alarm wasn't set. I disarmed the rest of the system—all of it. I didn't know which art had sensors that would set off the alarms. We filled some boxes, then Santos's mom came."

"Dulcie." Karen's voice was a whisper.

Grayson nodded. "She ran, and Ruben chased after her. I was hoping … I thought he would tell her what we were doing. That it was okay. While he was gone, I moved the boxes to the back door."

Grayson started rocking again. "Then in one box I saw something wrapped in fuzzy material. I unwrapped it and saw the Anonicelli between two other paintings. I knew then. His words were lies."

"What did you do?" asked Pete.

"I hid the Anonicelli, ran back, found another painting the same size, wrapped it again with the other two, and put it in the box. Then Ruben came back and took me home."

His voice dropped to a whisper. "He said … he said he'd kill my father if I told." He began sobbing again. "My father will die. It will be my fault."

"Grayson, this is not your fault." Karen took hold of his wrist. "Look at me. Look."

His eyes were desolate, hopeless.

"Listen. If you are guilty of anything, it is trusting the wrong person. He took advantage of you."

Pete leaned forward in his chair. "Grayson, Karen is right. Apparently, Ruben bears most of the blame."

Grayson's eyes met Pete's. Finally, he nodded.

"Can you help us recover the art?" asked Pete.

Grayson nodded. "The Anonicelli is still where I put it. All the rest is supposed to be hidden at Otto's."

"Good. I'm not going to lie and say there will be no repercussions," said Pete. "But if you tell us everything you know, it will be much better for you. It will help us arrest and convict Ruben. Then no one else can be hurt by his lies."

Grayson hung his head. "What will happen to me?"

"First we will have to talk with your father," said Pete.

Grayson crossed his arms to hug himself. "He'll hate me. I've been so stupid."

"Are you afraid he's going to hurt you?" asked Pete.

"I wish he would. I deserve it." Grayson sat back. "He'll just look at me. His eyes will be all sad. He won't say anything, just turn away. And I'll know. He'll never …" His voice dropped to a whisper. "Never."

"Grayson," said Karen, "You're his son. He loves you."

Grayson sagged, his posture the epitome of misery. Then his eyes met hers. "Could you and Dom be there? When I tell him?"

Pete cleared his throat.

"Could you?" Grayson's eyes held, pleading.

"Of course," she said.

Dom nodded. "If you want, we'll be there."

"Please." His voice was a whisper.

"Hang on," said Pete. "This discussion with your father will take place down at the station. I do have some leeway, but this is an active investigation. I have rules to follow."

Suddenly it became critical that Grayson should have support. Facing this alone was unthinkable. Karen swiveled toward Pete, aghast. "Are you—"

"I'm not saying you can't be there. I'm just saying I have to consider protocol. Grayson's father has parental say." He looked at Grayson. "And even though you don't want to hear, you have rights too." He looked at his watch. "I'm going to talk with Sam, then I'll ask Mr. Adams to meet us downtown. Grayson will ride with me."

"Does that mean he's under arrest?" asked Karen.

"Not yet, but this is a felony case. I need to get to the bottom of it, to learn as much as we can to go after Ruben. His threats shouldn't be taken lightly. It's important to keep Grayson and his father safe. That's all I will say now."

Grayson closed his eyes. "I want to get it over with. Just end it all."

CHAPTER SEVENTY-SIX

Karen followed Pete, Grayson, and Dom into a small conference room on the second floor of the Santa Fe Police Department. The room was uninspired with a curtainless window opposite the door. A rectangular table with six office chairs dominated the space. One wall, painted a soft gray-blue, held a flat-screen TV mounted above a credenza.

Pete set his laptop and a digital recorder at the head of the table. She and Dom sat to Pete's left and Grayson across from them.

The door opened, and William strode in with an annoyed look on his face. His eyes focused on his son. "What in God's name have you done now?"

Grayson didn't look up, but in Karen's eyes, he shrank further into his chair.

A woman wearing a casual business jacket and slacks followed William in and sat at the foot of the table with her portfolio.

"Mr. Adams," said Pete. "Your son has a right to an attorney. Are we expecting one?"

William looked at his watch. "No. I'm hoping this nonsense can be cleared up quickly. I have plans for tonight."

Karen felt a surge of anger. *Screw the opera!* Your son needs you.

"We'd best get started then," said Pete. "This meeting will be recorded."

Only then did Karen notice two bullet cameras tucked in the corners near the ceiling. Pete activated his recorder in the center of the table, and proceeded to read out loud the date, time, and case number. He stated the reason for the meeting and asked each person to identify themselves into the record.

The woman at the end of the table identified herself as Detective Ruiz. When it was Grayson's turn, he gave his name as Algie Adams. Karen bit her lip. He was back to being pond scum.

"Your legal name?" prompted Pete.

"Albert Grayson Adams."

"Birthdate?"

"August 10, 2001."

Dom's hand found hers under the table. Grayson's sixteenth birthday was yesterday? No one had said anything. What a horrible way to mark what should have been a joyous, hope-filled, looking-to-the-future day.

"Before we begin, I want to make sure young Adams understands our procedures." Pete reiterated his rights. "Do you understand?"

"Yes." Grayson's voice was firm. "Look. I told you before, I need to say this. Ruben has to be stopped. He has a gun. He tried to grab Santos. When Krista chased him, and Karen and Anton followed, he shot at them."

"Did you see this?" asked Ruiz.

"On the monitor, and I saw the bullet hole in her windshield when we left. You have to stop him from hurting anyone else."

William slapped his hand on the table. "What went on this afternoon? Sounds like a hell of a lot more than I was told on the phone."

Then William turned his cold-eyed glare to Karen.

"Lieutenant, what right do Karen and Dom have to be here?"

Grayson straightened. "I invited them."

"I object. I don't need outside interference with my child."

Grayson sent a beseeching look toward Pete.

Uff da. What would Pete do?

"Mr. Adams, I am in charge of this investigation, and I believe their presence is useful. Bear with us. It will become clear."

"Dad," Grayson's voice pleaded. "I *want* them to stay."

William's rigid posture relaxed only slightly as he moved back in his chair. "All right, but I don't like it."

"Thank you. We will move on. Ms Bjornson, will you share what transpired last Wednesday, and then today at your ranch?"

She told briefly about Sam being followed and Ruben watching with binoculars.

"None of us knew why someone would act like that," said Dom. "We worried about the possibility of kidnapping for ransom. All the children at that art class were from wealthy families."

Karen saw Grayson's eyes widen as Dom revealed what the surveillance cameras had caught and told them about Ruben's attempt to snatch Santos.

"That must be when he found out where Santos was," said Karen. "But how did this Ruben get Santos's phone number?"

"Santos's cell phone was stolen," said Pete. "It appears Ruben took it and got the information from it before he ditched it." Then he fixed his stare on William. "Allegedly, Grayson had a part in the theft of the art from your gallery on the night of August the fourth."

William jerked forward again. "Are you out of your mind? He was home watching TV. He was there all night."

"I wasn't. I snuck out. Ruben picked me up, and we went to the gallery."

"Nonsense. What tall tale are you telling? And who is this Ruben everyone keeps talking about?"

"Otto introduced me to him. At the Bistro."

"Otto? My manager? That Otto?"

"Yes. Otto told him about me. Said Ruben could help. At first, I thought he would, but—" He paused. "You're going to hate me."

"Why would I hate you?"

"When Ruben and I got to the gallery, the door was open. The alarm wasn't set. Bruno was sleeping, just like Ruben said in his plan."

"His plan?" asked Pete.

"It sounds stupid now." Grayson put his elbows on the table and covered his face with his hands. There were some sniffs, before his hesitant voice was heard. "The plan was to make my dad l-like me again."

"What?" William's voice held astonishment.

Ruiz spoke up. "Do you mean to say that Ruben had a plan to make your dad care about you?"

Grayson nodded. "It was my fault Mom died. My fault Swift died."

"Swift?" asked Ruiz.

"The borzoi," said Karen softly. "His dad's dog."

William put a hand on his son's wrist. "Algie, that wasn't—"

Grayson jerked away. "You told me you could hardly bear looking at me. That I only reminded you of Mom."

"I loved your mother and miss her every day. You look so much like her. She lives on through you."

"But you never see *me*!" Grayson thumped his chest. "Me! You turn away. You can't stand looking at me. Because it was my fault Mom died."

William's mouth dropped open. "I *never* said—"

"No. You never said anything. I miss her too, you know. I could never talk about her with you. I tried to be what you wanted me to be." He slumped back in his chair. "It doesn't matter anymore. My life is over."

Karen caught her lip between her teeth.

William rolled his eyes. "Don't be overdramatic."

"Grayson," said Pete, "can you tell us what Ruben's actual plan was?"

Grayson nodded. "He said he, Otto, and Bruno had worked out this plan together. He—"

"What?" William's voice was incredulous.

"Mr. Adams, let him speak."

"He said it was best if I didn't talk to Otto or Bruno about the details. Give it away."

Ruiz went to the credenza and returned with a box of tissues. "So, Ruben never told you how the plan would actually work?"

Grayson grabbed a tissue and blew his nose. "Just that the art would be at Otto's."

William sputtered again but desisted when Pete held up a hand.

"Then, don't know how, I would find the art. He said, said my dad … would be pleased. I'd be a hero." Grayson's voice trailed off in a tormented whisper. "And I thought … maybe … you could …"

"Could what, Grayson?" asked Karen softly.

"My dad could … love me. Love me again." He squeezed his eyes shut and shook in silent sobs.

"You fool!" William's anger rolled out of him. "How could you possibly believe a story like that? Have you no sense at all?"

Grayson hugged his torso, going back to the slow rocking. Back and forth. Back and forth.

Heated blood rushed to Karen's face. Could no one else see what was happening to Grayson? See what gashes their words were cutting in the young soul? She rose to her feet. "All he—"

Pete put a hand on her wrist. "Karen, please—"

She subsided to the edge of her chair, biting her lip as William lashed out at Grayson.

William's voice cut like ice. "Idiot, you let a thief into my gallery, let him steal millions of dollars of art. The exhibit had to be postponed. Everyone's plans were ruined. My gallery is still closed. For God's sake, Algie, the guard died. No son of mine would do such a stupid thing. You deserve what's going to happen to you. Shame on you." William sat back in his chair with enough force to roll it half a foot. He folded his arms.

Karen watched Grayson as his father's anger spewed at him. With each hurtful utterance, the boy withdrew. His eyes became dead coals in a pale sheet.

Karen's quick glance at Dom told her he was upset with William too. His nostrils flared, and his jaw was set.

Grayson bowed his head, and his shoulders shook with sobs. When the sobs reduced to sniffs, he began again in a small resolute voice. "I know it sounds stupid now, but I *wanted to believe* what he said."

Pete's calm, quiet voice broke the silence following Grayson's statement. "When you can, tell us what happened that night."

Grayson repeated what he'd told them in Karen's studio from the moment he'd disarmed the gallery security system to when he'd hidden the Anonicelli.

At that point, his dad glared at Grayson, but he didn't say a word.

What is wrong with William? Karen raged inside. Why isn't he objecting? His child is in pain. Why isn't he talking about getting a lawyer?

"After we left the gallery, Ruben dropped me off at my house. Told me not to say anything. Saturday night I heard Bruno died. Why? How? I still don't know. I called Ruben on Sunday to see if he knew. He was in a bookstore. No more helpful and kind. Told me never to call him again."

"The call the kids overheard," said Karen. She told them what Krista had told her.

Grayson nodded. "Then the next day after Dad left for work, Ruben came to our house. He wanted to know where the Anonicelli was. Threatened to kill my dad if I didn't tell him. He t-told me what was going to happen to me in prison. But I don't care. It won't matter about me anymore."

"Can you remember what he said in that phone call? Especially the threats?" asked Pete.

"Sure. I can give you the recording."

"*Gott im Himmel!* The recording?"

"After he took the Anonicelli, I didn't trust him. I recorded my call to him at the bookstore. I recorded him at our house." Grayson pulled his phone out and showed Pete how to access the recordings.

"Is Ruben's number in your phone?" asked Pete. "I'd like to check this out. We need this for evidence against Ruben to put him away where he can't hurt anyone else."

"Keep it. I won't need it."

Uff da. Grayson not needing his phone? That sounded alarming to Karen.

Pete put his hand over Grayson's. "Of course, you'll need it." His eyes held contact with Grayson's until the lad shrugged and turned away.

"I just have a few more questions," said Pete. "Grayson and I talked on the way over here I am going to arrest him for felony burglary and then we'll take him to juvenile detention. William, you will want to go with your son—"

"I have no son." William rose from his seat. "It's a good thing Gloria didn't live to see this day."

"William! You don't mean that." The rebuke burst from Karen's lips. "Grayson, he didn't mean it. Grayson!" She reached her hand across the table to him.

He didn't respond, just closed his eyes.

Dom took her other hand, giving it a gentle squeeze. Karen's eyes met his in anguish.

Pete's voice was firm. "Mr. Adams, sit down. As I was saying, first you, your son, and I, along with Sergeant Ruiz and a couple of patrol officers will go to your gallery to recover the Anonicelli. Then Sergeant Ruiz will take you and your son to the Juvenile Detention Center. While there, he will be assigned a juvenile probation officer. They will take it from there."

Karen watched in consternation as Pete talked. The boy seemed numb and accepting of his fate. When Pete finished, he read the time and stated that the interview was ended. Then he stopped recording. William's face held smoldering anger.

As they moved to the door, Karen took Grayson's hand. His fingers felt icy. "Grayson, we'll see—"

Grayson raised his head. The look he gave her was as bleak as she'd ever felt on her worst day.

"Goodbye, Karen, Dom. Thank you. D-don't worry about me." He turned and followed Sergeant Ruiz out the door.

William brushed past and left without meeting either her or Dom's eyes.

"My God. That sounded so … forever." Karen turned in anguish to Pete. "I hate it. *Just hate it.* It's Vidar all over again. We didn't have the right."

Dom took her hand. "Isn't there something we can do? Get him a lawyer? Anything?"

Pete shook his head. "Be an advocate. Keep on making noise. Keep on telling the boy that somebody cares." He stopped with his hand on the doorknob. His eyes closed. "His son. His only child. It may not be professional, but I wanted to grab William and shake him. I'll show you out now and call you when I can. It may not be until sometime tomorrow."

CHAPTER SEVENTY-SEVEN

Before Pete left the police station after their interview with Grayson, he started the ball rolling on a search warrant for Otto's home for the stolen exhibit pieces. While he did that, Ruiz took father and son to complete the paperwork concerning Grayson's arrest.

When they finished, Pete and Ruiz took William, Grayson, and the patrol officers to the gallery. Pete kept a watchful eye on Grayson as the teen pointed out the hiding place of the painting. He saw no signs of subterfuge in his demeanor or attitude.

The Anonicelli was in the kitchen, unharmed in a sandwich of aluminum serving trays upright in the cupboards.

Pete kept William under close scrutiny as the painting was brought to light and examined. Later he'd compare with Ruiz about their observed body language and expressions of the son and father.

Shortly after the find was documented, Ruiz left with William and Grayson for juvenile detention. Pete made a brief call to Tuttle with the news. By the time that call ended, Pete's search warrant had come through. He and the patrol officers left for Otto's home.

Pete's ringing the doorbell resulted in a shaky voice calling out, "Who is it?"

"Mr. Griffin? Lieutenant Schultz, Police."

The door opened and a sleepy-looking Otto stood there, his brows drawn together. "Why are you here so late? Has something happened?"

"Mr. Griffin, the Anonicelli has been recovered."

"Oh, my! That's wonderful. Is she all right?"

"As far as Mr. Adams could see, the painting is fine."

"Where was it found?"

"It never left the gallery. It was hidden there."

"That's amazing! Where? Was all the art there? I don't understand. Was Bruno involved?"

"We were told that the rest of the art may be here."

Otto did a doubletake, his eyes opened wide. "Here? At my house? Impossible. I had nothing to do with the robbery."

"We have not accused you. We have a search warrant, but it's easier if you allow us in."

"Sure, you can look."

Pete and the four officers began their search in the master bedroom, checking all the places big enough to conceal the missing art. In the guest bedroom, Kapaun's illuminated manuscript was found under the bed. An officer opened the walk-in closet to find it stacked with boxes.

"Those are my mother's things," said Otto.

The officers started taking cartons out of the closet and opening them. Knitting. Yarn. Needlecraft projects. Faded, folded linens and embroidered pillowcases. Christmas figures of carolers and angels.

"Mother liked to make things. She was always into decorating."

Behind the front stack of boxes was a large carton.

Otto frowned. "I don't remember that box."

The policewoman grunted in response to its weight. She lifted the flaps and pulled out the dark piece of fuzzy material lying on top. An outstretched bronze hand gleamed in the light.

"Oh, my." Otto's mouth dropped open. "Joaquin's sculpture."

The box behind it held the rest of the stolen paintings.

Pete looked at the list on the warrant. "The tapestry is still missing. It may be rolled in black garbage bags if my informant is correct. Check under the bed again and look in the other rooms."

"Your informant?" asked Otto. "Who told you the art was here?"

"I can't answer that, Mr. Griffin."

"Lieutenant!" An officer called from near the front-room coat closet. He held aside winter coats and pointed to a bulky, black plastic-wrapped roll stashed behind an assortment of table leaves and furled umbrellas. "I think we've got it. Man, it's really wedged in tightly under that shelf." He unloaded the things in front of it and worked it out.

The plastic on one end was abraded and torn. The finial hung out of the plastic, bent from the rod at an angle.

"*Mein Gott*." Pete touched it with a gloved finger. "Look, the pocket for the rod has been torn loose. Have the evidence technician note any damage."

He faced the little white-haired man still wearing a dumbfounded expression. "And now, Mr. Griffin. If you would be so kind, we need to go back to the police station and have a talk."

While Otto was turning on his security system, Pete excused himself to return one of the increasingly urgent calls in the last several minutes from Cecil.

"Sorry," Pete said when Cecil answered. "I couldn't answer you earlier."

"I suddenly started getting the signal from the tracking device that's attached to the Anonicelli. I called Tuttle and he says it's been recovered. Wouldn't tell me anything else."

Pete told Cecil where the painting had been hidden and described the circumstances surrounding Algie's arrest. "I only gave Tuttle the bare bones. We're still unraveling what happened."

"I can't believe Algie took the art. Holy shit. Yet it makes sense. He had all the knowledge to disarm the system. Poor kid. What he must be feeling."

"Dupre, I'm worried about him. I shared my concern with the folks at juvenile detention. I'm pretty sure they'll keep Grayson for a while, keep a watch on him."

"Best place for him at the moment, in a way."

"He's in pain, and his old man, well, to put it kindly, he's angry."

"Behaving badly?" asked Cecil.

"You didn't hear me say that."

"I'll have to go see William." Cecil sighed. "Tell me where the Anonicelli was found at the gallery."

"In a kitchen cupboard, completely hidden, nested between aluminum serving trays."

"Shit! A Faraday cage. The signal wouldn't go through all that aluminum."

"I thought so," said Pete. "Was going to ask you. I don't know how long it will take William at juvenile hall, but I'm sure he could use a friend. Look, I've got to go. I'll touch base with you later."

After Pete had Otto seated in one of the interrogation rooms, he quizzed the white-haired man again about the night of the burglary.

Otto dutifully repeated his testimony. Then he paused. "That's why! When I got home again after the robbery, I felt like someone had been in my house. Thought it was nerves, but I couldn't shake the feeling. I felt better after I asked Cecil to put in a security system. I was right. Somebody had broken in."

Pete made a note. Looked like Ruben had been setting up Otto. But no one ever mentioned Algie as a suspect. Why?

"I want you to think way back," said Pete, "to the day Dupre first went over the new gallery security system features with you. Who was there?"

"That was last February. I told you. Cecil, William, Guy, and me."

"Close your eyes. Picture who was sitting where."

"But—"

"Remember. Where were they sitting?"

Otto scrunched his eyes shut. "William was at the head of the table. Guy and I were on his right. Cecil and Algie were on his left."

"You didn't mention Algie knowing about the security. Why?"

"I didn't?" Otto looked bewildered. "He wasn't part of the meeting." Otto frowned. "He was just there. I guess I thought you meant employees."

Pete was chagrined. How did he and an ex-FBI agent miss that?

Pete set three photographs in front of Otto. "Look at these. Can you identify any of these men?"

Otto picked up the photo of Ruben and looked again at the other two. He handed Ruben's photo to Pete. "Don't know the others, but this man's a friend of mine. He's very helpful."

"His name?"

"Ruben Turner. I met him in our gallery."

"Do you know where he lives?"

Otto looked startled. "You know, I don't. He calls every so often, or I run into him. Everybody at the Hog Bristle Bistro and at the Blue Goose knows him. He's always helping people out and doing kind things."

"Can you give me an example of how he helps others?"

"We talked about his friend who owns a gallery in Dallas. He was gathering information on security systems for him. Asked me about what I liked and didn't like about ours. Things like response time and what set it off. He said his friend really appreciated the recommendation."

Pete avoided rolling his eyes. "Does anyone else at your gallery know him?"

"I would think so, but …" Otto frowned. "I've never heard William talk about him, but Algie knows him. I introduced them."

"You introduced them? Why?"

"Well, Algie was going through a bad time recently. You know how it can be between teenagers and their fathers. I thought Ruben could help. He's a good listener."

"Did they meet?"

"I'd told Ruben about William's bias against digital art. I know they talked, because …" Otto looked puzzled. "After that, Algie said the strangest thing. I didn't have a clue what he meant, but with young people, I often don't."

"What did he say?"

"He said, 'I know I'm not supposed to say anything, but thanks for your help with the plan.' What did he mean? What plan?"

"You never talked about a plan with Ruben involving Algie?"

"No."

"We heard of a plan, involving you, to store stolen art at your place. Being in possession of stolen property is a crime."

Otto's voice was emphatic. "I never heard of this plan till right now."

It looked more and more like Grayson was truthful. Pete sat back with a sigh. "I have other photographs you might be able to identify." He handed Otto several more stills cropped from the surveillance footage at the Bjornson Ranch. Sam and Anton had gotten them for him while the events that evening had unfolded.

As Otto looked, Pete wondered if Otto was mixed up in this mess or had just been duped by a mastermind. He suspected the latter, consistent with the Anonicelli thief MO.

"These are all Ruben."

"You're sure?"

"Absolutely. Lieutenant, why ask me about Ruben?"

"I should tell you this for your own safety. We have reason to believe he is armed and dangerous."

Otto laughed. "Oh, you're wrong. He's a good man."

"Do not get in touch with him. Contact us immediately if you see him."

"Ruben would never—" Otto's mouth dropped open.

"We're still investigating. Do not talk about this with anyone. We don't know yet who is involved. Do you understand?"

"Yes, but what if I see Ruben? What shall I do?"

"Call 911. Don't talk to him or get in his way."

"Oh, my."

CHAPTER SEVENTY-EIGHT

Saturday, August 12

William entered his home in the wee hours of Saturday morning. He couldn't figure out his dominant feeling. Was it anger or embarrassment? For certain, coming on the heels of Guy's arrest for embezzlement, his son's betrayal was devastating. His son, who'd never even skipped school, had been arrested, sent to juvenile detention to be charged with felony burglary.

The house felt strangely empty. William was unsettled. Sleep was out of the question, nor could he concentrate on anything. He wandered through the house, eventually into Algie's room. On his son's desk stood Didion, the old mechanical toy Cecil had made. He picked it up, fingering the smoothness. His eyes blurred and he set it down, none too gently, and turned away.

Blinking, he found himself in front of an oil painting on an easel. Though the painting was far from done, with some pencil sketches still visible, he could see it was of Dom and Karen. They were laughing, their poses natural. Like Gloria, his son had captured the subjects' feelings. This showed promise. It would be exquisite. And Algie was only sixteen.

What would happen now? Would the painting ever be finished? William left the room in despair.

He followed his feet to his own room, coming face-to-face with Gloria's portrait of herself, Algie, and Swift. Standing in silence, his eyes caressed Gloria's familiar features.

Unable to let her go, he often talked to her portrait in the privacy of their bedroom. Now feeling overwhelmed, he poured out his trouble to her.

"I need you. I can't do this alone."

Only silence.

Then with a jolt, he heard her voice in his head, *"You aren't alone. You have our son."*

"I've failed you. He's failed you."

His eyes closed. He sat on the edge of the bed, lowered his head into his hands, and rocked back and forth in anguish.

His cell phone rang. Who the hell could be calling at this hour?

Cecil. William pressed ANSWER.

"I know you're still up. I'm outside. Can I come in?"

William went to the door and opened it. "Don't tell me you were just passing on your way home. We live on opposite sides of the city. Can I get you something to drink? Scotch?"

"Fine."

Cecil followed William to the family room and sat on the couch, watching as William poured the scotches. The man's movements were jerky. He looked whacked, his eyes red-rimmed. Cecil couldn't blame him. William's week had been hellish.

"I heard Algie was sent to juvenile detention," said Cecil. "I'm sorry."

"Already? Who's been blabbing?"

Cecil coughed. "The FBI."

"What?"

"They'd asked me to consult. Long story, but now is not the time to tell it. I came because of Algie. He's a good kid."

William glowered. "Yeah. Good kid. Arrested for felony burglary."

"You know he loves you. All he wanted to do was to please you."

"Fine way of showing it. You don't understand what I'm going through. You've never had a wife or son."

Cecil leaned back and closed his eyes. Memories poured forth from the place in his head he kept private. He forced out the words he'd suppressed so long. "Not anymore. They were killed. A long time ago. Don't tell me I don't know what the hell you're going through."

"What? You never told me."

Cecil sipped his scotch. "No one knows in Santa Fe." He'd never wanted to talk about it. He wouldn't now, except the need was so great to help Algie and have his father understand. If breaking his silence would help, well then.

"My God, Cecil. What—"

"I was FBI. They were taken hostage. They died." Cecil swallowed. "I can't talk about it right now. Maybe later."

"I'm sorry."

"I envy you your son."

"After what he's done to me!"

"To you?" Cecil took a deep breath. "And what about what you've done to him?"

"Damn it. I haven't done *anything* to him."

"Maybe then, it's what you didn't do. William, he thinks you blame him for his mother's death, and for the death of Swift."

"Those were accidents. I never blamed him."

"But that's what he believes. All he wanted was for you to accept him."

William slid off his stool and paced back and forth. "He and some lowlife *robbed my gallery*. Keller is dead. They still don't know what happened to the cleaning woman."

"From what I can see, it's Ruben's fault."

"And yet I should accept what Algie did?" He spat out a crude epithet.

"Algie used poor judgment. He trusted the wrong person. He's living with the consequences. Shit, William, he just turned sixteen. Have you never trusted the wrong person?"

"I never let my judgment—" William paused and put a hand over his mouth.

His expression changed. "Hell, Cecil. Don't you say it." He shut his eyes and sat down heavily. "Guy. I trusted him. He stole a fortune from me."

Cecil didn't say anything.

"I've failed Algie. I told him I have no son."

"Are you shitting me?"

"He said it didn't matter anymore. His life was over. They just had to catch Ruben so he wouldn't ruin any more lives. I told him to stop being so melodramatic."

Slowly William's eyes raised to focus on Cecil's and then widened. His voice was a whisper. "Cecil, he wouldn't …"

His voice rose in volume and tension. "At juvenile detention, they said they would keep him this weekend for evaluation. Said he may be at risk for harming himself. I told them that was ridiculous. Jesus! What have I done?"

Cecil grabbed the bottle and poured them each another drink. "There's still time, William."

After William calmed, Cecil settled into the long haul of listening. Some was painful, bringing back his own losses, but cathartic too. William had never talked about Gloria with anyone. Her loss was still raw.

"All Gloria's talent," said William. "I saw in Algie that same spark she had. I thought if I bent his in her direction, her art would go on through our son."

"Her art. Don't you see, William? Algie isn't Gloria. He has his own unique talent."

"Don't you think I know that?" William slumped back in his chair. "But I miss her so much. How can I bear a world without her?"

"You keep her vision alive by doing your art for social change exhibits."

William traced the tiny puddle of scotch left on the coffee table from his unsteady hands, drawing the beads of liquid together. His head was still lowered, but he nodded slightly.

"A while back when Karen started those art classes, he wanted me to start calling him Grayson. Said he'd been pond scum long enough." William paused to sip his scotch. "Gloria always called him Grayson."

"It's tough being a teen. Any positive help with self-image is good."

"Karen was responsible for that change. How did she see what I didn't?"

"Different perspective?"

William nodded. "I yelled at Karen for interfering. Funny. Gloria would have done the same damn thing Karen did."

Chapter Seventy-Nine

At five o'clock on Saturday morning, Sam was roused from sleep by a phone call from a state police detective he knew from joint task forces worked in Santa Fe.

"Martinez, this is Captain Brower. I've been following your case with the missing witness to the gallery burglary. I was listening to chatter on the State Police channels."

Sam stifled a yawn. "You're up early." He took the phone with him into the bathroom.

"Sorry to wake you, but there's new information from the Cloudcroft area. I thought it urgent for you to hear right away."

"Captain, what is it?"

"A young immigrant woman from Guatemala was offered a ride from El Paso to Albuquerque by someone who appeared to be a nun."

Sam interrupted. "Appeared to be?"

"Turned out it was a man in disguise. He apparently drugged her and took her to an old farm outside Cloudcroft. He assaulted her repeatedly before dragging her off to an old mine shaft and leaving her for dead. When she came to, she was not alone—other women's remains were there."

"I don't like where you're going, Captain."

"I don't either. She was able to get herself back to the road. Someone found her and called the police. The man was long gone."

"Was the woman able to give a description?"

"Yes, especially of the nun disguise. Called himself Sister Mary Catherine."

Sam braced himself on the bathroom counter. "God, no. That's the name of the nun who gave a ride to our witness. Who's in charge in Cloudcroft?"

Brower gave him the contacts. "Give them a call. They will need your information."

Sam hung up, got dressed, then called the Cloudcroft PD. He learned the case was being handled by the Otero County Sheriff's Department. Cloudcroft didn't have the resources to handle a case of that magnitude.

Finally talking to the officer in charge, Sam emailed the picture of Sister Mary Catherine, Dulcie's description, and the leads he'd gained in tracing Dulcie and the so-called nun. They asked him to send a DNA sample of Dulcie's.

"Dulcie Rodriguez was wearing a distinctive yellow shirt with a cleaning company logo on it. Have you found anything like that?"

The officer responded. "No, but that doesn't mean it isn't there. They're searching other locations on the old farmstead. The police are following up on the property records. That may help identify who it is. This guy might have been flying under the radar for a long time, choosing victims with no one to raise the alarm if they went missing."

When Sam had given the sheriff the information, he checked in with Pete.

"As soon as you can, tell Santos," said Pete. "He should hear it from you, not the TV."

Sam went back to the bedroom. Farah rolled over and stretched her arms up sleepily to return his hug. "Bye, sweetheart. Sorry you were awakened."

"Is it about Dulcie?"

"Yes." He brushed her hair back from her eyes. "I had other plans for waking up with you."

"I know, but you must go."

"Love you."

"Love you too."

◆ ❖ ◆

Sam started the twenty-some-minute drive to the Bjornson ranch. How in God's name would he tell the kid about the possibility his mom had been a victim of this man and may not be alive? He believed in being honest with children, not sugar-coating the truth, but this held horrors for him, even calloused by years as a policeman. For a child it could be the stuff of nightmares for years to come.

He thought it would be good if Maria and Diego were there when he told Santos, and Dom and Karen too. He knew Dom and Karen were out late the night before with Grayson at the PD, but his grandfather would be okay being woken when he knew the reason.

"Santos needs support, but not a crowd when he gets the news," said Dom when Sam told him. "I'll give everyone heads up."

◆ ❖ ◆

It was seven o'clock when Sam arrived at the ranch. With Dom and Karen, he came down the long hall into the family room. The TV was off and no one else around. They found Diego, Maria, and Santos in the breakfast room. Santos obviously was braced for news he wasn't going to like.

God, what could he say to this youngster who was in such pain?

Sam sat across from him and accepted the mug of coffee Karen poured for him.

"Tell me." The boy's voice was fierce. "*Tell me.*"

"You remember we were told your mother was given a ride by someone? We think that same person offered a ride to another woman on Thursday."

"You mean that nun?"

"Everybody thought she was a nun, but she wasn't. It was actually a man in disguise."

Maria covered her mouth with her hand.

"He hurt this other woman very badly, and she passed out. She was left for dead in an old mine. But she survived and made her way to a highway where she got help. She was lucky because others died at that place."

"Where was this?" asked Karen.

"In the mountains, near Cloudcroft. Not too far from Alamogordo," said Sam.

"She got away?" said Diego. "Did they catch the guy?"

"Not yet. But thanks to Karen's photos, they know what he looks like. When this news breaks, it's going to be all over TV. But you can't believe everything you hear. They don't always get it right."

Sam watched as the boy processed what he'd heard.

Then Santos banged his fist on the table, making all the cutlery jump. He stood and yelled, "My mom would get away. She *would*."

"They haven't found her. There's still hope, Santos."

"She's not dead!" He kicked back at his empty chair, toppling it in a crash. "I won't believe she's at that place."

Diego quietly picked up the chair. Santos sank into it. His body slumped as he laced his fingers at the back of his head and brought his elbows forward. When he finally raised his head and met Sam's eyes, his look was pleading.

"Coach, what about what Ruben told me yesterday? That Mom was back in Santa Fe? Could he be right?"

"Ruben is a liar. He doesn't know what happened to your mom. He chased her the night of the burglary. Yesterday he would have taken you hostage to get to her if he could. He's already killed twice. He won't hesitate to kill again."

Sam leaned toward Santos, his hands cradling his mug. "You know you can ask me anything. If I don't know the answer, I'll try to find out. I have questions too."

Diego put his hand on Santos's shoulder and gave it a brief squeeze.

"We won't give up," said Sam. "We'll find your mom."

On Saturday afternoon, when Diego finally had a chance to talk with Maria alone, they went up to the swing with their coffee to make plans. Santos stayed by the alpaca pens. Thunderbump came running to the fence to lean into the boy and be stroked.

"Maria, I don't think we can wait long to get married. I want us to be able to move quickly if CYFD comes sniffing around." He met her eyes. "But I feel both good and bad about rushing our wedding. You deserve wedding memories to cherish, but how can we celebrate? That news this morning was awful."

"I agree we must move quickly," said Maria. "We could have a celebration later when it feels right. Now, no one's in the mood for dancing, big groups of friends, or elaborate meals."

Diego nodded. "I don't need anything fancy. But women think about things like wedding dresses and flowers. I don't want you to feel cheated."

"Cheated?" Maria looked into his eyes with warm affection. "Why would I feel cheated? I'm marrying the love of my life. I could celebrate by throwing rose petals from a mountaintop at dawn, with a judge saying the words, or with Sam playing his guitar, or reciting vows with you in our swing seat in the moonlight. I don't care. The important thing is in the doing and what is in our hearts."

"I like simple. It seems the wedding with a judge in the courthouse will have to do. Thank goodness there's no waiting period in this state." He lifted her fingers to his mouth for a kiss. "*Madre de Dios*, we do need to buy rings."

"An engagement ring seems silly. How about simple gold bands for both of us?"

Diego tilted up her chin and grinned. "I like it, and I do like the idea of Sam and his guitar. Maybe when we are ready to celebrate?"

Maria nodded. "When should we tell everyone?"

"Tonight after dinner?"

"Yes." Maria laid her head against his chest. "We'll make plans, but these days are so up and down. Flexible will have to do."

"So, Sunday for rings and shopping, get the license Monday morning. Perhaps a Tuesday morning appointment at the courthouse."

"Monday night is the barbecue at the middle school for new students and their families. Anton said we could ride with them."

"Our new responsibilities."

Movement from the nearby door caught his eye. Tuffy appeared, his tail an orange banner, waving proudly. He laid a mouse at Diego's feet. Then with a loud purr, he wound in and out of their legs before carrying the mouse down the steps to eat his lunch.

Diego grinned broadly. "New responsibilities, all."

CHAPTER EIGHTY

Sunday, August 13

Ruben slouched by a darkened upstairs window in the place where he was house sitting. He puzzled over that ranch in the country. He'd love to get close enough to watch and see the comings and goings. What he'd seen with his binoculars the day he'd discovered Santos convinced him there was something strange going on there. It felt like a personal threat.

Since it first occurred to him, the more certain he was that the Anonicelli was at that ranch. He hadn't heard about it being found, so it probably hadn't been with Purity's stuff. He'd carefully searched the Adamses' home. He was proud of that. Hadn't left a trace of his being there.

Algie, that devious brat, must have taken the Anonicelli to that ranch. Damn him. When Ruben finally had the painting, that kid's days on earth were numbered.

Many of the people he'd seen there carried computer cases or large portfolios. They could have been smuggling art in those cases.

There were a lot of people involved in whatever kind of scheme it was, and they seemed to be using children, holding them against their will. Certainly, they'd tried to keep Santos from leaving. Ruben thought by shooting at the others when he arrived to pick up Santos, the kid might have been able to break away and he'd have him. But that big blond bruiser had been too strong for the kid.

Many seemed to come and go. Did they have meetings of some sort?

Did the law know about them? He'd never seen a cop car there—oh, a couple in the area on that Friday afternoon. He hadn't stuck around after shooting at their car. They were smart, setting up operations out in the country. No cops in sight, and none could get there before you had time to finish what you were doing.

There was only one thing to do. He had to get close enough at night to check out what was going on while they slept. With luck, they wanted the Anonicelli themselves and it would be hanging on the wall someplace. Buyers for a prize like that took time to arrange.

His reconnaissance trip had to be soon. The homeowners where he was staying would be back by Labor Day.

The Florida thugs were getting harder and harder to avoid. Their calls had changed from annoying to threatening. They'd tracked him down, made it obvious they were watching. Waiting.

His heartbeat quickened as a car drove slowly into the cul-de-sac and stopped. The car lights were extinguished, but no one moved to get out. Ruben rubbed his stomach. The sick feeling was back.

He knew who waited in the night.

CHAPTER EIGHTY-ONE

Tuesday, August 15

The following night, Karen felt besieged from all sides. She lay beside Dom, staring into the darkness with eyes that would not close. Her tapestry woven with such hope had reaped only misery.

Dulcie had been missing for ten days, and the promise of her return was fading. If she was alive, why hadn't they heard? If she was dead, where did she lie?

Was Santos an orphan? What future did he face, robbed of both parents? Diego and Maria would do their best; they assured her their decision wasn't made only for Santos, but still.

The *Tapestry of Light*, stolen by Grayson. Held in an evidence locker somewhere. Recovered, yet at what cost? Grayson, bright, talented, but fallen prey to malevolent manipulation. Only because he wanted so desperately to have his father love him again.

How could William have rejected him? Now Grayson was in the juvenile detention system. She'd heard they kept him on Friday night. What would happen to him? Would he be charged as an adult? Face prison time? My God, the kid just turned sixteen. He should be going into his junior year of high school, learning to drive, learning more about his art, making friends, dating, and getting ready for college.

That look in his eyes still haunted her. That awful finality in his goodbye. She believed he'd been ready to take his own life.

Tears clogged her nose, her throat. Sobs threatened. Not wanting to awaken Dom, she folded back the blanket, rose, and tugged on her robe. She went into her sitting room and leaned back in the window seat. Holding back the sobs was impossible.

What would become of the Niemöller exhibit? What had brought tears of joy and hope at the Gala Reception was now despair and heartbreak. The artwork had all been recovered. But it wasn't back at the gallery yet, and who knew when the police could release it? Who knew when that exhibit, let alone the gallery, would reopen fully?

What went so horribly wrong? What could she have done differently? She hadn't sat back in apathy. She'd interfered. And yet...

Another image appeared in her mind. Her nephew, Vidar. Another life cut short.

Was darkness winning?

She felt Dom's hand on her shoulder. He sat next to her, and she turned into his arms, sobbing.

"Oh, Dom. Dulcie, Grayson, Vidar. The exhibit. All that promise. Taken away."

Dom held her, rubbing her back.

"Dulcie's face won't leave my mind. So full of life, warm, caring. The only parent her son had. Dulcie should be here. I can't bear to think she died in pain, alone, at the mercy of some ... evil monster. And left there."

Dom's hand continued its rhythmic pattern.

"And Grayson. I'm so frightened for him. Such emptiness in his eyes."

She felt Dom's head nodding against hers.

"I didn't have the right when Vidar was growing up either. He had to go back to his father, back to abuse, to bitterness. My husband and I couldn't do anything. We didn't have the right."

Dom sniffed. She put a hand to his cheek and realized he was crying too.

"There's a difference with Grayson," he said. "Friday night William was frustrated. He was shocked and embarrassed. But still he's the same man who set up the exhibits because of his wife's vision. He's not like Vidar's father. He will come to his senses."

"But in time?" She put her head back on his shoulder. "Even if I could give Grayson sanctuary here, I'm not equipped to help someone as depressed as he is. He needs professional help—the best there is."

"He should have that with juvenile detention. That we can push for."

"Dom, I held Vidar in my arms as he died. There was nothing I could do. He'd grabbed that gun and took that bullet for me, to save my life. I owe him. My life has to count for something."

"My love, don't you see?" He raised her chin and looked into her eyes. What little light there was caught the sheen of his tears. "You are making a difference. Your art, and the way you provide nurture and shelter. You care with your whole being."

"It's not enough."

Pressed so close to him, she felt the vibration in his chest as he spoke fiercely. "Then I will add what I can. Others you have touched will add more. It's a ripple. It grows larger. We will *make* it enough. Even if it takes a lifetime and more."

Karen pressed closer, held securely in his arms, feeling the conviction in his voice, and feeling the warmth of his embrace.

Images of Vidar, of Grayson, of Dulcie filled her mind. So precious—all of them.

How long they sat there she didn't know. His hand found and played with a strand of her hair, a soothing, tender touch.

But then a sound caught her attention.

She raised her head and listened.

Again!

"Dom! The alpacas are alarming. Something or someone's out there."

Chapter Eighty-Two

A low, throaty growl jolted Anton awake from a sound sleep. Then he heard another sound—a sequence of pings. Not Truman this time, but a biped.

Propping himself up on one elbow, Anton looked toward Twitch. Upright and bristly in the dim glow from the nightlight, his dog faced the outside door onto the deck. The clock by the bed flicked its digital numbers to 2:37. Pushing aside the light blanket, Anton slipped out of bed. The moon shed its waning light onto a quiet back yard.

"What is it?" Skyla's soft voice came from behind him.

The pings sounded again.

"Those pings. Biped. And Twitch knows somebody's out there." He glanced at the crib where Lucas slept peacefully. He bent and touched the dog's back. It was rigid. The growl came again as Twitch moved near the deck door, looking back at Anton.

"Uff da!" Anton pulled on his jeans, grabbed a sweatshirt, and jammed his feet into his loafers. "I'm going to check it out."

"Be careful."

"Always." He left their suite and walked swiftly down the hall.

Krista's door opened, and her dog ran past her. "Shadow woke me up all growly."

Both Airedales disappeared downstairs. Krista and Anton followed.

"Anton?"

Karen stood near the bottom of the stairs, Dom right behind her.

"Did something wake you too?" asked Anton.

"No, couldn't sleep. Then we heard the alpacas squeaking."

"Diego will be awake then," said Anton. "Call 911. Call Diego, make sure they stay inside. Then check the monitors."

Karen hissed in a breath. "Ruben?"

"Best to be safe." He started down the hall toward the garage workshop, looking over his shoulder at them. "I'm going to send up the drone from the garage roof."

As the drone lifted away from Anton on the roof, he watched the control screen in his hands, scanning the area around the house first, then the duplex, before searching near the outbuildings. This drone, which he and Skyla used for their archaeological exploration, had a thermal-imaging camera, not a regular one. It captured the blurry, green-colored heat signature of the alpacas lined up against the fence, facing one of the sheds near the duplex.

Uff da, that wasn't a good sign. When something alarmed them, alpacas habitually faced the threat. He heard Blanca's distinctive alarm call, a sound somewhere between a squeaky rubber dog toy and a dying seagull. Others echoed her.

He maneuvered the drone higher to include more territory. A figure emerged from one of the equipment sheds and ran toward their backyard gate. The man grabbed the gate latch and pulled. Anton knew it was firmly locked. Then the person backed up and took a short run at the fence, going up and over it, landing in the back yard and running toward the house. Motion-sensor lights came on illuminating the yard.

He heard the whoosh of the sliding glass door off the family room. The Airedales ran into the back yard barking like crazy.

God, who had unlocked the door, compromising that perimeter of safety and sending the eager dogs into danger?

Whoever the intruder was, he didn't get far. He turned and ran, the dogs jumping at him. Like quicksilver they darted—leaping on and bedeviling the creep. Then two bright flashes of heat preceded the sound of gunshots. The green blur of a person swung itself up to the fence top and fell into a heap on the other side.

Krista screamed from the house. "Shadow, come! Twitch, come!"

Anton's voice roared from the rooftop. "Krista! Stay inside." God, he wasn't even on that side of the house. All he could do was watch the green blurs in horror.

The dogs barked sharply a few more times, then they ran back to the house. Their movement showed no indication that they had been hurt. The sound of the door told Anton they had been admitted safely. Anton focused with growing rage on the figure that rose from the ground, turned, and fled beyond the range of the yard light and down the road.

Did the intruder realize he was being followed from the sky? This drone wasn't that quiet, and it had lights on it to keep track of it. He kept it high as he panned ahead to the driveway gate. There was no car waiting there, but he saw the large, faint block of heat from a cooling car engine about a hundred yards down on the side of the road.

He swept back to follow the green figure as it cut across the hairpin turn on the driveway, stumbled, fell, and slid down the slope. The figure got up, limped to the car, and drove away out of drone range. Anton brought back the drone and set it inside. The footage would be downloaded to his computer. His adrenaline rush was now being replaced by terror—that Krista had put herself, their dogs, and potentially all of them in mortal danger.

Downstairs, Anton flipped on the light in the family room and found Krista running her hands over Twitch's fur. Shadow crowded nearby, licking Krista's face.

As Krista stood and faced Anton, she caught her lower lip between her teeth.

"Krista, what did you think you were doing, letting the dogs out?"

"They wanted out, barking like crazy. I thought they could chase that guy away. I didn't know he'd shoot at them."

"Those dogs would give their lives to protect you, but by opening that door, you put them, yourself, and all of us in greater danger. It would have been better to keep them in with you."

Krista sniffed and nodded. "I'm sorry."

"Why didn't you ask your gramma?"

"She was on the phone, and Dom was watching the monitors."

"If that man had hurt one of the dogs, what would you have done?"

Krista's face crumpled, and she began to cry. "I don't know. I'd want to go to help, but I know that would be st-stupid. It'd be awful." She threw her arms around him. "I'm sorry, Daddy."

Anton hugged her close. What would he have done? Probably what Krista had, and it terrified him. "Are the dogs okay?"

"I think so. No blood."

"Did Quixote go out?"

"No. He stuck to Dom like glue."

"He's a wise old dog, Krista."

Anton never made it back to bed that night.

By the time the police arrived, the guy was long gone. They promised to send someone out in the daylight to check for bullets and casings near the fence, and would they keep the dogs out of the back yard until then.

Shortly after the sun rose, two patrolmen came. They took copies of the drone video and scoured the back yard, coming up with casings, and two bullets, which had been fired at the dogs.

They followed the cross-country trail the man had taken to his car. Then they left.

Not long after, Anton rode horseback, with Twitch and Shadow running alongside, down to the gate. He paused where the man had taken his unwise shortcut and fallen. Scuffs and gouges showed in the soil where the man had slid down the arroyo. The dogs went chasing through the marks, but it didn't matter, now the police were gone.

Twitch doubled back and ran by him, carrying something in his mouth. Shadow barreled after, but Twitch dodged and shot back toward the house with his prize, his littermate in pursuit.

When he got back, Krista and Santos were waiting by the stable. She held a stick from which dangled a dirty, rounded mess that used to be a tan flat cap.

"Twitch brought it to me," said Krista. "It must have been Ruben last night. Both times we saw him, he was wearing a cap like this."

"We're going to put it in a bag and give it to Pete," said Santos.

"Good idea," said Anton. "We can give it to him when we go into town with Diego and Maria this morning." Maria and Diego's wedding day. How strange and awful to be celebrating while grieving. And yet beautiful—to spit in the face of chaos and uncertainty—giving hope to the future.

He unsaddled his horse and brushed him down. Letting himself out of the corral, he rested his hand on the gate. His eyes swept over the alpaca pens, the duplex, and their house. How dare Ruben invade their home and bring danger so close. What the hell was his point in prowling around like that?

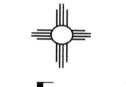

CHAPTER EIGHTY-THREE

Standing in the hall of the Juvenile Detention Center, Grayson flicked a questioning glance at Ms Garcia, the juvenile probation officer who'd been put in charge of his case. Her warm smile and the encouragement in her brown eyes bolstered him as she opened the door to a small conference room and moved back. He wiped his sweaty hands on his pants and went in.

Ms Garcia had told him his dad would be here for this preliminary inquiry. Grayson searched his father's face, looking for clues in his expression or his posture that might tell him if he still hated the sight of him.

The statement, "I have no son" echoed in his ears. As he'd lain on the hard mattress in his solitary room, alone with his thoughts in those long, dark hours of the weekend, those words still cut. Remorse for the stupid way he'd acted warred with building shields against ever feeling that same pain. He'd pushed away thoughts of ending it all, but he wasn't about to get close enough to be hurt again.

Another man sat next to his father. Grayson raised his brows.

"Grayson, my name is Liam Weber. Your father hired me to represent you."

The older man's quiet gaze met his. Grayson didn't see the smooth-talker type of guy he associated with TV lawyers. He wore a suit, but no tie, his collar open at the throat, looking casual like somebody's grandfather. The artist in him noted interesting coloring. Brown hair heavily grayed, dark mustache, but his neatly trimmed beard was almost totally white.

Grayson nodded once. A lawyer. What would that mean? To represent him? Or find ways to ease his father's embarrassment?

Ms Garcia motioned Grayson to a seat across from his dad while she took the one at the end, adjusted her reading glasses on her nose, flipped open her notebook to one of her endless forms, and started asking questions. Again. He'd answered lots about school, medical history, whether or not he'd ever been in trouble before, and had he ever used drugs. Now he'd be answering in front of his dad and this lawyer. At least now, his dad would be answering questions too.

And so it went. He didn't hear anger. Was it because his dad was playing nice? Both he and his dad probably were. He sure didn't want to stay here longer than he absolutely had to.

"Mr. Adams, you and I talked yesterday. Would you like to share with Grayson our previous conversation about rebuilding a relationship with your son?"

Ms Garcia's question brought a change to his dad's expression. His jaw flexed. When he spoke, his voice was hoarse.

"O-kay." His dad stretched out the word, like he was giving himself more time to form an answer.

She encouraged him. "What was it you were thinking?"

The simple follow-up question surprised Grayson. He could tell it put his dad on the spot. Did his dad care about him? Was it more than his looking like his mom?

His father sat, elbow on the table, hand over his mouth, looking into the distance. Blinking slowly and then more rapidly. Finally, he brushed under his eye with a knuckle.

"Because—" His dad heaved a big sigh, still not meeting anyone's eyes. "Because I don't think I know him, I mean, I know him, but—" He drew in another shaky breath. "He's part Gloria—" William cleared his throat and looked down. "And part me. It might surprise you to know that I see myself in him sometimes."

Grayson raised his eyes, let them wander over his dad's face. A thought, startling him with its objectivity, struck him. He'd never seen his dad show this kind of vulnerability. For a moment, he wished for a pencil and sketchpad, to capture that emotion. The expression burned into his memory.

His dad went on. "But I— It's like I've been away a long time, long enough for him to become a stranger. I've missed … I want to get to know my son, need to know him. I'm not saying this well."

I'm sitting right here. Don't talk about me like I'm not in the room. Look at me, Dad.

And then he did. Eyes dark, pleading. "I-I need you." His lip quivered like he couldn't quite form the words. What came out was a whisper. "Yes, I want that second chance."

Needed him? What was this?

Grayson's eyes dropped to the tabletop, his fingers rubbing the smooth surface lightly. His touch caught on unexpected roughness. The wood grain had been marred, the imperfection defying the ability of furniture polish to cover it. A deep scratch. He wondered if it'd been left by somebody like him. Had they dug into the table, inflicting damage to get back? In anger or frustration? How had they done it? Paperclip? Pen?

Ms Garcia's voice. "Grayson, are you willing to try again?"

His fingernail traced the line cutting across the grain. He wanted to leave. They called it a room—where he was staying— and there was a door instead of bars, but it might as well be called a cell. He couldn't leave, and they were watching him.

But try again? Risk that pain?

His dad needed him? Really?

"You told me—" His voice cracked. Crap. He hated that. "Told me you had no son."

William's eyes closed briefly. Shaky fingers covered his mouth again, and he cleared his throat. "I was angry. I should never … Grayson, I'm sorry."

"Grayson?" Ms Garcia prompted.

"I guess," he managed in a whisper.

"You aren't certain? Your wishes are important here, Grayson. If you aren't ready, we can work something out."

Grayson looked her in the eye, seeing only sincerity. What did that mean? Work something out? Going back to his cell? He flicked his gaze to his dad. "I do want to try."

His dad relaxed slightly as if he'd been tensed for the answer.

And then because the need rose inside, Grayson blurted out, "I'm sorry for what I did too."

"Thank you for saying that, but—" His dad's voice had gone hoarse again. "You shouldn't have felt you needed ... to do something so drastic," His throat worked. He finished, finally, in a whisper. "To know you were loved."

Grayson was stunned. He never thought he'd hear that.

"Good," Ms Garcia's soft voice slid over his thoughts. "We have work to do. At the detention hearing this afternoon, I will recommend that Grayson be released to your custody, Mr. Adams."

Mr. Weber leaned forward. "Ms Garcia, would you be open to my working out a time waiver with the DA?"

"Yes. In this case I would be. Perhaps you'd like to explain what that means to Grayson."

The attorney smiled at him. A real smile, holding warmth, not pasted on. "Certainly. Simply put, the children's court attorney and I may be able to work out an agreement, a time waiver, that will defer the charges for, say, six months. There will be requirements and goals that you must agree to. If you stay out of trouble and no new charges are filed against you, the judge will dismiss the charges."

"Dismiss?" Grayson's eyes opened wide. "You mean like, make them go away?"

Mr. Weber nodded.

"What kind of requirements?" Grayson wondered how bad they would be. The lawyer looked at Ms Garcia.

"This is what I'd require." She took off her reading glasses and looked at each of them in turn. "I would ask that you keep up your grades in school, abide by a curfew, do some community service, and meet with me on a regular schedule. And I strongly urge that Grayson and his father both enter into counseling. Separately, and also together. I'm not saying the process will be easy. It may be painful. Are you willing to do that?"

Grayson's gaze shot to his father's. "I am, but ..." Would his dad refuse and screw this up?

"Yes, I could agree to that."

A weight seemed lifted from Grayson's shoulders. He managed to smile at his dad and Mr. Weber.

Ms Garcia closed her notebook. "Good. I'm pleased by what I see and hear. Until this afternoon, then." She rose, motioning Grayson out before her.

She'd hinted before that all those horrible thoughts of trials and prison might not happen, but now Grayson felt he could believe it. Things felt lighter, like they really could be okay again.

Chapter Eighty-Four

Wednesday, August 16

Pete waved Loloma to a chair in his office. "Coffee?"

"Naw, I'm still jumpy from all I had last night listening to the gushy praise for Ruben at the Blue Goose. A bartender, Joe, identified him from the photo. He said the guy was helpful at first but had soured on him."

"At first?" prompted Pete.

"Joe said Ruben was always helping people, people going through chemo, elderly folks moving, artists needing connections. Talk, talk. That's all it was. Even helped Joe's own family. Their dog had died. Then Ruben gave them this cute, furry dog. He and his kids fell in love. Ruben went on and on about finding it a forever home. Said its owner had just moved into senior housing."

Loloma's mouth turned down. "Joe said when he took it to a vet, they discovered it'd been chipped. Some guy in a dark SUV had stolen it from a family in Albuquerque. Joe had to give it back. He guessed Ruben stole it."

"Had Joe seen Ruben recently?"

Loloma shook his head. "But we got lucky. Joe got Ruben to take pictures on his phone the day he got the dog. He insisted on showing me." He took out his phone. "I had him send me this one."

As Pete looked at the picture, he grinned. The dog was adorable—a Maltese, if he wasn't mistaken—but Pete's smile was caused by the car in back of the kneeling man. "Dare I assume this is Ruben's car?"

Loloma's dark eyes gleamed as he nodded. "Hyundai Accent Hatchback. If the dog weren't up on his hind legs licking Joe's face, we'd have a clear view of all the digits on the plate, but five out of six? Ain't bad."

"You should be able to get an address from what you have. Good work. Anything from Books and Bearclaws?"

"Same story, except he never spent much time there. He was well-known in the Hog Bristle Bistro. The bartender there said we should talk with Jimenez, the sculptor. He lives in the area and eats most of his meals at the bistro. They called him the Watcher. Doesn't say much but knows what's going on."

"I'm going over that direction today," said Pete. "I'll stop in at lunchtime."

◆ ❖ ◆

Rather than relying on chance, Pete called Jimenez and asked him to meet for lunch at the bistro.

"You eat here frequently, I'm told," said Pete once they had been seated. "What do you recommend?"

"The green-chile cheeseburger, if you've never had one here."

After they gave their orders, Jimenez said, "Can I ask questions about the investigation?"

Pete nodded. "I'll answer what I can."

Most of Jimenez's questions were about when the gallery and the exhibit could be back in business.

When their burgers came, Pete wasted no time biting into his. "Mmm." He wiped a bit of juice from his lips.

Jimenez looked amused. "So, what do you want to know?"

Pete swallowed. "Ruben was a regular here for a time. You know we're looking for him."

Jimenez snorted. "That guy's a sociopath. A puppet master, collecting people to dance for his own amusement. He tried it with me, but I've known too many like that. Wouldn't give him the time of day."

"Did you see him collect anybody?"

"Purity Gold."

"Really?"

"She used to eat here about once a week with the security guard before he died. I felt sorry for him. It was obvious he liked her, but she'd chase anyone wearing pants."

"Wait. He tried to collect you? Was this before you went on your east coast tour?"

"Why, yes— That effing bastard. Wonder if that's why the stolen painting ended up in my shed. Revenge because I blew him off."

"It might appear so." Pete took another bite of his cheeseburger. Delicious. He'd have to bring Akiko and his son here soon.

"The night Ruben collected her she was trying to pick up somebody. I was sitting at the window." He told how Ruben sabotaged her car to pick her up.

The men ate in silence for a while, before Jimenez went on. "Ruben was all show—wanted everybody to see what a helpful guy he was."

"Did you see him with other gallery folk?"

"Otto knew him, but I didn't see them here. Saw Ruben with William's son once. That worried me, but it was only the once, so I didn't say anything."

"When was that?"

"Hell, long time ago. Couldn't tell you. Before my east coast tour, I think."

Pete settled back with his coffee. "This has been a help, Jimenez." He gave him a card. "If you see Ruben, let us know."

"They don't call me the Watcher for nothing."

Pete was startled. "You know about that moniker?"

"Yeah. It was Cecil who told me. He's some kind of investigator. He was all full of questions about where I've traveled. Tried chasing round the bush to find out where my money came from, trying to ferret out if I'd gotten it by devious means. But he never asked in so many words, so I never said."

Pete shook his head, amused. "Okay, I'll bite. Where did your money come from?"

"Inherited it, invested it well, and I'm a damned hard worker."

"And good at what you do." Pete chuckled. "I've admired your work from the first."

Jimenez's eyes warmed as he smiled. "You know, I was waiting for Ruben to collect Roquet, the financial guy. Don't know what his problem was, but he had one. During the time he was here, he was well on his way to becoming a drunk. It was good Ruben didn't see it. Heard Roquet was arrested about a week ago. I'm glad he's gone. William is better off."

Later that afternoon, Pete escorted Tuttle and Cecil Dupre into his office. They sat at the round table with their coffee.

"Have you gotten any word back from your operatives about the other Anonicellis, Tuttle?"

"They went right to work as soon as you sent the photos to me. Good work, Schultz. We've tied all four thefts to the same person."

"Wonderful. What did you learn?"

"In each location, we got several positive identifications. In Minneapolis, a close friend of the murdered manager recognized him. Called himself Peter Singer. He and the manager fell in love and moved in together. But shortly after the theft, this Singer left suddenly. He said he had this wonderful job opportunity in Tennessee. He'd go down there, get settled, find them a house. They were planning a June wedding. But he totally disappeared.

She couldn't reach him and didn't know why. She became very depressed."

"Come in, establish a reputation, and reel in the victims," said Cecil.

Tuttle nodded. "Ballistics gave us a solid connection in Minneapolis too. The bullets from Ruben's shooting at Bjornson's car? Fired from the same gun that killed the Minneapolis manager."

Pete smiled in satisfaction. "We've got a few more bullets that I'm hoping will clinch this. Last night there was an intruder at the Bjornson ranch. The dogs chased him, and he fired at them. They weren't hit, but one of the dogs ended up with a tan flat cap, which we now have in evidence."

"Ahah!" said Tuttle. "In New York, one gallery employee said the guy loved that tan flat cap he was wearing in the photo. Always wore it—hot weather, cold, rain, outdoors, indoors—whatever. Never saw him without it."

"What else did you learn from New York?"

"They echoed the refrain—very nice guy." Tuttle paused to sip his coffee. "He was helping his cousin who was opening up a gallery in Dallas and looking for recommendations for security systems. The New York gallery had just gotten a new system, so this employee told him about it. Ruben wanted to know what he liked and didn't like about it. If it had any weaknesses, things like that."

"Did he go by the name Ruben there as well?"

"George Whistler. Then in L.A. more of the same. Very helpful. Said his brother's gallery in Tucson had been robbed. He was looking for a security system. What did they recommend?"

"His L.A. name?"

"Edward Constable. This employee said it was the name of a good solid person. He'd give you the shirt off his back."

Cecil let out a snort. "And here he was Ruben Turner. Steal a first name from one artist and the last name from another. That little vanity probably amused him."

"I believe he's unraveling under the pressure," said Tuttle. "Switching that obscure artist's painting for the Anonicelli seems to have knocked him for a loop."

"And a teenager did it." Cecil leaned back with his mug and looked at Pete. "I must confess that I was frightened for what the justice system might do to Grayson. This was a serious felony, and Keller died as a result."

"I was concerned too," said Pete. "But I hear they're pursuing the time waiver option. New Mexico tries to do what is best for the future of the child and for society. I see Grayson as a victim here. Nobody benefits by pressing charges against him. I heard William hired a lawyer. Who'd he find?"

Cecil nodded. "Liam Weber. Know him?"

Pete felt a smile stretch his face. "Excellent. He doesn't come cheap, but he's exactly who I'd recommend. Good man."

"Thank God. Grayson discovered something else you should know about, Schultz."

"Oh?"

"Before he confessed, he was badly frightened by Ruben's threats. He used a gimmick from thrillers and taped thread over doors and cupboards where no one would notice. He reset them when he got out of the juvenile detention center. A day later, he found all of them had been disturbed. Someone had gotten in and searched their house. He told me, and I talked with William. We contacted his probation officer. For safety, they are both staying at my house now. We've made it very difficult for them to be followed."

"Glad to hear it," said Pete. "I don't take Ruben's threats lightly. Let me ask—this bit about his skulking around the Bjornson ranch and firing off shots. Is Ruben losing it?"

Tuttle nodded. "The evidence left behind when Gold was killed—even a two-bit criminal wouldn't have left all that."

Pete smiled. "We surprised him there. He wasn't through erasing his tracks. She hadn't been dead long, and Ruben was frantically searching—no doubt for the Anonicelli. We must have just missed him. By the way, have you been able to get anything from that shipping label?"

"We're building a case there. That was a breakthrough."

There was a light in Tuttle's eye, an excitement that told Pete that Ruben wasn't the biggest fish the Art Crime Team hoped to net with this investigation.

"I'm looking forward to your ballistics findings from last night," said Tuttle. "Is there anything else?"

Pete shared what he'd learned from Loloma and Jimenez before gathering his papers together. "It's a damn shame this theft is holding up the Niemöller exhibit. The art is stuck in an evidence locker. The public should see this exhibit."

"In some states, don't know about New Mexico," said Tuttle, "the victim whose property has been stolen can go to the district attorney's office and request its release. There's a form for that. Perhaps each of the artists might have to go with their identification, and William with all the documentation from their contest entries. The work would be photographed, statements taken, yada, yada, but they get their stuff back. Then those photographs and sworn statements would be used in the eventual trial of this Ruben dude. The artists may be required to show up at the trial and verify the photos and the statements, but yes, it can be done."

"It's good," said Cecil. "Can you imagine having to keep all the evidence? For years, through appeals and all that?"

"Glad you reminded me," said Pete. "I'll encourage Adams to take advantage of that."

CHAPTER EIGHTY-FIVE

In the detectives' bullpen at the police station on Wednesday afternoon, Sam finished his report, leaned back, and stretched his tired muscles. Five o'clock.

Dulcie's brown eyes and warm personality haunted his thoughts. It was likely she was dead, and the thought made him sick. Since the news of the killer preying on immigrant women had broken on Saturday, what he'd heard was dismal. Deputies searching the property had found four sets of remains so far.

The only bright spot had been the capture of that so-called nun in El Paso yesterday. Good cooperation by detectives scouring property records, finding his car registration, and the El Paso PD, using their sharp eyes had resulted in his arrest. The creep wasn't cooperating but had been identified through a photo lineup by his escaped victim.

Life was moving on, even for those who knew and loved Dulcie. Today was the first day of school for Leyla, Krista, and Santos. Monday night he and Farah, Anton and Skyla, Maria and Diego, and the kids had attended a barbecue for the students, parents, and staff of their new middle school. Leaving elementary behind and venturing into middle school should have been an anticipated new adventure for Santos. They'd all done what they could to make it normal for him, yet he'd been subdued and distracted. Sam could hardly blame him.

Last night, Sam had stopped by the ranch and learned of Maria and Diego's wedding. Diego had sought him out for a private word, saying that no matter what they learned, Santos would always have a home with them. Sam was moved and glad for Santos.

Sam tidied his desk. He saw the lights in Pete's office go out. The phone on Sam's desk rang. Stifling an expletive, he picked it up.

"Sergeant Martinez?"

"Speaking."

"This is Deputy Vasquez, Otero County Sheriff's Department. I have a young woman here who wishes to speak with you. I'll give the phone to her."

"Sergeant, this is Dulcie Rodriguez."

"Dulcie!" Sam stood up, sending his chair rolling back to smack into the next cubicle. "Where are you?"

"*Halleluja!*" Pete hurried over.

"Where's Santos?" Dulcie's voice bordered on hysterical. "I've been trying to call him, but he isn't answering. Is he okay?"

"Santos is fine. He's at the Bjornsons'. Today was the first day of school. Teachers don't like kids to have their phones on. Maybe he didn't remember to turn it on again."

"Oh, thank God. I need—" He heard a sob. "To hear his voice."

"Dulcie, where are you?"

"In Alamogordo. I've been lost. In the mountains. Can I talk to you after I talk with Santos?"

The deputy's voice came on again, over the sounds of Dulcie's crying. "If you'll give me that number where her son is, we'll call you back."

"Sure."

"We're at the emergency room now. I believe she'll be at the hospital overnight."

They exchanged information, and Sam hung up. He sat, tilted his head back, and squeezed his eyes shut. He felt a strong grip on his shoulder and opened his eyes to see Pete smile broadly.

"*Danke Gott.*"

Sam's eyes were moist. "I was so afraid."

"So was I." Pete's voice caught. "S-so was I."

Sam took a deep breath. He felt curiously light; the burden on his shoulders had vanished like smoke.

◆ ❖ ◆

Thursday, August 17

"Almost there, *mijo*," said Diego, his eye on the antsy boy sitting next to him in the backseat of Anton's SUV. Anton was driving, with Maria beside him in the front.

"We're going to be late." Santos managed a bounce, even with his seatbelt buckled. "I want to see them land."

Ever since the astonishing call from his mother last night, Santos had been unable to be still. Diego couldn't blame Santos for his excitement—it was as if he and Maria, too, had been soaring with eagles, catching drafts of pure happiness.

Dulcie's homecoming was a miracle. First getting away from that murderous creep, then surviving ten days in the wilderness. The doctors had checked her out. She was lucky to be suffering no more than a sprained ankle, giardia, and dehydration—not to mention sunburn and numerous insect bites.

Anton had stepped in to make it possible for Dulcie to make it home sooner by arranging for his helicopter pilot friend to fly Sam to Alamogordo and bring them home.

"Hurry!" Santos urged.

"We're almost there. Just over this knoll," said Anton. He topped the rise and parked in an undeveloped cul-de-sac. "Look, to the south." He pointed to a speck on the horizon past miles of piñon and juniper. "They're coming in. Stay by the car. Even helicopters need space to land."

Diego opened the front door and squeezed Maria's hand as she stepped out. Joyful brown eyes met his briefly before dropping to the boy focused on the approaching helicopter.

Another car pulled up behind Anton's. Pete, who had come to give Sam a ride, and Karen joined the little group.

The *whump, whump* of the rotor blades grew louder. Diego grabbed the brim of his cowboy hat and squinted against the burst of grit from the landing helicopter's downdraft. He put a cautionary hand on Santos's shoulder.

The blades slowed, and the pilot got out to open the passenger cabin door.

"I see her!" yelled Santos.

Dulcie stepped down into the sunshine.

"Mom!"

Santos was gone, flying toward his mother to be caught up in her hug. The force of his greeting knocked her off balance, sending her backwards into Sam in the doorway. He steadied mother and son in their tearful embrace.

Diego blinked as tears blurred the sight. Dulcie leaned back, looked at her beaming son, framed his face with shaking hands, then pulled him close again. He heard incoherent words, fragments of speech. It didn't matter. It was all a part of coming home.

Maria slid her arm around his waist, looking at him through tears. Pure joy made a smile stretch his face. As Dulcie and Santos drew apart, everyone welcomed her home. Diego hung back, letting everyone get their hugs in first.

Next to him, Anton clapped the pilot on the shoulder. "Thanks, Glenn."

"No problem. Truly a pleasure."

Pete shook the pilot's hand. "The PD owes you thanks too. Thought you looked familiar. Met you about a week ago. How do you know Anton?"

"Ah, the FBI sting. Enjoyed that. Anton and I were roommates in college."

Santos was bursting to tell his mom all the news. "Mom, we're staying at the Bjornsons' until they catch that Ruben guy."

"I wanted to go home," said Dulcie, "but Sam says it's not safe yet."

"Maria says we can stay in her duplex."

"Oh, no!" Dulcie looked at Maria with shock. "We can't impose on you like that."

"It's not an imposition." Maria blushed. "You see, Diego and I got married Tuesday. We're living in his duplex."

Dulcie's mouth dropped open as she looked from one to the other. "I didn't even—"

Diego felt he needed to make this clear now, to everyone. "The news was bad from Cloudcroft. We knew you had gotten a ride from that guy pretending to be a nun. We knew he killed women he gave rides to."

"I told everybody you'd get away." Santos's voice was confident. "But Diego said I'd always have a home with them if I wanted."

"You married to give Santos a home? *Madre de Dios*."

Diego raised a hand to Maria's face. "Maria and I love each other. Sure, it happened fast, but we would have married in any case."

Maria smiled. "Of that, we're certain."

"Sometimes even in the darkest of night," said Diego, "a tiny star shines. It was right for us to marry and not just for Santos. We are so glad you're home."

Dulcie's eyes filled with tears as she raised her arms to embrace them both. Diego's eyes grew wet again as he heard her muffled words of thanks.

He pulled back to look into Dulcie's eyes. "You have no family nearby. Maria and I could use a little sister."

Dulcie drew Santos into the hug. "Coming home," she said, "I thought nothing could be better. But I was wrong. Coming home to family is more."

◆ ❖ ◆

As Pete drove Sam back to Santa Fe, Sam told him that Dulcie had given her statement about the nun imposter to the Alamogordo deputy and picked the correct photo from the lineup. Then, Sam had used his bodycam to record his conversation with Dulcie about that night at the gallery.

"Wasn't the helicopter too noisy for talking?" asked Pete.

"Fly in that bird," said Sam, "if you get a chance. Amazing. Not much noisier than a car. Dulcie recognized Grayson and was shocked to find out he was mixed up in a theft. I told her the other man, Ruben, had stolen Santos's phone and tried to snatch him. I said he might be after her to stop her from identifying him. She said she didn't even get a good look at him."

"But Ruben doesn't know that," said Pete. "I think Grayson is the one in greater danger now, though who knows how that pervert's mind works." Later he'd look at the footage from Sam's bodycam, but right now he reveled in the too-rare happy ending of a case. "We had some luck on our end today. We've ferreted out where Ruben has been holed up."

"Son of a gun! Did you get him?"

Pete felt a grim sense of satisfaction. "He wasn't there, but he's been housesitting for some professor on sabbatical. We have the white Subaru, but he still has the dark SUV, a gray Hyundai Accent hatchback. Both belong to the professor. Ruben must have stolen plates for them recently. The correct ones were in the garage."

Pete grinned as he told about Loloma getting the photo with the partial license plate. "At that point, Ruben hadn't yet switched the plate on the SUV. We got the address, talked with the neighbors, and got in touch with the professor through the University. He was horrified but has been cooperative. We got a search warrant. Found several interesting things: Purity Gold's purse and phone, Dulcie's purse, and the pictures he stole from the Rodriguez apartment. Also, IDs in the names of all three former aliases."

"Was his gun there or anything to tie him to the March attempt on the Anonicelli?"

"No gun, but we found a black ski mask with traces of black makeup around the eye holes. The property management company has changed the locks."

"His options are narrowing."

"Indeed. Tuttle believes he's becoming increasingly unhinged as we zero in. Evidently, he's getting squeezed by the person who paid him to steal the Anonicellis. Now he's dependent upon motels and so on for physical needs. His home now is the Hyundai, and we know about that too. He doesn't have much to lose if he's cornered."

"Volatile."

"Very." Pete listened to chatter on his radio, then went on. "Did Karen tell you about the gathering at the ranch tomorrow night to hear Dulcie's story?"

"Yeah, actually it was Dulcie's idea. She told me she wanted to tell her story, but not over and over again. We settled on this idea for both you and me as law enforcement and the Bjornson household. I cleared it with Karen. She suggested including Akiko, Farah, and Leyla. Dulcie liked that."

"Good."

"I've heard just enough to know it was a harrowing adventure."

CHAPTER EIGHTY-SIX

Friday, August 18

Though it had been a hot day, as evening came and they gathered to celebrate Dulcie's return and hear her story, the temperature dropped. Karen heard Dulcie make an offhand remark about feeling chilly. Anton started a small fire in the kiva fireplace. Karen picked up a soft throw, crossed her family room to where Dulcie sat, and placed it within her reach.

"Please, don't fuss." Dulcie's scold was negated by her snuggling under the softness, running her hand over the plush, and by her warm smile. "*Gracias.*"

"For two weeks I couldn't do much more than worry." Karen grinned at her. "You certainly fussed over me and my wrist enough while I was weaving."

Maria followed Karen closely, handing a mug of apricot-ginger tea to Dulcie. "We'll fuss if we want to, *mi amiga.*"

Santos tugged a hassock into place to keep her ankle elevated before he settled next to his mother. "Need anything else, Mom?"

Dulcie reached out to brush his hair back. "All I need is right here, *mijo.*"

"Do you mind if we record your story, Dulcie?" asked Pete. "I won't if you don't want me to."

Dulcie's look was steady. "It is okay."

"Can we ask questions?" asked Krista.

"Sure," said Dulcie. "You know the story up until ICE let me go in El Paso. That's where I'll start."

She sipped her tea. "It is hard to need help from strangers. It is even harder to know who to trust. I met a woman, a nun, dedicated to God's work. I thought I could trust her when she said she could give me a ride. I was so very wrong."

Dulcie shut her eyes. "I was exhausted after ICE let me go. I leaned my seat back and fell asleep. When I woke up, the nun was looking straight ahead, driving those uphill curves. I remember the light hit her face, and I saw the poor lady had to shave. She had a ... five o'clock shadow. I think that is how you say it. It looked funny with makeup."

"When did you know it was a man?" asked Santos.

"Then, against the light. She had a *nuez de Adán*, a nut in the throat. I do not know what you call it in English. When I realized she was a man, I was terrified."

A twig popped in the fireplace. Dulcie jumped, looked over at it, and took another sip of her tea. "Then something else hit me. The road to Albuquerque, Highway 54, is mostly straight, flat, and boring. My husband and I had been on it many times. The sun should have been on the left, but it was behind us. There should not be mountains, but we were climbing. Then I saw a sign, Highway 82. That goes east. We weren't going to Albuquerque at all, but into the mountain wilderness."

Pete's wife, Akiko, made a soft sound of dismay. The others were quiet, listening carefully to Dulcie's soft, accented voice.

"I pretended to be waking up. There were no houses, just high desert. No place to hide even if I could get away. If I did escape, could I stop a car? Or would that be worse trouble? Then the plants along the road changed. More brush, more trees. We got behind a car in a no-passing zone and slowed down."

"Could you have jumped out?" asked Krista.

"I thought of that. But I might be hurt bad and still not get away. Then he stopped on the highway, waiting for a car coming our way to pass, so he could make a left turn. Turning off the main road I knew was bad. I was afraid that if he took me to the wilderness, my chances of surviving after a horrible time were very small. I grabbed the bag with my jacket and water bottles, opened the door, jumped out and ran as fast as I could to the trees. He came running after me. Yelling, cursing."

"How did you manage to get away?" asked Pete.

"He couldn't leave the car on the road, and there was no place to pull off. I heard cars honking. I tried my best not to leave a trail, sticking to rocks or pine needles. I even splashed along the creek for a bit. I wanted to make it to the first ridge."

"Did you ever see him again?" asked Farah.

Dulcie nodded. "After a long way, I found a tree, easy to climb. I looked toward the road. I saw his blue car, creeping along. I decided to go farther from the road. I climbed the next ridge and went down to another little stream."

Dulcie paused to sip more tea. "I still feel that fear. I broke a strong branch from a tree. It made a good walking stick and a weapon if I needed it. I heard thunder and remembered this was the monsoon season. I hoped I'd come to a house soon. Then it started to rain. I couldn't hear traffic anymore, just noisy water and bugs buzzing. I thought about shelter for the night."

"Did you see any bears?" asked Krista.

"Bears?" Leyla sat up straight and looked surprised.

"I looked at a map on the internet after school today," said Krista, "when I found out where Dulcie had been. She was in the Lincoln National Forest, where Smokey Bear came from."

Leyla's eyes were wide. "Did you see bears, Dulcie?"

"Not that night, but later I did. That night was miserable. So cold. I needed a blanket like this." She touched the softness of the throw.

"Anyway, the next day I knew I was lost. I went to higher ground to look for the road. There was no sign of it. It's funny in the wild. I knew I'd gone two ridges away from the road, but ridges ran into each other and sent me out of my way. Rocky cliffs kept me from going the direction I needed. I had to turn because they did. I knew I had to go north to find the highway. Sometimes a bear or a rattlesnake would make me go a different direction. Clouds covered the sun, and I didn't know where north was. And I was hungry." Dulcie stopped, looked around at the concerned faces, as if she were surprised to see them there. She wiped at her eyes.

"Do you want to stop for a while?" asked Karen.

"No, I'm okay ... I think it's good to talk." Dulcie cradled her mug in both hands. "If I stayed by the stream, when I got thirsty, there was water."

"Is that why you got giardia?" asked Leyla. "Because you didn't have good water?"

"Probably. But you need water to live. I knew it could make me sick, but I drank it anyway."

"Couldn't you have boiled it?" asked Krista.

Anton smiled at his question-box daughter. "Boil it in what, Krista? And she'd need a fire."

"Did you start a fire?" asked Santos.

"I was no good at fires. I tried to rub sticks together. I got smoke a couple of times." She smiled. "At least I got warm, rubbing those sticks back and forth. Anyway, I walked all the next day, following the stream. Then I found what was left of an old cabin. Only the chimney was standing. Little trees grew in what used to be the inside.

"It smelled good—the fresh air, the sun-warmed trees with their dry, piney scent. They try to capture that in cleaning products, but it's nothing like the real thing."

Dulcie closed her eyes and smiled. "There were a couple of old scrubby apple trees. The apples on them were pretty ripe. The low-growing fruit was gone. Eaten by deer, I think. I picked a bunch. They had worm holes, but I was hungry. *Verdolagas* and dandelions grew there. My mother fixed those for us when I was little."

"Dandelions? E-yew," said Santos.

Dulcie squeezed her son's arm. "Food, any food, was important. I had to stay strong to get back to you, *mijo*."

"What's *verdolagas*?" asked Krista.

"Here we call it purslane," said Skyla. "It's common. A weed. Sometimes you can even find it in farmers' markets."

"Near the cabin ruins, there was a pine tree with low branches bending to the ground. Underneath was thick with needles. I added more branches to make a shelter, more needles and fresh pine branches on top. It was warm and dry inside, and I slept better that night. I learned lots of pine needles helped me keep warm. Animals, deer I hoped, woke me many times, sniffing around. I got up to pee—"

A warm wave of color flooded Dulcie's face. "*Dios mio*. I forgot. The recorder. I shouldn't say that."

"We're all human, Dulcie. We all pee," said Pete. "Please. Go on."

Dulcie nodded. "The sky that night was clear. Bright stars. Full moon. It made me feel good that it shone on you too."

Diego looked up, startled. "I remember a night like that. Maria and I were sitting in our swing seat, watching the moon, wondering where you were."

"I felt it. A connection somehow."

"I thought when you got lost, you were supposed to stay put and let the searchers find you," said Krista.

"That is good advice, and I thought about it. But only one person in the world had any idea where I was."

"And he was the last person you wanted to find you," said Akiko.

"You got that right," said Dulcie. "No, it was up to me to find my way home. My days blurred together. One day, I climbed and climbed. I got to the top only to find another ridge. I finally reached the top. As far as I could see—no people, no roads, no cabins ... *nada*. I went back down, built a shelter, and cried myself to sleep."

Dulcie dissolved into tears. "The next day, I saw turkey buzzards tearing at a furry dead beast ahead of me. It was horrible. I ran at them, just screaming. They flew off but didn't go out of sight. I yelled at them to go away. To let that poor, dead creature lie in peace. Then I just sat and bawled. They soared high overhead. Circling. Perching. Waiting. I thought maybe I would die out there in those miles of nothing." She sobbed again, deep wrenching sobs.

Maria leaned from her chair to cover her hand. After a while, Dulcie's sobs quieted to sniffs.

"The next day, I just walked, not paying attention. I slipped on loose rock and twisted my ankle. I made it back to a stream, where I could fill my water bottles again. I stuck to my plan after that—follow the water, go north when I could."

Dulcie looked down, scratching an insect bite on her arm. "Then I came to a real cabin. I broke in. It was heaven. Matches, a fireplace. Canned food. Aspirin. A real bed with warm blankets. I stayed there an extra day or two. Eating, sleeping, getting strong. I felt hope again. There was a road to this cabin. It would lead back to people. I left a letter behind for the owners—to tell Santos I loved him, to let everybody know what happened in case I never made it home."

"Oh, Dulcie." Karen felt tears forming in her eyes.

"I took some things when I left. Canned goods with pull-top lids. A knife. A jacket, warmer than the one I had. A few matches and a small blanket. I found papers with the name of the folks … Sam, if you can, can you help me contact them? I'd like to send them money to pay for what I took. And to repair the window I broke."

"Not a problem, Dulcie. Are you ready for a break?"

"I'm almost done," she said. "I was scared to trust anyone, but I knew I would have to in order to survive. I decided if I saw a car and it was not blue, like his, I'd flag it down. I would ask them to take me to a town where I could call police and Santos."

Dulcie smiled. "It was easier walking on the road. Eventually I came to a bigger road. But still, I missed the first car. I'd gone into the trees to— Giardia is nasty. The car went by so fast. The driver didn't hear me screaming. Then another car came. Those people were wonderful, gave me a ride to the EMTs in Cloudcroft. The EMTs got me to Alamogordo." She paused. "You know the rest."

She looked at Pete. "I thought about your last rule of survival. I repeated it over and over as I walked. Don't give up. Don't give up. You will survive."

"I'm glad," said Pete. "We're put on this earth to help each other."

"Amen," said Karen.

◆ ❖ ◆

Karen and Dom walked Pete and Akiko out to their car as the gathering ended at the Bjornson home.

"Have you had a chance to see the damage done to your tapestry rod yet?" asked Pete, as he opened the car door for Akiko.

"Yes," said Karen. "I picked it up yesterday. I'm almost done fixing it. I had extra finials." She tugged her sweater around her shoulders. "Meeting William was awkward. I haven't forgiven him for disowning his son like that. He didn't say much except that Grayson was released into his custody. Is Grayson at a better point mentally now?"

"Seems so. Because Ruben is still on the loose, they're staying with a friend."

"Cecil?" asked Karen.

"I can't say, but Cecil has been helpful. I'm staying in touch with Grayson's juvenile probation officer."

"Has William set the date for the Niemöller exhibit opening?" asked Akiko.

"Tuesday, August 29," said Karen. "He wants to get a jump on the fiesta events over Labor Day weekend. I'm all for that. The more people see it, the better."

"Sunday there was a big splash in the *New Mexican* about the recovery of the art," said Akiko, "but it didn't give many details."

"Got good cooperation," said Pete. "The lack of specifics was deliberate."

Dom's eyes glinted. "You're figuring Ruben will try again?"

"The FBI thinks so," said Pete as he started the engine. "Thanks, Karen, Dom. Good to have Dulcie back."

Chapter Eighty-Seven

Monday, August 21

Otto glanced at his watch. Quarter to five. Now that only the Near Room with the gift shop was open, the gallery closed at five. This day had lasted an eternity. He breathed a sigh of relief that it was coming to an end. William had gone to pick up Algie from his oil painting class and would be back soon.

An elderly man, bent and leaning heavily on his cane, crossed the portal and struggled with the heavy glass door. Otto hurried to hold it open for him. The breeze, as the door swung shut, stirred the man's graying fringe of hair.

"Thanks. Just looking," he mumbled and shuffled past into the Near Room.

Otto shook his head in pity at the tweedy sports jacket, fitting loosely on the hunched frame. When that jacket was new, the old man must have stood tall and muscular. Age had not been a friend.

The new security guard got up from the desk where he'd been monitoring all the screens. Otto peered outside through the door. In front, the young policeman in plain clothes casually sat on the low wall of the next-door gallery, looking as though he were waiting for someone.

The police believed Ruben would try again to nab the Anonicelli and had convinced William to increase security. The officer outside kept an eye on foot traffic and the driveway between the gallery and its neighbor.

Otto reluctantly followed the old man into the Near Room, watching his slow progress as he took in each painting in turn. Convinced the man wasn't going to buy anything, he motioned to the guard that he was going into the Middle Room. The guard nodded. He'd fetch him if he were needed.

Otto felt an urge to see the Anonicelli again. He stepped past the velvet ropes and flipped the switch that lit the lady's alcove. There was a noise from the outside, like a car backfiring. Nothing to be alarmed about. He looked upon his lady's beauty. How wonderful to have her back. Of course, she'd never left the gallery, but he hadn't known that.

My, was it just over a week ago when the police came knocking on his door, telling him the Anonicelli had been recovered? How shocked he'd been when they found the stolen art at his house. From the comments the police had shared, a few terse statements from William later on, and a bit more from Cecil, he'd pieced together what happened on the night of the Gala. At first, he was outraged with Algie, doing that to his father.

But then he'd found out about Ruben. He thought Ruben was his friend, but instead, he used Otto, charmed his way into making him share what he shouldn't. Otto had unknowingly set the poor child up.

His anger had deflated and turned to sympathy for Algie and guilt for the part he, himself, had played.

Otto thought about quitting his job, but felt he owed it to William to keep on working. Algie had been released into the custody of his father. William had been understanding about the part Otto had played by introducing Algie to Ruben. Otto was prepared to be sacked over that, but now that he hadn't been, he was determined to make it up to William by being an exemplary employee.

Even with increased security, Otto had to steel himself to come to work. Swallowing his fear, he jumped every time people came in. The cameras were always on now, recording every individual who entered.

Lost anew in his fantasy, a movement out of the corner of his eye startled Otto. The old man stood there. He shouldn't be in this room. It was closed to the public. Where was the guard?

"Well, well, if it isn't Otto."

The voice filled Otto with terror.

The voice, Ruben's, yet strange. Otto shook his head, trying to make sense of what was not right. The figure wasn't bent now, but straight. Otto looked into eyes, brown like Ruben's and scary. He heard Ruben's laugh, yet the face before him—wrong and curiously unexpressive.

"R-Ruben?" Otto's eyes dropped to the hand emerging from the baggy tweed pocket. Not an old man's hand. Holding a gun!

"Ruben!" Otto's heart began pounding, feeling like it might choke him. "Guard!" he yelled.

"I took care of him." Ruben's lips, which were not his lips, moved. "Your lady is leaving with me. Do as I say, and you won't be hurt."

"N-nooo!" Otto felt himself shrinking. He put his hands up in front of his face as though he could ward off an attack. "You will not take my lady."

Ruben grabbed him, spun him around to face the painting, gripping the back of Otto's suit collar with one hand. Otto felt the gun pressing against his ribs. He heard himself make whimpering, squeaky sounds.

"You will disarm the security and give me the painting. Call the cops, and you will be dead." He shook Otto's collar. "Now."

Jerkily, Otto swung the painting's placard to the side to reveal the keypad. With a shaking finger, he pressed the sequence of numbers, beginning with the digits that sent a silent alarm to the police station, and turned off the security features. *Please, this has to work. Please, please.* He lifted the lady from the wall and hugged her to him. He slumped in Ruben's grip, pleading, blubbering, "Not my lady."

Ruben shoved Otto down to cower against the niche.

"You pathetic little swine." He bashed the gun against Otto's head. Light. Pain. Otto succumbed to blackness.

◆ ❖ ◆

Karen had promised to drop off the repaired tapestry to the gallery this afternoon. She'd been fuzzy about the temporary shortened hours, but the sign still said OPEN.

As she crossed the street from the parking lot, a loud bang on her left startled her. It was followed by several more firecracker-like explosions. Dark smoke billowed under a car parked at the side of Canyon Road half a block down. People shouted. A young man who'd been sitting on the adobe wall near William's gallery put his phone to his ear and ran toward the car, now ablaze.

Good, plenty of help was on the way. Hopefully no one was hurt.

She opened the gallery door and carefully maneuvered her tapestry through it, avoiding possible damage to the new finials. She let the door shut gently behind her and walked around the corner into the Near Room. Otto wasn't at his desk, and a quick glance told her the fishbowl was darkened.

A voice, Otto's voice from the Middle Room, shrieked in terror. "Ruben! Guard!"

Karen retreated quickly to the statue of Swift in the entrance and set her tapestry on the floor. She texted 911 and told them Ruben was here. She hit SEND, picked up her rolled tapestry and turned to escape before Ruben saw her. She had to get help for Otto.

Then she heard Grayson's shout. "Otto! What the— Ruben! He's masked!"

It stopped her cold. Oh, my God.

William's yell followed. "Algie, run! He has a gun!"

Karen thought Otto had been alone in the gallery. Where had they come from?

"How nice to handle all the loose ends at once." A voice that could only be Ruben's. "Get down on the floor, or I'll shoot Otto."

No one knew she was there. Could she somehow stop Ruben?

With the tapestry furled tightly around its wrought iron rod, resting against her shoulder like a baseball bat, Karen crept into the Near Room on silent feet.

Ruben's voice was an evil taunt. "I'll shoot this scum. Now that I have what I want, he needs to pay for the trouble he caused me."

Not daring to peek around the corner and hugging the wall to avoid being seen, she took a stance by the archway into the Middle Room. Oh, my God. She had only one chance to get it right.

"No, not my son!"

Three shots rang out in quick succession.

"Dad!" A scream of horror.

An old man, clutching a painting, appeared in her vision. Had to be Ruben. He backed slowly toward the archway, around the two pedestals holding Joaquin's prizewinning pair of statues. He raised his gun, his voice a twisted snarl. "Scum, pre—"

She swung the tapestry with all her might.

The rolled tapestry hit Ruben below his knees, sweeping his feet from under him as she followed through, feeling the wrench in her shoulders.

Ruben flew backward; the Anonicelli arced through the air. The gun shot a bullet into the ceiling. He landed hard on his butt, whiplash sending his head back to crack on the tile. The gun was knocked loose from his hand.

Stunned, he started to sit up, shaking his head. Cold eyes, filled with hate in a face that was oddly immobile, met hers. He stretched his hand toward his gun.

Out of the corner of her eye, Karen saw Grayson, in a blur of motion, slam into the pedestals with Joaquin's statues, sending them careening toward Ruben. The bronze figures fell on him, knocking him flat again. He screamed.

She grabbed up the gun in both hands, trembling, and pointed it at Ruben.

Grayson rubbed his shoulder as he rose from where he'd landed.

She slowly lowered the gun. Ruben wasn't going to get up. Fifty pounds of bronze had taken away the threat. Ruben screamed again and writhed under the statues. The full weight of one statue rested upside down on his abdomen. The outstretched hand on the other statue had impaled Ruben's gun hand in a widening puddle of blood.

"Dad!"

She looked away from Ruben into the Middle Room. Grayson knelt by his father. So much blood! How could William possibly survive?

The memory of Vidar, as he lay dying, filled her vision. No, no! Not again.

Grayson snatched off his T-shirt and pressed it against the wound on his father's head.

"Dad! You can't die."

"My son ... Love you."

Karen heard sirens. Police poured into the room. One took the gun from her numb hand. She pushed past him and ran to Grayson, sinking to the floor at his side and putting a shaking arm around him.

William lifted a hand towards his son's face. Nearby, Otto struggled to sit up.

More police, then medics surrounded them. She clutched the one who helped her to her feet. She was crying, big, gulping sobs.

CHAPTER EIGHTY-EIGHT

This was too much for Karen to take in. Officers tended a man lying almost out of sight near the front desk. She hadn't seen him at all before.

She looked back at Grayson and his father, unable to focus on anything else.

William's eyes searched his son's face. One of Grayson's hands was now gripped by his father's in a bloody grasp.

A policeman shepherded Karen and Grayson back to make room for the medics. From somewhere, he produced two chairs.

Grayson turned to Karen. "Ruben was aiming for me." His eyes were dark and filled with pain. "Dad jumped in front of me." Then he sat, rocking slightly back and forth, focusing on his father.

A police officer handed her a Mylar foil blanket. She unfolded it and tucked it over Grayson's bare shoulders. His T-shirt was a bloody mess, discarded near the knees of the medic.

"Thanks," he whispered, sagging against her, still watching the medics. They rolled a gurney in next to his father.

♦ ❖ ♦

Another gurney left with the man who'd been lying near the desk. Then a policeman helped Otto as he walked unsteadily past.

"Is the Anonicelli, the painting, okay?" he asked the officer.

The officer steered him by where she lay on the floor face up.

Otto paused, nodded. Karen heard him plead with the officer to take good care of her as they left, presumably on their way to an ambulance.

Then Pete was there. "Can you tell me what happened, Grayson?" he asked gently.

"Will Dad be okay?" he asked. "Ruben was aiming at me. Dad tried to grab the gun." Grayson gave Pete a puzzled look. "Ruben and the gun went flying backwards, and I saw Karen. He reached for his gun again. I had to stop him." He drew in a shaky breath. "The statues. All I could think of. I pushed them over on top of him."

"You did good. You stopped him."

The gurney with his father rolled toward the door. Grayson rose. "I've got—"

Pete put a hand on his shoulder. "We'll see you get to the hospital. Can I call anyone?"

Grayson looked lost, before brightening a bit. "Could you call Cecil?"

Pete nodded. "Karen?"

"I was bringing my tapestry back. I heard Ruben … 911 … was leaving … Then William and Grayson. I had to do something. Ruben was backing up. I knocked him off his feet. He looked at me … his eyes. Murder." Karen put out a shaky hand to Pete's. Her tears wouldn't stop flowing. "Grayson saved us all."

"Ruben's in custody now. You're safe," said Pete. "Where's Dom?" The strength of his grasp steadied her.

"I was going to meet him after I dropped off the tapestry. He's at Sam's."

"I'll call him."

◆ ❖ ◆

Dom rested his eyes on his beloved Karen lying in his antique bed in the old Baca home. Light from the hall showed her resting peacefully now, her chest gently rising and falling. He still held her hand, holding it, stroking it, overwhelmed with gratitude that she'd been spared. Occasionally he ran his fingers over the smoothness of her ring, longing for the day when the matching band would join it.

She'd clung to him as she told the story, how all that blood brought back Vidar's dying in her arms. Her inability to make a difference then, her need to somehow make that up. She cried over Grayson and William. Kept on talking about William's sacrifice. He did love his son after all.

She wouldn't give up and rest until hours later when the word came that William was listed as stable. She fretted more about Grayson, until she was assured that Cecil would stay with him until his dad was home again.

Otto would be fine. They were keeping him overnight but expected to release him the next day.

Dom still couldn't believe Karen had attacked a gun-wielding madman with her *Tapestry of Light*. She shook as she told of having to get it right the first time.

"But your tapestry—against a gun? Were you out of your mind?" His voice had risen in horror. He'd been within a hare's whisker of losing her.

Her answer was simple. "It was all I had."

Farah knocked softly at his open door. "Sam's home. Pete's with him. If you want, I can sit with her while you talk with them."

"Thanks," he whispered. He tucked Karen's hand under the blanket. She sighed and slept on.

He found Sam and Pete in the kitchen.

"How's Karen?" asked Pete.

"Sleeping finally. Any news?"

"William's out of surgery. He was hit twice. Besides the bullet graze to the head, one shot went all the way through his left side below his ribs and above his hip."

"If you've got to be shot," said Sam, "that's not a bad spot. Didn't hit any organs or bones. Barring something unforeseen, he could keep the date for his rescheduled exhibit opening—that's more than a week away."

"That's good," said Dom. "The guard?"

"The security cameras caught what happened," said Pete. "Ruben had an astonishingly realistic mask. Made of silicone and went over his entire head. Movie quality. He and the guard had a brief conversation. Then as the guard turned away, Ruben swung his cane and knocked him out."

"I saw that cane," said Sam. "Had a solid brass cobra head on top. The guard was lucky he survived. He'll be okay."

"Glad to hear it," said Dom. "Karen remembered a car on fire down the street. Was that part of Ruben's plan?"

"Appears so. Explosion set off by a timer. Our guy out front fell for the distraction and went to help."

"Is Karen's tapestry okay? And the Anonicelli? Karen said it went flying out of Ruben's hand when she hit him."

"I didn't see any damage to the tapestry," said Pete, "even with what must have been a hell of a wallop. The painting is fine, but the frame is cracked." He sighed. "They're back in the evidence lockers."

"The Jimenez statues?" asked Sam.

"Both damaged. I'll have to talk with Jimenez."

"And Ruben?"

"Still in surgery," said Pete. "I gathered from the emergency room folks the statue that hit his gut really messed up his insides. Internal bleeding, perforated intestine. They'll have to watch for infection."

"He won't be happy when he wakes up about the damage to his hand either," said Sam, "Under arrest, under guard, in pain, and the prospect of many surgeries ahead."

"I suppose I should say I'm sorry," said Dom, "but I can't work up any enthusiasm for it."

Pete snorted. "I wouldn't even try. There was great satisfaction in arresting this piece of filth."

"How is Grayson doing?" asked Dom. "How does a lad recover from hearing a father say he has no son. That's a killer blow."

"While we were waiting for William to come out of surgery, Cecil and Grayson talked to me about that pain. That pain's not gone, but when his dad pushed him aside and took the bullets Ruben intended for him, Grayson was left in awe. That action spoke loudly and will help in healing." Then Pete grinned. "Grayson's actions brought a serendipity. The powers that be in New Mexico want to see troubled juveniles demonstrating change in a positive direction. Bringing Ruben down was a biggie."

CHAPTER EIGHTY-NINE

Tuesday, August 22

In Miami just before dawn, FBI agents, accompanied by a man in a courier uniform, surrounded a palatial estate. Several frenetic minutes later, Agent Tuttle confronted the rheumy-eyed man he'd startled awake. The elderly man cowered against his pillows, crying out in vain for the two bodyguards who lay handcuffed in the hall.

Tuttle listened to the words of Miranda. His eyes swept the walls in the dim light and feasted on the three paintings hanging opposite the bed. The rising sun's rays touched the face of the nursing mother and the child leaning against her. Such skill. Such luminosity.

Outside, the courier unobtrusively watched as the old man was taken away in handcuffs. Through the flurry of activity, the agent with whom he'd dealt emerged from the door and caught the courier's eye. Tuttle tilted his head and nodded.

The courier faded into the shadows with grim satisfaction and walked quietly away.

All had gone well.

No more loose ends.

CHAPTER NINETY

Tuesday, August 29

A little over a week later, Karen woke with a sense of serenity in her own home. The room and the predawn light angling through the window were familiar, but the bed posters standing sentinel cast different shadows than the slender maple posts they'd replaced. These were dark, massive, and spoke to her of history scrolling back hundreds of years.

She smiled, imagining the people who had slept in this bed, all the couples who contributed their genes to the warm, beautiful person lying beside her. The scope of history, which had unfolded since this wood had been living walnut trees, left her in awe.

She remembered Saturday, August 26, the day this old bed had finally moved to the ranch with Dom's things, as an exhausting but satisfying milestone.

Moving day had actually involved three households. The Circle Sleuths had all been on hand with organizational skills, willing hands, and muscle power. Dom's things joined Karen's, Maria's joined Diego's, leaving one half of the duplex as a new home for Dulcie and Santos, who vacated their apartment in town. The cleaning company had not held Dulcie's job for her. She was now employed full-time at the ranch, helping Maria and assisting Karen in her weaving business.

A hand covered hers with a gentle squeeze. Dom's voice softly rumbled, "Good morning."

She rolled to him and rested her head on his shoulder, content to listen to the robins sing to the rising sun, *cheery, cheerily, cheerily.*

"I forgot to tell you," said Dom. "Sam said to thank you for letting Leyla stay here last week."

"She's always welcome. Did he and Farah finally have a chance to get away together?"

Dom chuckled. "They stayed home. While we were busy on this end getting ready for the move, they took advantage of the privacy and my not-so-subtle suggestion. He said they gave this bed a good send-off, before it moved here."

Karen raised her head to grin at him. "Good for them. Dare we hope their efforts met with success?"

He pulled her down in a hug. "Wait and see. God willing, they made us another grandchild."

The robin's song was joined by distant mourning doves and then the mundane sounds of the sliding glass door and happy Airedales. Quixote got up from his bed and padded over to theirs.

Dom grumbled. "I can hear him looking at us. How is it that a dog's stare speaks with such volume?"

Karen laughed and sat up, reaching back to caress Dom's tousled hair. "I'll let him out. This day will be fun. The opening of the Niemöller exhibit."

"Finally, the public gets to see it. William got a jumpstart ahead of the Labor Day festivities."

"Nice to spread it out, and I'm glad Herb and Yolanda can come over Labor Day weekend to see it."

Dom stretched. "This morning let's take another look at those travel brochures. We should get our reservations nailed down."

Karen pulled on her robe and opened the door onto the portal for Quixote. "For someone who has been complaining about living out of suitcases, you're awfully pleased about more of the same."

"Not the same at all. It'll be our honeymoon. Visiting with Ana Sophia in Spain, finding out what or who so fascinates my granddaughter that she's grown roots there? Prowling around all the places in Germany we've been reading about while immersed in Niemöller? Going to Norway, looking up your relatives, finding more museums to discover, and the piéce de resistance— a chance to see the Northern Lights? That's worth packing my woolies."

"I totally agree. An October wedding. It will be here before we know it."

CHAPTER NINETY-ONE

Karen accepted the compliments of two weaver friends from Taos with a smile and turned to Dom. "People are feeling the overall effect of the exhibit. Just what I'd hoped."

She and Dom had spent much of the afternoon of opening day at the gallery as family, friends, and the art community cycled through the Niemöller exhibit.

"Here come Pete and Akiko," he said.

"They've been here more than an hour." From time to time, Karen had looked away from her conversations with others to see them, quietly moving through the exhibit.

Akiko gave her a heartfelt hug. "I knew it would be special but seeing it all together— such an impact."

Then Pete folded her into a warm embrace. "*Ausgezeichnet*," he whispered. "Excellent." He pulled back, his hands resting lightly on her arms. His eyes were wet. "You, with your light, and all these other lights. You give strength to the rest of us to keep going."

He took Akiko's hand in his, and they left, swallowed up in the swelling crowd as families with school-age children filtered in.

Dulcie, Diego, Maria, and Santos arrived with the after-school visitors. Karen introduced Dulcie to Joaquin. He seemed taken with her, falling into step beside her and talking as they wandered through the exhibit. Karen wondered if Dulcie might be an inspiration for a future bronze.

Sam and his family came. Krista came with Anton, Skyla, and the baby. They were still here, experiencing at last what they'd heard so much about.

Grayson arrived with Cecil, who must have picked him up from school. They stopped to talk with Joaquin, who was standing near Karen. The crowd was thinning; it was near closing time.

William walked toward them, stopping to lean heavily on one of the podiums that held a different numbered edition of Joaquin's set of bronzes.

"Are you doing okay, Dad?" Grayson asked. He went to fetch one of the rolling office chairs from the fishbowl. "Here. You must be tired."

"Thanks. I could sit for a while, even though this day has been marvelous medicine."

"William," said Karen, "I'm glad to see you're looking so well. I was worried about you."

William touched his bandaged wound gently. "I'm afraid I'll be stuck with a dreadful-looking scar."

"Good conversation piece," said Cecil.

William moved his hand over his bald pate. "There's no way I can comb my hair over it. Maybe I'll have to get a toupee."

"Don't bother, Dad. The scar means something. Wear it proudly."

"Let your light shine?" asked Dom.

Cecil laughed. "With William's head, it's let your light reflect."

"Yes, it does reflect well on him," said Karen with a gentle smile. "Grayson, may I ask what's happening with your case?"

"I'll be on probation for a while."

"I'm confident we can put the thoughts of trials and prison time aside," said William. "So many people have spoken up for Grayson." He blinked a few times and swallowed hard. "Even Otto. He actually went to Lieutenant Schultz and said that it was his fault for introducing Ruben to Grayson. Ruben fooled everybody and why blame a child for what an adult couldn't see. If they had to arrest somebody, arrest him, and let Grayson go."

"Really?" Karen was impressed. Maybe there was something of a protector-of-children-Tomten in Otto after all.

"They've made the probation contingent on a few things," said William. "Grayson and I are both in counseling— separately and together."

"I can see value in that," said Cecil. "William, your Niemöller exhibit has touched us all. He was a man who acknowledged he was wrong and was willing to change. It made me take a hard look at my life. I want to live again, not just exist, if that makes sense."

"I'll be doing community service," said Grayson. "Maybe using my art or computer skills. My probation officer said I can even use that experience on my college application."

Karen smiled at Grayson. Had he grown taller in the past week or was he carrying himself differently? Maybe his dad's sacrifice, acting to save his son? Maybe Grayson knowing he was loved made the difference.

She looked at these friends gathered around. "What I got from this whole experience was something far greater than I expected. In the beginning I was focused on what I could do, *my* art, *my* voice, *my* light. I was thinking about what physical object I could create. That's important." She waved her hand at the art surrounding them. "But the people behind the art are more important. When it came to stopping Ruben, I didn't even think twice. I bashed him with my tapestry and would do it again."

Joaquin laughed. "I know. If I'd been there, I would have clobbered Ruben with my bronzes before Grayson could think of it. I would have used my statue on him in a heartbeat."

"What I discovered," said Karen, "was artists everywhere, all the ones in this exhibit, musicians like Yolanda, and others are doing what they can. William's creation and Gloria's vision work together with my tapestry, with all this."

"I see hope in that collective action," said Dom. "There's a ripple effect."

Karen grew quiet, her eyes moving from one art rendition to another, from one artist to another around the room. A smile played on her lips, growing broader.

"What are you thinking, my love? Your face is glowing with happiness."

"I know what I'd like to tackle next." She turned to Dom. "I see a small child wading in serene shallow water. There's color reflected from the sky. Maybe it's dawn. The child is joyful, in action, skipping a stone. Each time it hits, the water ripples spread out. They meet, intermingle, the contour changes as they intersect."

"How cool," said Grayson. "I could paint it, but mine's different. It has two people. One has just skipped his stone. Now the other tries. The ripples from the first have widened, gotten gentler. The second stone left fresh, deeper ripples. Wow! Think of how the water would reflect the sky's color. Think of how the ripples would intersect and change it. I could do a great digital art painting with that. How fun that would be."

"Might the two be father and son?" asked William.

Grayson looked at him. "Maybe."

"A ripple effect," said William, stroking his chin. "I like it. Can you see how artists would respond to that? To show the many ways what we do affects those around us?"

"Another exhibit?" asked Dom. "Would you allow fiber arts and digital arts?"

Karen caught her lip between her teeth as she saw William's eyes rest on his son.

"Hmm." William took a deep breath. "Maybe I'll begin the call list with digital art."

"Really, Dad? You mean it?"

William nodded.

"Do you know what you're saying?" asked Dom. "Remember the ripple effect."

"I'm counting on it," said William.

"Thanks," said Grayson. "I'll take that as a compliment."

Karen caught Grayson's eye, and they both laughed.

Karen's gaze drifted back to her tapestry. How satisfying it was to see it hanging with all the other Niemöller works again.

Then Krista, holding baby Lucas, walked by to stand in front of the tapestry. He grabbed a strand of her long blonde hair and pulled it into his mouth. She gently extricated it from his fingers, and with her hand over his, pointed at the tapestry.

"Look," she said, "that's Gramma's *Tapestry of Light*. Isn't it beautiful?"

Lucas stuffed his free hand into his mouth, but his eyes followed his hand tucked in Krista's as she pointed them toward the light held by the kneeling Statue of Liberty.

"Follow the light, Lucas. It's always there, even when clouds get in the way. Let yours shine. That's what's important."

About the Author

Betty Lucke holds a Bachelor's degree in elementary education from Macalester College, St. Paul, MN, and the Master of Religious Education and the Master of Divinity degrees from Princeton Theological Seminary, Princeton, NJ. She has fond memories of summers worked in New Mexico. She lives in northern California with her husband and a Welsh terrier.

She is a co-founder of the Town Square Writers, a weekly writing group associated with the public library.

Made in the USA
Middletown, DE
06 November 2023

41897456R00265